Island of Secrets

Patricia Wilson lived in the village of Amiras in Crete where the book is set. She was inspired to write when she unearthed a machine gun in her garden – one used in the events that unfolded in September 1943 – and much of the novel is based on real stories told to her by the oldest women of Amiras. Women who've never spoken of their experiences before. Patricia still spends much of her time in Greece. This is her debut novel.

First published in Great Britain in 2017 by
ZAFFRE PUBLISHING
80–81 Wimpole St, London W1G 9RE
www.zaffrebooks.co.uk

A CIP catalogue record for this book is available from the British Library.

Paperback ISBN: 978-1-78576-278-9
Also available as an ebook

5 7 9 10 8 6 4

Typeset by IDSUK (Data Connection) Ltd
Printed and bound by Clays Ltd, St Ives Plc

Zaffre Publishing is an imprint of Bonnier Zaffre,
a Bonnier Publishing company
www.bonnierzaffre.co.uk
www.bonnierpublishing.co.uk

Island of Secrets

Patricia Wilson

ZAFFRE

For Berty, with love.

STARS DON'T CRY FOR ME.

Stars don't cry for me,
Because I sing at night.
Because I hurt in my heart, for the dark-haired girl.
Stars don't tell me off
Because I lament at night.

I'll tell my pain to the stars,
Because they're discreet.
Because they have patience
And listen all night,
While I tell them about my pain, and you.

Moon, you've never been
In the mess that I'm in.
And you have the right to ask
What I've become, why I'm unhappy.
But you can't understand, it's never happened to you.

Chapter 1

Crete, Present Day.

The village of Amiras was still, like a theatre waiting for the curtain to rise. Heat shimmered from the cobbled streets. In front of the kafenion, empty chairs stood in haphazard groups between square tables. Outside the closed supermarket, hessian olive sacks hung over boxes of potatoes and vegetables, protecting them from the fierce Mediterranean light.

A herd of long-haired goats shifted into the shadow of the hilltop chapel. For a few seconds, the dull clatter of their bells broke the peace and quiet of siesta time.

In the lower village, a blue door squeaked open and a wide hipped, middle-aged housewife hurried up the narrow streets. From the shade of a vermilion bougainvillea, a skinny white cat sniffed the air, narrowed its eyes and watched the woman.

Inside one cottage, an elderly couple sat as still and silent as the stone walls. A crucifix hung over a garish icon of Saint George. The martyr seemed distracted from his dragon slaying by an object in the living room. A chocolate box overflowed with photographs, letters and mementoes in the centre of a low round table.

The old woman, Maria, reached for a faded picture of Poppy cradling her baby. She studied the image and recalled Poppy's last words, still fresh in her ears, although decades had passed.

Forget me, Mama. Forget I ever existed.

A shaft of sunlight streamed through the window illuminating Maria's scarred hands – an ugly reminder of the fire. It took time for those wounds to heal.

Her wizened face hardened with a decision.

'I will write to them, Vassili,' she said to the Einstein look-alike sitting by the fireplace. 'Voula can help me.' She replaced the picture and closed the box. 'God's getting impatient, and I'm tired of it all.' She crossed herself three times and prayer-locked her arthritic fingers.

Vassili nodded as though he understood, but passing years had eroded his grief. He dropped his amber worry beads and hobbled to her side.

'Don't waste your thoughts on what's dead and gone, old woman.' He kissed her forehead.

Despite his words, scenes from the past returned and filled Maria's head.

'I can't forget,' she whispered, staring at ghosts that crowded into the whitewashed room.

Vassili followed her gaze, unable to see those who haunted her.

Recognising his confusion, Maria wished the spores of old age would moulder her mind too. Regrets were useless now. The time had come for forgiveness and, before she died, Maria hoped to touch the cheek of Poppy's child.

'Angelika has a right to know the truth, old man, she's our granddaughter.'

'Mama, Papa, your dinner's here.' Voula crashed through the doorway, the multi-coloured fly curtain whipping around her faded black dress. She gripped a casserole pot against her belly and grinned, her face a friendly gargoyle.

'No need to shout, Voula, we're not deaf,' Maria said.

Vassili cupped a hand behind his ear. 'Eh, what's that? Ah, the food. No chance of any meat I suppose? I'll be glad when Lent's over. I can smell the lamb already.' He shuffled to the kitchen table.

'Only a few more days until Easter, Papa. I've made stuffed peppers. Will you have a glass of Demitri's wine?' Voula clattered the dishes and then helped Maria out of the armchair. 'Anything else?' she asked, pouring cloudy red *krasí* into tumblers before serving their meals.

Maria cut open a green pepper, hunched over her plate and sniffed the food.

Voula stopped bustling and watched Maria taste the rice stuffing flavoured with herbs, currants, and pine nuts. When she approved with a nod, Voula took a breath and smiled.

'I want to write to Poppy and Angelika,' Maria said flatly

Voula's eyes widened. She glanced around the table top and then at Vassili who guzzled his food. 'Are you sure, Mama?' She lowered her voice to a whisper. 'What if it starts up again, the trouble, after all these years? Isn't it better to forget? We can't bring back the dead.'

'No,' Maria said, her face drawn and thin above the mound of colourful vegetables. 'I've decided.'

* * *

The next day, Voula asked, 'How do you want to start the letter, Mama?' Her pencil poised over a child's exercise book.

Maria grunted. 'I've thought about it for hours. The beginning is the most difficult part. If it's not perfect, they'll screw it up and throw it away. We've got one chance at this, Voula. We should address the envelope to Angelika and put both letters in it. Otherwise, I fear her mother might tear it up unopened. Now, let's see, how shall we begin?'

'I know, what about: *Dear Angelika*?'

Maria rolled her eyes. She wondered if her daughter-in-law had lost more of her marbles in sixty-five years than

Maria had in ninety. 'Yes, very good, Voula,' she snorted. 'And then?'

Voula lifted and dropped her shoulders, which made her breasts quiver against her belly.

'Write this then,' Maria said. 'I have wanted to send you a letter for a long time. I hoped to see you before I die, but I realise our meeting is unlikely.'

'Mama!'

'Oh, face the facts, Voula; I'm on my way out. Let's get on with the letter before the Angel Gabriel replaces you as my personal assistant.'

Voula scratched her lip and nodded.

'Now, write this, Voula: Angelika, please tell your mother I have never stopped loving her. Put your arms around her and kiss her from me. Poppy is in my heart. Say that I am sorry. *Truly sorry*. If I could have changed things, I would.'

'Mama, how do we know Angelika reads Greek?'

'We have to trust Poppy will have taught her. Anyway, we can ask Demitri to translate for us. What shall we write next? Perhaps something about Angelika's father.' Maria tilted her head to one side. 'Yeorgo,' she sighed. 'Wasn't he a beautiful man, Voula?' Silent for a moment, Maria's eyes became glazed. 'That's another difficult part. I wonder if Angelika knows.'

* * *

At the kitchen table, Voula sat opposite Maria and opened the exercise book. 'It's been a week and we're no further, Mama. Perhaps we should write *To Be Continued* on the bottom and post it, just in case . . .' Their eyes met.

Maria shook her head. 'The letter to Poppy wasn't too difficult, but I'm struggling with what to say to Angelika. Let's keep working on it. I don't want it posted until it's perfect, Voula, but it isn't as easy as I thought. What do you think we should write?'

'Tell her about her aunts, uncles and cousins. What about me and my children and grandchildren?' Voula said.

'No, I want it to be something important.' Their eyes met again. A cockerel crowed outside the door. '*Tut*, you know what I mean, Voula. Considering I was a teacher, I shouldn't find a simple letter so difficult. Make us a coffee and then we'll sit in the garden and crochet.'

They settled in the shade of an ancient olive tree, opposite the cottage door. Maria gazed down, over the village rooftops and the bell tower of the church of *Agios Yeorgios*. Her eyes followed the local bus, miniature in the distance, travelling the pale, dusty road beyond the village. Barely two cars wide, the road snaked between silver-green olive groves, descending to the beach and fishing village of Arvi. The sound of a tootling horn drifted up as the bus neared a bend. The Arvi gorge, clearly visible, was a deep slash in the red rock. From the sheer-sided canyon, griffon vultures launched off their narrow ledges to circle up, over Amiras, on the thermals.

The view drew her in, so peaceful and calm, showing no hint of the horrors Maria had witnessed from under that very tree, long ago. She sniffed the air and caught the scent of burning wood, lamb, and rosemary. Chops on someone's BBQ. The memory of a fire, her darling boys in mortal danger and the worst day of her life hit her with such startling clarity she whimpered.

Voula looked up from her crocheting. 'Are you all right, Mama?'

Maria huffed. 'Why shouldn't I be? Let's keep thinking about this letter.'

'Why don't we tell Angelika about the village, it might make her want to visit; or about the olive crop, or that the school is closing.' Voula's crochet hook flashed and dipped through a half-made tablecloth.

'So much to say, but nothing seems worthy of such a significant letter.' Maria struggled with her work, the silk snagging on her crooked fingers, but if she lost a day she'd never return to her crocheting.

'I know!' Voula said, making Maria jump and two hours' work unravel as it fell to the ground.

Maria took a swipe at her daughter-in-law, but missed. 'Now look what you've made me do! This had better be good, Voula.'

Voula had trouble picking up the crocheting, her legs too fat to bend, and her belly too round for the reach. 'Start by telling Angelika about Poppy and Yeorgo's wedding day. Tell her you still have Poppy's dress. Ask if she'd like to have it.'

'Bravo! That's a good idea, Voula. Let's aim to get the letter finished in time for next Monday's post.'

Grunting and panting, Voula reached for Maria's work and came up flushed but triumphant. The moment she plopped into the garden chair, one of her black knee highs rolled to her ankle and the house telephone rang.

'Virgin Mary!' Voula cried.

They both crossed themselves three times.

Chapter 2

Flight EZY1105, The Same Day.

THROUGHOUT THE FOUR-HOUR flight to Crete, Angie worried about her trip. Suppose she found her mother's family, how might they receive her? She wished there had been some form of communication before her visit to the island, but Angie had no way of contacting her Cretan family. What if they misinterpreted her good intentions as meddling? Who were her father's family? Why did her mother leave Crete and break all contact with her family so many years ago? The answers, she believed, lay in the remote, mountain village of Amiras.

Outside the arrivals terminal, Angie tilted her head and closed her eyes allowing golden sunlight to wash over her face. Things would work out. Anyhow, they could hardly get worse. Her mother – Poppy – seemed to be on the verge of a breakdown. Angie worried about her all the time. The doctor had prescribed sleeping pills for Poppy and Angie feared if she didn't do something to help her, the next prescription would be tranquillisers.

To add to this, Angie had just lost her job – the career in publishing that was her lifeblood.

With Poppy's illness, and her own redundancy, Angie wondered if her wedding would ever take place. Until now, she hadn't realised how much of her life revolved around her mother and her career. Despite always trying to appear confident, privately she struggled with everything that had happened.

What would she have done without Nick to lean on? He promised they would have their wedding, house, children, and happy-ever-after no matter what. Angie couldn't wish for a more supportive or loving man. But, in the aftershock of her redundancy, she realised she needed to prove her value in the whole scheme of things, mainly to herself.

She *had* to get another job soon, but, more importantly, she must find out what was troubling her mother so much that it was making her ill. It seemed the closer Angie got to finalising her wedding plans, the more Poppy suffered.

Angie hated the idea of looking for employment. What if she wasn't considered good enough for a major publishing house? Would she become sad and lonely because life had been unfair, and end up on medication like her mother?

At least now she had time to try and get to the bottom of Poppy's wretched unhappiness. Her mother so vehemently objected when Angie said she was going to Crete to find her grandparents that Angie almost cancelled.

'Don't go! Angelika, please, I'm begging you!' Poppy had pleaded, and then she had cried – breaking Angie's heart. Thank goodness Nick had promised to keep an eye on her.

The situation was awful. In all her thirty-seven years, Angie had never gone against her mother like this. If she was honest, though, She was using her wedding as an excuse to find Poppy's estranged family. She suspected the root of her mother's worsening illness lay buried in Poppy's self-exile from her homeland. Every time Angie brought up the subject of Crete, her mother would have a relapse.

Angie took a breath and studied her surroundings. The airport seemed dangerously close to the city of Heraklion. Perhaps less than a mile away, she could see the hotels and buildings of

Crete's capital quite clearly. Through the airport's chain-link fence, she gazed across the runway to the blue sea beyond. From her window seat on the plane, for a horrible moment, Angie had feared they were landing on the water.

She turned and faced Crete's interior. Past rows of shiny coaches and parked hire cars, Angie studied a backdrop of high mountains. On the south side of those peaks, which surrounded the Lassithi Plateau, she hoped to find her mother's village.

Suddenly, Angie saw a window of opportunity. Alone in Crete with no fiancé, no mother and no job left her completely unrestricted. Free to find direction. She could decide what she wanted most from life; a career, the commitment of motherhood, or the wellbeing of her mother. Was a three-way compromise possible?

Happy tourists dragged luggage and lively children around her. Slightly light headed, but calmer, Angie absorbed their holiday mood. Her shoulders dropped and the grip on her suitcase relaxed.

Angie's confidence gathered strength. Her plan was simple, and so long as she could find her grandmother, she couldn't foresee any problems. Hopefully, in the mountain village of Amiras, she would discover the cause of her mother's anxiety attacks. Then her family could reunite and Poppy's health would improve in time for the wedding.

When Nick and Angie had children, they would be her everything, and her mother would make the perfect Granny Poppy. In her mind, she could see the loving environment that would surround her family and it filled her with happiness.

Angie realised these things didn't just happen, they had to be worked on, earned. This week in Crete, she had to forget about herself and try to get to the bottom of her mother's unhappiness.

Yet the feeling of loss and shame over the job severance hurt like a great emotional bruise in her chest.

She hired a car from smiling, helpful Greeks. They welcomed her to Crete with a map of the island and then hauled her suitcase into the boot. She set off for the island's south coast.

To drive on the 'wrong' side of the road seemed weird. At gear change, her left hand searched for the gearstick and bumped against the door panel. By the time her right hand found the gearstick, she had inadvertently taken her foot off the clutch and she crunched.

'Come on, Angie, you can do this,' she told herself, trying to calm down.

On the outskirts of the city, traffic thinned and the modern infrastructure with its magnificent fountains, glass buildings and palm-lined streets disappeared. Traffic lights didn't work. Pavements crumbled. Roadworks, shopping trollies, and old cars lay abandoned along the highway. Deciding to stop and practise her gear change, she pulled over at a broken kerb, turned off the engine, and closed her eyes.

Clutch, right hand down to the gearstick, change, de-clutch.

Startled by the sound of the passenger door opening, Angie swung around in her seat. An elderly couple bundled themselves, and two bursting Lidl supermarket bags, into the back of her car. In heavy Cretan dialect, the man was saying something Angie didn't understand.

'Wha . . .' she stammered, glancing about for help, and then realising she had parked at a bus stop with a three-legged plastic chair tie-tagged to the post.

The man, gruff voiced and ancient, flapped his hand at the windscreen and said, '*Páme!*' which Angie remembered meant: Let's go.

Ten minutes later she dropped the old couple and their shopping at a small stone house. An enormous pink-painted cement swan dominated the front garden, and a row of supermarket bags, pegged to a clothesline, fluttered in the breeze. They offered her coffee. She explained, in halting Greek, she had to get to Amiras. The man kept hold of the car's door handle while the woman toddled indoors. She returned with a napkin full of fat shortbreads and a plastic water bottle.

'She make!' the old man shouted in English, pointing at the biscuits, then at the bottle of clear liquid. 'Is raki here, I make! Very good, very strong, like me.' Beaming, he slapped his belly.

Angie said goodbye and continued her journey, laughing and looking forward to sharing the incident with Nick.

When their children came along, Angie could see them stalling at bedtime, as all youngsters do. 'Mummy! Tell us that story about that old couple in Crete.' She imagined a glance and a smile from Nick as she took her darlings to bed. She could see it all. The perfect family.

Angie thought Poppy must have found it difficult adjusting to life in London when she came from such a friendly environment. Once again, she wondered what had made her mother leave all the sunshine and laughter of Crete. Despite Poppy's claims of family discord, Angie decided that enough time had passed. A line needed to be drawn under that era and the family reunite.

Spring flowers grew everywhere, exploding from roadsides, nodding a welcome as she passed. Lines of ochre earth separated olive trees and vine trellises across a quilted, undulating landscape. The countryside shimmered under a densely blue sky. In the distance, snow-covered peaks rose majestically to challenge the afternoon sun. The island seemed much bigger, and more intense, than she had expected.

Angie pulled onto the verge of a mountain road and gazed over a plateau. Hamlets of whitewashed houses clustered in the valleys of rolling green foothills. She noticed red-roofed churches with domes and bell towers which rose from the centre of each village. Angie got out of the car and took a panoramic picture with her phone, drinking in the captivating scenery.

In an olive grove just below the road, a flock of sheep stopped grazing and stared with curious, unblinking eyes. Their mouths twitched as if about to speak, and the clanging bells that hung from their wide red collars were silent for a moment.

Warm sunlight rested on her shoulders like her mother's arm. Angie wondered if Poppy had ever stood on that spot and admired the picturesque countryside. She considered her mother's forty years of self-exile. Could Angie heal old wounds without knowing the cause?

The photographs she planned to take were a start. Pictures of Crete were sure to bring happy memories to Poppy. A good feeling settled over her. In the bright sunshine, everything seemed so much more simple than it had at home.

Back in the shade of the car she reached for the ignition key, hesitated, and rested her head on the wheel as doubts set in. What possessed her to go against Poppy's wishes? Angie feared her stupid, self-centred plan could lead to even more heartache.

Her grandmother knew nothing of Angie's arrival in Crete. She could leave for a tourist area, have a few days of sun, sea, and sand and return to London refreshed. Her mother would be happy – on the surface. Angie dwelled on the deep-rooted secrets tormenting Poppy. Thinking of her from such a great distance, she realised the intense loneliness of the woman who had given her everything.

Angie remembered when she'd had a splinter of wood in her finger as a child. All that she touched gave her pain, even the things she loved. It hurt when her mother took the tweezers to it and prodded around. Angie had begged her to leave it alone.

If Angie could find the cause of Poppy's unhappiness, despite the discomfort of her digging about, healing would be possible. Relief flooded through her. She started the car and pulled away from the tranquil scene.

* * *

Half an hour along the deserted road, cleaved into the muted red and green mountain rock, the landscape became sparse and rugged. A flurry of silky-haired goats with long mismatched horns skittered across her path. Kids romped and skipped around long-bearded nannie goats. Roadside poppies and rockroses gave way to clumps of sage and vast swathes of pink anemones. Neat rows of olive trees, so iconic of the Mediterranean, were replaced by tangle-rooted pine or holm oak that towered precariously overhead. Her adrenalin peaked as the uneven highway twisted and turned, always climbing steadily.

She rounded a bend and suddenly, far below in the distance, she saw the sea. The majesty of the scene took her breath away. She wanted to stop but the road, dangerous and unforgiving, had an ornate religious shrine on each hairpin. She guessed many motorists had lost their lives on those sharp corners. When the road levelled, starting a gentle descent, Angie spotted a Shell sign. Horrified to see her petrol gauge showing red, she turned off the air-con to save fuel. With her palms wet on the wheel and her hair stuck to the back of her neck, she drove into a dusty forecourt.

Glad to be out of the sweltering car, Angie reached for the petrol pump. She gave a friendly nod to a pensioner sitting in heavy shade outside the garage shop.

A young man dashed from the workshop. 'No! I'll do it. How much?' he said.

'Full, please.'

He shoved the nozzle in place, dragged a chamois from a bucket, and washed her dusty windscreen.

'Lovely, thanks,' Angie said admiring the sparkling glass. 'Can you tell me how far it is to Amiras Village?'

'Ten kilometres. It's just past the town of Viannos.' He glanced at her cabin bag complete with flight labels on the rear seat. 'Why Amiras? It's not a holiday place.'

'I'm looking for my grandmother, she lives there.'

'What's her name? My grandfather's from Amiras, he'll know her.' He nodded towards the old man.

'Kondulakis Maria, but I don't have an exact address.'

While he spoke to his grandfather, the fuel clonked to a halt: forty-nine euros. Angie pulled a fifty from her purse and looked up to see the pensioner spit into the dust. The dense shade hid his face before he turned into the shop.

'Keep the change,' Angie said. 'Thanks for the clean glass. Did your grandfather know my grandmother?'

'No.' Sullen now, the youth avoided her eyes and walked away.

Angie glanced in the rear-view mirror as she drove onto the road. The two men stood together, watching her.

* * *

In the main street of Viannos, the last town before her grandmother's village, Angie reversed into a tight space behind a red pickup. A goat stared from the back of the battered vehicle, bleating its lack of confidence in her parking. She crossed the road and sat at a kerbside table, grateful for the cooling shade of an enormous tree. Tangled branches overhead were bursting with spring's first leaves. Electrical wire and fly-speckled bulbs snaked through the boughs and swayed in the light breeze.

Angie didn't expect a problem with her next task, to find accommodation. On the web, she had seen many rooms for rent in the town of Viannos. But for now, she needed to relax with a coffee.

A waiter approached and followed her gaze. 'Is more than a thousand years old, this tree.'

'Wow, so old!' Angie placed her palm against the trunk and felt the warmth of the day in its gnarled bark. She soaked up the atmosphere of the town square. Perhaps Poppy had also relaxed there, touched the tree and smiled up into its branches.

The waiter snapped her back to the present. 'You want a drink, lady?'

Too tired to try speaking Greek, Angie said, 'Coffee, please.'

'Frappé, Nes, Greek coffee?'

'Frappé, thanks.' An iced coffee would cool her and perk her depleted caffeine level.

'Where yous from?'

Angie patted her chest. 'England, English.'

'Ah, I am Manoli. I speaks perfect English. You want something, you tell me, okay?'

While he made her drink, Angie enjoyed the town chaos, amused that such a narrow street was part of the National

Highway. Viannos, scruffy, dilapidated, yet postcard-picturesque, charmed her. Honeysuckle crawled up a whitewashed building and tangled around blue louvre shutters. Perfume from the spidery flowers drifted on the early evening air.

Upright old women with proud faces wore widow's weeds and shuffled across the street, halting traffic. Occasionally, a stream of cars reversed so that oncoming vehicles could continue along the pothole-ridden thoroughfare. Local pensioners greeted each other with the vigour of intense friendship. Everyone smiled – and everyone shouted.

Manoli, broad, sun-drenched and handsome with come-to-bed eyes, brought Angie her frappé and then sat uninvited at her table. 'What's your name? Where you from in England? Are you married? You have sister? Why you here, holiday?'

Angie answered the questions, amused by his interest. 'No, I'm here to find my grandparents.'

'Your grandparents, who are they?' Manoli asked.

Angie hesitated, remembering the atmosphere at the garage. 'Kondulakis, in Amiras, it's near here, isn't it?'

Manoli's head jerked back as if slapped. 'Kondulakis, you is the granddaughter of Kondulakis Maria?' His eyes widened.

Angie gulped. 'To tell the truth, I'm not sure where they live, and they don't know I'm here. Do you know them? I mean, I might not even . . .' she stuttered.

'Wait.' Manoli loomed over her. He placed his big hand on her shoulder, pinning her to the seat while he pulled a mobile phone from his jeans and thumbed numbers. Moments later, he bellowed into the phone, his free arm gesticulating.

Angie thought of running but someone had boxed-in her car. She had trouble understanding Manoli's Cretan dialect but caught, 'I'm telling you, she's here, in front of me!' He thrust his open hand towards Angie as if the person at the other end of the conversation could see her. 'I'm sure, *malákas* – the granddaughter!'

Unsure of what to expect, Angie placed both feet flat on the floor and shifted to the edge of her seat. Several people appeared from nowhere, almost surrounding her table. She glanced from one to the other. Blankly, they stared back.

Manoli turned to Angie. 'Your mother's name?'

'Poppy,' Angie said. 'It's short for Calliope.'

He rolled his eyes. 'Father's name?'

'Yeorgo, but he died,' she said.

Manoli squinted at her. He took a breath and then continued on the phone, throwing in the occasional *malákas* – a common expletive meaning wanker. His animated voice made pedestrians turn. More people stopped and gawked, heads cocked to one side.

An old man rested on his stick in the middle of the road. He glared at Manoli and then Angie. A truck pulled up with a hiss of airbrakes. Traffic came to a halt and tailed back. Everyone stared at the waiter.

'You go to Amiras tonight?' Manoli said.

Angie glanced at her watch and shook her head. 'No, in the morning.'

After a few words, Manoli ended the call. 'I telephone Demitri from the supermarket of Amiras. He is family of Kondulakis. Tomorrow, he will take you to your grandmother.'

'Thank you, you've been so kind,' Angie said.

The old man who had stopped traffic hobbled to her side. He glared at Angie, his mouth tight, eyes hard and narrow. His jaw thrust forward in a lined face that appeared to have seen the worst of life. After a moment of contemplation, his look softened and his mouth relaxed into a smile.

'Welcome,' he said reaching out and shaking her hand. 'I am Thanassi Lambrakis.'

Angie's heart seemed to leap into the back of her throat. 'Lambrakis . . . I'm Lambrakis too!' she cried. This was so unexpected. Was he from her father's family? Could her quest to find her relations be so simple?

'Of course you are,' Manoli scoffed, with a smile. 'Lambrakis and Kondulakis are the two most common names in this area. There are hundreds of us living here, and thousands spread around the world. We go back to Byzantium.' He poked his chest with his thumb. 'I am Manoli Lambrakis. Manoli comes from Emmanouil, meaning God. Lambrakis means the light.' There was no doubting the pride on his face, as if the name Lambrakis was exclusively his.

'The *little* light,' the pensioner corrected. 'Akis means little.'

Manoli stood taller and broadened his chest while throwing the pensioner a scowl.

He turned back to Angie. 'Here, the surname comes first so, translated, my name becomes: The light of God.' He spread his hands piously.

'The *little* light of God,' the pensioner said.

'Go and sit down, old man!' Manoli shouted.

Angie could hardly contain her excitement. 'Manoli, are we related?' she asked, the words tumbling out.

Manoli huffed and turned his head away, as if the thought of being related to an Englishwoman disgusted him. He replied with a sneer. 'Plato said: if you go back far enough, you will find we are all related.'

Angie's elation died. Nothing was ever that simple.

The old man chuckled, nodded amiably, and sat at another table. With a cough of black smoke, the HGV pulled away and traffic moved along the street.

Children swung on the back of Angie's chair, touched her arms and stroked her long hair while chattering to each other.

'Go, go,' Manoli said, flicking the backs of his fingers at the youngsters. He turned to Angie. 'The frappé is from me, you no pay, okay? You need anything, you tell me,' he said in what appeared to be a complete change of mood. He showed his palms in a gesture of openness – and then made an exaggerated wink.

Angie still needed a room. 'Is there a tourist information office?'

'Tourist information, what you want? I am tourist information. We no need office, we have kafenion, tell me.'

She hesitated, feeling vulnerable after the suggestive wink and not wanting helpful Manoli to know where she would sleep. 'Is there a hotel?'

Manoli grinned and whacked himself in the chest. 'Ah, I have room.'

Oh, crap.

'A very good room – special price for you – over my kafenion.' Manoli glanced at her breasts, then back to her face. A triumphant smile blazed across his face as he pointed to a flaking balcony.

'Thanks, Manoli, but I need a quiet place away from the road.'

His smile fell and with less enthusiasm he said, 'Okay, my cousin have rooms, very nice, very quiet. How many days? I call her.'

* * *

Angie hauled her suitcase up a steep backstreet. The four-by-three white-painted room contained a new pine bed, a wardrobe, and a tiny modern bathroom that had surely been tiled by a blind man. Finding only one small towel, a coat hanger, and no soap, she locked the door and went in search of a store.

On her return, Angie's stomach rumbled and Manoli's kafenion seemed the easy option.

'Welcome back, lady. The room is good, yes? What you want?' Manoli peered at her supermarket bag. 'What you buy?'

'Nothing exciting, Manoli, but I'm hungry, is there a menu?'

'Why you want menu? Tell me what you like, I am menu.'

'Moussaka? Lamb chops? Sardines?'

'Ah, all finished, we have pizza, any sort of pizza except four seasons, because we only have three,' Manoli said.

Angie couldn't figure out that little gem. 'What about Greek salad?'

'But of course, Greek salad. This is Greece. Always we have the Greek salad! I don't have to say, because *I* make the best Greek salad in Crete. Everybody knows it.'

Angie laughed. 'And a glass of dry red, please.'

While he busied himself preparing her food, night fell. She studied the locals and realised she didn't look out of place at all. With her olive skin, brown eyes, and long dark hair, she could easily be mistaken for a Cretan woman. She had just arrived, yet already the wish to belong stirred inside her.

Bathed in harsh light from the bulbs in the old tree, Angie wondered about the village of Amiras and her grandparents. Then, she thought about her mother and hoped she was doing the right thing. If only she had better understood Manoli's phone call. Still, her mother's parents and family were *her* family too, she had a right to meet them, to know them. Yet, despite her internal pep-talk, a niggling spark of anguish flickered in the back of her mind.

* * *

The following morning, Angie checked herself in the mirror. What would they think of her? First impressions were so important. Her sigh steamed the glass.

Calm down, she told herself. *They're family, why get stressed?*

She wore her best clothes and jewellery, and slicked her hair into a ponytail. Ashamed to realise she had forgotten to bring a gift, she decided to buy something from a local shop. First, she needed a coffee.

At the kafenion, Angie dropped into a chair.

'Madam, you go to see your *Yiayá* now, yes?' Manoli beamed.

'Coffee first. I'm nervous, Manoli. Do I look all right?' Her skin felt damp, her heart fluttery.

'Very nice.' His grin was ridiculous.

A pretty donkey trotted along the road. An old man in dusty dungarees and a black leather cap rode side-saddle, drumming his heels against the beast's belly. Bits of fodder fell like confetti from a mound of vegetation roped over the donkey's hindquarters.

Iridescent in the Mediterranean sunlight, a bright yellow petrol-tanker crept along behind man and beast. An occasional hiss of airbrakes interrupted the steady clip-clop. Angie noticed the tanker driver was reading his newspaper while he inched down the street. These people are so laid back, she thought.

Angie's grandparents would surely be pleased to see her, after so many years. This early step towards a family reunion was down to her. It hadn't been easy, and she regretted hurting her mother but she hoped Poppy was going to thank her for making this first move.

'Should I buy my grandmother cakes or chocolates, Manoli?'

'Bah! Take something that will stay when you've gone. You see the flower shop? They have beautiful lemon trees. You cannot have too many lemon trees. I make coffee, you buy a tree. Fetch it here and I'll put it in your car when you pass.'

Angie bought her tree, over a metre high and bearing four fat lemons.

'What you pay?' Manoli asked.

'Eight euro.'

'They rob you.' His outspread fingers stretched towards her. 'These are not the clothes to wear for shopping.' He plucked a lemon and took it into his kitchen.

* * *

Angie drove out of Viannos with the tree sprawled across the passenger seat. Leathery, dark-green foliage bounced against the hatchback window, filling her car with a citrus zing. The horseshoe-shaped village of Amiras huddled on the mountainside and overlooked the Libyan Sea.

She saw the WW2 memorial, a simple procession of larger-than-life men cut from slabs of cream marble. The figures lined the road that led down into the village. Angie wondered if the monument was built after Poppy had left. She pulled over and took a photo through the car window.

With the phone still in her hand, she flicked back to the last image captured at home. Nick's sleeping face, calm, dreamless, satiated. His thick dark hair falling boyishly over his forehead. His mouth, relaxed in slumber, reminded Angie of his wide, honest smile and beautiful, even teeth.

Angie adored watching him sleep. It had seemed slightly weird to photograph him without his knowing, but she had wanted something of the moment, with all its preceding pleasure and encompassing happiness to take to Crete with her.

They had made love, *really* made love. The room filled with flickering candle light. Puccini playing in the background, champagne on ice, and creamy Belgian chocolates on the bedside table.

Perhaps because they were about to be parted for a week – for the first time in their three years of living together – they seemed even closer than ever. An intense, yet gentle passion grew between them. This new experience was nothing like their usual boisterous sex; noisy, athletic, and breathlessly enjoyable.

They had sprawled on the sofa with a Greek takeaway before them and their favourite old movie playing. Between feeding each other stuffed vine leaves and tiny lamb chops, they sang along to; 'As Time Goes By' and 'It Had to Be You'. Nick did his Humphrey Bogart impression growling, 'Play it again, Sam,' at Angie. She tried to flutter her eyelashes and look sad, but ended up giggling.

They murmured words that meant everything and nothing; odd lines from films, snippets, sensual promises and shared dreams.

They found themselves laughing, touching, and frequently kissing. When night drew in, their caresses became urgent, stirring a deeper desire to be closer, naked, and wrapped in each other's arms.

Finally, as an aria from *Madam Butterfly* filled the bedroom, Angie clung to Nick, while a crazy emotional rollercoaster both melted and exploded inside her at the same time. Tingling surges of passion raced through her body. Every nerve ending set afire. She lost focus, breathing heavily, consumed by overwhelming pleasure so intense she called out his name. Again and again, she almost surfaced, and then drowned in painfully sweet euphoria until she lay, limp and exhausted, on damp sheets.

After making love, she had cried, unable to say why. He held her to his chest, stroking her long dark hair until her tears were spent.

* * *

Angie sat back in the car seat, closed her eyes, and allowed a great wave of emotion to wash over her. She remembered his last words before a goodbye kiss at the airport.

'I love you Angie Lambrakis. I'm going to miss you,' he said. 'You must call me *at least* ten times a day.'

Angie sighed, dropped her phone onto the passenger seat, and returned to the mission in hand.

The small chapel next to the war memorial appeared quite modern and new. Through the open doors, she could see hundreds of highly polished gold lamps that hung from the ceiling. She took another picture, wondering about the significance of so many lanterns. A question to ask if conversation got awkward at her grandmother's.

Angie realised she was stalling. This plan to find out what had upset her mother so much, for all these years, was only the half of it. She also hoped to learn about her father, Yeorgo. Poppy said he was killed. Died in the army before she was born. There had to be more than that, but her mother would never talk about him.

Angie needed to connect with her Dad. Was that so hard for Poppy to understand? She wanted to see her father's birthplace, where he grew up, if any of his siblings were still alive. And discover Poppy's Cretan life and family too. She was searching for her roots and knew she couldn't be completely happy and able to start this new phase of her life until she found them.

A coach pulled up, tourists tumbling out, camera phones at the ready. Angie put the car in gear and drove down into the village of Amiras.

A bakery, kafenion, supermarket, and post office clustered around a central square. She parked opposite the supermarket. Men, sitting outside the neighbouring kafenion, stretched their necks and stared.

'*Yia sas!*' Angie called, knowing the stranger should greet first. They grinned and reciprocated.

She slipped into the dimly-lit shop, blind for a moment after the bright sunlight. Behind the counter, a handsome, thickset, forty-ish man looked up from a basketball game on TV. He stubbed his cigarette into a full ashtray and stood.

'Angelika? I am Demitri, welcome.' He shook Angie's hand, his smile cautious, eyes curious. 'Your grandmother's waiting.'

'Thank you, Demitri. I've brought her a lemon tree. It's in the car.' Angie blushed, wishing she had bought cakes too, or a nice piece of cut glass. Elderly people liked to receive ornaments. She had heard the Cretans were exceedingly generous. Now she was going to look mean and penny-pinching and she realised how much she wanted them to like her. Almost overcome by the longing to meet her family and be accepted, she watched Demitri's face.

'A lemon tree?' His smile widened. 'Maria is going to like that. Leave the car open, someone will bring it to the house.'

He didn't bother to close the supermarket door. They walked fifty metres along the narrow road and turned left at a row of green rubbish bins. Skinny, long-legged cats with grubby noses searched among the refuse. They stared with glassy eyes, their tails straight, the tips flicking. Angie followed Demitri up uneven cement steps flanked by trees that met overhead.

The air chilled in the shade. Angie's thoughts returned to her mother. Poppy had grown up here, played as a child and walked with Angie's father. What made her mother leave Crete? Why wouldn't she talk about Angie's father or her homeland? Muddled by melancholy, and a sudden dread of meeting her grandmother, Angie felt apprehensive about what lay ahead.

She searched for an excuse to turn back, afraid there was more to the family breakup than a simple quarrel. What if deep hatred awaited her? Why hadn't she thought of this earlier? Her grandmother might be deranged, angry and violent, and as much against a reunion as Poppy.

Perhaps this was the reason Poppy objected to the visit with such vehemence? Despite the shade, sweat prickled Angie's forehead.

She jumped when a rust-coloured hen ran across the path. Her legs seemed leaden, her body reluctant to move forward. At the top of the climb they broke into sunshine. A short walk took them to a red-roofed cottage. The garden overflowed with flowers. Riotous clumps of reds, pinks and purples fought for space, plants bursting from an odd collection of buckets and cans.

Two gnarled olive trees threw mottled shade over the area. In the corner of the plot was a white-painted stone oven. Long nails driven into the mortar supported an axe, scythe, and mattock. The glint of fresh steel along age-blackened blades suggested the tools were newly sharpened. From one stout olive branch, a length of chain with a couple of heavy butcher's hooks hung as still as death. Behind the trees lay a freshly-turned rectangle of red earth furrowed by neat rows of vegetables.

Aware of her breathlessness after the steps, Demitri asked, 'Are you okay, Angelika?' The overweight smoker seemed unaffected by the climb.

'Give me a moment, I'll be fine.' She filled her lungs and blew slowly.

'Don't worry, it's the altitude,' Demitri said. He nodded at the house. 'This place is about two hundred years old, and the trees are three times that.' He pulled a multi-coloured fly curtain aside and shouted, '*Yiayá!*'

Angie pressed her hand against her chest and felt her heart thudding. She was about to meet her grandmother. Through the low entrance, two stone steps led down between cottage walls half a metre thick. She entered a cool, white-painted lounge with simple furniture. A gaudy icon of Saint George, displaying his dragon slaying skills, hung on the longest wall and a converted copper gaslight was suspended over a round, wooden table. A sharp-eyed matriarch sat on the sofa.

Chapter 3

ANGIE'S GRANDMOTHER, MARIA, WORE a faded blue dress and a washed-out floral scarf over her white hair. In the dim living room, the old lady appeared strangely fragile, almost ghostly, as if she had appeared in a dream.

'Hello, *Yiayá*.' Angie cranked up a smile. 'How are you?'

The old woman fixed Angie with a squint. Her sharp eyes darted over Angie's face, scrutinising every detail. She frowned at Angie's hands, stared at her feet, and came back up to meet her eyes.

Hardly breathing, Angie chewed her lip. A bead of sweat slithered down her spine.

After a moment, Maria's tension fell away and her eyes twinkled. She patted the seat beside her. When Angie sat, Maria cupped her chin, peered at her again and pressed a shaky hand against Angie's cheek.

'Oh, Poppy . . . your precious child has come to me after all these years,' Maria whispered. 'It's a miracle. I've waited so very long.' The old lady's eyes brimmed.

Angie's excitement peaked, then, to her dismay, her grandmother's tears spilled. She pulled a pack of tissues from her handbag and gently dried the old lady's face, worried that her grandmother might not be strong enough for so much emotion. But despite her tears, Maria seemed genuinely pleased to see her.

'Sorry, sorry, please don't cry, *Yiayá*,' Angie pleaded. 'I didn't mean to upset you.'

Despite her great age, the high cheekbones and classical beauty of Maria's youth shone through her deeply-lined face. She sniffed and nodded, taking the tissue from Angie and dabbing her nose.

'Hello, Angelika,' she finally said, her voice weak but clear. She pulled Angie forward to kiss her cheeks and forehead. But then her emotions rose again. 'Oh my poor child . . .' she muttered, shaking her head, allowing fresh tears to fall. 'How I've missed you all these long years.'

That would be Poppy, Angie thought, wrapping her arms around her fragile grandmother and allowing Maria to cry on her shoulder. A great rush of relief, and love, coursed through her and, as she held the old lady in her arms, she found herself sniffing back tears too.

Before they had a chance to chat, the neighbours arrived. Angie dried her grandmother's face, and then her own. They held hands and smiled at each other as the room filled with local women. All the questions for her grandmother went on hold and, deep inside, Angie found herself bursting with affection for the woman she had only met minutes earlier.

'*Yia sas!*' or, 'Welcome, welcome!' the local women shouted. Several were proud to speak English, eager to practise the language, others were shy and smiling. No one came empty-handed. Supermarket bags, stuffed to their over-stretched handles with local fruit and vegetables, lined the wall. Plates of cookies, candied peel and olives for Angie to take to England, covered the round table. The village people with their broad smiles and curious eyes had no concept of 'Luggage Allowance: twenty kilos'.

Two hours passed before Angie was finally left alone with her grandmother.

Maria studied her, stern for a moment, and then affection rolled in and softened her features. 'You look like your father,' she said, sliding a shaky hand down Angie's face. 'How often I prayed that one day I would touch the cheek of my granddaughter.'

Angie smiled, desperate to hear about her father.

'How is Poppy?' Maria said.

Angie threw her head back and smiled. 'I'm so lucky. I couldn't wish for a better mother. She worked hard to put me through university, really made some huge sacrifices. Not just that, she's become more of a friend, recently. Nothing's too much trouble. We share almost everything.' Angie smiled again, proud. 'I moved in with my partner, Nick, three years ago, but I go home regularly and often stay over with Mam. She's amazing . . . makes the perfect Sunday roast, and always bakes something special for me.'

Maria seemed to glow.

'I'm getting married soon,' Angie continued. 'That's my big news, and Mam's a bit het up about the wedding. She adores my fiancé, Nick; "a fine Greek boy", she calls him.' She hugged herself. 'He *is* wonderful; kind, handsome, hardworking, everything I could wish for. I can't wait for you to meet him.'

'So Poppy approves?'

Angie nodded. 'Mam sends her love,' she lied.

Maria's eyes narrowed.

Angie turned away, hiding her guilt.

Glancing over the gifts that cluttered the room, she tried to change the subject. 'I'll never be able to take all this to England, *Yiayá*.'

Maria wasn't distracted. 'You were saying, about Poppy?'

Angie tried again. 'I'd like to draw my family tree, and perhaps write about my ancestors' history. Nick and I want a family, *Yiayá*, that's one of the reasons we're getting married. I'm thirty-seven, so . . .' She shrugged. Maria nodded. Angie continued. 'It's important that children are familiar with their roots, don't you think?' A weak excuse for digging into the family's past – would her grandmother see through it?

'What was Poppy's reaction to this family tree idea?' Maria insisted.

Stubborn, Angie thought, a trait she recognised in herself. 'To be honest, she's reluctant to help me with it.' She sighed and met her grandmother's eyes. 'In fact, she refuses to discuss it.' The truth brought heat to her cheeks.

Maria nodded. 'Understandable.' She pulled a bag of crocheting from under the table. Despite her poor eyesight and crooked fingers, she worked the fine crochet hook through the lace.

'How beautiful, *Yiayá*.' Angie fingered the filigree. 'What are you making?'

'It's the last item for your dowry, Angelika. A tablecloth. May God give me time to finish it.'

'My dowry? But how did you know I was getting married?'

Maria seemed to shrink a little, her eyes flicking to the icon of Saint George. She bowed her head and continued crocheting as she spoke. 'Naturally, you must have your wedding linen, Angelika, but I'm not aware of what my daughter has made.'

The words were forced and Angie heard pain in her voice.

'Mam wanted to come too, but she has the influenza, *Yiayá*. Perhaps next time.'

Maria looked up. She had recognised another lie. Angie's cheeks burned and she turned away.

Yiayá reached over and patted her thigh. 'Don't worry; it's not your fault.' She sat with her thoughts for a minute, stiffened, clamped her mouth and shook her head.

Again, Angie wondered what had caused this terrible rift between her mother and grandmother. 'I'm sorry,' she said quietly.

'No need. I know you mean well.' Maria shrugged.

'Was it wrong of me to come here, *Yiayá*?' Angie watched her grandmother's face as she continued. 'I've wanted to meet you for a very long time, but Mam became upset when I told her. I'm sorry to say we had a huge fight.'

'I was waiting, Angelika, *hoping* one day you would visit. About your mother, what was said? Don't spare my feelings, Angelika. I need to hear the whole story.' Maria stroked the scars on her hands.

Angie hesitated, but then thought if she wanted her grandmother to be totally honest and tell her everything, she owed Maria the truth.

'Me and Nick, we have a small flat in the city. It's fabulous, and he's lovely too.'

Angie closed her eyes for a moment and recalled the first time she met Nick. He had walked into her office, smartly suited-up, arm outstretched, and caught her eating a sandwich while playing Candy Crush on her computer.

'Hi, I'm Nick; new head of department,' he had said with a twinkle in his eye.

'Oh, sorry, lunch break,' she replied through a mouthful of egg mayo. Crumbs, brushed from her chest, sprinkled her keyboard. He looked on, grinning as he so often did, eyes bright and face full of amusement. Heat rose in her cheeks. Being flustered was something Angie rarely experienced.

At his first staff meeting the next day, she had scribbled notes, her hand on automatic while her heart did somersaults every time he glanced her way.

She fingered her engagement ring and said to her grandmother, 'We've lived together for three years, *Yiayá*. I love him to bits.'

Maria patted Angie's leg again. 'I see it.'

'Sometimes, Nick takes in freelance editing and works from the flat. The extra money is to pay for our wedding and a house we've set our hearts on. It's better if I'm not home, distracting him, so I usually go out with my friends or visit Mam. Me and Nick, we're employed by the same company, so we're practically together all day.' She stopped, her shoulders drooping as she remembered her jobless situation. 'Except that I've been made redundant, so that's all changed. I haven't had time to adjust yet; but I hope to find employment with another publishing house soon,' she added quickly with confidence she didn't feel. 'I've always had a nice time at Mam's, until recently.' Angie tugged her lip, thinking about her mother. 'Things haven't been so good lately.'

'Tell me about it,' Maria sat back. 'What started the trouble with Poppy?'

Angie recalled life before her redundancy, when everything seemed perfect. At her mother's house, she searched for her birth certificate. That was the afternoon when her problems really began.

Chapter 4

London, One Week Earlier.

PERCHED ON THE BALLS of her feet, Angie pressed against the wardrobe mirror and reached for a cardboard box. She tightened her grip and pulled. A dust avalanche cascaded over her head. She sneezed, banged her forehead against the glass and fell back onto her heels.

Exasperated, she tried again. Once the carton had tilted past the point of no return, the contents slid to one end and Angie couldn't keep hold. The cardboard split and a lifetime of documents bombarded her.

Guarantees, instruction books and Greek paperwork that belonged to Poppy littered the floor. Angie spotted a passport application leaflet. Hadn't she needed her birth certificate when she applied for her first passport? Her sigh sent airborne motes percolating towards the window as she recalled signing the bottom line. Her mother had taken care of the rest.

She noticed an old A4 envelope caught in the base of the box. If her birth certificate was inside, she could complete the form for her wedding licence.

In the packet, Angie found a bundle of letters, pages smoothed flat and tied together with ribbon. The first, dated with the year of her birth, and the last one; quite recent. She blinked at them, curious and then excited. Perhaps they were from her father. But no, he had died before she was born. Angie had nothing of his, not even a picture. The sheets of pale Greek handwriting were almost undecipherable, each one signed: *Love and kisses, Stavro*. Disappointed, she wondered who this Stavro could be.

'Angelika, what on earth's going on up there? Dinner's ready,' Poppy shouted up the stairs.

Angie slid the letters back into the envelope and placed them on the bed with the other documents, respecting her mother's privacy.

Downstairs, she sat opposite her mother in the Victorian kitchen. Perhaps Stavro was an old friend, she mused, glancing at Poppy. Clearly her mother had been very beautiful. Now, in her mid-sixties, she was still attractive with a good figure and smooth olive-coloured skin; but a boyfriend? Angie didn't think so.

'Mm, roast lamb, it's making my mouth water,' Angie said, suddenly hungry. She noticed a dish containing two red-dyed eggs and a simple white candle in the centre of the table. 'Ah, of course, it's Orthodox Easter. I'd forgotten.'

'It is. What were you doing in the spare room?' Poppy said.

'Searching for my birth certificate. Sorry about the mess. Any idea where it might be?'

Poppy glanced at an empty chair before concentrating on her food.

'Can't think . . . why do you need it?'

'My marriage licence application,' Angie said.

'Fill the form in and leave it here. I'll find your certificate and post it tomorrow. That room needs a seeing-to anyway.'

'Mam, you're a star. Nick's meeting me at the estate agent's later. We're going to view the property again before making an offer. It's perfect; in a good school area, too.'

Poppy's eyes widened. 'You're not . . . ?'

'No, but I hope I will be soon. Thirty-seven, Mam. My biological clock's ticking away. Perhaps you'd like to come and see the house with us?'

'Another time. I'll sort the spare room, get your paperwork done, and look forward to seeing you sometime next week.'

'Thanks. Promise you'll help me choose the dress,' Angie said.

'Of course.' Poppy looked up, brown eyes filled with pride.

'And the invitations, I need the addresses of everyone in Crete.'

Her mother's smile fell, and her cutlery clattered to the plate. She slapped a hand over her mouth, swallowed hard and blew through her fingers.

'Mam . . . what's the matter, are you all right?'

'A bit of food down the wrong way, that's all.' Poppy frowned and thumped her chest. 'Angelika, can we forget your wedding for an hour and just enjoy Easter by ourselves?'

The annual return to Greek Orthodox tradition made Angie smile. 'Come on then, let's crack the eggs against each other,' Angie said. 'See who'll get their wish granted this year.'

They each took an egg and banged them together. Poppy won, her egg remaining intact while Angie's shattered.

'Make your Easter wish, Mam,' she said, thinking her own silent prayer that her mother would find the peace and happiness she so rightly deserved.

Quiet for a moment, Poppy closed her eyes and buried her face in her hands.

Angie wondered what her mother wanted. 'I hope your wishes come true, Mam. Thanks for seeing to my wedding licence; another job crossed off.'

Poppy took an apple pie from the oven and passed Angie a knife before she filled the kettle.

'Can we tackle the guest list this week?' Angie said. 'I've seen the most gorgeous invitations, white parchment framed with the Greek keys in silver. The wedding planners are going to write everyone's name in calligraphy.' She grinned at Poppy, pausing for effect before she continued. 'And listen to this, Mam, you'll love it. Not only will the Cretan invites be written in Greek, but also using the Greek alphabet! What do you think? Fantastic, or what?'

Poppy flinched.

'And then next week, we can talk about the cake,' Angie said. 'You're such a great cook, Mam. Can you make the actual wedding cake? Three tiers on Doric columns, and I thought the Greek keys pattern around the sides to tie in with the invitations. Simple, but classic.' She stopped, suddenly concerned by the anguish on her mother's face. 'Mam, are you all right? What's the matter? Don't worry, we can buy the cake.'

Poppy turned away. 'Look, Angelika, I'll tell you straight, I don't want you to invite the Cretans.' Giving the tea her full attention, she shared a teabag between two mugs. 'We haven't seen them since before you were born. Save your money towards the house.' She fished out the teabag, stared at the drinks and scratched the back of her hand.

Angie cut generous portions of pie. The delicious smells of apple and cinnamon clouded around her. 'They're your parents, we have to ask them. If my daughter got married and didn't invite you, you'd be terribly hurt, Mam. Don't worry about the money. We've saved for this for years. Nick, God bless him, is still putting in lots of extra hours, so we can have the wedding we want.' Angie glanced about the room realising she couldn't remember seeing anyone but her mother, and occasionally Nick, in the big old house.

Since Aunty Heleny had died, Poppy seemed to have become something of a recluse. Perhaps she found the thought of so many guests descending on her suffocating, or even frightening. Poor Mam. Angie made a mental note to research agoraphobia and then help Poppy to get over whatever was making her so anxious. After all, there was no point in having the perfect wedding if her mother did not enjoy every moment of it too.

'Well I don't want you inviting them,' Poppy said, tension making her voice brittle. 'I haven't asked for much concerning your marriage, so do this one thing for me. Invite Aunty Heleny's folk, God rest her soul. Your godmother was all the real family we ever had.'

'Why? It makes no sense. I'd like to meet *Yiayá* and *Papoú* and show them my husband,' Angie said. 'You've kept them from me all my life, Mam, and I've no idea why. But now we're talking about our wedding. It's important to me and Nick.'

'Just save yourself the stamp, Angelika.' Poppy stared into the distance, her voice softening as she spoke about her father. '*Papoú* is ninety-three, love, they'd never make it to London.'

'No, Mam. They don't actually have to come here. There's no need to fret about finding accommodation for dozens of people you haven't seen in decades.' She watched her mother's face, slightly ashamed that she hadn't given Poppy's lack of social life a thought before now.

Poppy's shoulders dropped and Angie realised how tense she was.

'Mam, you don't have to worry. I'm all organised. I've been dying to tell you all week.' She grinned, sure her mother would love this latest idea of hers. 'One of the girls at work got married recently and her family were from Jamaica. You can imagine the problems, because they all wanted her to get married there.'

Poppy stared at the empty chair at the head of the table and then glanced around the room. Whatever Poppy was so concerned about, was sure to be nullified by Angie's plan.

'My colleague's wedding planners organised a little reception in Jamaica for those that couldn't come here. Then, they called her grandparents on video conferencing, shortly before she left for the church. Isn't that a brilliant idea?' Simply talking her wedding through with her mother uplifted her. 'They'll see me and Nick the morning we get married, and be part of the celebration. I'd love to hear them wish us health and happiness. And when we honeymoon in Crete, we can take them cake and favours. I can't wait –'

'Honeymoon in Crete?' Poppy screwed her eyes and shook her head. 'No, you're not listening. *NO!*'

Angie's elation fell away. 'Please, stop this nonsense, Mam. A wedding is all about families and love and bringing people together. I won't let you spoil it. As for Dad's family, I don't even know their names, so you can at least allow me this!'

A cry caught in Poppy's throat while she raked at the back of her hand.

'Mam, stop scratching, you're bleeding.' Angie's stomach rolled at the sight of her mother's blood. She took a napkin and tenderly dabbed at the lacerations. 'You silly thing, it's really deep. Come and put it under the tap.'

'Please, Angelika, forget your mad ideas, they're simple people. I'll bet you won't find a computer in the entire village. You build things up in your head. They don't know you, and you don't know them, leave it alone now.'

'What's the matter? Where's your heart? You're saying I can't even speak to my own family?' They stood at the sink, cold water running over Poppy's wound. 'Tell me why you insisted I learned Greek, then? What was the point?'

Angie dressed the hand and then made fresh tea. The silence built up like an ugly wall between them until, frustrated, she blasted through it with words louder than intended. 'Come on, Mam, we have to talk about this. Why are you being difficult? Why shouldn't I invite them? I have a right –'

'Stop it, don't push me,' Poppy interrupted. 'Let me speak in my own time.'

Angie recalled her teenage years when they last argued about this. Angie had wanted to go to Crete for a holiday with her university mates. Poppy went berserk and Angie and her friends eventually booked a week in Benidorm. Crete became a taboo subject.

But this had nothing to do with holidays. This was about roots, love, uniting the family and celebrating solidarity. She tried to find the words to explain but her mother cut in, glaring at her.

'You know I don't want to discuss it. Why won't you leave it? I spent years burying the past – my past – and now you're digging it all up, opening wounds. You're so stubborn and selfish. You couldn't care less if you break my heart, just so long as you have what you want.'

Shocked at her mother's outburst, Angie stared at the untouched apple pie. Ashamed, she admitted to herself that Poppy was right – she was stubborn and selfish. But why couldn't her mother see the wedding was so important to her? Still determined to understand Poppy's angst, she blocked the emotional blackmail and did her best to keep the dialogue going, even though she knew it would probably upset her mother further. 'Mam, I'm an adult, please trust me. Explain what turned you against your family.'

'You don't want to know!'

'I do want to know!'

Her mother's shoulders dropped and she picked at the edge of the dressing on her hand. 'If I do, will you promise not to ask me again?'

Angie hesitated. 'Can't you see I need to understand, Mam? Tell me. Why are you so against me contacting them? Then I can make up my own mind.'

Poppy nagged her lip for a moment. 'Okay, I'll tell you the bare bones but don't you judge me. And let that be an end to it, all right?'

Angie wavered. The past couldn't be that bad. 'Mam, whatever happened, it won't change our relationship. I just need to know, that's all.' Over the years, surely a minor incident had escalated in Poppy's mind. Angie hugged her tea and watched her mother stare around the room.

Poppy gathered herself together. 'The trouble started after our marriage. A terrible feud built up between my family and your father's. I can't describe how awful, Angelika, honestly, you've no idea. Everyone was fighting. Things got steadily worse until the situation became impossible. Better if they all forgot me, so I left.' Poppy stared at the floor.

'A feud, you mean you had a quarrel with your in-laws? Is that what's upsetting you?' Angie sighed with a mixture of relief and disbelief.

Poppy's head snapped around, eyes narrow, her skin seemed to bleach and tighten over her face. 'No, damn it . . . a real feud. People suffered the most terrible consequences. People I – we all loved. It divided the village.' She inhaled sharply, fighting a wave of emotion. 'That they might come after your father next, terrified me so much. I tried . . .' Poppy closed her eyes. Her throat and chest made little convulsions against sobs.

Terrified? Surely she's exaggerating?

Angie hated herself for dragging up the past but she was determined to get to the bottom of her mother's distress.

Poppy took a damp cloth from the sink and wiped the worktops, the front of the fridge and around their plates of pie. Angie remained silent, allowing Poppy to gather her thoughts.

When her mother reached for the broom, Angie's heart went out to her, 'Mam, stop. Come and sit next to me.'

Poppy studied the spotless floor for a moment and then returned to the kitchen table. After another minute of silence, she said, 'I tried to put a stop to the fighting but everything started to go wrong.' Her voice fell to a whisper. 'If only I could live my life over, love. Things would be different.'

Poppy stared hard at Angie, reached out and touched her daughter's cheek. 'But then, perhaps not.' Her eyes softened. 'I probably wouldn't change a thing.' She pushed her hair back and white roots flashed at the base of her dark curls.

Angie covered her mother's hand with her own and spoke softly. 'Go on, Mam; don't stop now, share it with me, you'll feel better.'

'My brother, Matthia, lay unconscious in hospital when I left, his face so swollen I didn't recognise him. His ribs were smashed and his lungs almost punctured. Your uncles had tried to kick him to death.'

'What!'

'The surgeon said he'd live but the police told us, when the doctors discharged him, he would go to prison. My own brother locked up, because of my actions. I should have been jailed, Angelika, but don't ask why. Don't put me through that.'

Angie found it difficult to know what to say when she didn't have all the facts. What had her mother done? She slid her hand over Poppy's again, and stroked the plaster. 'Wounds heal, Mam.'

'Not these wounds.' Poppy thumped herself in the chest. 'You can't bring back the dead!'

Shocked, Angie wondered who had died, but knew that to interrupt now would stop Poppy from opening up.

'Poor Matthia! If you had seen the state of him.' She shook her head. 'They forbade him to marry their sister, and they sent her away to Athens. He loved Agapi so much, it broke his heart. I told them all to forget me and I believe they have, Angelika. How else could I stop the vendettas? I begged Stavro, my other brother, for money and I ran away to London.'

Stavro . . . the letters.

Poppy closed her eyes and pinched the bridge of her nose. 'Your father signed up for life in the army. I didn't see him again, and that's my punishment. I don't know when he died or where his bones are. It broke my heart, smashed it to smithereens.'

Angie tried to imagine not seeing Nick again, never visiting her mother again. 'I wish you'd told me all this before, Mam. I'm ashamed to have doubted you. I never imagined . . . how awful.' How could she have been so naïve and selfish? 'What an awful tragedy to go through by yourself, Mam.' She slipped her arm around Poppy's shoulders and gave her a squeeze.

'You still don't understand, Angelika, but get this into your stubborn head.' She shrugged from under Angie's arm. 'I do not want to see my family. It's too painful for me and it would be too painful for them. Let's drop it now. Please.'

'But why did Dad go and join the army? Couldn't he work here so that you'd be together?'

'You and your damn questions! Why are you doing this to me?'

'Look, I'm sorry, okay!' She had pushed Poppy too far. Her voice softened. 'No, really . . . I am sorry, Mam. I didn't mean to hurt you.' Concerned to see her mother so emotionally distressed, Angie wished she could take on Poppy's pain. She reached out a comforting arm.

Poppy gulped, stiffly shrinking away from her with an air of pathos. 'Can't you understand it's a tragedy that I want to forget? Haven't I suffered enough?' She stared, hurt and sadness etched around her eyes. Her mouth worked but it took a few moments before she put sound to her words. 'All right, for God's sake I'll tell you.' She paused, screwing her eyes closed again. 'Your father left because, when he came to London and found me, *I* sent him away. Before you were born, *I* sent him away.' She shoved her plate. It skidded across the polished table and teetered for a second before it crashed to the floor.

Angie jumped up.

'Leave it!' Poppy shouted and then she whispered, 'Why can't you just leave it?' She hugged herself. 'You can't imagine how often I've regretted that . . . sending my darling Yeorgo away, seeing you grow up without a father. I hope you'll never experience such heartache.' Tears rolled down her face and then her voice dropped. 'I've thought about him and missed him every day since, for all these long years. I don't want the Cretans to know why he re-enlisted and left for Cyprus. Don't stir it all up again.'

'You sent him away?' Shocked, she held back her own pain at this revelation, understanding a reprimand would only worsen the situation. She tried to comfort her mother, calm her down.

'Mam, it happened so long ago. Things change – people change – they're our family. They'll understand.'

'No,' Poppy whispered. 'I can't come to your wedding if they do. You'll force me to go away until they've returned to Crete. I swore they'd never lay eyes on me again. Invite them if you must. It's your choice. I can leave. That's my ultimatum.'

Riddled with guilt, Angie tried to push her mother into a family reunion with a counter ultimatum. 'Are you saying that they're more important than me, than what I want? Just for our whole family to be together for one special moment? Is it too much to ask? If you don't come to my wedding, you know very well I won't get married.'

'That's not fair,' Poppy said. 'It's you that's saying the Cretans are more important than me. You don't know them. I do. Trust me, Angelika, please! It's for the best. You're my life. Don't bring back the past. I'm begging you.'

Chapter 5

Crete, Present Day.

Forlorn, Angie stared at her hands. 'We never used to argue, ever, but I wanted to know why Mam left Crete. It sounds crazy, but the more she refused to talk about it, the more preoccupied I became. In the end, it was as if I'd become obsessed by her secrets.' She closed her eyes for a moment, recalling all the tension of previous weeks.

'Then, last week, I had a car accident on my way home from Mam's. I ran a red light, too busy thinking about our argument instead of concentrating on the road. Nobody was hurt, thank God, but it could have been worse.'

Yiayá crossed herself.

Angie continued, 'I got myself in a state and Nick caught me having a cry about it. He said enough was enough. The time had come to get to the bottom of Mam's distress. He's such a darling, *Yiayá*, so sensitive. He couldn't stand to see me upset when I returned from Mam's. I realise I've hurt her, and I feel awful, but for some crazy reason that I don't understand, I can't let it go. Nick was the one who suggested I came here to find you.' Angie took a deep breath before she asked, 'Will *you* tell me my family history, *Yiayá*? I want to know what's at the root of Mam's terrible unhappiness.'

Maria squinted at the window and contemplated. Early afternoon sun pierced the handmade curtains and lacy shadows danced over her. 'I'll think about it, Angelika. Now, it's time for my sleep. I'm tired. Come back tomorrow and meet your grandfather.'

Angie returned to her car, preoccupied by her grandmother. *Yiayá* seemed so nice. Surely she would want to help Poppy recover from whatever had hurt her. The idea that Angie could arrive in London with new understanding, and the seeds of resolution, and healing made her so happy she wanted to pull on her sweats and jog through the streets.

In the shimmering heat, siesta had settled over the village. Angie heard a raucous dog and an egotistical rooster, then the place became as still and silent as an abandoned film set. She drove back to Viannos.

* * *

'My grandmother's amazing, Manoli,' Angie said the next morning when he brought her coffee under the big tree. 'She's going to tell me about my family's past, today. I'm quite excited.'

Manoli blinked. 'Your history? You mean you don't –'

Cretan music jangled from a megaphone on the roof of a pickup, drowning Manoli's words. The vehicle contained several boxes of fish and an old-fashioned brass scale dangled from the back. Manoli shoved his thumb and forefinger into his mouth and whistled. The truck braked, crunched gears, and backed-up to the kerb.

'Take your grandparents some fresh sardines. They are very good now,' Manoli shouted over the jangle of music.

* * *

In Amiras, cats sniffed the air as Angie passed. Several felines leapt from the bins and stalked her, mewing and peering at the bag of fish. She chucked a sardine as far down the steps as possible and then she ran. Angie reached the top of the climb wheezing like an asthmatic donkey.

In the garden, behind the cottage, Maria sat at a long, grey, marble table that had a jagged crack through the centre, dividing the table in a strangely artistic way. Delighted with the sardines, she said, 'Let's sit inside, Angelika. It's cooler.'

Angie felt sharp old bones through the cotton dress when she helped Maria out of her white plastic chair. In the living room, she broached the family history again.

'Are you sure you want this, Angelika? You may regret it. You can't return my words like an unwanted gift if you change your mind.'

'I have to understand, *Yiayá*. It's important to me, and Mam refuses to talk about what happened here.'

'Poppy has her reasons,' Maria said.

'But I don't know them. If I ask, she becomes distressed and hurts herself. She scratches the backs of her hands until she's bleeding. It's a nervous habit she has and it's truly awful. Sometimes, I hear her crying in bed at night. The doctor has given her sleeping pills, and I'm terribly afraid it will be tranquillisers next.

Maria took a sharp intake of breath and touched her mouth.

'I can't bear to see my mother so unhappy. It breaks my heart. I want to help her find peace,' Angie explained with all sincerity.

Maria's face clouded. She stared at the floor and then brushed a tear from her eye. When she spoke, Angie heard both hurt and irony in her voice. 'And you think if I tell you what Poppy doesn't want you to know, it will make her feel better?'

'Put like that, possibly not.' Angie leaned back in her chair and thought about it. 'But I do believe, if I understood why Mam's so unhappy, I could try to ease her pain. I'm desperate to help her.'

The silence seemed heavy in the room, but then the old woman spoke kindly. 'Has it occurred to you that perhaps Poppy's protecting you from something?' Maria stared at Angie and crossed herself three times. 'If you understand what happened here, in the past, it might alter your future, Angelika.'

'*Yiayá*, I love my mother. She's a good person, wonderful, generous and kind, and I admire her greatly. Nothing anyone tells me can change that.'

Maria patted Angie's knee. 'May those thoughts always stay with you, child.'

Angie frowned.

'If I tell you, then you'll get the whole story, Angelika. I won't leave out the unpleasant things. I haven't the strength to pick and choose what you should hear, and I'll astonish you with the cruelty of it all. It won't be something you can put out of your head.'

Angie hesitated, for a moment unsure of what she might stir up. But in the end, she had to know the truth – everything – for her mother's sake. She supposed the truth must come with a truckload of tragedy, because Angie did understand how much the past still upset Poppy.

'Don't worry about me, *Yiayá*. Let's concentrate on getting Mam sorted.' After living in a big city all her life, Angie doubted anything that happened in the picturesque village of Amiras could shock her.

Maria studied her for a moment and then her eyes narrowed. 'You underestimate this wizened old woman, Angelika, but that will change.'

A white-haired man with a kind, open face leaned heavily on his stick as he tottered into the room. Before sitting in the corner by the fireplace, his great, shaggy moustache spread in a horizontal grin aimed at Angie.

Maria lifted her eyebrows and stared at him.

He shook his head as if replying to a question.

'I have to,' Maria said, 'before I die. It's important.'

Shocked by her grandmother's words, Angie waited to be introduced.

The old man frowned at the floor.

In the stillness of the cottage, Angie sensed emotion pass between the couple.

Maria pointed a bony finger towards the pensioner. 'Angelika, meet your grandfather, Vassili.'

My grandfather, my Papoú, *at last.*

Vassili tossed amber worry beads over the back of his fingers while his other hand gripped his *bastouni*, the traditional Cretan walking stick.

'Hello, *Papoú*.' Angie stood and kissed his white-stubbled cheeks.

The concern fell from his face and his eyes twinkled. 'Hello, *koritsie mou*.'

Koritsie mou – my girl; the words thrilled Angie. She had found her family.

Maria smoothed her skirt and glanced around the room.

Angie's excitement escalated.

Her grandmother went through an assortment of facial expressions, both happy and sad. After a few minutes, the old woman seemed to reach a decision.

'First, I need your promise, Angelika. When I'm dead you do as you like but, until then, keep this story to yourself. It's a tragedy worse than you can imagine, and I won't see anybody else hurt by it. Will you abide by my wishes?'

'Absolutely, *Yiayá*, but may I take notes while you talk? I want to remember everything to tell my future husband and children.'

'Ah, you remind me, there's a notebook on the shelf. Pass it to me.' Angie did and then watched her grandmother remove a sheet of Greek writing and hand it to her.

'I was writing you a letter, but I didn't get it finished,' Maria said.

'That's quite a coincidence.'

'The fates guide us,' Maria said. 'Here's the one I wrote to Poppy. I was going to post them together. Don't look at it now. Wait until you're in England. Read it to your mother.'

Angie folded the page and slipped it into the zip pocket of her handbag. Was she about to learn the cause of her mother's distress and something about the father she'd never known? She hoped so. Then she could return to London and Poppy would realise the past didn't matter as much as the present and the future.

Uplifted by relief, Angie hugged her grandmother. 'Thank you. You've no idea what this means to me.'

Maria hesitated and Angie realised she was still uncertain.

'Please, *Yiayá*,' she said.

Maria peered into Angie's eyes. 'I need time to think, Angelika. Go with your grandfather.' She turned to her husband. 'Old man, take Angelika through the house. Show her how we lived in those days, so she understands everything.'

Vassili nodded, pulled himself up and rested on Angie's shoulder. 'My grandfather built this place.' He waved his cane at the beamed ceiling. 'The roof was made with tree trunks and clay back then. Very strong; it kept the heat and rain out. Now we have foam stuff that mice eat and tiles that crack.'

He snorted. 'That's progress, hey? The youngsters always know better.'

Angie looked at him and remembered her mother's words: Papoú *is ninety-three*. She hadn't expected this jovial old man.

He poked the wall. 'No plaster or electric in those days. The walls were lime-washed every Easter, to stop fleas, and we lit the place with oil lamps.' He nodded at the fireplace. 'That's where we cooked, in one big pot. My grandfather built a kiln outside, for baking, but it used too much wood. It's still out there.' He lifted his chin to the window. 'The oven had a food safe on the back for the rusks and honey. If you keep sweet things in the house, you get pestered by bees and ants.'

'Tell her about the bread,' Maria said.

Angie smiled. *Yiayá* could talk about these things, but she wanted to include *Papoú*. She imagined herself and Nick as doddery old people, still caring about each other's feelings.

'Look up the chimney, *koritsie*,' Vassili said. 'There's a nook for the dough. It went in at night and we woke to a fresh loaf each morning.'

Angie peered up the flue but it was dark and soot-laden.

'Go through there, Angelika.' Vassili nodded at a curtain draped over a narrow archway.

The super modern kitchen with its faint smell of vanilla, coffee and roast meat surprised Angie.

Vassili stood taller and squared his shoulders. 'It's new, and this . . .' They turned and faced a small dining area with the largest plasma TV Angie had seen in a house.

'Oh my God!' she said.

Vassili crossed himself, stuck his chest out and said, 'A gift from our eldest son, Stavro. We don't see very well, *koritsie*.'

They grinned at each other but then Vassili's eyes dimmed.

'This used to be the bedroom, very traditional. All the houses were the same. One big wall-to-wall bed as high as this.' He leaned on her shoulder and waved his stick over the kitchen worktops. 'The mezzanine had wide steps and cupboards underneath for the clothes and linen. My father built it. Nice carving on the front. We were proud of that woodwork; the finest bed in the village. The baby slept in a hammock above us so that Maria could reach him.'

Vassili spoke with sadness. 'The Nazis destroyed it, burned everything. Nothing left of that bed but the children conceived there.'

'The Nazis . . . they were here? I didn't realise.'

'There's a lot you don't know, Angelika.'

'I kept meaning to do a little research, to understand where I came from, but I'm afraid my work and the wedding always got in the way. I never progressed much further than tourist information, *Papoú*.'

Vassili seemed sad, lost in his thoughts for a moment, and then his gloom lifted. He flashed a smile towards another handwoven blanket nailed across the opposite wall. 'The next room is more interesting.'

The third part of the house was a peculiar contrast to the steel and pine kitchen.

The dusky bedroom hinted of mildew and mothballs and myrrh. An odd collection of furniture, from polished walnut to pink marble Formica, stood side-by-side. Every flat surface supported a white crochet tablecloth and framed photographs of stiff-faced people. Jesus, and an iridescent 3D of a blinking Virgin Mary, featured prominently. Purple and red silk flowers with petals tipped in gold glitter, paid homage.

'This was the *appothiki*, the store room,' Vassili said. 'We kept the animals, olive oil, and the dried food here. The walls had recesses for cheeses.' He caught Angie's puzzled look. 'Because, in the thick wall, the cheese stayed cool for most of the year, ripening nicely.' He waved his stick. Angie ducked. The Virgin Mary blinked.

'There was a door where the window is. We had a goat for milk and cheese and we fattened her kid for meat, if the Nazis didn't get it first. Our chickens roosted here at night, safe from vermin. Polecats are *malákas*, that's why we have dogs. Polecats kill the fowl and steal the eggs. Do you have them in England?'

Angie shrugged. 'I've never seen one, *Papoú*.'

'You must have because I hear the English have many dogs.' He poked his stick towards the corner of the room. 'I buried our largest terracotta pot there, below the floor. In war time, it's important to have a hidey-hole, everyone knows that.'

Vassili lowered his stick. Jesus remained in place. His upturned eyes gazed at a mildew patch on the ceiling as he offered his bleeding heart.

Back in the lounge, Angie sat next to Maria. Vassili closed the cottage door and then settled into his chair. Concern returned to his face.

Maria glanced around the room. 'This journey will take me down a path of pain, child. If I shouldn't make it to the end, you mustn't feel guilty, Angelika.'

Startled, Angie stared at her grandmother, and then at her grandfather. He nodded and then shook his head. A spark of fear exploded in Angie's chest. She took her grandmother's bony hand.

'*Yiayá*, I don't want to –'

'Quiet now, Angelika. The decision's been made.' Maria closed her eyes and when she spoke again, decades had fallen from her voice.

'As I remember, the story started at dawn on the fourteenth of September, 1943 . . .'

Chapter 6

Crete, 14 September 1943.

At six o'clock in the morning, hunger woke me. In the musty warmth of the big bed, I listened to the breathing of my two boys, Stavro and Matthia, beside me. My thoughts settled on my husband, Vassili, fighting in Albania. After ten long months, I missed him enormously. Would he remember his son's name-day today? Should I cook the remains of our beans to celebrate the feast of The Holy Cross, Saint Stavro, or should I plant them? This war wouldn't last forever.

The thought of a bean casserole with wild herbs and a splash of lemon made my belly rumble so loudly I feared it would wake the children. Baby Petro stirred in his hammock. He would cry for my breast soon. I rocked the fabric cradle, hoping he would sleep longer.

I slipped from our bed, crept into the living room and pulled the front door open. Cool air drifted in, earthy and fresh. In the wide fireplace, embers flared and flames danced into life. With a small copper *brickie,* I scooped water from the pail before settling the long-handled jug in the ashes. Coffee would be wonderful but we had none. I added chopped olive leaves and a pinch of mountain herbs to the *brickie* and then reached inside the chimney stack. The bread had baked hard overnight. I lifted it to my nose and inhaled its sweet, nutty smell. I had used the last of the flour and bulked the loaf out with sunflower seeds and crushed chickpeas. Thank God the wheat harvest would start in a few weeks. If I found work in the field, I hoped payment would be in flour. Money had little value now.

The oil lamp flickered into life and I sat in peace with my warm bread drizzled with olive oil and a sprinkle of salt, and my cup of herb tea. If I didn't eat, my milk would dry up and my baby starve.

Stavro wandered in, sleep-tousled and innocent-faced.

'Come here, my boy.' I hugged him and kissed his damp cheeks. 'A big year for you, son. It's your name-day today, Stavro. Your father will be thinking of you. Let's eat bread together.' I gave him my knife, an honour to the child. 'Cut yourself a slice.'

Stavro stood taller, the seven-year-old boy trying to be a man. While he hacked at the loaf I had to turn my head, fearing for his fingers. I stood the bucket of water in the embers, a treat to have a warm wash this morning.

Petro slept after I'd suckled him. An easy baby, content to feed and sleep through his days and nights, oblivious to our troubles. I tucked him back into the hammock and set about my chores. The sun appeared over the mountains. Long shadows through the golden sunlight reminded me to water our struggling crops, before the earth became hot.

I carried the pail to our vegetable patch but, before I emptied it, a scream came from behind the house. My heart leapt. I dropped the bucket and raced to the back plot. Stavro and Matthia were a tangle of limbs rolling in the dirt. I wanted to smack them both.

'Stop it! What are you doing?'

'He put a snail down my vest!' Matthia, almost five, pointed at his brother.

'I did not!' Stavro said.

'Act your ages and get on with your chores or you'll have no dinner.' They *were* acting their ages, of course.

There wasn't a cloud in the sky and I didn't expect to see one before late October. Until then, every drop of water was precious. I poured the contents of the bucket into a hollow of pale earth, hard and cracked, around a spindly tomato plant. The soil sucked down the scummy liquid. Three heavy tomatoes, bigger than my fist, hung from the vine but the fruit needed a few more days to ripen. I licked my lips thinking of the feast: chopped tomato on rusks with wild oregano, olive oil and salt. I hoped the soldiers wouldn't find them and reminded myself to keep a few pips for replanting. About to turn back to the house, I noticed the heel of Matthia's shoe sticking out of the dirt.

'Matthia!' He trotted to my side. 'Look, why is your shoe in the ground?'

'They're too small, Mama, they hurt. If we water them they might grow like the tomatoes.'

My tension lifted. 'It won't work, son. I'll put a piece of wet sack inside each one, to stretch them. You go and see if you can find any eggs.' Our hens suffered from the heat but, if we were lucky, we found an occasional egg. Perhaps Saint Stavro would bless one of the fowl today. I returned to our back plot and showed Stavro how to dig a trench in the hard earth with the *skapáni*. I had decided to plant half the dried beans.

'I'm going to search for herbs,' I told him. 'Take care of Matthia while I'm away.'

'I'll try, Mama, but you know he's a little devil. Don't blame me if he gets up to no good.'

'I will blame you, Stavro, so watch yourself, son.'

Petro slept soundly. With my folding knife, cold in the palm of my hand, I slunk behind the houses to the nearest olive grove. Wild greens and snails, if I found them, would supplement the small amount of food we had. The Germans forbade us to venture outside Amiras, but I had three growing boys to feed. Around the trees, dandelions and nettles grew in the watered circles, where the rest of the September landscape lay barren. Like the Italians before them, the Nazis confiscated our goat's milk and most of our potatoes and vegetables.

I hurried down to the village road and then turned up into an olive grove. A clump of sow thistle beckoned me. Lush and green, both roots and leaves were tasty when boiled. Such a small find, yet it thrilled me. I dug my knife into the soil, cutting around the base of the stalk. At that moment, with my nose close to the ground and my behind in the air, I heard an unusual sound. At first I couldn't make it out, a pounding, more of a vibration than a noise. Although hardly louder than the cricket chirruping somewhere near my feet, the strange clattering worried me.

I tugged at the plant and stood, recognising the 'whoomp-whoomp' as studded jackboots slamming against the metalled street. The thud grew more powerful with each heartbeat. I peered between the trees, horrified. I had never even seen a full German platoon. This was countless soldiers marching along the main road that ran above our village. For over a year, we only had two or three soldiers in our area, the ones that took our food. This sounded like thousands.

In the crystal-clear morning air everything seemed intense – the noises and colours, the words of my children, the smell of the earth in the grove. A couple of ravens passed overhead screaming their black-hearted croak, then the strangest thing happened. One bird half closed its great wings and rolled onto its back, as if dead in the road, but still sailing horizontally across the sky. I had never seen anything like it and knew I had witnessed an omen, a most terrible warning. What did it mean? A drop of sweat trickled past my eye and I realised I had crushed the herb in my tight fist.

A double stamp of feet crashed my attention back to the soldiers, and then . . . silence, for a second almost tangible. I panted, my mouth dry. Had they seen me? The platoon waited – what for I couldn't imagine. My belly knotted and then I heard, from far away, another steady rhythm breaking the hush.

More marching boots approached our village from the west. I stretched my neck, peered through the trees and across the rooftops. Distant noises grew louder and then lines of soldiers loomed up on the opposite ridge. They stood for a moment, before pouring down onto the houses like ants from a disturbed nest. We were surrounded. Why?

My neighbours told us truckloads of Nazis had arrived in Viannos the previous day. Two thousand, they claimed. One Nazi came into Amiras on a motorbike with a sidecar. He stuck a poster on the kafenion window and then continued to the next hamlet. The notice said nobody would be harmed if we stayed inside our village. Anyone found outside the boundary would be executed.

I had broken their rule!

A breeze rustled through the grove. Trees swayed, their dark shadows performing a hideous dance around me. The ravens circled back, flying devils that ate our precious corn. I wanted to screech a warning but kept quiet, afraid of capture and terrified of the consequences.

The soldiers stopped below the olive grove, the road between my children and me. I cowered behind a stout tree, trembling like a dog, looking for a way out but scared to move. The men stood to attention, filling the street, three abreast and at least thirty deep. Their white faces cold, eyes with the emotionless stare of Charon. The captain gave orders, foreign words, dull as a funeral bell.

In the kafenion the day before, Andreas the shepherd had told of a battle in the neighbouring village of Simi. Enemy soldiers had fought Cretan Andartes, our self-appointed freedom fighters. Many locals referred to them as renegades and draft-dodgers, others claimed they were heroes. Men had died in the fight but details were vague. Our elders warned us to prepare for reprisals. I didn't understand what 'reprisals' meant. Perhaps they would take more food, or threaten to shoot somebody. But I doubted they would go that far, not in our small community, yet a feeling of dread overcame me.

My precious boys!

Thinking of them spurred me into action. I dashed to the next tree, following a back route to the house, lifting my heavy skirts from the dragging vegetation. I staggered, my legs hobbled by intense fear. In the name of God, please, don't let my children see anyone shot.

The Nazis were marching again. They turned towards me. I dived behind another wide trunk, afraid they could hear my thumping heart. They came too close. I dared not move, if they saw me . . . The church bell rang a warning knell. I pressed my back against the rough bark and crossed myself. *Saint Stavro protect us.* The enemy were almost upon me.

If they kill me, who will take care of my boys?

Invading forces continued to pour into Amiras. The sound of a gunshot rattled me, and then another echoed around the mountains. My knees buckled. I tripped on the front of my skirt, fell hard on the ground, pushed myself up and stumbled onward, glancing across the village and then down to the road. They were still coming, endless streams of uniforms.

I wondered if the entire German army had invaded Crete. My stomach rolled and I'm ashamed to say my bladder emptied before I could squat. Hot urine ran down the inside of my thighs, tears sprang in my eyes and my mouth tasted gun metal. Amiras was in trouble. Where were our soldiers? My boys needed their mother. What kind of fool would disobey the regulations and go out of the village?

Because our house and the olive trees were above the main street, I could see the events happening below the grove. The heady scent of thyme, oregano and rosemary was gone. The air now reeked of cordite and fear.

I quickly realised these were not the German soldiers that we knew and tolerated. These men were the evil Nazis. They stomped past me. I peeked from behind the tree and watched them force their way into the lower village houses. They dragged the occupants out.

Women shrieked, their husbands, sons and fathers shouted. A bedraggled hen ran down the road, squawking and flapping outstretched wings. A dog gave chase. Evangelia, a respected elder of Amiras, tried to talk to the militaries. They knocked her to the ground with a rifle butt to the face.

I had never seen anything so shocking. Her walking sticks clattered across the street and blood streamed from her nose. I wanted to reach out, help her up, the noble old lady. A machine gun fired into the air. The rattle echoed from every mountainside and valley, petrifying us all. A second of silence followed before the chaos continued.

I had worked myself up into a terrifying conviction that if I didn't get back to my boys right then, something terrible and irreversible would happen. I ran, thighs chafing from the friction of pissed fear, frantic to reach little Petro in his nightgown, and Matthia and Stavro attending to their chores.

My legs shook so badly I could hardly stand. I had no time to make sense of things. Instinct told me to protect my boys at all costs. Hide them from the approaching evil. I sensed the troops were closing in all around us. I glanced over my shoulder and saw the Nazis advance. More screaming and shouting followed them. Old women fought strong young soldiers.

Children cried. Dogs barked. The roosters were silent. Bewildered men and boys, pulled from the houses and forced together, were marched up the road like a gang of convicts.

I ran back up the grove, took a shortcut through my neighbour's garden and found Stavro and Matthia behind our cottage, hugging each other, confused by the ruckus. The Nazis were already at the end of our street. The commotion in the village below grew louder.

'Get inside the house!' I yelled, running frantically towards my boys. Go to the *appothiki*!' Baby Petro bawled in his hammock over the bed. We raced past him to the third room. I ripped the top off the buried urn.

'Climb in, and don't make a sound, no matter how long. Stay quiet until I come for you. Do you understand?' They nodded but Matthia started crying. 'Shush!' I said sternly, my heart breaking. I wanted to comfort him but knew if I put my arms around the four-year-old, I would be unable to let go.

I dragged the lid and sack back into place and shovelled goat droppings over the top, hoping they had enough ventilation. For good measure, I picked up the goat's bucket and slopped a little water over the dung. Nobody would investigate that slimy heap.

After throwing the wooden shovel to one side, I dashed to the bed and lifted Petro from the hammock.

Where could I hide? The dry ditch next to our plot! I wished I had thought of that earlier, for my boys. We could have escaped along the gully. As I passed the window, I saw the Nazis, now only metres away.

Too late!

I backtracked, sat on the wooden bed-steps, pulled out my breast and clutched Petro to my teat. If we were quiet, perhaps they would pass the house. The child, always hungry, latched on and guzzled. His small pink hands opened and closed against my skin. He gazed up, the innocence in his wide brown eyes tugged at my maternal instincts.

For a second I forgot the danger and ran a tender hand over his head. His soft dark hair already covered a liverish birthmark on his scalp. The midwife called it a stork mark although it appeared to be an eagle with outspread wings.

The door crashed open and my mind snapped to the present. Soldiers barged into the house.

'Your boys and men, where are they?' the captain demanded in poorly pronounced Greek.

I stammered, confused, unable to answer. My sons were all I had. My husband, my father, and my father-in-law were in the army, fighting Italians in Albania. The Italians had changed sides a few days back, but we didn't understand if that would affect us.

Terrible dread rose inside me. My children were too young to work at the Nazi barracks. They couldn't take my boys. Vassili would say I did right to hide them.

Enemy soldiers charged through the house, filling the rooms, barging for space while they delved into every conceivable hiding place. They pulled cupboards open, tipped drawers out, and even looked up the chimney. I feigned unconcern but, demented, begged the Fates to keep my precious sons safe. When the soldiers stomped through to the *appothiki* I prayed Matthia had stopped crying.

The soldiers returned empty handed and I struggled to hide my relief, but the nightmare continued. A Nazi leader, his expression as nasty as gangrene, suddenly pulled Petro roughly from my breast. Embarrassed, I was quick to cover myself but the milk, still squirting from my nipple, made a dark wet patch on the front of my cotton dress. A young soldier laughed, his face flushed, twitching, nervous.

I reached for Petro but hard white hands slapped my arms away.

'Name?' the leader shouted.

'Petro.' Paralysed by fear, I could hardly shape the word. What did they want with a baby? I stretched out for him again.

The Nazi threw Petro to another soldier. His little limbs jerked out stiffly before he started yelling.

'No, damn you all – give him back to me.' I launched myself at them, pulling at their stiff uniforms, frantic to hold my baby Petro. They could kill me for saying such things but I didn't care, feeling, somehow, I would be more powerful dead. A vicious push slammed me to the ground.

When I struggled to get up, a rifle butt bashed me hard in the shoulder and sent me sprawling. I scrambled onto my feet, fought a scream of pain, and caught an apologetic glance from the last soldier as they marched away. His eyes were wide with thinly disguised anguish.

'Why?' I shouted after him. He turned away.

I hurriedly fastened my dress buttons before I ran after the soldiers. I wondered if my shoulder was broken; the pain was barely tolerable. I grasped the top of my arm and held it against myself.

The road was packed with mothers, wives and daughters following the herded males. Women tugged at my clothes in an attempt to get in front of me. In the frantic shove of desperation down the narrow street, the rough stone walls grated skin from my cheek and elbow. Everyone yelled the names of their men and boys, and so did I.

'Petro! Petro!'

The grandmothers tried to keep up, their walking sticks knocked away in the surge. Several clutched their chests and collapsed onto concrete doorsteps. They stared, futile and defeated, after their doddering husbands and bewildered sons.

I had to find my baby and get him back.

Ahead of us, two Nazis dragged crippled and bedridden Philipo out of his house. His sunken eyes, wide; his false teeth exposed in a ghoulish grin of confusion. They yelled at him to stand. He couldn't. The Nazis pulled him around the corner, out of sight. His legs, like empty trousers, flapped in the dirt behind them. A pistol fired and the soldiers returned alone. Only a warning shot . . . surely?

I didn't dare to think what had happened to the old man.

As the street inclined, I saw a Nazi ahead with two small babies. One might have been Petro, I couldn't be certain. He held them in each hand, by the wrists. The infants hung at his sides like a child's empty mittens threaded on elastic. Should

I go after him, the Nazi with my baby, or return to my terrified children in the buried urn?

Caught in the throng of village women, unable to turn, I followed that macabre procession. Pleading with the Nazis, like screaming gulls behind a fishing trawler, we begged for our men and boys.

Pelagia seized my arm and yanked me around, her face inches from mine, breath hot, eyes wild.

'Where's my Yianni . . .? Yianni, have you seen him, Maria? He's six, what could they want with him?'

'No, but Petro, did you see who had my baby, Petro?'

She released me, shook her head and continued yelling, 'Yianni! Yianni!' Panic-stricken, she attempted to shoulder her way through the mob of daughters, wives and mothers.

The street narrowed. Everyone shoved, desperate, somebody up front shrieked. Women at the back pushed. Something crunched underfoot and I stumbled on softness. I peered between a sea of hips and legs and caught a glimpse of old *Kiria* Anna, the cobbler's grandmother. Trampled beneath our feet, her eyes screwed closed and her nose ran with blood. I realised I'd stepped on her hand and felt the snap of brittle bones through my worn-out shoes. I couldn't stop for the love of God and the force behind me. Blessed Jesus please forgive me. Petro was more important. At that moment, I would have trodden on my own mother to rescue my son.

The soldiers stopped on a rise at the village perimeter. They forced the men to stand together. The able-bodied, pale with fear, supported the old and infirm. I stretched my neck, searching among the terrified group of men for my Petro. A young boy called out, his frightened bleating drifted from between the surrounding males.

'Mama, Mama!'

Pelagia screamed out from behind me, 'Yianni! Oh, God, it's my Yianni.' And then I caught an unmistakable sound, my baby's cry. My womb cramped, the distant echo of a labour pain.

The Nazis held us back.

'Please, I must get to my baby. I'm begging you!' I cried, but they wouldn't let me through the guards. I ran around the perimeter of soldiers again and again, like a worried dog herding sheep.

'Petro!' I shouted, but I couldn't see him. His cry addled my brain and madness overcame me. I made a plan to charge through the uniforms, then through our men, grab Petro, drop to my knees and somehow escape from the other side. I hauled in several deep breaths, rocked back and forth, ready to launch myself.

Someone grabbed me from behind: *Kiriea* Joanna, the baker's wife.

'They'll kill you,' she said, her mouth pressed against my ear, her hair smelling of sweat and yeast. 'Don't let the men have to see that.' I couldn't get free of her arms, their incredible strength gained from years of dough kneading.

'I have to try,' I sobbed. Tears raged down my face as I struggled against the weight of her. 'My little one, Petro, is in there with the men. He's crying, frightened, he needs me . . .'

'Be still, pray to God!' She shook me hard and kept a bruising grip.

Our men and boys were silent except for the weeping of children and a few consoling voices from the elderly. I strained to listen for Petro but couldn't hear him. Since war had broken out, only the disabled or those too old or young to fight remained in the village. Now they stood, bunched before us in a huddle of helplessness.

The commandant reached into the horde and dragged out Pavlo Petrinakis. A young man of twenty-five, our local doctor. He slammed the poor doctor against the chapel wall. Another Nazi, standing to attention, translated the commandant's barked words into faltering Greek.

'Now, we make example. You all take notice of what happens when we are crossed!' he yelled.

I held my breath, straining for the sound of my son. I think most of the other women were crying, screeching, but they weren't important to me. I wished they would stop their noise. I stretched up on my toes, trying to see who had Petro, hoping he would cry again so that I got a direction.

We begged the soldiers to show mercy, prayed to the Blessed Virgin, crossing ourselves repeatedly in a futile effort to instigate divine intervention. I think all the women shared my emotional relief, better for Pavlo to die, rather than my own son. I remembered the man had a weak heart, failed the army medical, and now he would have immortality as our village martyr.

Sickening remorse rose in my throat. I would lay flowers of guilt on his tomb. Every Nazi aimed his machine gun at the doctor. Pavlo's wide eyes turned to heaven, his face gaunt as an El Greco icon.

'Oh, Virgin Mary, make it quick.' My head screamed with the horror of it all. Where were our soldiers? Where was our God? Where was my baby?

The Captain yelled, 'Name?'

'Petrinakis.' He gulped and shook violently, barely able to stand.

My heart pounded in my ears. Time must stop. Wake me from this nightmare.

The doctor searched our faces for his wife and child.

'Katarina, come to the front!' one of the women shouted, choking on the words, she as guilty as me – as guilty as the rest of us. 'He needs you. Your husband wants to see you!'

We parted, dragged her forward, bearing her weight and blocking her whimpering from our minds. She clutched their baby girl and shuffled through the women, stiffly reluctant, tears streaming. Older women, standing behind, wrapped their arms around her waist. Others were ready to grab the infant if Katarina collapsed.

Old *Kiriea* Petrinakis, the mother of Pavlo, dropped to her knees and hugged herself. She rocked, her arms enfolding the belly that once contained her son. Her toothless mouth in a wretched salivating grimace.

Pavlo nodded at Katarina. His thin face taut with anguish, yet he appeared to take succour from the line of eye contact. Their life together should not end like this. I remembered their wedding a year ago. We danced all night in the village square.

The Nazis prepared to fire, pulling their weapons to their shoulders in unison. Our village priest, at the front of the men, led them in prayer, their eyes fixed on the young doctor.

Get it over with, God have mercy. I must find my baby, take him home and suckle him.

'Now, and at the hour of our death . . .' the men sang in plainchant.

The commandant shouted a three-word order in German.

The soldiers turned on their heels and fired. The deafening rattle of bullets went on, and on, and on . . .

Apart from Pavlo Petrinakis, every male fell to the ground.

The hot Mediterranean air stank of gunpowder and dread.

'*Petro! My baby! No!*'

My body shrank with horror. A woman's arms wrapped around me and mine about her – grasping at each other's clothes in a kind of manic hysteria. Screaming. The endless screaming that only ceased with the need to breathe. Unable to turn away, my eyesight blurred and re-focused, each vision worse than the last. Cameos of death branded into my memory for eternity.

They fell, wave after wave before my eyes. My friends' husbands hunched over babies and infants in an effort to save them. Old men clutched adolescent boys against their chests. Familiar faces twisted with the terror of realisation.

I caught sight of my grandfather, Matthia, my second son's namesake. My arms stretched out towards him although he stood more than ten metres away. I had such a strong compulsion to embrace the gentle old man, to protect him. Yet the short space between us amounted to an abyss. He turned to me and nodded, bitterly sad. I saw his ribcage jerk forward in one violent movement. Disbelief flickered in his wide eyes as he sank lifeless to the ground.

'No, *Papoú!*' I shouted.

And somewhere real or ethereal, my voice cried to the heavens.

'My baby! Somebody save my baby!'

I stared at the men intently as they fell, desperate to see Petro, afraid I would miss a glimpse of him, my mind blocking the inevitable. And then I saw with my own eyes, a flash of the bloody red nightgown of my son, clutched against the broad chest of the baker. He spun his back to me and fell to the ground, a puppet with his strings cut.

Sick to my stomach, I knew with certainty that this was my fault – I let the soldier take my baby. As long as I lived, I would never forgive myself for allowing such a nightmare to happen. Why did I go into the grove that morning? Why didn't I hide in the ditch with my children? We could have escaped. I had been stupid and irresponsible.

Bullets rattled and crashed. In the deafening noise, pieces of flesh flitted and dropped like pale pink butterflies over the vibrating bloody mound of one hundred and fourteen men and boys.

I knew all of them. I had taught most to read and write. I'd praised them for the smallest improvements and basked in the light of their grateful eyes.

I stood on the ridge with the other women of Amiras, empty, bloodless. The life sucked from my body leaving only a shell, hot and dry like a long-dead crab. My baby, poor Petro. God take his soul. He'd come into this world, bloody and screaming only eight weeks ago and now he left the same way.

Why had I always been so eager to put him in the hammock after suckling? I could have held him, rocked him against my bosom and told him about the father he had never seen.

* * *

When exhaustion brought a respite from the screaming, nobody spoke. The only sounds were shuddering sobs when somebody forgot to breathe and then juddered air into their lungs at the last moment. It might even have been me. A dog bayed in the lower village, its piteous yowl echoing from the mountainsides. The beast cried for us all.

A wall of soldiers surrounded the dead.

I stared at the devastation surrounding me. Many of my friends had collapsed having seen the murder of their children, fathers, husbands, brothers and grandfathers. Other women, on their knees, pounded the earth, or raked the skin from their faces with jagged fingernails in a terrible fit of madness. A few remained on their feet, tearing their hair out, beating their breasts and howling prayers to God.

The soldiers forbade our approach.

From the corner of my eye, I noticed the doctor had fallen to the ground. His wife and mother were trying to drag him away. Nobody helped them. Petrinakis, now cruelly ostracised for surviving.

Occasionally, we saw twitching in the blood-soaked mound. Each of us hoped for a miraculous sign of life from one of our family. Prayers answered. But the Nazi commandant took out his pistol and fired into the skull of any half-dead man or child. An abomination or a blessed relief . . . who could ever know?

Day bled into night, the sky turning deep red. We all waited, wretched, desperate to find our loved ones. I fretted about my two boys, buried in their dark earthy tomb at the house. Stavro and Matthia would be terrified, hungry and thirsty but, thank God, they were alive. A day seemed an eternity in the life of a child. I had to go back to them. Petro, dead, was beyond my help, I could do nothing. Even if, by luck or miracle, he had survived, I remained helpless. I could not stand to watch that final Nazi bullet. My baby's feeding time had passed and my breasts ached, heavy with milk. What sort of mother would leave knowing her baby lay underneath that mound of bodies? But I knew I had to get home, rescue my boys, take them far away from the dangers of Amiras.

Another pistol shot cracked the night. Ashamed and broken hearted, I turned away from my hysterical neighbours and started a fast walk to our house. I wanted to race back, but sensed I shouldn't draw attention to myself. An explosion in the village caused the ground to tremble. Somewhere up ahead, flames leapt into the dark sky. Grit and small pebbles fell through the air. Were they blowing up houses? I broke into a run. Hardly below the ridge, a hand caught me and swung me around by my elbow.

'Halt!' a soldier barked. He pulled so hard I pirouetted into his grasp and found myself slammed against the grocer's shop wall, staring into ice-cold Aryan eyes. He mumbled words that I interpreted as lustful and his obnoxious breath cloyed about my face. Another explosion sounded. I choked on panic. My boys trapped in the terracotta pot, Petro trapped beneath a mound of dead bodies, me, trapped in the grip of a Nazi.

'No, please . . .' I begged.

Chapter 7

Crete, Present Day.

Tears shimmered on Angie's eyelashes. Maria's shocking revelations were almost incomprehensible. Suddenly angry with her mother, Angie wondered why Poppy had never shared her grandmother's history with her. She glanced around the simple living room that, as *Papoú* pointed out, had hardly changed since that appalling September day.

Maria looked up, nodding, as if confirming the atrocities she had witnessed. Or perhaps she displayed nothing more than the doddery reflexes of her ninety years.

Angie fought her emotions. 'I'm so sorry, *Yiayá*. Mam didn't tell me any of this. I had no idea . . .'

Maria bowed her head and sighed. 'Ah, poor Poppy . . . The past was terribly cruel to her too. She suffers in silence.' A solitary tear rolled down her cheek.

Angie, desperate to hear about her mother, noticed her grandmother was exhausted. She struggled to keep her voice even. 'I've asked too much of you, forgive me? I didn't realise, didn't know . . . we can stop now if you prefer?'

Maria lifted a bony hand with knuckles distorted by arthritis and patted her granddaughter's thigh. The old woman's golden skin, tissue-thin and dotted with brown freckles, bore vast white patches. Angie recognised the evidence of third degree burns and imagined the appalling pain. Wondering what had caused the disfigurement, she recalled her mother's hands and the frantic scratching until they bled.

Maria shook her head and said in a tremulous voice, 'You need to hear the whole story.'

Angie glanced across to her grandfather who sat in the corner, his worry beads still and his eyes shining. Maria turned to him.

'Old man, I don't want you here when I tell the next events to Angelika. You are too nosy and it's women's talk. Get yourself to the kafenion for your coffee and give us a little peace.'

'I will.' He pulled himself to his feet. 'I'm proud of you, old woman. This story isn't easy.'

Vassili shuffled across the room and kissed Maria on the cheek. Before he straightened she whacked at him with the flat of her hand, nearly knocking him off his walking stick. He lurched backward, teetering to keep his balance while retreating from her assault.

'Don't start with your nonsense, you old devil,' she yelled in her weak, high-pitched voice.

Behind Maria's back, *Papoú* turned to Angie and winked. 'Did you see that, Angelika? My wife, she beats me! I'm a martyr.' He grinned a set of yellow mismatched teeth before shambling out of the house.

Maria kept the anger on her face until he had gone and then she took on a gentle, mischievous look. 'Don't let this man of yours become too familiar, *koritsie*. Men, they're always trying to take advantage, no matter how old they get. You have to keep them in their place.'

Angie nodded and offered a feeble smile, not trusting herself to speak at that moment. Yet she recognised the kindness of these elderly folk, lifting the weight of emotion from her. She scrabbled in her handbag for a tissue, dried her eyes and blew her nose.

'*Koritsie*, I hope you never feel the torment I had that day.' Maria stroked the white patches of skin on her hands. 'But you know, if ever you need it, The Almighty will give you a giant's strength and huge endurance to save the fruit of your womb.' She held her hands out. 'God gave me these scars to wear like a medal. Whenever I have a problem, they remind me of what I can overcome, and then my difficulty becomes dust – nothing.'

Angie needed a break to collect her emotions. 'Shall I make you a drink, *Yiayá*? All this talking, you must be thirsty.'

'Yes, bring the iced tea from the fridge, Angelika.'

In the kitchen, Angie noticed the silver larder-fridge rocked as she pulled the door open, and understood why it rattled every time the chiller motor started. Didn't they know it had adjustable legs? She would sort it out before she left Crete. The thought of doing this small thing for them gave her an inexplicable amount of pleasure. She brought a couple of cans of iced tea into the lounge. Her grandmother pointed to a box of multi coloured straws on a shelf.

They drank in comfortable silence.

Chapter 8

Maria shook her head. 'Whatever you learn while you're here, Angelika, I want you to remember: the circumstances surrounding your mother's wedding were not her fault. Poppy was completely innocent.' She glanced at the icon again. 'I realise you don't understand, but be patient and everything will become clear.'

Alert to a connection, but not understanding what it was, Angie nodded at the garish image. 'It's Saint George, isn't it?'

'Yes, *Agios Yeorgios*,' Maria said. 'A Christian martyr. His parents were Greek; did you know?'

Angie felt she had missed something. 'My father's name was Yeorgo.' Saint George and the dragon, she thought. Was her mother the dragon, or her grandmother, or was she being ridiculous?

Maria turned her face away. 'Poppy wasn't born until after the war. With girls, you must provide a dowry. It's expensive and, in the end, you lose them anyway because they go and live with their husband's family.'

Angie only half listened, wondering why her mother had refused to talk about all this. Surely, as her grandmother's story progressed, she would understand everything.

Maria continued. 'Every day at sunset, as the fierce heat weakened, I sat outside with the other mothers to crochet bed linen and lace.' She smiled, closed her eyes, and seemed lost in her memories of warm summer evenings.

'It must have been hard to find the thread after the war, *Yiayá*.'

Maria nodded. 'We kept silkworms then, and fed them on mulberry leaves. All the women worked together to produce the yarn.' She dropped the needlework back into her sewing bag and crossed herself three times.

'Let's return to the story. I'm ashamed of the next event, *korit-sie*. I know you want to hear, and you have a right to learn everything, but don't judge me too badly.'

Angie nodded and then shook her head, unsure of herself. Fearing she was about to put her lovely grandmother through more stress, and humbled by the old woman's past, Angie waited. She found it impossible to imagine how Maria had felt after seeing her grandfather, and then her baby, so callously murdered.

Maria closed her eyes and sat, trance-like, hands on her knees, palms up, like some unwritten yoga pose. Angie sensed her grandmother's thoughts were returning to that evening of the 14th of September and her astonishing fight for the lives of her children.

* * *

Crete, 1943.

THE NAZI IGNORED MY protests and overpowered me. He forced my arm up my back while his other hand snatched under my skirt. I tried with all my strength to push him away and remembered the folding knife I had used to cut weeds that morning. I could plunge it into his neck. Kill him the way we slaughtered the village pig.

I pulled the knife from my apron pocket but the Nazi grabbed my wrist. He bashed my hand against the grocer's wall until I let go of the weapon, then his knuckles smashed into my face.

Pain blinded me. A second blow, under my ribs, knocked the wind out of me. My knees folded. My lungs screamed for air. I couldn't breathe and collapsed to the ground.

The mortifying shame . . . Tears stung my eyes and I tasted blood in the back of my throat. He mumbled something in German. At first, I tried to fight, but he seemed energised by my efforts to push him away. In seconds, he had my skirt lifted, his knees forced mine apart and he savagely took me.

Some kind of bizarre grief, that I am unable to understand, made me cry out my husband's name. '*Vassili!*' At that moment, I hated my man for not being there to save me. Then I hated the grunting pig that rammed into me, painfully, too soon after I'd given birth. I cried for baby Petro, cried for my husband who had never held his third son, and I cried because of the terrible thudding ache below my belly.

I cannot recall the end, only that I recovered my senses on the hard ground. I opened my eyes, tentatively, afraid he was there, but I discovered myself alone. Dirty, frightened, and fearful for my children. I loathed my body and still cried for my husband. Grief welled up and rolled through me in waves, each surge weaker than the last until eventually I struggled to my feet.

I used the hem of my skirt to wipe away most of the blood and semen that ran down between my trembling legs. Crouching, I tried to pee, hoping to cleanse myself internally, but dehydration made it impossible. Using the sleeve of my dress, I wiped my blood-streaked face. The boys would be frightened enough. They shouldn't see their mother in such a state.

I staggered towards home, thinking of Petro, his little body, a life hardly started and yet so cruelly ended. Poor *Papoú* too, my gentle grandfather to whom I should have said many things but didn't make the time. I never told him, 'I love you, *Papoú*.' How terrible to leave that simple truth unspoken.

I hoped someone would bring them to me, or perhaps later the soldiers would go and I could return to the ridge. As I turned off the village road, a flash of blinding light illuminated everything around me. The following explosion vibrated the air. Ahead, sparks rose like red shooting stars against the night sky.

The sickening smell of smoke grew stronger. I raced towards our house. Fire! My boys were trapped. They couldn't get out of the urn without help. I didn't know how much more of this atrocious day I could take.

The incline leading home seemed steeper than ever before, yet my abused body found astonishing strength. I gathered my skirts and ran. The only flammable things in the animal room were the wooden spade and the herbs drying on the wall, and the roof. Then, I remembered the *pithoi* half full with olive oil.

By the time I got there, the *appothiki* door lay on the ground and most of the ceiling had collapsed inside. Sparks fizzed and flew up in the hot air. My boys would surely suffocate in the urn. I wanted to scream their names, but the Nazis might hear me. Perpendicular beams blazed against the stone walls and a litter of twigs crackled and spat across the floor. Smoke rose in red swirls and twists.

I ran to the *appothiki* doorway but shimmering heat pushed me away like the hands of a blistering spectre. The firelight projected demonic shapes that leapt about me. My mind flickered, returning to the devilish shadows in the olive grove. Yes, God had sent me an omen. Why hadn't I acted on it immediately? Then I remembered the water barrel behind the house.

I snatched the enamel pail that lay next to our trampled tomatoes and raced to the back plot.

At the butt, I poured water over myself. Rigid and gasping from shock, I repeated the process until my dress and hair were drenched. Then I refilled the bucket and returned to the *appothiki.* The water slopped and my wet clothes slapped a hindrance around my limbs.

A chunk of clay roof had fallen in one huge block. The slab had knocked the door off and jammed against the corner of the room, making a triangular space over my buried children. The layer of manure over the urn had baked white and the rising steam should have warned me of its heat. I raked it off with my bare hands, oblivious to the blistering of my scalded skin.

'Stavro, Matthia . . .' I called as loud as I dared, and I had almost loosened the wooden lid when the pain of my burns registered. Such agony, terrible, I submerged my fists into the bucket of cold water for a moment's relief before emptying it over the lid of the urn.

Clouds of hot, dung-stinking vapour billowed around my face. I could see nothing and heard only the crackle and splutter of fire, so loud it drowned the wailing of distraught women on the ridge. I scrabbled in the scorching manure. The water turned it into viscous bubbling glue that fried my hands.

Gripped by the intense dread of finding Stavro and Matthia cooked alive in the terracotta pot, where I had put them, I fumbled for the edge of the jute olive sack. It tore the skin from my palms as I yanked it away. I wished I had more water but I would not leave the boys until I had removed the lid.

My pathetic whimpering poured out like the bowels of a butchered lamb. Smoke stung my eyes and I could hardly see.

Again, I jabbered their names, 'Stavro! Matthia!' My fingers found the ventilation holes and I pulled back with all I had. It cracked from the baked dirt. I hurled it aside.

Blinded by the smoke, it was impossible to see inside the *pithoi*. I heard no sound from my children.

I threw myself onto the smouldering earth, reached into the urn and touched hot motionless flesh. Grabbing a limb, I lifted and dragged Matthia up and out. I'll never forget the feel of his little body against mine, his head lolling in the crook of my neck as I carried him. My burden felt so precious. I laid my darling boy on the cool ground under the olive tree.

Please, God, spare me sweet Matthia. He is such a gentle child, only four years old.

At that moment, I would have traded my life for his. That is the absolute truth.

My tears fell onto his face. I felt his chest for a heartbeat but most of the feeling in my burned hands had gone. Sinking into despair, I knelt beside him.

All alone on that dark night, with no notion of what to do, I wanted to scream for help but dare not. I was only an ordinary woman, but at that moment, I needed to be so much more. Stavro, still in the urn, might be seconds away from death, or dead already. Should I leave Matthia and give Stavro all my attention? Yet, I refused to accept Matthia had gone to God before his time. My mind snapped and the most appalling anger consumed me.

What sort of Christ would allow this to happen? I thumped the ground with my raw fists. Gaia, Mother Earth, how could she let this abomination take place, the deity a mother herself?

An explosion of pure rage went off inside me. I would fight the Gods and all their angels for the life of my boy! In my madness, I'm ashamed to say, I directed this fury towards my child.

Uncontrollably angry that he had died, I pounded my fists against Matthia's chest. 'Breathe, in the name of Jesus, breathe!' Years later, a doctor told me the action had possibly restarted his heart. Perhaps there is a God after all.

I used the wet fabric of my skirt to wipe Matthia's hot face, mortified by my own violence. I didn't deserve to be a mother.

Thinking he was dead, I opened his shirt to the cool night air and found it almost impossible not to cry out. I can't describe the combination of joy and hope that coursed through me when he made a slight, fluttery movement of his hands. I pulled my cotton underskirt off and ran to the back of the house where I dipped it into the water butt. When I placed it over Matthia, he moaned. Then, in the light of the fire, I saw the rise and fall of his chest.

'You're safe now,' I said through tears of relief, not knowing if he heard me. 'Lie still while I rescue your brother.'

I returned to the *appothiki* and reached inside the urn for Stavro. I tried to lift him out, but my burned hands combined with his weight defeated me. Weak and desperate, frazzled by heat so intense, in any other circumstance it would have been unbearable, yet I had to rescue him somehow. The extreme temperature quickly dried my clothes. I pulled myself to my feet, grabbed the pail and returned to the butt. After soaking myself, I filled the pail again.

Racing back, I tripped and my burned hands lost their grip on the heavy bucket. Most of the water spilled over thankless earth. I dashed onward and threw myself down next to the *pithoi*.

Lying on the floor with my upper body hanging inside the urn, the proximity of the burning roof felt as though it were searing the skin from my back. Courage left me. Exhaustion and the atrocities of the day took my last smidgen of fight. My baby dead, my grandfather too. Me, sullied by a dirty Nazi. And now my first-born son cooked alive because he did, without question, what I'd told him to do. All my remorse boiled up and I howled into the urn.

'Stavro!'

Bewildered and defeated, I let go of my boy's arm. Water ran from my wet hair, dripping onto his hot body at the bottom of the *pithoi*. I just wanted to lie there and die but, as I breathed out, hardly able to inhale the searing air inside the urn, I felt the most glorious movement beneath my injured hands. Then, from somewhere behind me, I heard a mumbled word from Matthia.

'Mama . . .' he croaked weakly.

His voice grabbed my heartstrings and an enormous sense of relief flooded me. I pulled myself away from the urn and staggered over to him. His eyes were open and, although dazed, he focused on me.

'Thirsty,' he said

I remembered they hadn't had a drop to drink since daybreak. Torn between him and my eldest, I said, 'I'll get you some water.'

I took my soaking underskirt from him, dashed back to the urn and dropped it over Stavro to cool him. My hands seemed to explode with pain as I drew closer to the burning cottage. At the butt, dizzy and muddled, I suddenly realised my own raging thirst. I slurped water from my palm. Bits of skin from my hands stuck to my lips like wet paper. At the urn, I splashed a little water over Stavro, promising to get him out soon, not knowing if he could hear me. I returned to Matthia's side, held him to me and scooped water into his mouth.

'Lie still while I help your brother,' I said, desperate to get Stavro away from the fire.

A deafening crack, followed by a vroom, thundered the air. Red sparks streamed towards the night sky and a wave of heat rolled over me. Another beam had exploded into flames. More of the ceiling collapsed.

Stavro!

Just when I thought I had reached the pit of this dreadful day, things turned worse.

A slab of fallen roof, jammed against the corner of the room, was inching down the wall. My insides seemed to drop too. What was I supposed to do? The chunk of clay was half a metre thick and three metres long. The slab would kill us both if it fell while I tried to get Stavro out. But I had no choice – and I had to act fast.

Earlier, a fallen beam, jammed under the clay, had supported the heavy slab. Now, that length of wood had almost burned through and the charcoal crumbled under the weight pressing on it.

I grabbed the bucket and threw myself at the urn, chucking the remains of the water down, dropping the pail inside and hauling my cotton petticoat out.

'Stavro, Listen to me! We're both going to die if you don't do what I say right away.' Acrid smoke burned my throat and eyes, but I no longer cared. Nothing could stop me getting Stavro out of there. 'Take the bucket, turn it upside down and stand on it so I can pull you out.' He didn't move.

The roof slid closer, now less than a metre above the urn, and closing.

'Stavro, I love you. Help me to get us out of here.' I reached down and yanked on his arm. He stirred. 'Come on, son, Matthia needs you, I need you, be strong and stand on the bucket.'

I pulled myself clear of the neck of the urn. The falling roof might flatten me over the urn, meaning Stavro would have no escape. I hunched over, on my knees, next to the rim. Perhaps there would be enough crawl space for him, made by my body, if the roof collapsed. I felt crumbs of earth and small hot stones fall on my back, stinging like little bullets.

My mind went to baby Petro and I believed I would see him in heaven shortly. The intermittent scraping sounded like a saw through wood as the clay inched down the wall. The noise brought me back to the urgency of the situation.

'Stavro, we only have seconds. You have to stand on the bucket. Do as you're told, son!' Through the smoke, I could see his hand reach the rim and hold on. 'That's a good boy, now step onto the bucket and I'll help pull you out, quickly!'

Another sliding sound and then the roasting clay touched my hunched spine. 'Now, Stavro!' The top of his head appeared. I reached down to grasp his belt and hauled with all my strength. He slid out of the opening like a cooked snail on a bent fork. The pressure on my back increased.

'Crawl out, go!' I cried, fearing I would not make it.

The moment he escaped, I flattened my body and rolled through the space, now barely more than half a metre. I've never been so glad to see the night sky. A million stars blinked down at me.

A loud smack and then dry earth filled the air. A dust cloud billowed over us. Grit clung to my nostrils and scratched my eyes and it took a few seconds for the shock to die down and the tears to spring up.

I don't know how long I lay on the ground under the big olive tree, perhaps I passed out for a while. I would like to say my children's needs stirred me into action but, in truth, thirst got me up. I listened to the distant crying and wailing of the women still on the ridge, afraid of what else could happen on this dark night.

Matthia wobbled to his feet. He must have given his big brother a drink. I don't know.

Several hours had passed when cold water splashed onto my face. I sensed the approach of dawn and opened my eyes. My sons sat at my side, dipping their fingers into the bucket and shaking them over my head.

For a second I thought we had all died and gone to heaven, but then the disgusting state of us registered. We were certainly alive – yet the glory of our survival did nothing to slake the heartache of Petro's death, the pain of my hands and the fresh burns on my back.

To the west, a full moon seemed to have the face of a skull as it crept like a cowardly dog behind the village ridge. A row of wind-bent cypress trees, silhouetted witches' fingernails, reminded me of the baby snatched from my breast and murdered. Fear shoved my grief to one side. We had to get away and find a place of safety.

To the east, a hint of pink shone through the black gown of night and revealed Mother Earth's gentle curves. I felt we had passed our darkest hour. We were alive, and dawn promised a new day filled with hope.

Chapter 9

Crete, Present Day.

ANGIE PLACED HER NOTEBOOK and pencil on the low table. She tried to swallow, her throat hard and painful from halting sobs. 'You have a wonderful way with words, *Yiayá*. You should write a book yourself.'

'No time left, *koritsie*, you do it. Many years ago, I taught reading and writing in the schools of Amiras and Viannos, but my passion lay in ancient Greek, the poems of Homer.' She smiled and broadened her shapeless bosom. 'My father – a great scholar – gave me lessons. Girls were not usually trained to read and write, but my father had no boys so he educated me.'

'Did you teach your own sons?'

'I did, Angelika, and everyone in the village that wanted to learn.' Angie caught the pride in her grandmother's eyes. 'I got Vassili reading and writing too, and he went on to be a teacher. Most adults were illiterate then, some old ones still are.' She stared at Angie's notebook. 'Promise you'll write my story, *koritsie*. I fear what happened will be forgotten. Only now, I realise the importance of our local history. We all want to forget. It's understandable when many of us continue to grieve.' She shook her head. 'Young people don't know the real pain war causes, and there's great danger in that.'

The door banged open. A short, wiry man, with a thick grey moustache and angry brown eyes, lurched through the strip curtain. His dazzling white shirt seemed oddly out of place.

Sharp rectangular creases down the front told Angie it had come straight from the packet. He leaned on his *bastouni* and stared at the women.

'Oh dear, now I'm in trouble,' Maria said. She lifted her drink and sucked iced tea and air noisily through the straw.

'Mama, who's this?' the intruder asked, holding out a stiff hand with fingers spread – first in Angie's direction – then at her pencil and notebook on the table.

'Calm down, Matthia. Show some manners to our guest. Angelika is your niece, Poppy's girl.' Despite the aggravation in her voice, Maria's mouth softened with affection.

'Welcome,' he said. His brusqueness suggested the opposite. 'I heard you were here.'

Angie stood up and offered a nervous smile. 'Hello, I'm pleased to meet you, Uncle Matthia. Your mother has told me so much about you.'

He frowned for a moment and then peered towards the kitchen. Hope glimmered in his eyes and his voice softened. 'Is Poppy here?' He smoothed his shirt-front.

'No,' Maria replied gently, 'your sister isn't here.'

'Humph.' The asperity returned as he faced Angie. 'Don't believe anything the old woman tells you.' He shook his walking stick and threw an icy glance from under a bank of frosted eyebrows. 'She eats too much *glystretha*.'

He scowled at bags and bottles cluttering the room and then turned like a white tornado, whacked the strip curtain with his *bastouni* and disappeared through the parting.

'Eeh,' Maria sighed, glancing at the ceiling. 'Take no heed of Matthia. He still tries to pretend the past never happened, especially to foreigners.'

'What did he mean, you eat too much *glystretha*?' she asked, hoping the conversation would come around to her mother.

Maria giggled. The vertical creases that pleated her face upended into hooked fingers of mirth, beckoning Angie to join in her amusement.

'*Glystretha* is the local name for one of the wild salad herbs. It grows in September. You'll know it as purslane. The stalks are slimy inside. In fact, *glystretha* means slippery in Greek. When a woman talks a lot, the men say she's eaten too much *glystretha* because it makes the tongue slithery fast.'

Maria's eyes flashed with pleasure and contentment where Angie expected to see bitterness. She found it humbling to listen as her grandmother recalled the tragic events. Silent with her thoughts, she waited for Maria to return to the morning of the 15th of September.

* * *

Crete, 1943.

THE AIR, ACRID AND sour with the smell of smoke, held none of the pleasure of a fresh new day. The time had come to plan our escape while we had darkness on our side.

'Who's hungry?' I asked trying to lighten the mood, knowing they hadn't eaten for almost twenty-four hours. They both nodded. 'Stavro, bring the goat and kid from the back plot, and don't let anyone see you.'

'Now we must eat as much as we can,' I said to Matthia. His little face lit up. 'We need to be strong, son. Fetch me the rusks and the honey from the food safe.' He trotted to the outside cupboard behind the stone oven.

The sky grew lighter by the second. I guessed it to be around four thirty and knew the importance of filling our bellies before we escaped from Amiras. I got to my feet and plopped to the ground again, dizzy from lack of sustenance. We had two choices: up the mountain, or down. Up, the safer option, would lead us to the plateau of Little Omalos, or even further to Lassithi. However, Omalos would be snowed in soon enough, making it safe from the Nazis, but would we survive without salt or vegetables?

South, towards the canyon of Arvi, would be warmer, with food and shelter. But it carried the risk of discovery and death if the Nazis planned to stay in the area.

Stavro returned and clumsily milked the goat, proud to demonstrate a hardly acquired skill. The creature stared over her shoulder, twitchy, unhappy to have her teats pulled by unfamiliar hands. My boys took their fill, drinking the warm frothing milk straight from the pan.

The dishes, in the garden sink, were covered in ash and cinders. I had a large dish, blue glazed pottery with painted yellow flowers; a miracle that it wasn't broken. I soaked the rusks in the remaining goat's milk and drizzled honey over the meal. I allowed my boys to poke their fingers into the honey pot and enjoy the special treat of sucking off the stickiness.

Fortified by the food, I pulled myself to my feet and told Stavro to bring me the slaughter knife from the outside sink. I grabbed the goat's kid. It had enough meat on its bones to be a viable kill. I straddled its back, gripped its ribcage between my knees and clamped its snout against my chest with my chin. Stavro passed me the knife, staring at my burned hands. Although they looked terrible, black blistered with raw flesh, the pain had subsided a little.

Once I had sliced halfway around the animal's neck, I snapped the spinal cord. The creature went through the usual spasmodic kicking reflexes and then relaxed into death. As it was with all the village children, since my early childhood, I had grown up with this routine – never thought twice about it. But, after witnessing recent horrors there seemed something almost satanic about the ritual. Horrified, I stared at the blood-ied knife in my hand, unable to continue with what had always been a mundane chore.

The mother goat skipped sideways and then looked on, as docile and bewildered as ever.

'Mama?' Stavro said, perceptive as usual. 'What's wrong?

'My hands are painful, son. Can you take over?' I tried to keep my voice steady but, inside, my heart was breaking.

Petro, my child, so cruelly slaughtered! A desperate urge to turn my face to the sky and howl with grief was almost overpowering.

With my guidance, Stavro butchered the carcass into small joints. We wrapped the portions in mulberry leaves and placed them in the smouldering ashes near the entrance to the house. In an hour, the meat would be cooked.

Before sunrise, my boys and I would feast as kings. The fire had consumed itself now and the interior smouldered and glowed through empty windows like a fat and satisfied Satan. The screaming and wailing from the ridge, across the village, had quietened, as eventually even the most powerful grief must. I remembered that I had my own demons to face, and to explain to my children.

I wiped the axe and leaned as far inside the *appothiki* as I dared. My blistered hands throbbed in the heat as I slid the hatchet under a black glob of melted cheese in the nearest wall nook and lifted it into the cool air. It soon solidified on the iron blade. Stavro cut away the burned exterior and divided the warm yellow insides into three. That cheese remains one of the most delicious mouthfuls of food I have ever eaten. I can recall the taste in an instant.

We filled our bellies and wrapped the remaining meat into a bundle that Stavro tied onto the end of the axe.

'I can carry it over my shoulder, Mama,' he said eagerly.

'Mama, where's baby Petro?' Matthia asked, staring at the burned-out house and looking panicky.

My insides seemed to plummet. Unable to speak, I struggled against a sob as overwhelming grief held me in its grip. Stavro's eyes read mine. I could see he understood nothing but tragedy and, in that fleeting moment, the seven-year-old boy became a man before his time.

'Don't ask questions,' he said sharply. 'Now, you're in charge of the goat, mind you do a proper job, brother.'

Bless you, Stavro.

A tattered blue coverlet lay over the woodpile. We spread it on the ground and placed on it every useful item we could find. The petrol lighter, knife, a small can of fuel and flints, all stored in our outside oven, went into my apron pocket. The beans, corn-cobs, *skapáni,* and a dented pan that belonged to my deceased mother, were tied into the blanket.

'I'll carry that,' Matthia said, mimicking his brother and nodding at the bundle. Stavro and I exchanged a look. The parcel weighed as much as him.

'You bring the goat, Matthia, and put your shoes on.' They were hanging in the olive tree. I used my teeth to pull out the damp sacking, hoping they had stretched a little. 'Hurry, boys. Let's go quietly.'

Despite the food, we were incredibly weak. I had to explain the importance of getting away from the village. Quite possibly, my sons were the only two boys still alive in Amiras. The Nazis were bound to search.

I had nothing to tell them but the truth, so terrible for a child to hear.

'They'll kill us if they find us,' I said.

Their brown eyes widened. Stavro chewed his lip, glanced at me and then spoke to Matthia. 'We must be very quiet, brother. No crying, okay? It's time to be a man, like me.'

'Here's my plan,' I said. 'We'll go up, along the ditch as far as the church, and then stop until it's safe.' They nodded, wide-eyed and frantic. 'We need to cross the road and hide in the trees opposite, before sunrise. Come on, let's move.'

Was I doing the right thing? I prayed for God's guidance.

In dawn's early light, we started our trek towards Omalos Plateau. The gully ran along the side of our patch. It channelled water from the melting snow that cascaded down from the plateau in spring, and then gushed through the village. The ditch, dry in September, concealed us under a dense tunnel of wild fig, damson, mulberry trees and myrtle shrubs. With the bundle tied like a sling on my back, I went first, crouching, sometimes crawling, torn strips from my petticoat wrapped around my hands. Stavro followed with Matthia and the goat behind.

We struggled along, snagged by branches and stabbed by vicious damson thorns. I realised, although we could not be seen, perhaps someone would notice the branches moving above us as they caught our clothes and hair. Would the Nazis be waiting at the end of the tunnel? We could not go back, yet I was afraid to continue. Clouds of fruit flies, attracted to the moisture of our sweating faces, tickled our nostrils and flew into our eyes.

The trench passed a small Byzantine church where a couple of laden mulberry trees covered the roadside edge of the ditch.

'Good so far. Now, tether the goat and sit quietly while I go into the church.' Stavro nodded and Matthia copied him. They were glad to rest after the arduous slog.

I slipped into the chapel and prayed for Petro, asking God to keep him safe, in heaven. The reality of the last twenty-four hours seemed to hit me all at once. My heart shattered at that moment and I hugged myself with arms that should have held my baby. Tears broke free and raced down my face and I fell into the depths of despair. Why had this terrible thing happened to us? All the prayers in the world could not reverse it.

Falling to my knees, I begged God to keep my family safe. I had to believe he heard my prayers and would protect us. He had his reasons for taking Petro, and perhaps I would understand them one day. For now, my sole job was to get my poor frightened sons as far away from danger as possible.

I slipped a bundle of beeswax candles into my apron pocket and returned to Stavro and Matthia.

My boys were feasting on ripe mulberries. They slurped at sweet juice that ran to their elbows and they blindly swiped burgundy tongues around their mouths. The goat, a rapacious ruminant, pleated heart-shaped leaves into its mouth; the rectangular pupils in her yellow eyes stared stupidly at nothing. We heard the bell in the church tower ring out six o'clock and then toll the funeral knell. Village dogs barked with hunger and several goats bleated to be milked. My engorged breasts echoed their pain, swollen, hot and throbbing with a need to suckle my child.

Terrible wailing from the bereaved women drifted up on the morning air. I wondered if anyone had found Petro. I hardly dared imagine his little body. My tears ran freely, reminding me that we had no water. *Poor Petro.* How could I explain to my husband? What would he think of me, to have lost his child before he had even seen him? My emotions were all over the place but I knew, for the sake of our family, I should pull myself together.

We had to cross the road, visible from most of the village; a dangerous but necessary manoeuvre. In the open, we risked capture and certain death.

Stavro and Matthia stared at me, waiting for instructions.

'We'll dash across, quick and quiet, when we're sure no soldiers are coming,' I said. A difficult call to make and its consequences rested with me. Bad timing would mean the end of everything.

The sky became lighter by the second. My heartbeat raced as the urgency built. We loitered under cover at the edge of the ditch until there was no sound of approaching traffic, donkey hooves, or soldiers' boots. The boys' wide, unblinking eyes fixed on my face, anticipating the command.

'Now!' If God was with us, the Nazis on the ridge would be looking the other way. We raced across the tarmac and into the bushes on the upper side of the road.

The goat, skittish for fresh vegetation, didn't stop and dragged Matthia off his feet. Stavro and I dropped our parcels and made a grab for boy and goat as they came tearing by. I snatched the goat and Stavro caught Matthia. The brave little lad had clung to the rope even as the skin shredded from his knees. My burns had dried but, somewhere along the ditch, I'd lost my bandages.

Reaching for the goat had cracked my flesh and blood oozed from my knuckles. Stavro stared at them.

'You look like that painting of Jesus in the church, Mama.' I didn't know whether to laugh or cry. 'Do they hurt?' he asked. His young voice, soft with concern, touched me deep inside. I had to take a calming breath before I could answer.

'Not as much as before, son, but they're getting stiff and it's difficult to close them.'

At this point, after so little sleep, I saw the risk of travelling in daylight. I spied an unruly old fig tree a short distance up the hill. It gave me an idea. The branches and big leaves drooped to the ground like a giant green umbrella. Dark violet figs hung heavy from the boughs. Many of the fruits were fat and overripe, their suede skins split to reveal succulent pink and golden flesh.

'Come on, boys, let's rest in there,' I said.

Matthia fought tears for his bleeding knees.

'Spit on them,' Stavro ordered. 'Spit's a natural healer.'

The words made me smile and gave me strength.

We tied the goat to a sapling, knowing she'd bleat a warning if anyone approached, and then we hid in the dark, leafy cave. The warm earth, cushioned with pale dead grass, made a soft bed. The sweet smell of hay, and the dim light, was calming and we soon relaxed. We shared the space with a cloud of gnats but didn't care. The ground, sturdy as ever, gave us strange comfort and, after eating a couple of figs, my boys curled up close to my side and soon drifted off to sleep. I wished we had some water and remembered the cool spring in upper Amiras. The brass tap was not far away and would be our first call when darkness came. In a matter of minutes, I too had fallen asleep.

* * *

I woke suddenly; tense, listening. Judging by the shadows, it was around midday. A gentle wind soughed through the trees and whispered up the mountainside. l pondered, perhaps that very breeze bore the souls of our dead heavenward. Sadness shivered through me despite the heat. While I thought of Petro, the warm draught caressed my skin and felt like the breath of my sleeping baby. *Goodbye my son. Rest in peace.* The baby was not baptised, yet God would surely let the innocent into his Kingdom. I drifted back into the sleep of exhaustion and dreamt of what could have been.

Chapter 10

Crete, Present Day.

ANGIE PICKED UP HER NOTEBOOK from Maria's table and dropped it into her handbag. She had hardly written a sentence. The sharpest pencil in Greece could not record the emotions that swarmed around her grandmother's words. They needed time before they went on paper.

She too could taste the soft, warm cheese and feel the fierce passion of a mother determined to protect her children. As she pulled the zipper across her bag a stray sunbeam caught her engagement ring. Diamond-white sparkles spiralled and flashed around the whitewashed walls as if Nick's spirit were in the room with her. Angie had so much to tell him. She recalled the day, a couple of years ago, when he gave her the simple solitaire engagement ring.

They had taken part in a seven mile fun run in aid of the local hospice. Nick didn't run, just the idea of exercise made him wince, but he had wanted to do it for Angie, and got everyone at work to sponsor him. He said it was absolute proof that he would do anything for her. They ran side by side, and at the halfway mark, she could see he was really hurting, but he dug in and carried on. At the end of the race, he took a medal from the official and put it around her neck himself.

'I love you, Angie Lambrakis,' he said, and then he went down on one knee, right there on the finishing line, and pulled the ring box out of his shorts pocket. 'Will you marry me?'

The local press loved it, spectators too, all taking photos.

Angie, flustered, tears rising, couldn't speak.

'Say yes, love!' a woman with a twin buggy shouted.

Angie blinked at Nick, still down on his knee in the churned mud. 'Oh, Nick . . .' she said, the tears springing free, 'of course I'll marry you!'

Poppy came rushing over. 'Did I miss it? You great lummox! You could have waited for me!' She whacked him playfully around his head and then, pulling her phone out, she said, 'Go on then, get up, slip the ring on, and give her a kiss. I want a photo!'

Angie smiled with the memory. How she loved them both. How she missed her Mam being so carefree.

Maria's eyes also followed the glinting light from Angie's engagement ring. Her face took on a transcending absence. 'Lost souls,' she said quietly, as if praying. She lifted the hem of her apron and dabbed her eyes. 'Each of the hundred and fourteen bodies on that ridge belonged to somebody's family. Hundreds of hearts were broken that day, lives smashed, and for what?' A sigh came from deep inside her. 'How could I have known what would take place while I was up the mountain with Stavro and Matthia? How could I, Angelika? I wasn't there.'

Maria dabbed at another tear.

'Please don't get upset, *Yiayá*,' Angie said. 'You saved the lives of Matthia and Stavro all by yourself. That's something to be very proud of.' Angie regretted bringing all this tragedy back to her darling, sweet grandmother. The old lady had been through so much.

Remorse deepened the lines on Maria's face. She stared ahead as if seeing into the past. 'I shouldn't have left the village, Angelika. Your mother said that to me the day she left here. She suffered as much as anyone on that ridge.'

'But, *Yiayá*, my mother wasn't born then.' Angie couldn't figure out what was going on in her grandmother's mind. She considered Maria's great age and told herself that, at ninety years old, her grandmother was bound to experience some confusion. It seemed Maria was muddling Poppy with Petro.

Maria shook her head, reached for Angie's hand and read her palm. 'No, Angelika, I'm not senile yet,' she said, smiling.

Angie felt the heat of a blush, ashamed of doubting the astute old woman.

'You'll understand when you've heard the rest of the story.' Maria placed Angie's hand back in her lap and pointed at a pool of sunlight on the floor near the window. 'You see that? Every afternoon the sun shines through that big olive tree outside and marks the spot in here, where your poor mother stood nearly forty years ago. She said it was all my fault.' Maria smiled sadly and turned to Angie. 'When you go back to London, don't forget to tell Poppy I've always loved her. I always have and I always will. And say I'm truly sorry.'

Angie wondered if she had missed something. Her grandmother wasn't making sense.

'Tell me about my daughter, is she happy living in England, Angelika?' Maria's chin quivered, and Angie sensed her grandmother's enormous pain.

She thought for a moment. It seemed rather odd to talk about Poppy's life. She had never considered it before. One thing she knew for sure; if her mother was around, Angie's world ran smoothly. In a flash of realisation, Angie understood she had taken Poppy for granted, all these years. Poppy had dedicated her life to her daughter and nothing had ever been too much trouble, until the wedding.

Maria waited, her eyes pleading.

'Mam has always lived by herself, *Yiayá*. She has a house in Camberley, that's near London. A semi. I grew up there.'

'Does she still make her own clothes, Angelika?'

Angie smiled. 'Funny you should ask. Mam turned the smallest bedroom into her sewing room. She did her accounts in there before she retired. Did you know she was an accountant?'

Maria nodded.

'She does alterations and repairs for the local dry cleaners, and she always has some dressmaking of her own on the go.' *Not that she ever goes anywhere that requires dressing up*, Angie thought sadly. That was about to change. 'Mam doesn't get out enough, *Yiayá*, so I'm thinking about taking her for a meal, or to the cinema, now and again.'

Maria smiled and nodded. 'Poppy learned to use my sewing machine when she was eleven years old. She fashioned peg bags from odd scraps of material.' Maria chuckled. 'I think every woman in the village had one of her fantastic creations.' She stared into the past, her eyes sparkling. 'When your *Papoú* had a hole in his trouser pocket, he asked her to fix it. She was so delighted, she made him extra-large pockets.'

Proud of her mother, Angie tried to imagine Poppy as a young girl sitting at an old treadle machine.

'Every time Vassili dropped anything in his pocket it went all the way down to his knees, which meant comical contortions to get it out again.' Maria chuckled. 'Everyone joked about him having deep pockets, but he hadn't the heart to ask her to change them.'

Angie was telling her grandmother about Poppy's latest creation, a copy of a Chanel jacket she had seen in a magazine, when she realised Maria was dozing. Her putty eyelids had descended and the face that had shown so much emotion, relaxed. A soft smile rested on Maria's lips. Angie noticed how peaceful she looked, and fancied she might be dreaming of Poppy.

For a moment, she felt an aching sadness. How terrible to be parted from your child. No matter what your age, or what distance divides you, your daughter is still your own. Sadly, she imagined never seeing her mother again. Then she tried to imagine having an estranged daughter, and realised that must be heart-breaking. The thought renewed Angie's determination to reunite Poppy and Maria.

On the wall, an old clock ticked the minutes away. Angie wondered if a week was long enough to get to the bottom of her mother's secrets.

Angie could hear her grandmother's gentle snore over the hypnotic chirruping of cicadas from outside. Other village noises drifted in through the cottage door. Nearby, a cockerel thumped its wings against its body and then crowed in the warm midday air. Somewhere a man shouted and a cat screeched. A dog, probably on a short chain guarding chickens, barked and from a distance, another replied – canines conversing over the valley. Angie contemplated her grandmother's story that had travelled across three generations, bridging a gap that she was yet to understand.

After a few minutes, she decided to slip away for a walk around the village. As she shifted her weight forward, Maria's eyes opened. The old woman blinked, tears and tiredness gone.

'Don't leave. Let's move on with the story, Angelika,' she said.

* * *

Crete, 15th September 1943.

THE NEXT TIME I woke, under the sprawling fig tree, the boys were at my side. Stavro had his hand pressed over my mouth while Matthia shook my shoulder. With hardly enough light to see, Stavro put his face close to mine and placed a finger across his mouth. I understood at once.

He took his hand away and I sat up. The sound of marching on the road, only about twenty metres away, grew closer. Matthia started to whimper and at the same time, the goat bleated. I pulled Matthia to me but, just as the Nazis were level, he wriggled free. He barged through the umbrella of leaves and bolted up the hillside away from us and the soldiers.

The men came to an abrupt halt. I prayed they hadn't seen Matthia and wondered if I should stay put, or go after him? Stavro and I heard barked orders in German. We peeped through the branches and, in the failing light, could see two Nazis start up the steep hill in our direction.

They swept the ground with torchlight and called, 'Stop, or we shoot!' in textbook Greek. Through the large fig leaves, I saw their silhouettes come closer.

Hidden in the depths of the tree, we were terrified. The Nazis saw the goat and an argument followed. I guessed they were deciding to take or leave it. We peeped through the branches and could see a soldier heading our way. Had he realised we were there? He would put his pistol to our heads if he found us.

Take Stavro first, I prayed. I couldn't bear for my boy to see me shot and understand what would happen to him.

I shook so badly it's a wonder they didn't hear my bones rattling. Stavro sidled up to me. I folded my arms around his thin body and held him tightly. He stuffed his knuckles into his mouth, his heart pounding against my ribs.

The soldier stopped beside our tree. I could see the round tips of his jackboots poking beneath the branches. We hardly dared breathe. The Nazi balanced himself firmly, planting his feet on the soft earth. Judging by his silhouette, I saw him reach for his pistol. The coup de grâce . . . We were about to be slaughtered.

For a second, I considered pleading, but then I decided on a silent prayer and inched Stavro's face against my chest. At least it would be quick and the boy would not see the end coming. Perhaps the same bullet would finish me off too. I hoped so. Death seemed a blessed relief at that moment.

I prepared, said a mental goodbye to Vassili and prayed Matthia had found a safe place up the hillside and that the Nazis hadn't seen him. I trusted my husband would survive the war, find Matthia and live in peace. I concentrated on the boots less than a metre from me, not wanting to see the features of our executioner.

The Nazi grunted – pig, I thought – and then came the sound of piss hitting the ground. I felt warm splashes sprinkle through the leaves onto my bare legs. The man fumbled with his buttons and then turned away.

I didn't know whether to laugh or cry.

The goat, skittish in the presence of strangers, bleated nervously. My relief was so enormous that before I could stop myself, I had sighed louder than intended. The Nazi spun on his heels and returned to the tree, shouting something to his partner at the same time. I pushed Stavro's head down to my lap and flattened myself over him. Perhaps in the dark, he would not see my boy and only shoot me. There was always hope.

The torchlight shone in our direction. Small dots of light broke through the dense canopy and jerked around our leafy cave as the man with the torch walked over uneven ground. A hand thrust between the thick silver branches above us, struggling to part the tangled leaves. I closed my eyes, held my breath tightly, knowing if I opened my mouth now a whimper would escape. If I had to die, I would go with dignity. The tree shook with a rustle, once, twice, three times . . . Then I realised, the Nazis were plucking figs from over our heads. I prayed for Matthia to be still, wherever he was.

The Nazis laughed, talking to each other as they returned to their troop, leaving the goat behind. Moments later, the group of soldiers continued their march towards the village of Pefkos. I shivered and couldn't stop sobbing. My senses seemed to run away through me like a dropped stitch in a knitted blanket.

Stavro, young and strong, wriggled free of my grasp.

'Shush! Come on, Mama.' He tugged on my apron and the candles rolled out. Stavro gathered them and shoved them back into my pocket. 'We must find Matthia, quickly, let's go.'

We left the goat on its tether, and our belongings beneath the tree. Under cover of night, we rushed up the hillside in the direction Matthia had taken, moving as quietly as possible. Every snapping twig underfoot seemed like an explosion. Sick with fear for Matthia and what might have happened, I called his name softly as we moved along, aware that he may have crawled under one of the many scrub bushes.

Keeping Stavro close beside me, I hurried towards the upper village of Amiras. Hidden in the trees, this sparse cluster of houses with its spring of sweet water could have been overlooked by the Nazis. I prayed to the Blessed Virgin to keep my son safe, to keep us all safe. Surely we had lost enough.

Although the moon had not yet appeared, our eyes adjusted to the dark and we could see a sufficient distance to travel quietly between the trees. I knew the first house Matthia would come across belonged to the local shepherd, Andreas. This maverick Cretan and guardian of the village flocks was the subject of many outrageous stories.

Perhaps Andreas lay dead, along with the other men on the ridge, or would we find him inside? I didn't recall seeing him with all the unfortunate men, but thought it best not to call his name. I used my elbow to press the latch, put my shoulder to the wood, and then bit on a cry of pain. I had forgotten the slam of the Nazi rifle. The door opened.

'Kérios Andreas?' I whispered in the dark, conscious that he may have shut some goats in there and I could instigate a racket. Greeted by silence, we crept inside.

In the gloom, at chest height next to the entrance, I recognised the semi-circular shape of a water-deposit with its small brass tap. I knocked the galvanised container with my elbow, relieved to hear a dull timbre that told me the tank was full. Luck had stayed with us. Stavro tripped over an enamel jug and washbowl below it, sending them skidding and clattering across the floor.

'Shush, be careful, son.'

'Sorry, Mama.'

I sensed Matthia's presence. 'Matthia, are you in here? It's your Mama and Stavro,' I called softly.

Stavro closed the door, took a candle from my pocket, and lit it. We found Matthia under the shepherd's low table, curled tight into the corner, sucking his thumb, eyes wide with fear.

'Poor child, don't be afraid, we're safe now,' I said to calm him.

Matthia stared at me and whimpered.

'Come on, it's all right, brother,' Stavro said. He held the candle while I stretched under the rough wood.

After a moment, Matthia crawled out of his sanctuary and clasped his arms around my neck. I pulled him to me, holding him so tightly he squealed and wriggled free.

'Mama, I thought the soldiers were coming to kill me. I was scared.'

I hugged him again, rocking, never wanting to let him go. Such relief exploded inside me, feelings so intense I found it difficult to keep my composure.

'Don't squash me, Mama,' he cried.

I held him while my eyes adjusted to the meagre light. Stavro took the candle and investigated the nooks and crannies of the small room.

The cottage, sparse and windowless, had rough lime-washed walls. A simple fireplace had a wooden shelf across its breast that supported a single china cup. A black metal pot hung from the wall and old baskets from the roof beams. Ashes filled the hearth. A cluttered collection of eating and cooking implements, bottles and an oil lamp were stuffed into a square alcove, and kindling scattered the floor. We poured water and drank our fill, gulping and sighing over the cracked and grimy cup. Its contents sweeter than the finest wine.

A stone bed that we call a banquette ran against the wall opposite the door and a couple of grubby sheepskins and some olive sacks lay on it.

'Stavro, help me to make a bed. You boys need some sleep,' I whispered.

They climbed onto the fleeces, and Matthia clutched Stavro around the waist. In the candlelight, I tried to sound calm.

'I have to go back down to the fig tree for our belongings and the goat, Stavro.'

'I'll come with you, Mama, you can't do it alone.'

'No, son. You look after your brother. I'll make two trips. Now get some sleep. Once I've brought the food up, we'll eat.'

'But, Mama, I'm afraid. The soldiers might get you.'

'I will be fine. Matthia needs you with him. If I'm not back by sunrise, leave here and continue up the hillside. Find another tree like the one that we hid in and stay there while it's daylight. Don't let anyone see you, right?'

He nodded.

'It's important. The Nazis will probably search the houses tomorrow.' I ran my burned hands over my boys, finding it hard not to tell them my real fears. How I missed Vassili at that moment. If ever Stavro and Matthia needed their father, it was now. I tried to imagine him with us, looking over us, and it gave me great strength.

I heard his voice in my head. *You can do it, Maria. Stick to your plan. Go and get the things you'll need, woman.*

Once again, I was almost overcome by the urge to gather my sons in my arms and crush their young bodies against me. I didn't want to leave them knowing, if things went wrong, this could be the last time I ever saw them.

I gazed into Stavro's eyes and tried to imagine how he would think of me if I never returned. 'Always remember that I love you, son. Now, go to sleep. We have to move on before daylight.'

They curled up together and I covered them with a couple of hemp olive sacks, tucking the rough edges around their thin bodies. A final sack went over their heads to keep the September mosquitoes off their sweet faces. I sat on the edge of the bed for a while, listened to their even breathing, and wondered how I would ever cope if I were to lose them, too.

Life had been good to give me these precious children. Petro came into my heart too. The numbness of fatigue did nothing to relieve my overwhelming sense of loss.

There would be time for grieving. But at that moment, I had to protect my two remaining sons. Heavy hearted, I blew out the candle and turned to leave. Yet as I reached for the iron handle, it twisted and the door flew open. The great bulk of a man blocked my exit.

Chapter 11

Crete, Present Day.

THE OLD WOMAN YAWNED, her pale tired face stretching like *The Scream*. 'Enough, Angelika,' she said.

'But, *Yiayá*, who found you, a Nazi soldier, or the shepherd?'

'Ask me later. It's time to sleep.'

Angie sighed louder than she intended.

Maria looked up, a smile on her lips.

'All right, Angelika, I'll tell you, it was Andreas, the custodian of our sheep and goats. Now, I need my siesta. I'm tired.'

'Of course. You must be exhausted.' She lowered her eyes. 'I'm being selfish. Sorry. I've recently come to realise it's my worst fault. I could blame my mother for always giving me what I want but, at my age, I really should know better.'

Maria dropped her head to one side and smiled again.

Angie got to her feet. 'To recall all this tragedy has to be absolutely awful for you. I can't imagine how you're feeling.'

'Yes, it's very hard, *koritsie*. But I'm glad to do it. The story needs to be told.'

Angie helped her grandmother out of the chair. The ninety-year-old stood and stared at Angie for a moment, her expression turning sad.

'Can you bring my daughter back to me, Angelika? Our hearts are broken. For as long as you have lived, we have waited for Poppy's return.'

'I promise to do my best, *Yiayá*.'

Maria sniffed, shook her head, and shuffled through the curtained arch to her bedroom.

Angie waited for a moment, listening to her grandmother moving about, before stillness settled on the cottage.

In the dim light, she soaked up the atmosphere of the place and inspected a collection of ancient wedding photographs in tarnished frames. The pictures hung on the wall near the fireplace. She searched the brides' faces for Poppy and the poker-faced bridegrooms for Yeorgo. Despite never having seen a clear photo of him, she guessed she would recognise her father. Angie had longed to hear her mother talk about him, especially when she was a child. But Poppy always broke down when Angie broached the subject. This made young Angie feel guilty, as if a tragedy, which seemed to destroy her mother, was her fault.

Why, Mam? I wanted a daddy so much when I was a kid. You could have invented one for me. Yours is lovely, my Papoú. *A Greek Einstein with twinkly eyes and a quiet sense of humour. Why have you abandoned him for these past thirty-seven years? You've broken his heart.*

Angie studied the photographs on the wall. The black moustaches, clean-parted, heavily-greased hair and the dark eyes of the bridegrooms had no effect on her. He's not there, she thought. Disappointed, she slipped through the strip curtain and closed the cottage door.

The bone-deep silence of the village at siesta time made every small noise seem like a clash of cymbals. Angie realised Amiras was a natural auditorium. When she looked over to the ridge, she understood how the sound of marching feet and the women's tragic wailing would not only carry across the rooftops, but also halfway up the mountain.

She turned left at the bottom of the steps and continued along the street. Heat from the tarmac pulsed through her thin sandals. Antirrhinums and poppies grew from cracks in the doorsteps. She stepped around a giant rosemary bush that spilled into the street, the shrub covered with pale mauve flowers. When she caught the sweet, soapy scent of the herb, she was instantly transported to her mother's house; Sunday lunch, roast leg of lamb, roast potatoes, minted peas, buttered carrots. Her mouth watered.

The whitewashed houses lining the road appeared quite modern, yet she noticed the walls were half a metre thick. Angie guessed that behind the smooth plaster and white aluminium window frames stood stone and clay walls that had also witnessed the day of the massacre.

The narrow street, quiet with its secrets, seemed to push Angie onward. A tightly packed gathering of small, square houses with double-glazed eyes that watched her.

Beyond the dwellings, Angie recognised the field of olive trees her grandmother had mentioned. Stepping off the road, she enjoyed the shade of the grove and walked up the gentle slope between gnarled trunks. Like a new bookmark in an old history book, she felt slightly incongruous but soon slipped back in time. What age was Maria when all this happened? If she married at sixteen, and had Stavro the same year, that would have made her twenty-three. Although ninety now, Angie was very aware of Maria's earlier beauty.

She visualised herself in her grandmother's place on that September day in 1943, and rested her hand against a wide trunk. Looking up, she whispered to the overhead branches. 'Did my grandmother stand right here, old tree, terrified for the lives of her children?'

Like young Maria, Angie peered through the canopy of silver-green leaves and olive blossom, searching for a sign or an omen. A swallow dived past, glossy black, skimming the ground before it ascended with acrobatic grace, trawling the sky for aerial plankton.

Turning to look the way she had come, Angie imagined the sound of two thousand marching soldiers. The scene Maria had described seemed to appear through the dappled sunlight. Shadows shapeshifting, ghostly around her. Sounds filtered in from the back of her mind, until she found herself totally immersed in her grandmother's past.

Pictures from Maria's story flashed and clashed before her eyes. She moved behind the tree, as her grandmother had done, and then peered towards the road. Her heartbeat quickened and a shudder raced through her body. The deep shadows took on a menacing air and a cloud seemed to drift over the sun. Minutes slid by, her head full of Maria's words. Visions of that terrible day appeared before her. Then, she realised she was crying, sobbing bitterly. All the emotion she had fought against in the cottage poured out.

Angie was not a crier. She didn't turn on the tears when things went wrong. She usually became angry, analysed, got organised, and addressed the issue. Yet there she was, for the second time in a week, sobbing her heart out. She buried her face in her hands, blocking the tragedy, damming her tears.

She hurried down to the street, gulping in the warm air, turning her face to the sun. Back on the tarmac, she experienced a loss of purpose and, for a moment, found herself overwhelmed by loneliness. Once again, she had a terrific sense that the street watched her.

You're just missing Nick, she told herself, continuing along the road until she came to a cemetery.

Her thoughts returned to her mother. How terrible for Poppy to lose the man she loved. Angie yearned for Nick, and they had only been parted a couple of days.

As a child, she had bouts of longing for a father. Sometimes she hung around the playground to watch her friends being dropped off at the school gate. Some would give their dads a peck on the cheek, or a quick hug. Older girls would rush from the car, embarrassed to be with a parent. They didn't realise how lucky they were.

Poppy often glanced at the empty kitchen chair, or stared vacantly with a smile on her lips. Ashamed to have thought nothing of it, Angie now realised some of her mother's loneliness.

When she returned home, she would stop taking Poppy for granted. The time had come to spoil her mother, for Angie to show her appreciation for all the care and attention she had received over the years. First, she would phone the local florist and have a nice bunch of flowers delivered on the first of each month. She smiled, satisfied with the plan.

Then she remembered: Poppy was prone to hay fever, and Angie, being newly jobless, had cut up her credit card in a fit of self-righteousness. Still, she'd make it up to her mother somehow. She had to.

Steep cement steps rose to simple rectangular grey marble tombs decorated with gaudy bunches of silk or plastic flowers. Despite an urge to read the inscriptions, Angie couldn't muster the energy. Overwhelmed by a desire to speak to Nick, she decided to return to Viannos and call him.

She closed her eyes and remembered his handsome face, when he held her at the airport. As he stood, looking down at her, she knew he was remembering their night of love making.

'Will you miss me?' he asked, placing a finger under her chin and tilting her face.

'Not at all,' she replied, smiling. 'Forgetting you already.'

Laughing, he hugged her, lifting her off her feet.

'In fact, who the hell are you?' she continued, teasing him. 'Never mind. Kiss me, handsome stranger.'

He did, laughing. 'Stay safe, Angie. You know I love you.' Then he embraced her, full of love and tenderness.

Oh, Nick.

* * *

The moment Angie saw her hire car, the flat tyre registered. Because of siesta time, the road lay deserted. Could she change the wheel herself? She imagined Nick's disbelief when she told him she'd done it on her own. The thought lifted her spirits, and gave her the confidence to get on with the job.

She lectured herself: if a woman can't change a tyre, without breaking a nail or making a fuss, at the age of thirty-seven, then she had absolutely no right to yelp about equality – had she? After all, she told herself, you didn't need a penis to change a tyre, you needed a wheel nut spanner and a jack.

Angie opened the boot, hauled out the spare, and winced when she felt a nail snap to the quick. She glanced around.

A lace curtain fell and a cottage door closed. A bent and aged woman in black shuffled down the street, pulling a fat sheep on a rope with two lambs skipping around its rear. The stranger stopped by the rosemary bush and pulled the sheep in close.

'You want help?' she rasped. The lambs took advantage of the stilled ewe, butting her udder and suckling.

The woman looked older than Maria. Angie smiled and whacked the stubborn wheel spanner with a lump of rock. As the nut gave way and the spanner clattered to the road she said, 'Thanks, but I can manage.'

A door across the street opened and a heavy, middle-aged woman, also in black, hauled a kitchen chair out and plonked herself in it. In a few minutes, a small crowd of elderly females had gathered, keeping their distance but watching with an expression of wonder and admiration. When Angie had the new wheel in place, and the wheel nuts hand-tight, she lowered the jack and finished the job with a last turn of the spanner. Mission accomplished.

One of the old dears handed her a small water bottle. After thanking her, Angie unscrewed the cap and took a well needed glug. Too late, she realised it was raki. She swallowed and coughed. The women laughed, slapping their thighs and nodding.

Another pensioner brought her cold water in a glass, another, a bottle of olive oil, and yet another, half a dozen fresh eggs splattered with chicken shit.

Touched, and humbled by their kindness, Angie placed the gifts on the car bonnet before rolling the flat tyre towards the boot of the car. A shout made her look up the road where she saw Demitri, rushing in her direction.

'Wait, Angelika, I'll do it.'

'Yeah, right, typical man!' she said, throwing a grin. 'Too late, Demitri, I've done the job myself.'

He stared at the wheel and then at her. 'Alone? You changed the tyre, you, without help?'

'Well, no, actually these kind ladies lifted the car while I got the punctured one off and the new on,' Angie said, smiling.

The women nudged each other, grinning. Demitri's eyes flicked from Angie to the amused matriarchs and then back to her.

'Are you sure the nuts are tight?' He reached for the spanner.

'I'm sure.' She took the tool from his hands, and passed him the water bottle, glancing at the women.

Demitri took a gulp of raki and spluttered. The old women laughed with Angie.

'Where can I get the puncture fixed? Do I have to go back to that garage on the Heraklion road?'

Demitri's head snapped around. 'You called in there?' Lifting the wheel, he elbowed her to one side and put it in the boot.

'I needed petrol,' Angie said.

'Avoid that place, they're mad, pull up at the supermarket and I'll get it fixed this afternoon.'

'Thanks. Demitri, do you think I could get a wifi connection at *Yiayá*'s house? I'd like to videocall my mother before I leave.'

He shrugged. 'I'll ask my cousin, he's the local telephone engineer.'

Angie dropped the wheel at the supermarket and then drove to Viannos to collect her tablet. She smiled to think how great it would be to see her mother and grandmother reunited before she left Crete. With her mood still buoyant, she arrived at Manoli's kafenion and, in the shade of the big tree, she relaxed.

'Hello, lady, welcome back. I believe somebody slashed your tyre, hey?'

Here comes the Manoli interrogation, Angie thought.

'Don't start rumours, Manoli. I had a puncture, my own fault for parking by the bins. I'll have a beer, please.'

Manoli reeled off six brands of lager. 'What you like?'

Angie chose the only name she recognised. 'Small beer, small glass, please.'

'This beer is not Greek, lady. Is German beer,' Manoli sneered. 'I call it Angela Merkel beer, is pale, all gas and no good taste. You want, I bring.' His smile dripped away like melting butter, leaving something rancid.

'No, sorry, I want a local beer,' Angie said.

The cartoon grin returned. 'Okays, you want a large or small beer . . . large glass or small glass? What you like?'

'I'll leave it to you. I don't suppose you have wifi, do you?' Angie slid the tablet out of her bag.

'What you think? We are in Europe now. Of course we have wifi,' Manoli said.

Angie searched for logic in his answer but found none.

Manoli stared at her tablet. 'Holy Virgin, very nice. How much memory? It takes pictures? You buy in England? How much this cost you?'

'I wouldn't know, Manoli. My fiancé bought it for me.'

'Fiancé?' He scowled. 'You put "Manolis" then "e" then "x" for the password. I bring you beer.'

Angie typed in the password, realised what she had entered and giggled. *Manolisex.* Suddenly, with laughter on her lips and the hot sun on her face, Angie felt that everything would work out. Soon she would discover why Poppy had left the island, what had upset her so much, and how she could fix it. She'd bring her family back together once and for all.

Angie thought about Nick. She recalled their first date. Not a date at all, really. The new boss had just broken up with his partner and had to attend a wedding.

Shortly after he had joined the company, he had slipped into her office and said, 'Would you do me the greatest of favours?'

Angie, unable to speak after one glance into those eyes-to-die-for, had nodded far too eagerly.

In the church, he had whispered the first line of *Pride and Prejudice*, '*It is a truth universally acknowledged, that a single man in possession of a good fortune, must be in want of a wife.*' She had giggled, noting he happened to be a single man in possession of a good job, which she decided was worth a fortune these days.

She asked if he had read *The Hunger Games*. He had, and their literary discussion then led them through a range of best sellers and classics, which continued through the main meal and culminated in hushed exchanges through the speeches.

Finally, as the bride and groom cut the cake, they discovered they were both avid *Doctor Who* fans, and they spent the rest of their night revelling in clips of their favourite episodes.

'Baker!'

'No-no, Pertwee!'

Angie realised the sight of Nick's handsome face on her tablet would have her snivelling. She should phone him instead.

Her mood continued to lift as she keyed his number. His deep, honeyed voice uplifted her, and she could not help grinning as she reassured him everything was fine.

'Don't feel you have to do this, Angie. If anyone upsets you, or you want to drop the idea and come home, do it – okay? Promise me, you have my credit card, just buy a ticket at the airport,' he said. 'Give me a call and I'll pick you up at Heathrow. Don't make me worry.'

'Nick, you're so lovely, but please, I'm absolutely fine.' She recounted events so far, avoiding the massacre, which still lay heavy in her heart. Nick seemed tense, probably overworked and not getting his full eight hours, she thought.

While Angie talked, Manoli returned with her drink and three saucers with little round meatballs, stuffed vine leaves, and a mound of tiny olives.

'Is from me. Real Cretan mezzé.' Manoli's familiar grin radiated.

Angie thanked him and returned her attention to Nick.

'Who was that?' he asked, an edge to his voice.

'Nick, don't fret! It's just the kafenion guy, Manoli. He got me a cheap room at his cousin's place, here in Viannos.' Sensing his concern, she tried to inject a smile into her voice. 'I'm having a beer under the biggest tree I've ever seen. A thousand years old, can you believe it?'

'Be careful, sweetheart,' he said, his voice softening. 'Remember that old film, *Shirley Valentine*? Make sure you don't go anywhere near his brother's boat!'

Angie giggled. She recalled cosy winter nights when she would lie in Nick's arms and they would watch old films together. 'I wish you were here with me, Nick. I miss you.'

A woman's voice in the background said, 'Nick, what time would you like –' The rest of the conversation muted. Angie strained to hear but guessed Nick had his hand over the phone.

'Who's in the office with you?' Angie asked.

'Nobody.'

'There is, and her voice sounds familiar. Who is it?'

Nick hesitated, then said, 'I'll get back to you. Can you give me a moment?' to somebody.

'Sure. I'll be in my office,' a woman's voice spoke. Angie heard the office door close.

'It's the transitions manager from Whitekings Judy Peabody,' he said tensely. 'Don't sound so suspicious, Angie. I'm having a hard enough time dealing with this woman, without you implying I'm up to no good. You wouldn't believe the changes around here. You're better off out of it, sweetheart, believe me.'

Angie stared at a discarded cigarette butt at her feet. 'Whitekings . . . but I thought you had that sorted. You're stressed, Nick. What's really going on?' In a flash, the fun was gone. Nick had problems. This harpy from Whitekings was putting him under pressure and Angie wasn't there for him. She feared he would toss and turn and fret all night, and then be wrecked by the time he had to go to work. He wouldn't eat breakfast, would worry too much, and make do with crisps and a beer for lunch.

Manoli sidled up asking if she wanted another beer.

'Please, Manoli, give me a minute,' Angie pleaded.

'Nick? Why didn't you tell me?'

'This trip's important to you, Angie.'

'That's true, it is, but you're far more important.'

'I thought, under the circumstances, better if you take your holiday while I've still . . . anyway, let's forget it. Tell me, what are you doing tomorrow?'

'Hang on. Are you telling me you're about to lose your job too? Oh my God, Nick! That's terrible. You must be out of your mind with worry.'

'I doubt it will come to that, Angie, but it *is* a time of uncertainty. That's why I'm working all the hours they want.'

'I guess I'd better not invite all these people to our wedding,' she said quietly. 'If we're both unemployed, we can't afford to go crazy on a big razzmatazz affair.' Let alone afford a baby, she thought. 'Oh, Nick . . . what about the mortgage?' she said, regretting it immediately. He didn't need the added pressure.

'Angie, calm down. We'll know one way or the other by the time you get back.'

'I'm so sorry, darling. I imagine your stress level is high enough, without me adding to it. What an awful situation, I can't believe it, Nick.'

'Trust me, Angie. I'm doing everything I can to secure our future.'

'It's such a shock. I feel useless. Is there anything I can do, darling?'

'Just find the answers to your questions and enjoy yourself,' Nick said.

After the call, Angie stared at her phone. Poor Nick. Everything they'd dreamt of hung in the balance. Their big wedding, their new house, and their baby plans. He must be going through hell all by himself.

'You don't like my mezzé? Why you look so sad, lady?' Manoli put two tiny glasses of raki on the table and then pulled up another chair. *Yammas!*' he cried, banging his small glass onto the tin table in the traditional salute. But the rattle sent the tablet sliding, knocking the drink towards her.

Horrified, Angie caught the glass in one hand, before it spilled, and the tablet in the other.

'Bravo!' Manoli clicked his fingers in the air. 'Now tell me, what's wrong, lady?'

Angie had an irresistible urge to talk. 'Terrible news, big problems, Manoli. We may have to cancel our wedding, and give up the house we planned to buy.'

'You see, when you tell somebody, it is not so bad.'

She blinked at him, unable to speak.

'These things are not a catastrophe. You are a beautiful woman; you have health, friends and family. The rest are dust, not important, and we can fix some of them.'

'Are you crazy?' She knocked back the raki, a spark of anger flaring, immediately doused by misery.

Manoli grinned and nodded. 'I might be crazy; how can I know?'

'I've lost my job, Manoli. Our wedding costs run into thousands. Now, my fiancé may lose his job too, which means we can't afford to get married.'

'What is this, afford to get married? Come, get married here. You have more friends here anyway.'

'I don't know anybody here.' She thought about her Facebook friends, the plan to upload her wedding pictures, and then enjoy reading their comments. She also thought of Shelly and Debs, her very best friends. All through Uni, they'd been incredibly close, almost like sisters, sharing everything. Now they met less often, usually for an Indian, Vietnamese, or the latest Nuevo food place. A meal, accompanied by laughter, gossip, and occasionally tears, but *always* ending with two puddings

Angie smiled. One thing was sure, wherever she got married, her friends would be there too.

Manoli banged his glass on the table, breaking her thoughts. 'You are the granddaughter of Kondulakis Maria; everyone in Amiras village is your friend. Because you don't know them yet, doesn't mean they don't know you, doesn't mean they are not your very good friends. Get married here.' His eyes narrowed, he stared at her for a moment as if deciding something then he dived back into the kafenion and returned with the raki bottle.

'Manoli, coffee!' someone shouted from a table behind the tree.

'Go somewhere else, I'm busy,' he yelled back while refilling Angie's glass. 'Lady, when you get married, why you want job? Have babies, they are a big job.' Manoli frowned for a moment then slapped himself on the forehead, a look of conspiracy in his eyes. 'Or, work for me. Make coffee for these *malákas.*' He waved his arm towards the big tree and its surrounding empty tables.

'But what will you do if I take your job?' she asked, the very thought breaking her mood and making her laugh.

'Me, I have a plan. I am a big businessman.' He stuck his chest out and did a head waggle. 'I'll cut down my olive trees, because *malákas* co-op pays nothing for the oil, borrow money from the *malákas* bank and plant photovoltaic panels for solar electricity. I will be rich. A good plan, yes? Everybody's doing it, even the ones who still owe the bank for the ostrich farms, from ten years ago.'

'Ostrich farms?' Angie blinked at him.

'Yes, *malákas* Government gave us grants and said we would all get rich quick. To get rich quick is the national sport of Greece. But the *malákas* Government didn't mention the *malákas* giant birds were not as daft as chickens. They scared the shit out of us all and everyone chopped their heads off and ate them. Not the heads, the rest, before they'd even laid an egg or paid any loan money back to the *malákas* bank.'

Angie started to giggle.

'You laugh. Is not funny. One of the *malákas* nearly killed my old aunt who had the job of feeding them for me. I bought two chicks.' Manoli winced. 'Okay, perhaps I should not have told my old aunt they were a new type of chicken from Europe. They grew so fast . . .'

Angie laughed. 'Thanks, Manoli.' Their eyes met and he nodded knowingly.

As Angie drove back to Amiras, she thought what a great guy Manoli was, cheering her up like that. Nevertheless, she often got the impression he was simply a one man theatre act. Her thoughts returned to Nick and the looming uncertainty about their plans. With a sinking feeling, she wondered what they would do if he lost his job too?

Chapter 12

AMIRAS HAD WOKEN FROM siesta. Men played cards or backgammon outside the kafenion. Women, mostly dressed in black, sat in small groups on the shady side of the street, gossiping while they crocheted. Children, with a length of rope tied to a tree, played a skipping game in the narrow road. They stopped and moved to one side so that Angie could drive past. If it hadn't been for the childrens' Nike trainers and Benetton hoodies, she thought the scene could have been from decades ago.

Halfway up the village steps, a cluster of young teens jostled for space on a makeshift bench under a mulberry tree. As she approached, panting from the climb, they fell silent, glancing shyly with wide, curious eyes. 'Hello, lady!' one of the older ones called in English. They giggled and bunched together, tangling limbs around each other like puppies in their playful wrestling.

Angie placed a hand flat on her belly. How long before she and Nick would have their own family? Children would bring a whole new dimension to their lives.

The sun had morphed into the deep yellow of a nursery school painting, and honeyed light flashed starbursts through the olive branches. Angie walked around to the back of the house. In the garden, dishes of food and mismatched plates covered the cracked marble table.

Nearby, Uncle Matthia turned a row of souvlakia on a barbeque that looked suspiciously like half a hot water cylinder.

Chunks of pork sizzled on sticks of rosemary. The scent of herbs, lemon, and roasting meat teased Angie's taste buds.

Yiayá sat in the shade of the olive tree, concentrating on her crocheting. Before Angie could greet her, a very fat woman, wearing dark stockings that hardly reached her knees and a black dress that barely came down to them, dashed out of the house. Thrashing her arms above her head, she launched herself at Angie.

'Angelika! Angelika!'

Angie supressed an urge to turn and run. The animated, jovial woman grabbed Angie's shoulders and kissed her cheeks forcefully.

'*Yia sas . . .*' Angie stammered at the grinning face.

'I am your Aunty Voula, Matthia's wife. They are my grandchildren,' she yelled, gleefully waving at the youngsters under the mulberry tree. Voula steered Angie towards the food and shouted at Matthia to bring the meat.

Yiayá smiled and dropped her needlework into its bag. With Angie's help, she got out of the white plastic chair and tottered to the table. Angie wanted to talk to her but Voula dominated the scene, gathering her grandchildren and forcing meat and salads on everyone. '*Eat! Eat!*'

Matthia scowled from under his frosty eyebrows.

The children, as rowdy as Voula, snatched food from the plates and then ran wild in the garden. They threw olive stones into the barbeque and screamed with laughter when the pips exploded under Matthia's kebabs. Although incredibly noisy, their happiness infected everyone. Sometimes the boys swore, '*Malákas!*' and then Voula would run at them making chopping movements with the side of her hand. Her dimpled knees flashed white, like risen dough, over the black half-stockings.

Neighbours arrived with more food and vied for Angie's attention. Tumblers, filled with red wine poured from cola bottles, were passed along the table. 'Without chemicals,' Voula yelled. 'Every day you must drink two glasses, Angelika.'

Eventually, Matthia joined the party, eating like a lion. He shoved more meat into his mouth before he'd swallowed the last and managed to sip raki while his cheeks bulged with pork. The fury Angie had seen on his face the first moment she'd met him hadn't shifted.

When Voula filled Angie's glass with acidic wine for the third time, she found the courage to talk to her formidable uncle. She walked around the table and sat beside him. He stood and returned to the barbeque. Determined, she followed him, thinking it would be better to have a conversation with him away from the present company, anyway. The thought of a confrontation made her nervous, but she needed to get to the bottom of his anger, or there would always be this tension between them.

'Uncle Matthia, can I speak to you?' she said.

'Why do you want to talk to me? My mother talks enough for everyone.'

Angie tried to smile but the corner of her mouth ticked nervously. Humility did not come easily to her. In a moment of tense silence, Matthia ignored her and turned the last six souvlakia.

Exasperated, she cleared her throat. 'Uncle, I was very excited to meet you, but you've been so cold to me since I arrived.' She glanced at the glowing coals that were spitting and flaring as the pork fat dripped. 'What did I do that made you so angry?'

Matthia glared. 'You don't know?' He huffed and turned towards her. 'You rich people, you come here . . . These honest villagers have brought you all they have in gifts. Your grandmother has told you that the Germans took all that we had, every single thing; our crops, our possessions, our houses, our men . . .' his voice dropped, 'and more.' His face pinched. 'Have you noticed how many blue eyes you see in Greek faces, around here? Two generations later, and we are still not allowed to forget the worst of it.'

Angie blinked, slow to understand then shocked. She shook her head.

'Now, they cut my pension to dust, raise the taxes on everything, and give us a pittance for the olive oil. We struggle again because of the upper-crust Europeans. I can't even put petrol into the car to take my grandchildren to the beach. It's a catastrophe.'

Angie, speechless for a moment, glanced at the heaps of food still on the table. She struggled to keep the conversation going. 'I realise it must be painful –'

Matthia interrupted. 'Painful? You don't know what you are talking about!' he shouted. His fingers stuttered down buttons before he threw his shirt off, spinning away from her. 'This was painful!'

Angie gasped. Matthia's back, pale gold Mediterranean skin kept out of the sun for a lifetime, had many white, spear-shaped scars.

'Good God, what is that?' Her hand covered her mouth.

'Ask my mother,' Matthia shouted. 'She's so eager to talk about the past and how lucky we are; stupid woman.'

Maria's voice reached them. 'Matthia, be careful.'

He glanced at his mother, then back to Angie, before speaking quietly but with no less anger.

'We weren't to blame then, and we aren't now,' he said, pulling his shirt over his shoulders. 'Politicians, Europe, they claim to work for the people, they are liars. And you lot, you don't know anything. If we had black oil, you'd be on your knees slobbering with respect, but olive oil . . . you screw us.

'You have no idea what's going on here, and you couldn't care less. You didn't then, through the wars and the junta, or perhaps you did, I suspect that's why you supported our oppressors, the regime of the Colonels. I'll bet you don't even know we have the Nazis back here now, at this very moment.'

Angie shook her head. 'No, you're right, but I've come to Crete because I want to know and understand, Uncle Matthia.' She blinked at him. 'What do you mean, the Nazis have returned?'

'Golden Dawn, racist monsters that use our Greek keys symbol like a Nazi swastika. They attack, even kill people who say anything against them. Well, they won't stop me saying what I believe. You Europeans look the other way while we struggle, but you still expect us to defend Europe's borders against the Muslims and terrorists.'

Angie wondered why he grouped Muslims with terrorists, but she decided not to antagonise him with political or religious questions.

He continued to rant, his voice low and hard, eyes flicking towards Maria. 'Cretans, gullible fools with short memories, or village people who should know better, give these anarchist-thugs their support. They swap their vote in exchange for a bag of potatoes. Potatoes! It's ironic that the excuse the Nazis gave for being here in the Viannos area, in '43, was also potatoes. Bah, Judases.'

'I'm sorry. There's so much I don't understand,' Angie said.

'You shouldn't have come here. The journey was a stupid waste of your time and money.'

'I wanted to invite you to my wedding, Uncle Matthia, it was important to me. But now . . .' Angie didn't want to tell him she might have to cancel the wedding. Not only that, but also her Pilates class, her interior design course, and God only knew how she was going to pay off her credit card debt. But, she told herself, she hadn't just come to Crete to escape her own worries; she was here to try and help her mother find peace. To resolve whatever had driven poor Mam away from her parents.

Suddenly, she realised her own shallowness. Her entire life revolved around herself, her marriage, and her happy-ever-after. Poppy had been right, and so had her Uncle Matthia, she shouldn't have come.

She saw herself in a new light and didn't like it. Shocked to recognise the person she had turned into, she stared at the people who were giving their all to make sure she had a good time. Matthia grabbed her attention again.

'But now . . .' he scoffed, 'you realise we couldn't afford to bring our families to England, or buy the wedding clothes. We'd embarrass you. Can you imagine how my Voula feels – you in your fancy get-up and gold jewellery?' Matthia's eyes flicked from Angie's face to her shoes and back again.

Angie lowered her eyes.

Matthia continued, 'And my hard-working and selfless wife in the same dress she's worn for years? I don't have the money to get her another. You probably think it's quaint, ethnic. You'll take your photos to London and say, "They are real village people, Greek peasants," like we're tourist-postcard freaks. Well, let me tell you, Angelika, we are Cretans first – proud Cretans, Greeks second, and Europeans last of all.'

Angie felt the heat of a blush burn into her cheeks. 'No, you misunderstand me. What you wear to our wedding isn't important. It would be wonderful if you came, for Mam's sake as much as ours.' She halted for a moment, realising that might not be quite true. 'I'm so sorry. I didn't mean to . . .'

Angry and sad at the same time, she struggled to find the right words. She wanted them to like her – wasn't that childish? She'd had her own way, always been given anything she wanted, by the two people she loved; Poppy and Nick. Now, when the time had come to be honest and open and selfless with her estranged family, she floundered.

Angie's desire to belong, and to understand, hadn't weakened, yet she found it impossible to relate. She should stand on her own two feet and speak to these lovely people with sincerity, on an equal footing, but she didn't know where to begin. She had absolutely nothing in common with them, apart from her bloodline. How shallow she was, the realisation cut her deeply. Choked on frustration, she decided to drop the subject and leave.

'I'd better go, Uncle. I'm sorry, it wasn't my intention to come here and upset you.' She reached out and touched his arm, but he turned away, sniffed hard, and flipped his souvlakia over the blazing coals.

She'd hurt him – although unintentionally – and Angie felt bad. Defeated and drained, she stared at the ground for a moment, and then returned to the table for her handbag. She couldn't think of any way to reconcile herself with her uncle and staying would only worsen the atmosphere. Yet oddly enough, she had a sudden suspicion Matthia's angst was more to do with Poppy than herself.

'Where are you going, Angelika?' Voula screeched.

'I've a headache, too much wine, Aunty. It's been lovely, thank you.'

'No! You sit here. I will bring you aspirin. My *malákas* husband upset you, yes? I'll kill him.' She reached into the olive tree and peeled a slender branch from the trunk. The tiny white blossom showered over her like Princess Shrek in a snow globe. She ran at Matthia, yelling in Cretan dialect beyond Angie's comprehension.

The children came running and gathered to watch. Matthia crossed his forearms in front of his face while Voula whacked at him with the branch.

'Voula, stop it.' Maria called as loud as she could manage.

Voula froze mid-swipe. She started back to the table but Matthia crept up behind her and gave her such a hefty slap on her massive bottom it made Angie's eyes water.

Maria giggled, Voula yelped, lurched forward and then spun around, threatening to chop his head off with the side of her hand.

The kids clapped, laughed and whistled.

Angie met her uncle's glance and, for a second, their differences were forgotten. She saw the small, skinny child who had planted his shoes. A boy whose innocence had kept his mother focused through their darkest hours.

Everybody returned to eating and drinking. Voula's two daughters arrived with their husbands. The occasion seemed dominated by each guest trying to talk louder than anyone else until somebody yelled, 'Quiet! The phone's ringing.'

Voula jogged indoors. Everyone's eyes involuntarily fixed on her bovine buttocks. They listened to her squealing and shouting into the phone until she returned to the table, her face flushed and her body jigging with excitement. 'Stavro is coming. He'll be here tomorrow evening.'

Maria crossed herself and then squeezed Angie's hand. 'Good, you will meet your Uncle Stavro.'

The prodigal son? Angie wondered, remembering the letters at her mother's house.

* * *

Angie drove through Viannos at midnight, surprised to see several bars open in the main street. Back in her room, tanked on Greek coffee and emotionally drained after her fracas with Matthia, she found sleep impossible. As twelve o'clock in Crete meant ten o'clock in London, Angie decided to call Nick. She imagined him lonely in the flat, his calming voice telling her of his day, saying everything would work out. Sleep would arrive with a smile.

'Hey, it's me,' she said, before recognising the background noise of a public place. 'Where are you?'

'Hey you, I've missed you. How's it going?' He sounded tired.

'I'll bring the car around, Nick,' a woman spoke in the background.

Angie recognised the voice. The transitions manager from Whitekings, again.

'Where are you, Nick?'

'The Meadows, we've just finished a meeting over dinner.' Angie heard alarm bells. *How many people are at this meeting Nick; just two?* He continued, 'It's been a long, long day, Angie and I can't talk now. I'll phone you tomorrow, okay? Got to go. Love you.' He ended the call.

Nick, at the Meadows with another woman. Their special, romantic, candlelit restaurant.

Another woman? No way. She was overreacting. Pulling herself together, she dismissed the entire conversation, put on her sassiest little black dress and heels, and locked the room. At half-past midnight, she marched down the high street of Viannos with purpose.

⁂

At three thirty in the morning, with Manoli standing behind her, Angie fumbled to get the key into her door. What a night! Who would have believed a bunch of isolated village-Greeks were such party animals? She had never danced on a table in her life before, and did that middle-aged man really drink Cava out of her shoe? Wow!

The quaint, traffic clogged, pensioner-populated Viannos underwent a transformation at midnight. Nondescript doors, plastered in peeling events posters, were flung open. Super modern, neon-lit bars were revealed. Music blared. Scantily clad, stunningly beautiful women of all ages danced as if their spines were latex. People filled the high street.

An elderly man with a receding hairline wore an open shirt that showed too much chest hair, and a heavy gold neck-chain. He actually kissed the back of Angie's hand and presented her with a red rose. Mad, or what? Manoli appeared and seemed to think he stood a chance. A couple of musicians walked down the street, playing bouzouki and lira.

Manoli leapt into the street and performed the solitary *Zeibekiko* dance, blatantly showing off his skills. He waved his arms above his head, his eyes serious, concentrating on the ground. A ring of appreciative Viannos revellers surrounded him in a big circle, a few went down on one knee, clapping the rhythm of a stoic, sombre tune. Someone threw a glass of raki that smashed at his feet. Someone else set fire to it. Manoli fearlessly danced through the flames, his arms swaying above like seagrass in a swell. The audience shouted, 'Opa!' after each dramatic twirl or leap.

As the key turned in her door lock, Angie said, 'Thanks for seeing me safely back, Manoli. I appreciate it, goodnight.' Then she quickly ducked inside, and turned the key.

He knocked. 'Aren't you going to offer me a coffee?'

'Sorry, Manoli, early start tomorrow,' she called through the door.

Angie took a bottle of chilled water from the fridge, sat on the bed, and listened to Manoli's departing footsteps. She half turned the key in the lock so, if he had a duplicate, and she had no idea why she thought he might have, he wouldn't be able to use it.

She wanted to be at home with Nick, but then told herself to stop pining. She only had another four days to learn the truth about her family. Angie pulled the rose from her hair and dropped it into the pocket of her suitcase. Nick would laugh when she told him about her night on the town.

Then she remembered what had prompted her need for a crazy evening. Her fiancé had taken another woman to *their* special restaurant. How could he do that? She recalled their first proper date. They arrived in their own cars, ate there and kissed in the car park before parting. The following week she'd suffered palpitations whenever he came near her desk.

He did ask her out, and later told her he was just as afraid she would say no.

She rapped her knuckles against her forehead. What on earth was she thinking?! How could she be such an idiot? Of course she could trust her man. He loved her . . . he'd been on a business meeting, nothing more, and anyway, he happened to be the most reliable person she had ever known.

* * *

Angie woke with a headache after a few restless hours, ashamed of doubting Nick. After a cool shower, her thoughts rationalised and her head cleared. She dressed in an Indian cotton skirt and washed-out T-shirt, abandoning all jewellery apart from her engagement ring.

At the cottage, she found her grandmother dozing in her chair.

'I thought you weren't coming, *koritsie*,' Maria said. 'Did you have an enjoyable time last night?'

Angie's eyes flicked up to meet her grandmother's. What did she mean? Had she heard about her Viannos party night?

'Um, yes, thank you.'

'Good, I feared Matthia had frightened you away.' She patted the cushion next to her and when Angelika sat, Maria leaned towards her and peered into her eyes. 'Angelika, what's troubling you?'

'Me?' Angie laughed lightly. 'Nothing at all, honestly, I'm completely fine.'

'You can tell me your problems; you know? That's what grandmothers are for.'

Angie blinked at her grandmother, and then changed the subject. 'Would you like a drink, *Yiayá*? I've brought a box of loukoumades from the cake shop, they're still warm.' She placed a box of small golden doughnuts sprinkled with toasted sesame seeds and slathered with local honey, on the table.

'Make us a coffee to go with the cakes,' Maria said. 'The beans are in the fridge.'

Coffee beans? '*Yiayá*, I don't know how to fix coffee from scratch. My mother drinks instant and I have a coffee machine.'

'Then go into the garden, stand under the olive tree, and call "Voula," as loud as you can, towards the lower village.'

Angie grinned and did as Maria instructed. Outside, she called, 'Voula!' while feeling stupid and hoping no one would hear.

'Pathetic. Shout!' Maria's voice came from behind the strip curtain.

Angie hauled in a great breath and bellowed, 'Vooo-laaa!' over the rooftops. She blushed, unable to remember ever hearing how loud she could actually yell. On the village's lower level, she recognised the broad figure of Voula climbing outside steps that led to a flat roof.

Voula cupped her hands around her mouth and replied, 'What?'

Angie hauled in another breath. 'Can you make Greek coffee?' Immediately realising the stupidity of the question. The words flew from deep inside her chest, great cannonballs of voice that left her with a peculiar sense of relief. No wonder these Cretans are always happy, they shout all the time, she thought.

'What do you think?' Voula replied. 'I'll come!'

Angie laughed, returned to Maria and placed a stack of napkins next to the doughnuts. 'I enjoyed myself last night, thank you, *Yiayá*.'

'You're very Cretan, Angelika, you say what you believe people want to hear, even when it's not the truth. Matthia upset you. He has a lot of anger and you remind him of Poppy and your father.' She patted the seat. 'You look very like Yeorgo. We all loved him very much.'

Angie glanced at the icon of George and the dragon, before she sat next to Maria. *At last.* Her father, the man she hadn't known but never stopped loving. 'Is it true he died in the army, *Yiayá*?'

Maria did the Greek down-sideways nod. 'It's difficult to accept ... but let's not leap ahead. We're not up to that yet.'

Angie sighed. 'I'm eager to learn why my mother left here, *Yiayá*. I want to understand her.'

'Patience, we'll get there, Angelika. The important thing is for you to hear the whole story, so that you realise nobody was to blame.'

Blame? To blame for what?

Voula barged through the plastic curtain. 'Ooh, Angelika, come here you lovely girl, I could eat you.' She threw her arms around Angie and kissed her cheeks.

'I brought loukoumades to say thank you for last night,' Angie said.

'Ooh, look at that, I'll get too fat if I'm not careful.' Voula's dimpled hand scooped a doughnut out of the box while the other snatched a napkin to catch the dribbling honey. She plopped onto a chair, her muffin-top knees wide apart and her thighs settling with considerable overhang.

Angie caught the glint in Maria's eye. *Yiayá* loved her daughter-in-law. After feasting on three doughnuts, Voula gave Angie a lesson on how to make Greek coffee and then left to prepare the family's lunch.

'Where were we up to, *koritsie*?' Maria said, dipping pieces of doughnut into her small cup.

'You and the boys had escaped the Nazis and were hiding in the shepherd's cottage and he came crashing through the door,' Angie said.

'Ah, yes, I remember it well . . .' She sucked the top off her coffee and then her face relaxed with a reminiscent smile. 'Poor, poor devil . . . I'll never forget him, Angelika, as long as I live.'

Chapter 13

Crete, 1943.

A GIANT FILLED THE DOORWAY. He grabbed my shoulders with his shovel-sized hands. I struggled to reduce a cry of pain to a whimper, afraid of waking the boys. The man's goat-stink invaded every corner of the room. I certainly didn't have to see him to recognise the shepherd.

'What are you doing here, woman?' he whispered angrily.

Andreas was a great barrel of a man, all hair and belly. With his bushy beard and long goatskin coat, he seemed more closely related to his own rams than humanity. I threw myself against his wide body, desperate to make physical contact with another adult, even the infamous shepherd. He had earned dubious fame as a local character: dirty, illiterate, and usually drunk.

The Amiras gossips, who could never be relied on to tell the truth, claimed this Goliath could kill a man with one punch, had sex with goats, and that he stole people's sheep. On the rare occasion he came into the village, children ran to hide. I didn't care what people said, I felt myself in the arms of Hercules himself.

Mother Nature worked her conniving trick that morphs us women into weak and helpless beings in the presence of strong men. I turned my face into his musty chest to muffle my cries, and my grief gushed like a flash flood. He patted my back clumsily, made awkward shushing noises, and then steered me to the end of the banquette.

Andreas slid the heavy wooden bolt across the door and waited with patience until I stopped my snivelling.

'I've a candle, shall I light it?' I said, pushing my damp hair from my face and composing myself.

'Best not, *Kiriea*, the Nazis are still on the ridge.'

My sight had adjusted to the dark and I saw him fumbling in the nook by the fireplace. When he returned to my side, I realised he had a litre bottle of raki, a glass, and the cracked cup. I dried my eyes on my apron, glad he couldn't see the state of me.

Nodding at the sacks that covered Matthia and Stavro, he whispered, 'Who's that?'

'My two boys, we escaped.'

He nodded. We were nothing but lonely shadows in the dark. He poured a couple of drinks and passed me the small raki glass.

'I can't hold it, my hands are burned.' I took the cup between my palms. The fiery liquid relaxed me. Its warmth flowed and my anxiety ebbed.

'All the Amiras men and boys are dead,' I said. 'The Nazis rounded them up and shot them to pieces in front of us . . . more than a hundred of them. My baby too – poor little Petro. I still find it almost impossible to believe.'

Fresh tears spilled down my cheeks. 'Perhaps you're the last man in Crete, Andreas, and why? I don't understand . . . old men and children too, madness.' I steadied the cup in my lap, not having the grip to hold it in one hand while I crossed myself.

He sat next to me, his arm against my throbbing shoulder, reminding me of the moment when Nazi soldiers had snatched Petro from my breast.

'It's true, *Kiriea* – murdered – all of them. Also in the villages of Simi, Pefkos, Vachos, Viannos and God knows how many others. Two thousand Nazis, they say, marched in to kill us all. There's no news about the rest of Crete. We have no idea what's happening elsewhere.'

'How do you know all this, Andreas?'

He threw the raki into the back of his throat and poured another.

'The midwife told me this very day. When she can, she passes . . . passed information on to the resistance. Poor woman. Oh, the poor woman!' He made an odd little hiccup noise, rolling his head and wringing his hands. 'She said I should contact the *Andartes* in the mountains and explain the situation here, but I can't find anyone to tell. The rebels seem to have disappeared, like our allies. Where are the British? They must have known what was happening here. Tell me, why did they abandon us? Why have they allowed this terrible murder of innocent people to take place? They could so easily have come to our rescue. You must leave. It's dangerous here. Go up the mountain with your children, while it's dark.'

'They're killing the men and I am afraid for my boys, but I'm safe, Andreas.'

'You're wrong.' He rolled his head as if in pain and hiccupped again. 'They're murdering all the women they find outside the villages.' He put his raki glass down, blew a gust of breath that hinted of rotten teeth and then rubbed his hands over his face.

My sense of dread grew. What was that he said about the midwife?

'Two women are hanging from the trees on the Pefkos road, just below here. Can you believe it? What evil possesses those men?'

My throat closed. No! Why hang defenceless women? The Amiras wives and mothers were not freedom fighters or terrorists. We were uncomplicated people who didn't know or care about politics. My only ambitions were to bring up my children, grow vegetables, and harvest enough olives for a year's supply of oil. I took pleasure from simple things: laughter, a word of praise, the grunt of satisfaction from my husband, and attending church on Sunday.

I couldn't make out Andreas's expression in the dark, but his voice dropped. He gulped raki straight from the bottle and made a strange mewling sound. After a moment's silence, he slapped his big hands over his face and rocked back and forth. He sobbed. I realised he was struggling to speak. Then his torment gushed out. The lump in my throat hardened and I found myself sharing his grief.

'Why?' I asked, the word only a whisper. 'What reason had they to hang women?'

Consumed by his own horror and rage, Andreas didn't hear me. He shuddered and then his sorrow erupted. 'God forgive me, I watched. I couldn't look away,' he said, sobbing between the words. 'The Nazis . . . Blessed Virgin Mary . . . I saw . . . I saw, but there were twenty soldiers with machine guns so I crouched in the bushes. What could I do? They'd have shot me before I got near.'

His breath caught, he swallowed hard and then swigged the raki again. 'I failed to help them – useless – I hid like a coward. A stinking dog with my tail between my legs. I recognised the older woman and did nothing to save her. I'll never forgive myself. I watched for a chance when I could rescue them.'

'You said one was familiar to you?' I knew everybody and couldn't be left wondering. Desperate for my suspicions to be incorrect, I awaited his answer.

Andreas nodded, understanding my fear. 'Yes. It was the old midwife, *Kiriea* Kiriaki . . . we had spoken not half an hour before. She warned me to stay hidden. The other woman, I don't know, young, sixteen or seventeen, so beautiful, so utterly terrified.' He groaned, pushed his hands up into his mass of long matted hair and, keeping them on the back of his head, he hunched over his belly as if speaking to his knees.

I realised it must have been the platoon that almost found us under the fig tree. My stomach churned to think what might have happened to me and my boys.

'They fought hard, the midwife and the girl . . . hitting out and kicking the soldiers. The midwife spat in one of their faces,' Andreas said. 'May they find peace in heaven, poor creatures. The Nazis tied their hands behind their backs, tore all their clothes open and poked them with their guns – taunting them. Pitiable sight, the humiliation of them; a woman should not know that shame. Filthy men, sneering at their exposed preciousness.'

I remembered the grunting pig who had raped me and, hearing of the terrible thing Andreas had seen only an hour before, something changed inside me. It took away a little of my own pain and disgrace. I had survived and that Nazi who sullied me now seemed like nothing but spit in the dust – a worthless disgusting memory to discard. Andreas continued to bawl out his tragic story.

'They put ropes around their necks and hoisted them up into the trees.' He whimpered, shook his head and kicked the heels of his boots rhythmically against the stone banquette, trapped in reliving the nightmare.

He had forgotten my presence. In his mind, Andreas crouched in the bushes and saw the defilement and murder of two innocent women.

'The commandant and his men shone their torches on them, watching. They . . . they shit themselves, the women, shit, it flew out of them as they kicked and struggled and choked. God, I've never seen anything so awful. Their tongues poked from their mouths like strangled chickens and their eyes bulged while they thrashed in the air, mad dancing puppets. It took so long . . . minutes. Why didn't they just shoot them? Poor Kiriaki, poor old mother . . . she brought so many babies into the world yet she left it in that terrible way. Those evil *malákas* laughed!'

I knew Kiriaki: she had delivered Petro.

The shepherd clenched his fist and slashed with an imaginary dagger. 'I want to kill every single one of those Nazi bastards with my gutting knife.'

Silent for a moment, his broad rounded shoulders shuddered as he battled to overcome his emotion. Then he spoke with a leaden voice. 'I'll never forget them. God forgive their sins, poor women. When it happened, I couldn't do anything, do you see, *Kiriea*?'

'I understand, Andreas. You can't blame yourself.'

'Blame myself? Of course I blame myself! There had to be a way to stop it from happening. I've gone over and over it. I'm not being boastful but I'm very strong, *Kiriea*, I don't believe there's a stronger man in Crete, but I paid for my strength with intelligence. There is a balance in these things. I've been called stupid.'

'You're not stupid, Andreas.'

'You're kind, but I know what I am.' He sighed, his shoulders falling forward and his chin dropping to his chest. 'Now I think . . . now that it's too late!' He made a piteous howl. 'I could have started a bush fire; they would have run from that. Why couldn't I have thought of that earlier? They died because I am a slow, lumbering fool. I want to go and cut the innocent women down, it's my fault they hang there, but two soldiers with guns are standing guard.'

He shook his head violently, all the emotion returning. The torture in his voice was so intense that, afterwards, I realised it would be impossible to bear. I could say nothing to wipe the atrocities from his mind.

Andreas broke down, went on and on, blaming himself. 'Please, dear God, forgive me . . . I should have saved them. Why did he give me this great strength if I can't even save a helpless little old woman and the other, hardly more than a child? Tell me, *Kiriea*, why am I so strong? What's the point?' He knocked back the raki and threw his glass across the room.

With the shattering, both boys jumped from their sleep. 'It's okay,' I said, patting the sacks, trying to keep the pain from my voice. 'Andreas the shepherd is here, we're safe. Close your eyes and rest.'

'Sorry, *Kiriea*, I shouldn't have told you those disgusting things. I hadn't intended to, it just poured out of me. Forget it. But of course, you can't forget it, it's impossible. You see, I am stupid.'

He sniffed hard. 'You have to look after yourself, and your boys. That's the important thing,' he said. 'My best dog is tied to a tree. If he barks, you must all leave this house, fast. Go up the mountain and hide. Me too, but I'll take a different way, better we are not together.'

I nodded in the dark. Gaia prodded me into the role of woman. 'Have you eaten, Andreas?'

He sighed, shook his head. 'Not today, nor yesterday, plenty of carobs but not proper nourishment. My goats are on the hillside. The Nazis will see me if I go there. I fear they're watching the flock.'

'We have food hidden between here and the road.'

Andreas hauled his bulky frame from the edge of the banquette. 'Tell me where and I'll fetch it.' He swiped his arm across his face, blew the glutinous contents of his nose into the palm of his hand and then slid it down his trouser leg.

I imagined him crashing through the olive grove to the fig tree, alerting every creature of the night and our goat too. She would kick up a racket if taken by a stranger. A sentry, half a kilometre either way along the road, would surely hear the ruckus.

'Better if I go. Guard my sons with your life, Andreas.'

'*Kiriea*, what's your name?' he mumbled.

'*Kiriea* Kondulakis Maria, school mistress, wife of the soldier, Vassili, daughter of The Teacher.'

'You belong to Kondulakis Vassili, and these are his children?' His head jerked towards the boys.

'Yes, why?'

He grunted. 'Fuck the Vir— '

'Andreas, my children!'

He swallowed the blasphemy and continued in a dramatic whisper. 'Sorry, *Kiriea*, but I've dreamt of smashing my fist into that ugly man's face.'

'Why, what did he ever do to you?' I knew my husband had his moods but, in general, he held a good reputation as a peacekeeping member of the community.

'Kondulakis beat me six times straight at *tavli* – go to the devil – and me the best until he started playing. *Malákas*.' He snorted. 'My one chance to prove I wasn't an idiot and he took it from me. Now I have to guard his sons?'

Suddenly, I recognised the pretend anger in his voice, a decoy from the atrocities. I blessed him for trying to counteract the effect of his outpouring and realised this man would be a lifelong friend.

I had an urge to laugh, cry, and explode with hysterical emotion. I wanted to hit somebody, beat them cruelly and scream until my lungs burst. Tears rushed back. Life before yesterday. My dear Vassili was always crazy to play backgammon before he left with the army. He spent hours each evening drinking raki and throwing dice across the *tavli* board in the kafenion.

I recalled the victorious crash when he slammed his opponent's tiles onto the tin tabletop. We women, crocheting in the street, would raise our heads and nod to each other knowingly. 'Kondulakis is winning!' It made me proud.

I never entered the kafenion, a place reserved for men. I would peer through the door, make a 'dinner's ready' sign by moving my hands towards my mouth, crab-like. Pensioners in rickety chairs circled the challengers. Vassili always shooed me away, refusing to be told what to do. Nevertheless, his belly got the better of him and, when the game finished, he came home manly and triumphant.

Tears trickled down my face. The comforting arm of Andreas fell over my shoulders. We sat in silence, in the dark, each with our thoughts, coming to terms with the situation.

The memory of life before the war heartened me. My despair lifted a little. I stood, ready to start my journey back down the hill.

'Wait, *Kiriea*, I'll bring my dog in. He'll bark if he sees you out there.'

The shepherd fumbled around his feet, which he could hardly reach because of the size of his belly. He pulled off a boot and then a sock, replaced the boot, took a rope from the wall and crept outside.

After a few minutes, he returned with his dog, a beast of a black Alsatian with the sock over its muzzle and the rope around its neck. The creature yanked on the makeshift lead, resisting the drag indoors. I glanced at the olive sacks. My sleeping boys were as safe as they could be.

It must have been near midnight. The moon, full last night, would be almost as bright tonight. I had to be quick.

After spending so much time in the dark, my sight had adjusted well. I crept down the hill, racing between trees for cover, and then standing still, straining my ears for any sound of movement. About halfway down, I threw myself against a stout carob trunk. A large tree mouse leapt from one of the branches, then a polecat bounded into the clearing, pounced and clamped the rodent in its jaws. The polecat's victim made a high-pitched squeal into death. I caught a flash of white face with glinting coal black eyes from the polecat before it sped into the parched vegetation. I waited until the rustle of dried thistles had faded.

Fear bubbled inside me, my heart thudding in the silence. Barely perceptible noises seemed to come from all directions. I couldn't get a fix on the source of any one sound. What if soldiers surrounded me? Perhaps troops hid in the undergrowth, waiting for the likes of me creeping about in the dark?

I thought of my precious children and leaned against the carob trunk until the natural sounds of the night returned. I hitched my skirt and raced to the next tree. Each footstep seemed loud enough to wake all Crete. The moon made her appearance and I studied the hillside below, searching for the unmistakable shape of the old fig. Before I spotted it, I heard the snoring of our goat.

'Na . . . na . . .' I called, softly, not wanting her to kick up a fuss if startled. I recognised a shuffle and a double thump as she got to her feet and, following the noise with my eyes, I picked out the tree.

My plan to collect the goat, the axe, and the food parcel, proved difficult. The burned flesh of my hands had dried. They were so stiff and painful I couldn't close them over the axe handle, so I used my teeth and forearms to unknot the bundle from the hatchet.

Eventually, I struggled up the hill. The goat's leading rope was tied around my waist, and a sling containing the food over my good shoulder. It took much longer than I had expected.

Andreas waited in the doorway, his face anxious in the moonlight. Inside, the Alsatian whimpered.

'Take the goat to the back patch,' he whispered.

I slipped out of the blanket and dropped it where I stood, finding great relief in being told what to do. Andreas fetched the dog and tied it to a sapling, and then he took the bundle of food into the hovel. My boys were awake and hungry. I guessed the time to be near two in the morning. We closed the door and lit a candle.

'*Kiriea*, you must take care of your hands. If they get bad, the black rot – think, what use is a mother with no hands? Here, clean them with this.' He opened a filthy bottle and poured some yellowish water into the enamel bowl.

I understood his meaning. Gangrene, or worse, leprosy, which would have me shipped to the local colony on the other side of the island for the rest of my life. I would never see my family again.

'What is this?' I asked.

'Chamomile. Clean your burns, let them dry without touching anything, and then apply this honey. It's going to sting, but that's the purity. It will keep your hands supple and stop the flesh from cracking.' He gave me an equally dirty stone pot with barely an inch of honey in the bottom.

'Mama, my knees hurt,' Matthia said, pushing for attention. I bathed his knees and glanced sideways at the shepherd. The big man smiled. All the terrible things people said about this malodorous giant, yet I wondered how many of them would give the remains of their honey to a stranger in wartime.

'Thank you, Andreas. I'll never forget your kindness.'

How we ate! The four of us stuffed as much food inside ourselves as possible. Andreas fed me chunks of meat. He softened half of the rusks with a little water and then sprinkled olive oil, oregano and salt over them. That simple meal was a banquet. Andreas belched with enormous gusto and my boys, full of admiration, tried to do the same.

We laughed so hard I had to hush everyone. The shepherd lit a fire and brewed coffee made from roasted acorns. It tasted good, not exactly like the real thing, but still bitter and strong and near enough to be enjoyable. He sweetened it with black syrup derived from boiled carob beans.

Surprised that Andreas knew so much about living in the wild, I realised that I could learn a lot from him. I paid attention while he explained how to make flat bread from acorn flour.

'In the summer,' he told me, 'I take the sheep up to the plateau and live there all season without supplies. If you know how, it's not difficult.'

Stavro and Matthia gazed at him with open admiration and when he said, 'I need to piss', my sons looked at each other, nodded, and stood either side of him in the doorway. I blew out the candle and sat on the banquette watching the backs of the three, silhouetted by the moonlight, pissing into the night.

The boys, with their heads turned up to Andreas, copied every grunt and shake. Then the shepherd spun around, bent over, and farted noisily into the darkness. My sons caught a whiff and with a 'Phaw!' and 'Yuck!' they were back at my side – my dear children. That silly hour strengthened all four of us.

'Andreas, how do you stay so big and strong in these hard times?' I asked.

'I eat carobs and acorns every day,' he said. 'They keep my belly full and stop the hunger pains.' He scratched his armpit vigorously, then his head. 'They're free food, and if these things are good enough for pigs and rabbits, they'll do for me.' He opened the door and peered up at the moon. '*Kiriea*, if you want to get the remains of your belongings, you only have a few hours before first light.'

'I don't think I can manage it, Andreas. I need to rest before we go up the mountain.'

He grunted. 'I'll bring the olive sacks in for my bed. You squeeze on the banquette with your boys and I will sleep on the floor.'

We settled down quickly, bolted the door and blew out the candle. Soon, judging by the sound of their breathing, they were all asleep. I lay in the dark and tried to make a plan. How could we survive on the mountain with so little? Perhaps if we could find an old shepherd's shelter, or even a cave, but we couldn't go too far up because there were only pine trees on the higher slopes, and then nothing but rock. We needed carobs, acorns, figs and mulberries, herbage for the goat and water for us.

Thinking of water, I longed to wash my body. The village spring waited for me, about a hundred and fifty metres uphill. Dare I go and bathe? A metal bucket stood in the corner of the room, it would only take twenty minutes or so; nobody would miss me.

Chapter 14

I HELD MY BREATH, slid off the banquette and made a big stride over the shepherd, asleep on the floor. Just as I straddled his huge body, he reached out and clasped my ankle firmly.

'Where are you going, woman?' he whispered.

'I need to wash, Andreas.'

'Be still; wait until you are further up the mountain.'

'Please, I can't delay any longer. You see the Nazis, they didn't only kill my baby yesterday morning, they got me too. I lowered my voice to hardly a whisper. 'One of them dishonoured me, right after they murdered poor little Petro. My boys have no idea. I feel so filthy, Andreas, I have to wash away the Nazi stench.'

He released my ankle. I completed my stride and stood between him and the door. He pushed himself onto his elbows and, in the dark, I sensed his eyes on me.

'How can you clean yourself with those burned hands? You have to keep them dry.'

He seemed to hesitate before he spoke again. 'I have a well under this floor. If you let me, I'll help you.' A moment of silence passed between us. I analysed his motives and I guess he realised my suspicion. 'Trust me; I'm honourable, *Kiriea*.'

I remembered the gossip about him, but then for some obscure reason, I became calm and almost serene. Perhaps a spirit inspired me and guided me to do the right thing by

Andreas without my understanding, morals, or judgement. 'I would be embarrassed, I don't know if I could,' I said.

'*Kiriea*, I am a simple person, a man of nature and not educated like you, but my word is true. You can depend on it.'

I thought for a moment. If I didn't wash my personal parts, I would almost certainly suffer from debilitating infection. I needed to be strong for my boys and the ordeal that lay ahead. 'Thank you, Andreas. I know, at least I hope, you'll treat me with respect.'

The shepherd opened the door. Moonlight flooded into the room. He pulled an old woven rug away from the corner of the floor and lifted a couple of planks. Then he took a coil of rope from the wall, tied the rope to a bucket that had stood in the corner, and dropped it into the well. A minute later, he had filled the enamel jug and bowl. 'Wait while I take them around the back,' he whispered.

I hesitated again and glanced at the sleep-soft faces of my boys who trusted me to keep them safe. Andreas returned and refilled the bucket. He threw a couple of sacks over his shoulder and told me to follow him. Behind the house, he spread one sack and hooked the other onto a nail in the wall.

'Wait,' he whispered, and then he reached into the low hanging branches of a nearby olive tree. He came back with a tin bath, a sea sponge, and a block of soap. 'Do you trust me, *Kiriea*? I will be like a brother to you, I swear.'

'I have faith in you, Andreas, thank you for your kindness.'

'Then stand in the bath.' He took off my shoes and then my apron and top clothes. I saw his passive face become puffy in the moonlight, his eyelids drooped softly and his mouth slackened. The breath caught in his throat and I understood the look of want that every woman recognises.

A spark of fear flared inside me. How stupid were these actions of mine? What possessed me? Attempting to obliterate one disgusting episode by almost encouraging another had to be madness. Trying to convince myself that, despite everything, I remained in control. Endeavouring to prove that all men weren't the same.

When he reached my undergarments, he stopped, soaped the sponge and said, '*Kiriea* Maria, I must tell you, until I saw those poor hanging women, I had not seen a naked female. Thank you for having faith in me, but I confess I'm burning with desire to hold you against my body, to know what it's like to have a real woman in my arms. I have never before . . .'

'Hold me now, Andreas, I'll not deny you that experience, but I can't give you more, do you understand? I am trusting you, Andreas.'

He bit his lip, dropped the sponge, threw off his sheepskin tunic and wrapped me in his arms. I listened to his soft moan, strangely confident with his promise as he lifted me off my feet and rocked me. His hands slipped down, cupped my bottom, and he crushed me against his massive body. He covered the top of my head with his bearded chin. With my ear pressed against the thin fabric covering his chest, I heard his big heart hammering.

'Why did God make man so wicked?' he asked, his voice thick with desire. His manhood swelled and grew against my belly.

'Remember your promise, Andreas? I trust you're strong enough to keep your word.'

'Virgin Mary . . . forgive me, *Kiriea* Maria.'

I glanced around anxiously, vulnerable, in my undergarments.

Andreas, shy and innocent in his way, took a deep breath and then removed the last of my clothing. With surprising tenderness in his big calloused hands, he soaped my body. In a state of wonderment, and inquisitiveness, he washed every inch of me, as a new mother would bath her baby. I admit I found a little, inexplicable, pleasure in satisfying his curiosity.

When I lifted my arms so he could wash beneath them, he gasped and stepped back, gazing at my white breasts and then at my entire body in the moonlight.

'Madam, forgive me for looking, but I have never imagined such beauty . . . Adam must have been alone for a long time, while God created woman. The Almighty made such a thing of perfection,' he said.

When I squatted and parted my knees so he could clean my privates, he screwed his eyes and turned his head away. He thrust the sponge between my legs, nearly pushing me off my feet.

'Andreas, please,' I whispered. 'You may look. I trust you, and I'd rather you used your hand. These hidden parts of me are tender and sensitive, especially after all that has happened. The rough sponge hurts too much.'

He took a shaky breath, sat on his haunches and washed my most intimate parts. His eyes flicked up to meet mine. 'Tell me if I cause you pain, *Kiriea*, I'll try to be gentle.'

The shepherd was a gentleman, in every sense of the word.

He dried me with the olive sack, dressed me, and then bowed slightly, thanking me for my trust. We returned to the room and he patted the sacks spread on the floor.

'Rest here, *Kiriea*, next to me. I will keep you safe.'

I lay beside him, my head on his big arm. Feeling protected and secure, I fell into a deep sleep. In the night, I had a strange dream about the old midwife and the young woman hanging from the tree. I saw Andreas cut them down, wash them, and then take their hands to lead them along the pathway to heaven.

Great rumbling snores coming from the shepherd woke me, the vision still vivid in my head. The warm room was stuffy and hummed with body odour. I pulled myself up and opened the door a crack, to let in a little fresh air. Dawn light sliced across the floor.

'Get up, everybody, it's morning!' I said.

We scrambled to gather our bits and pieces together. Andreas let the dog off his rope for a runabout. I thanked him for his help. Our eyes met and for a moment we shared something special that will always stay with me. Sweet and honourable Andreas.

'Go straight up, *Kiriea* Maria. You'll find an old ruin with no windows and the door has gone, but it has a roof. Rest there, out of the sun and, tonight, continue up the track. Once you are higher than Simi, pull right a little. There is an archaeological site with a long-drop waterfall, dry now, but it's easy to spot the smooth plunge of the rock face. There is a cave to the left. Look for flocks of small birds flying close to the ground and follow their direction, they usually lead to water. If I can, I'll bring your bundle up in a couple of days.'

Andreas, the praiseworthy shepherd that kept me safe. Who else could have cleansed me of the Nazi's atrocity and enabled me to relax into deep sleep.

I kissed his hairy cheek tenderly. 'One day soon, when this war is over, I want you to come to my home and play *tavli* with Vassili. Will you do that, Andreas?' I wanted him to realise how much he had restored my sanity, but there seemed no words to explain.

Our eyes met and, holding my gaze, he considered for a moment before making the down-sideways nod. 'And if you'll pardon me, I'll beat the *malákas*!'

My boys grinned at him, loving the sound of his swearing. His countenance relaxed a little and his rough hand came to my face and stilled. His eyes covered my body and then pierced mine. 'Thank you,' he said, his voice soft and sincere. The dog barked, and barked again. His smile fell away, replaced by a flash of fear. 'Go now, hurry!'

We scooted around the back of the house, collected the goat and started up the slope, quickly and quietly, trying to keep under cover. Just before we pushed into the dense thicket, I swear I felt a tap on my shoulder. There was nobody behind me, of course, but I peered down to the ramshackle cottage that had kept us safe overnight. Andreas stood on the spot where he had washed me. Too far away for me to make out his eyes, but I knew they met mine. The enormous shaggy man, as noble yet humble as his largest ram, stared up at me and nodded his hairy head. A great surge of sadness rushed through me as I understood, at that moment, my dream had been a vision. He intended to go and cut down the hanging women.

Would I ever see the big shepherd again? I didn't think so.

I found it almost impossible to turn away and break the thread between us.

'Mama . . .' Stavro said, pulling me back to the urgency of our situation. He sniffed, and I sensed his distress.

'Are you all right, son?'

The boy turned to me, his face pale. He worried his lip, glanced at Matthia and then at me. 'I wasn't asleep,' he whispered, his voice catching.

Oh, the poor child, what had he seen? Perhaps he came out of the room while Andreas washed me? How would a seven-year-old interpret such a scene? Because of the darkness, I wouldn't have known he was there.

'Matthia, take the goat up ahead,' I said quietly, sick and ashamed of not being more cautious. I watched them go, afraid the cantankerous creature would drag Matthia off his feet again. When he had moved out of earshot, I asked Stavro, 'What do you mean, about last night? Tell me, son.'

'You know, when Andreas told you about *Kiriea* Kiriaki . . .' Tears broke free and rolled down his face. 'I thought I had dreamt it when I woke up later, like I'd had a nightmare or something, but you were gone so long. I really feared the German soldiers had got you too and torn your clothes off and hung you from a tree.' He wrapped his arms about my waist and squeezed hard. 'Mama, I'm so ashamed. When I believed you were dead, I nearly cried in front of the shepherd . . .'

I caught a glimpse of life through his young eyes and, at that point, I had to put my hand over my mouth to cover a smile. To think, your mother may be hanged by the neck but how terrible for a shepherd to see you crying about it.

Stavro continued – his voice quiet and sober. 'When you returned with the food, I was so happy.' He stared at the ground and spoke earnestly. 'Please don't get killed, Mama. I'm trying very hard to be a man but . . . promise you won't tell anybody?' His brown eyes turned up, pleading.

'Not a soul, son.'

'I'm scared all the time, really afraid.' He held me in his gaze and nodded forcefully, but then shook his head. 'I won't be much good as a man. I'd better tell you now, Mama, so you don't get your hopes up. I'll never be as strong and clever as Andreas the shepherd.'

'Come here, my big boy.' I dropped to my knees and wrapped my arms around him tightly. 'There's no need for you to be grown up just yet, Stavro. You're my first-born son and I love you more than anybody, exactly as you are at this moment. And I'll tell you something, a secret between us, sometimes I'm afraid, too.' I pulled back and looked at him. 'But let's put a brave face on for Matthia, hey? Even though we both know he's a little devil. We should find him, before that goat drags him away through the bushes.'

We discovered Matthia on his haunches, examining his scabbed knees.

'They'll be ready to pick in a few days. Don't start now or they are sure to bleed,' Stavro said.

Matthia nodded earnestly.

The goat's leading rope had tangled in a thorny, scrub lemon tree. Stavro untangled it and, just as we continued our journey, we were drawn to the sound of the big dog somewhere far down the hill. The Alsatian worked itself into a frenzy, yapping and snarling.

The distant stomp of marching feet rose on the morning air. A flock of crows took to the sky; wings flapping, they banked on a turn to the opposite hillside. My blood chilled.

Troops were on the road. God knows how many soldiers' boots hit that tarmac. The noise thrummed up through the trees, through my bones. I concentrated on the tone. So long as they stayed down there, we were safe. The chilling rhythm got louder, and then it stopped. The dog went mad.

A burst of machine gun fire cracked the silence. The sound bounced off the mountainsides, each reverberation fainter than the last, echoing with the essence of death. A second later, a high-pitched whimper squealed into the morning light. The most remorseful, soul-destroying whine that ever came from an animal.

A single gunshot with its choir of echoes silenced the beast. In that instant, I knew my dear friend Andreas and his dog were dead.

Stavro's head jerked back as if he had received a slap with the last retort.

We stopped where we were, listening, my boys not understanding. I glanced up at a waning moon in an insipid sky, almost expecting to see the great ghost of Andreas the shepherd ascending. Even the dawn chorus had quietened. We peered down the hill but only saw the trees that hid us from the enemy.

Stavro turned his sad eyes to me and asked, 'Did they shoot the dog, Mama?'

'I don't think so, Stavro. They probably just frightened it away. Stop worrying, son, you've seen how those two take care of each other. Nothing will separate Andreas and that big old Alsatian.'

Stavro nodded, comforted.

'Now let's go and keep an eye on your brother,' I said.

The path, a jagged wound in the scorched landscape, had partly healed over with nettles and saplings. We scrambled onward. The air, previously perfumed with thyme and rosemary, became resinous with the scent of pine. A gentle breeze refreshed us. Andreas drifted into my heavy heart. I wanted to shed tears for the big man at the end of his life but, like Stavro, I had to appear strong.

I made a plea to the Virgin Mary.

Take Andreas into God's Kingdom, he was a kindly man, a shepherd the same as your own Son; a very good person.

Chapter 15

Crete, Present Day.

Angie considered her grandmother's words. 'Imagine watching them hang the women and not be able to do anything, *Yiayá*. I'd never sleep easy again. A thing like that could drive anyone insane. The poor man.'

Maria crossed herself. 'I can't explain the effect that Andreas had on my life. I only knew him for a few hours but I learned we shouldn't judge people by how they look. Nor should we believe everything we're told.'

'Thank you for telling me what happened; it can't have been easy for you.'

'Yes, it was difficult, but somebody should hear what war really does to families, and the effect it has on local people. They're the ones that suffer. All those Nazis too, they were some mothers' sons, probably nice boys with loving parents. I can't forgive them though, even now. I'm sure I never will.'

'I hadn't thought of it like that. It must have been so upsetting for *Papoú* too, to hear all this when he returned from Albania.'

Maria nodded, blew her flaccid cheeks out. 'Very hard indeed; it took a few years to get back together as man and wife. Having him home should have been wonderful, but war twists us up inside. Difficult times, *koritsie*. I see films of conflicts on the TV, and toy guns in the shops. It's all become unreal, even a little glamorous.'

Maria shook her head, silent for a moment. 'To train people to kill others and brainwash them into believing it's something to be glorified is wrong. Corrupt governments and greedy politicians have taken our children and used them in their bloody, power-hungry, war games. Bah! This island is mine.' She thumped her chest with alarming ferocity. 'It belongs to me, we – the Cretan people, not those leaders in Athens, or the neo-Nazi fanatics that are using fear or bribery to capture seats in parliament right now, or those bureaucrats running Europe.'

Angie stared at Maria. She had seen her as a sweet but decrepit old lady when she arrived in Crete a few days ago. Suddenly, she realised the fiercely patriotic, political animal that was her grandmother. She still held strong views and ideals, despite her great age. Maria had defied orders by going into the olive grove to find food for her children. Her grandmother was a selfless, brave and determined woman. Pride rushed through Angie. What an honour to belong to such a family.

Poppy should feel the same, so why didn't she?

Suddenly ashamed, Angie recognised the triviality of her own life. She'd never held a political conviction, nor bothered to vote – though she knew, now, that would change. 'What difference will my one vote make?' she asked herself. As for her children's future, she had hardly thought past the colourful pages of the Babyland catalogue, and deciding which pushchair to buy.

Uncle Matthia came to mind. Now, Angie understood him. He saw her as shallow, self-centred, materialistic, and it made him angry. She shook her head, feeling slightly sick and humbled. She was all those things. Her life amounted to nothing more than superficial detritus floating on a sea of commercialism.

Yiayá patted her knee. 'Don't worry about it,' she said and smiled straight into Angie's eyes, as if she knew everything that had gone through her mind.

Angie told herself she could change. Glad to have had this epiphany now, before her children arrived. She would set an example to the next generation that would make her grandmother proud. Nick did not vote either, nor had he any political leanings. In a nutshell, like Angie, when it came to politics he wasn't interested, didn't care, changed the channel.

'I want to tell you that, whatever I find out at the end of all this, I promise I'll try to write your story, *Yiayá*.' Angie paused to consider the awful personal details, and wondered how it would affect other family members.

How would she react if she read about the rape, or humiliation and hanging of, say, her own mother? She shuddered. How would her children or grandchildren feel to discover they were connected to this tragedy? Yet, she decided, it would be cheating the victims to exclude the distasteful details.

'Should I change the names of the women, *Yiayá*?'

'It makes no difference to me, Angelika. I'll be dead. Perhaps Poppy . . . you must ask her, and those others who were involved. A few people may want you to alter their names, but who knows? As we get older, we learn to tell the truth, things aren't so embarrassing. After everything, we all shit and have sex, et cetera.'

'*Yiayá!*' Angie gulped and bit her lip.

Her grandmother giggled. '*Koritsie*, one day you'll understand. Meanwhile, you have to judge for yourself about the names, but don't sell them cheap. Those martyrs deserve to be remembered and have a true and complete account of the facts told.'

'I'll do my best, I promise.'

'I know you will,' Maria said.

What could have affected Mam so much that she might want her name changed in a story about her life? Poppy wasn't even alive in the war. Angie realised the futility of asking. *Yiayá* would tell her to wait. She hesitated, unsure if she could stand to see 'unsavoury' things about her mother in print, if the manuscript were published.

At that moment, Angie noticed the mosquito on her shin, slapped at it and, unexpectedly, saw it flattened on the palm of her hand. 'Ugh!' She cleaned it off with a napkin and then spotted the smear of blood on her leg. After spitting on the napkin, she wiped it away.

Her grandmother pointed to a decanter and six tiny glasses on the shelf over the fireplace. 'Get some raki, *koritsie*. It will stop you scratching later.'

Angie nodded, poured a small glass of the clear liquid and knocked it back quickly.

Maria hooted with laughter, her bony shoulders jigging up and down and her hand over her mouth.

'No, Angelika, you rub it on the mosquito bite.'

Angie blushed and then saw the funny side. She dispensed a little raki onto the napkin and dabbed her leg.

'Angelika, Angelika!' The strip curtain in the doorway seemed to shiver with the force of Voula's voice as she screeched over the rooftops. Angie stepped outside and peered across to the lower village. Voula waved from the same flat roof as before, standing at the end of a clothesline of white sheets flapping in the breeze. 'The lunch is ready, come!'

Back in the cottage, *Yiayá* glanced up from her crocheting. 'Voula cooks our food every day. She's a good woman. You can collect it, to save her traipsing up here. Tell Vassili to stay at Voula's. I haven't finished telling my story.'

'How will I know the right way to Voula's house, *Yiayá*?'

'Don't worry, the house will find you. Just walk in that direction. If you get lost, ask anybody for Kondulakis Voula.'

Down the main village road, Angie tried to figure out which side street would lead to Voula's. She turned towards a woman, watering a clump of salmon-pink geraniums, when a group of schoolchildren distracted her. They held hands like a chain of paper dolls and skipped up the steep cobbles.

'Aunty, Aunty!' they chanted. It took Angie a moment to realise they were calling her.

She waved and greeted them in Greek, which led to great hilarity.

When the youngsters reached her side, they lifted their arms and Angie stooped to receive their hugs and kisses. The physical embrace comforted her; they were so affectionate and unselfconscious. The girls skipped and pranced as they tugged her down the sloping street towards Voula's.

Several old people, sitting on verandas that exploded with flowers, or pegging out their laundry, waved and called, 'Come for coffee, come, come.'

'Tomorrow, tomorrow!' the girls replied, explaining their aunty had to collect Maria's dinner.

A battered red pickup, loaded with small bananas, chugged and spluttered up the narrow road. Bouzouki music blared from a loudspeaker on its roof and the driver hung out of his window shouting the price of his fruit.

Voula's granddaughters and Angie flattened themselves against a house as he came close. The truck stopped. The middle-aged driver jumped out and snatched a viciously sharp knife from the back of the 4x4.

Blocked in by the wall behind, the pickup in front and the girls either side, Angie stared about wildly, looking for an escape. The man with bulging, bloodshot eyes and wild, grey hair ran around the vehicle. Sunlight flashed off his knife blade. The children huddled in close to Angie, squealing as they clung to her; their voices inaudible over the jangling music.

The Cretan grabbed a hand of bananas, sliced half a dozen off the bunch and thrust them at her. He grinned a set of strong, tobacco-stained teeth, jogged back to the cab, and drove away without a word.

Stunned, Angie remained flattened against the wall, staring for a moment at the bananas in her fist. Still very unsettled by her grandmother's story, she had completely misjudged the poor man. The children, carefree and happy, continued to tug her towards Voula's house. By the time she reached her destination, her heartbeat had steadied.

A net curtain hung over the open door and, inside, the warm air smelled of fried onions and cinnamon. Voula rushed towards her, clasped her head, kissed her viciously on both cheeks and then pinched one of them so hard Angie feared a bruise.

Everyone grinned, except Matthia, of course.

Voula handed her two plates of food covered in aluminium foil. 'Chicken in the oven,' she yelled.

Angie placed her bananas on the gold satin tablecloth. She told them about the pickup, her fear of being attacked, and the charity of the banana man.

Papoú, sitting in the corner, banged his stick on the floor. His black eyes sparkled, his wrinkled face radiating glee. 'You did right to be afraid, *koritsie*. Beware of strange Cretan men who put their bananas in your hand!'

Voula and the children laughed. Matthia got up and walked out.

Angie watched him and sighed.

Voula took the plates from her, dropped them next to the bananas on the table, and rubbed Angie's back. She turned away from her father-in-law and lowered her voice. 'Don't let him upset you, Angelika. Sometimes Matthia's a nasty old bastard and I hate him to death.'

Shocked by Voula's vicious tone, Angie glanced up and saw squinting snake-eyes flicker with animosity, immediately replaced by an affable grin directed at her slightly deaf father-in-law. Surprised to see a dark side to the plump, Greek chuckle-bunny, she said, 'I can't help being upset, Aunty. He always seems so angry with me.'

Voula shoved her into an overstuffed armchair. *Papoú* shook his head and then struggled to his feet.

'Maria must tell her,' he said, his voice steady and unemotional. 'Not you, Voula.' He grasped his walking stick and hobbled outside to join Matthia on the terrace.

Voula lowered her eyes and Angie sensed a conspiracy.

Voula measured *Papoú*'s words for a moment and then shouted, 'Matthia, take your mother's lunch, and sit with her while I talk to Angelika.'

Matthia came through the door, glared at Voula, then at Angie, then at the food. After a moment's consideration and a complaining grunt, he took a plate and left.

'Coffee?' Voula asked when Matthia had gone. She folded her arms under her bosoms, raising them like foothills in an earthquake.

Angie shook her head. What must Maria tell her?

'Okay, *koritsie*, you have to understand, your grandfather's right, I can't tell you much,' Voula said. 'Your grandmother will explain everything. Matthia is angry because it's your mother's duty to take care of *Yiayá* and *Papoú* and we have done it ever since Poppy left.'

She patted the back of Angie's hand. 'Also, Matthia and Poppy were very close. He would never say so, but he misses her and wants to blame everyone because she upped and ran off to England. Perhaps he holds himself responsible; there was an argument about money before she left.' Voula shrugged. 'He won't talk about it. Sometimes it's better to let things go. We all hope she'll return one day. He misses your father too. Matthia and Yeorgo were good friends before your father joined the army.'

'Can you tell me about him?' Angie glanced at a collection of photographs on top of the fridge. 'Do you have a picture? My mother has a small passport photo in her purse but it's so battered I can't see what he looked like.'

Chapter 16

VOULA STARED AT ANGIE for a moment and then seemed to come to a decision. 'You must wait for Maria to tell you about Poppy. Your poor mother, such a terrible tragedy, so unfair. I don't know what I'd have done.' She rolled her lips inward, bit on them and gazed into space.

Angie cleared her throat and Voula snapped from her daydream. She reached for a picture and passed it to Angie.

'Here's your father when he joined the army.'

Angie took the sepia photo. She stared at the strongly built man with dark eyes and thick lashes, handsome in his uniform. He appeared to be in his thirties – her age now – and that small thing seemed to draw her closer to him.

She studied her father's face and recognised her own similarities, his brown curls, strong jaw, and full lips. She imagined herself as a youngster at his side, his arm around her shoulders telling her how much he loved his daughter.

Her eyes misted as childhood fantasies came back. Hide and seek. Angie would flatten herself behind a curtain or curl under her bed, imagining his search for her, her name on his lips. 'Where are you, Angelika? Where's my girl? I'm getting closer . . .' She would wait, grinning, expecting her phantom father to appear with a 'Boo!'

Eventually she would crawl out of her hiding place with nothing but pins and needles and disappointment.

When she played shop, her Daddy's ghost always appeared as her first customer, buying everything and telling her to keep the change when she held out plastic coins. Angie smiled now, remembering dolls' tea parties on a blanket in the back garden, an empty place set between teddy and her Sindy doll, where she served lemonade and iced gems to her father.

Angie had a secret belief: if she could get him to eat, the food would put flesh on the phantom. Her father would fill up and become real. Once, when her mother joined her on the blanket, she revealed her plan, but Poppy had jumped up, snivelling, blaming a bout of hay fever.

Poppy never played tea party again. She watched from the kitchen window, waving occasionally and blowing her nose.

Angie remembered comprehensive school, when she wrote an essay about her father. Eleven-year-old Angelika claimed her Daddy was an astronaut who had gone to the moon. She said he worked in a secret spacestation, somewhere up there, and looked down on the world and his family.

The prize she won for her writing made her mother proud, and probably sowed the seeds of her ambition to work in publishing. Angie desperately wanted her father there when she received that school trophy, at the end of term awards. She imagined his ghost clapping in the audience, unseen by the masses. She stared across the sea of applauding parents and threw a special smile to the invisible man, sensing his spirit in assembly hall, watching.

Now, Angie could put a face to the entity. She battled with a lump in her throat. 'I wish I'd known him. It's not fair. As a child, I had ways of dealing with not having a father.'

'A child's imagination can be a great consolation, Angelika,' Voula said.

Angie nodded. 'I accepted his death and built a fantasy father in my head. But, here's the weird thing. I'm thirty-seven years old, and quite suddenly, I really wish I had a dad. Now, I want to learn as much as possible about him. For example, I wonder if he thought of me, before he died. Mam has always refused to talk about him. She says he left for the war before I was born and never came back, and that's all there is.'

Angie held the old photograph. Her fingertips brushed across the glass over his face and her eyes misted.

'Of course he thought of you, *koritsie*,' Voula said. 'In fact, I know he did. Your mother sent a picture of you to Stavro, just after you were born. Stavro told me he gave it to your father when he was on leave. Stavro always feared Yeorgo might not return from the army. We all did.'

'Can anyone tell me where he died? Is there a grave I could visit?' Angie said. 'I'd like to lay a wreath. It would make me feel closer. Perhaps my mother would come with me.'

Voula dropped her bulk into an armchair, one of her stockings concertinaed to her ankle and she groaned, reached over her belly and tugged the black nylon up to her knee.

'The year you were born, we had difficult times in Greece, Angelika. We'd had a war with the Axis and then, from '46 to '49, a civil war. That was terrible.'

'But it can't have been as bad as World War 2?' Angie said.

'Worse. Crete had always been communist, it still is, but in those days the British wouldn't tolerate it so they, and the USA – who are even more paranoid about commies – backed the Greek government to wipe out communism. Everyone was afraid; our own people – against us.' Her eyelids lowered. 'You've never lived through civil war, when you don't know who you can trust and fear your neighbour's breadknife in your back. Anyway, then we had the junta.'

'Matthia mentioned the junta last night, what is it?' Angie said.

Voula's eyes widened. 'Did you go to school, Angelika?'

Angie nodded. 'Of course, but . . . sorry . . .'

Voula sighed. 'In 1967 a Greek coup d'état was led by a group of Colonels. We had military rule. Anyway, the dictatorship ended in 1974 but then the Turks invaded Cyprus. But, with Archbishop Makarios –'

'Archbishop Makarios?' Angie tried to keep up with the details.

'Angelika, are you telling me you've come here to discover your family's past, and you don't even know your own country's history?'

'To be honest, I can't remember learning much more than British history at school. I wasn't interested. I'm ashamed to admit it, Aunty Voula.'

'So you should be. Anyway, that's when your father left for Cyprus with the army.' Voula shook her head, sniffed and then took Angie's hand. 'Thirty thousand Greeks were killed. May God forgive their sins. The Turks made another twenty thousand of our men refugees.

'We all feared for our boys. Trouble here – conflict there; madness. Many simply disappeared, Yeorgo amongst them. That was at the end of the 1970s.' She rubbed her hands over her face. 'A generation lost to war.'

Voula lowered her voice. 'After seven years, we had a memorial service for soldiers that hadn't come home. Matthia hoped Poppy would return for the commemoration, but she probably didn't have the money, and you were in school by then.'

'I wonder why Mam never kept in touch with Uncle Matthia.'

'Stavro and Poppy corresponded. That also hurt Matthia. Poppy didn't contact Matthia after leaving Greece, not once. It dented his pride so much that he refused to write to her.'

Angie recalled the bundle of letters from Stavro stashed in her mother's spare room.

Voula stared at the floor for a moment. 'You know, it would mean such a lot to Matthia if Poppy did call, just once, to say she hadn't forgotten him.'

'I'll do my best, I promise. Mam continues to mourn my Dad. On the anniversary of their marriage she goes to the local park and lays a copy of her wedding bouquet on the tomb of the Unknown Soldier. She's worn black for as long as I remember. I know she still loves him, with all her heart.

'Tell me, Aunty Voula, why isn't *Yiayá* wearing black after losing Petro, is it because he wasn't baptised?'

'At the time of his death, she didn't have a choice.' Voula shrugged, then lifted a hand. 'Don't ask me any more questions, Angelika. I don't want to get into trouble with my in-laws. The events of that year were so tragic. Poor Poppy,' she repeated before passing another photo frame. 'Here are your parents on the day of their marriage. Poppy was incredibly beautiful, the double of her mother. What does she look like now?'

Angie held the picture and gasped, hardly hearing Voula. She saw her mother and father together for the first time in her life. Although stiff, and staring at the camera, she recognised a slight tilt to their bodies, leaning in towards each other. They were very much in love, she sensed it from that fraction of body language. She stared at the photo, bringing it close to her face, her breath misting the glass and emotion misting her eyes.

'Angelika, what does Poppy look like now?' Voula repeated.

Angie swallowed hard, not wanting to speak – the moment was so precious to her. 'Mam, Dad,' she said, her finger tracing their faces, linking the two words together for the first time in her life. She couldn't take her eyes off the photograph, and then she realised Voula was waiting for an answer.

For all her literary skills, Angie found it difficult to describe her own mother to someone who hadn't seen her for forty years. 'I wish I'd brought a photo, thoughtless of me. She's sixty-something now, of course. Curly dark hair, like mine, but hers is short.' She made a sawing motion at jaw level and then she stared at the photograph again, unable to get enough of her parents together.

'Mam wears glasses to read and she's gained a little weight.' Suddenly, Angie saw her mother as if for the first time. 'My mother's very beautiful for her age.' She flushed with pride and wished Poppy had come with her to Crete.

Voula nodded. 'I knew she'd keep her looks, good bones – like Maria.' She seemed to be talking to herself and Angie realised Voula also missed her friend.

'On her wedding day, Poppy wore a gown made by your *Yiayá*, silk and handmade lace.' She held out another picture.

Angie stared at it. 'Wow, *Yiayá made that?* And look at Mam. She reminds me of somebody . . . Emilia Clark.' Voula frowned. '*Game of Thrones*,' Angie said.

'Ah, I haven't time for those game shows,' Voula said and then frowned again when Angie grinned.

'You know something, Angelika, that wedding dress would fit you. Your grandmother still has it, a very special keepsake. Poppy and Yeorgo had a wonderful day. I wasn't with Matthia then. I taught a new breed of Greeks who planned to become travel agents in Heraklion. Matthia was engaged to my friend Agapi, but that's another story. Poppy chose me, Agapi, and Yánna for her bridesmaids – we were all best friends.'

'Yánna?'

'Poppy's sister-in-law . . .' Voula's eyes opened wide. 'She . . . um . . . died later.' She took a breath, frowned, and then smiled at the photograph. 'Such a beautiful wedding, before all the family trouble, of course. The whole village came together. A perfect day, apart from the donkey's penis . . .'

'*What?*' Angie blinked rapidly.

Voula started a giggle that grew until she laughed real tears, her huge breasts bouncing while she flapped her hands in the air.

'I can't say. You heard your grandfather, Maria must tell you.' She set off again, chuckling hysterically. 'I'll bet she doesn't though.' Voula sniffed and wiped her eyes.

Angie thought about her own wedding plans, and her fiancé, and her emotions took a dive. She had to face the fact; if Nick lost his job, they must postpone the wedding, and put the house buying on hold. Heart-breaking, yes, but not the end of their future together. It was more important for them to support each other in their individual quests to find employment and get back on their feet. She held up the photo of her parents. 'Can they make copies of this in Viannos? I'd like to take one home for Mam, and I'd love a copy for myself.'

Voula bit her lip, still trying to murder the laughter, and if merriment hadn't danced in her eyes, she would have succeeded. 'Why don't you go back to your grandmother for the rest of the story? I'll gather the pictures I have of Poppy and Yeorgo and you can look at them all later.'

'Thank you.' Angie said. 'Also, I'd like to meet my father's parents, my other grandparents. Are they still alive? Do they live in Amiras?'

'Virgin Mary, that's a big one . . .' Voula hesitated. 'Leave it until you've heard the whole story, *koritsie*. Then, if you want to contact the Lambrakis family, we'll talk about it, but don't say that to Maria, will you? It might kill her.' She crossed herself.

Shut out again, why?

Maria had only spoken affectionately about Angie's father. She remembered the soft wistful look when her grandmother said Angie resembled him. Why would mentioning her father's family upset Maria so much it could be the end of her?

'Now go back to your grandmother,' Voula said. 'Send your grumpy uncle home. Here, take your lunch with you.'

'Stavro's coming for dinner this evening, may I provide the food? Everyone's been so kind and generous, I feel it's the least I can do.'

'It would save me a lot of work, but don't go crazy with lots of fancy dishes, or you could offend Maria.'

'Why, how?' Angie asked.

'She may think our food isn't good enough for you, Angelika. I'll give you a list of dishes, and you get them from Seli Taverna, near the monument; then everything will be homemade. Bring it here after five and I'll put the food into my own bowls.'

They grinned at each other, happy with the conspiracy.

The children rushed at Angie when she stepped into the street. They skipped alongside her as she panted all the way back up the road. When they passed one of the other houses, a wide-faced woman came rushing out with a misshapen square of something wrapped in aluminium foil.

'Take, take!' she said in English, handing a parcel over her red-flowering hibiscus shrubs. 'Cake, cake, I make, for you – for you!'

Angie smiled and said 'thank you' twice, in English, as it seemed traditional to repeat everything.

The lady beamed and the girls clapped, chirping, 'Thank you, thank you,' to each other, mimicking Angie who wished Nick were with her, to see how welcoming everyone was.

Angie speculated as she walked: how were things going back at the office? She wondered about cosy meals with the woman from Whitekings in 'their' restaurant, and questioned how far Nick would go to protect his job.

She was being stupid. Hadn't she *always* trusted him? He'd never given her a moment of worry. How often had he said, 'You're my world, Angie, I couldn't live without you'? Why was she doubting him now? Pre-wedding nerves, that was probably it.

Back at her grandmother's, Angie saw no sign of Matthia. Maria appeared pale and tired and Angie realised siesta time had arrived. '*Yiayá*, I'm going shopping, is there anything you want?'

'I have everything I need, *koritsie*, now I must sleep.'

Papoú tottered through the door, clacking his worry beads. He stood for a moment, and then opened his arms wide. Surprised, Angie went to him and he hugged her. The scent of mothballs and fabric softener filled her nostrils.

'Thank you, *Papoú*. I needed that,' she said softly. 'It's been a difficult day.'

He nodded knowingly. 'Patience, Angelika, patience,' he muttered.

Chapter 17

Athens, Present Day.

STAVRO SAT IN THE DEPARTURE lounge, waiting for his flight to Crete. He hardly noticed the people that bustled around him with their luggage trolleys and tired children. A sign caught his eye: Cheese Pie and Greek Coffee, 3 Euro.

That will do for me.

He dragged his suitcase across the highly polished floor.

After buying the snack, Stavro settled at a table with his food and drink. He reached inside his jacket for a small notebook. Once again, his investigation had come to a dead end. Although he had little proof, he remained convinced that Yeorgo hadn't died.

There must be a way to find him. Stavro had ploughed through the usual army channels but Greek administration was slow with abysmal recordkeeping. Eventually, he followed advice found on the web, sending letters addressed to Yeorgo to every battalion. He had included a return envelope but nothing came back except for one reply.

His unopened letter was returned from Yugoslavia with a note from an officer saying Yeorgo had been sent to Serbia.

For the first time, Stavro knew for sure that Yeorgo was alive. He hadn't died in Cyprus. He felt close to finding him, but then Stavro's investigation fell apart when he was hospitalised for a triple heart bypass. By the time Stavro had recovered, and was well enough to continue his search, the Serbian battalion had relocated. The thread was broken.

He bit into his cheese pie, golden flakes of filo pastry fluttered over the pages of his notebook and grease spots soaked into the paper.

Stavro never told his family. They had come to accept Yeorgo had died. He wondered if Poppy ever found the courage to tell Angelika the truth about her father. Yeorgo's decision, to disappear, had been hard to take. But, considering the circumstances, and with the feud still going on, Yeorgo had feared that somebody else would be killed.

Yeorgo's brothers had forced Matthia to break his engagement with their sister, Agapi, and beaten him almost to death. An action that made Stavro determined to become a criminal lawyer and fight against injustice. A profession he had practised in Athens and enjoyed right up until retirement. However, if Yeorgo *had* survived the wars, Stavro thought the time had come to return home and heal the rift, before his mother and father died. He knew his parents still hoped Poppy would come back one day.

Stavro brushed the crumbs away and glanced around the airport. A group of soldiers loitered in fatigues, their bulging kitbags piled against the wall; scrubbed young men in their twenties, clean-shaven with thick necks. He smiled, remembering his own national service.

When were the Yugoslavian wars? He couldn't remember. He got up, and dragged his bag over to the young men.

'Excuse me?' he said.

The soldiers turned to him. One said, 'Yes, sir?'

'Can any of you tell me when the Yugoslav war started?'

They glanced at each other. 'Early nineties, perhaps,' one replied. 'Ninety-one, two?'

'Before our time, sir,' added another.

'Before I was born,' said a third soldier.

'Thanks.' Stavro returned to his table. How the years had raced past him. It hadn't seemed so long ago since he received that officer's reply.

He caught a reflection of himself in the black glass-fronted café counter, slightly shocked to see a stooped old man. He sat up straight, pulled his stomach in and squared his shoulders. *I'm getting on*, he admitted to himself, *sometimes I forget*. After a quick calculation, he realised Yeorgo would be retired now. Where had the years gone? Perhaps Yeorgo lived in an army-sponsored retirement home.

And then it struck him. Of course, he could trace Yeorgo through his army pension. Stavro had always imagined Yeorgo as a soldier still serving his country. *What a stupid mistake*. He should try going through those channels, retired service men.

At that moment, he wanted to leave the airport and find the army pension records building. They were probably located in Athens. His heart pounded. Take it easy, he told himself, you've a stent and you're knocking on, old man.

Damn it, Yeorgo, I'll find you if it kills me.

His chest tightened.

Chapter 18

Crete, Present Day.

As she was about to enter the cottage garden, a clatter of sheep-bells made Angie look up. To the right of the monument, on the rocky ridge overlooking Amiras, stood a picturesque chapel. Black and white sheep hurried past in single file, disappearing over the hilltop. Moments later, an old shepherd and his dog appeared from behind a row of cypress trees.

Angie remembered how Maria had described those very trees on the night of the massacre: *A row of wind-bent cypress trees, silhouetted witches' fingernails, reminded me of the baby snatched from my breast.* Heart-breaking, Angie thought.

Even over that distance, she could hear the shepherd's commanding whistles. She sensed his urgency to get the flock back to their pens before nightfall. The orange sun slid behind the chapel and the light turned down a notch. Angie felt a sense of urgency too. The end of another day. Time was ticking on. Still, she was no further in her quest to find out what had made her mother exile herself from these lovely people.

The cracked marble table supported a mismatch of plates and dishes. The aroma of moussaka, pasticcio, salads, bread, and dips drifted on the warm, early evening air.

Papoú grinned and clacked his worry beads. Voula's son-in-law, Demitri from the supermarket, played his lira under the big olive tree, and Voula's six grandchildren danced in a chain. The two boys and four girls kept time with delicate steps, the girls feminine, pretty; the boys leaping and kicking, their faces incredibly serious.

When the music stopped, the children crowded around Angie, stroked her hair and touched her bare arms as if confirming she was real.

'Will you teach me to dance?' Angie said.

They clapped and pulled Angie to her feet. Delight shone from Maria's face, and Voula joined in the lesson. 'You're so light on your feet,' Angie called to Voula who seemed to skip on air.

'The basic step is easy, Angelika, kick left, kick right, step behind. Say it as you go.'

They danced with their hands on each other's shoulders, and moved in a circle to the right. Voula, in the lead, flicked a napkin in the air with her free hand. The last child in the chain held his arm behind his back.

They took turns to break away, come to the front, and perform a solo. Angie danced a little hiphop zumba, rolling her hips and shoulders while punching the air. Laughing. Showing off.

'Bravo!' Demitri called out, encouraging Angie.

Demitri's wife whacked him playfully around the head and Angie noticed a rare grin from Matthia.

Vassili clattered his stick against the table and shouted, 'Opa! Opa!' and one of the older boys stuck two fingers into his mouth, pleased to demonstrate his deafening whistling skills. Everyone clapped and whooped.

The boys made an elaborate display of flicking dust from their shoes in time with the music, and then they launched into high kicks and spins. The girls were delicate, tripping intricate steps that ended with a twirl.

Demitri played a slow *Sitarki* on his lira, the dance she'd learned. Angie stared down at her feet, pleased to keep up with the other dancers. She fell into the rhythm, smiled at Maria, and caught a glimpse of Matthia's pleasure, his eyes fixed on his wife.

When Angie had mastered the dance, Demitri winked at her and the lira picked up pace. The old folk kept time, *Papoú* banging his stick and Maria slapping the table. Faster and faster, the music played until Angie whirled around in the chain. Then, suddenly, the music stopped.

Everyone clapped, laughed, and returned to their seats. Angie, dizzy and red-faced, stood with her hands on her hips, bent double, gasping for breath.

Voula waddled back and forth shouting words of affection and radiating her love of life with a periodic chorus of, 'Eat! Eat!' Matthia scowled at anyone who looked his way and complained the souvlaki meat was tough and the charcoal rubbish.

Darkness fell quickly. The girls lit nightlights and placed them on every available surface. A stout woman arrived carrying a basket of eggs and Voula invited her to stay. Angie sensed an awkward moment as glances were exchanged around the table.

Demitri broke the sudden tension. 'Angelika!' he called out while still playing his lira. 'Meet your father's sister, Agapi.'

Instantly excited, Angie had to think where she had heard the name before. Then she remembered her mother saying; Matthia was forced to break his engagement to Agapi. The woman seemed so like Voula, they could have been matching bookends, except for Agapi's mass of dark hair, twisted and wound around her head.

'I'm so pleased to meet you, Aunty,' Angie said.

Agapi kissed Angie's cheeks, and then greeted everyone, apart from Matthia. He, in turn, hardly looked her way. Angie suspected remnants of their bygone feelings remained. Even now, they were intensely aware of each other's presence. She smiled to herself, caught her grandmother's eye, and saw the slightest nod. *Yiayá* had sensed it too. That old woman was so astute, Angie thought.

Voula let out an exuberant screech and they all followed her direction. 'Stavro!' She launched herself at the tall stranger coming into the garden, her arms thrashing about over her head.

Angie laughed, recognising her uncle's urge to turn and run. He stooped and allowed his sister-in-law to kiss him before he came over to the table.

'*Yia sas!*' Stavro addressed everyone and then cupped Maria's face in his hands and kissed her gently on the lips. 'How are you, Mama?' Their eyes met, she smiled and nodded. Stavro greeted his father next, kissing cheeks and patting each other's backs, and then he embraced Matthia. Lastly, he offered an outstretched hand to Angie. 'Welcome to Crete, Angelika.'

'Thank you, Uncle Stavro. It's such a pleasure to meet you.' She kissed him, shy for a moment – in awe of the trim and upright old man who had experienced such a lot as a young boy. Scenes from Maria's story rushed back. How Maria had saved his life, and how in turn, he had rescued her from mortal danger. They had come very close to death, yet together they had survived.

To be a member of this noble family, relatives who overcame so much adversity and still had iron ties of loyalty to each other, was tremendous. And Poppy was part of it all too. Her mother, the kindest and most honourable woman Angie knew. However, a rift remained. A thorn in Poppy's shoe that prevented her from taking a step closer to the people who loved her. What could possibly have caused such pain? She studied her Uncle Stavro and remembered the letters in the spare bedroom. He had kept in touch with Poppy for decades, and perhaps he still did.

Would Angie ever get to the root of the problem?

The party continued long after the children, *Yiayá* and *Papoú*, and Voula's daughters had left. Agapi pulled Voula up to dance. They held hands and stepped daintily side-by-side to a very fast tune from the lira. Angie couldn't believe that the two stout women, both in their sixties, were so light of foot. Occasionally they would break away, twirl delicately with their arms raised like music box ballerinas, and then come back together as gracefully as black swans gliding over water.

On one such occasion, Agapi's amazing hair worked loose and tumbled over her shoulders, reaching past her waist. A dark wavy cloak that shimmered as she danced. Angie heard Matthia gasp. The dancing women's faces glowed, their expressions otherworldly, serene. Once again, Angie desperately wished her mother was with her.

They sat around until deep into the night, drinking raki and telling stories. The streetlight on the steps went out and the village below plunged into darkness. 'A power cut,' Matthia grumbled, satisfied.

Angie couldn't believe her eyes. 'Look at the stars . . . Wow.'

It seemed like they were under a black, moth-eaten blanket in a brightly lit room. In the ebony sky, thousands of diamonds blazed and twinkled.

'That's so amazing,' she whispered.

Stavro reached for her hand. 'Come with me,' he said as someone blew out the last of the flickering candles

After leading her cautiously to the end of the garden in the pitch dark, he stood behind her. Holding her shoulders, he turned her to face the horizon of the Libyan Sea.

'See how it spirals away? That shimmering powder arching through the sky is the Milky Way, our galaxy, 400 billion stars.'

Stavro stepped back. Night closed in and surrounded her. Below and all around, there was nothing but darkness and silence. Above, millions of brilliant pricks of light in a great coil of stardust exploded into infinity.

A melancholy chord broke in as Demitri pulled his bow across the lira strings and proceeded to play a slow Greek melody. Angie recalled the words of one of her mother's favourite songs, 'Stars Don't Cry For Me'.

Overcome by the moment, her heart ached with longing for Nick and a surge of emotion filled her chest. 'Uncle Stavro,' she whispered – her voice catching. 'I don't think I've ever seen anything so beautiful, thank you.'

'The stars are here every night, waiting for your return, *koritsie*. You must bring your bridegroom and show him, and we all hope your mother will come back and see this once more. Please remind her of it, Angelika.'

Angie nodded. Everyone seemed to miss Poppy. Perhaps time had changed them all and her mother's fears, whatever they were, no longer mattered.

They returned to the table and relit the candles. Shortly after, the village lights came on and the magic of the night sky disappeared.

Demitri took up his lira again and played as Stavro and Matthia danced 'Zorba the Greek' with their arms over each other's shoulders. Then, Matthia danced alone, waving his hands above his head and spinning on his heels while Voula knelt on one knee, grunting and calling on the Virgin Mary to ease her arthritis. She raised her arms towards Matthia and clapped the rhythm – a traditional salute of admiration.

They were all slightly drunk, yet Angie saw great dignity and pride in these people. She felt immensely honoured to be a part of this family unit.

Agapi patted her arm. 'I'm going now. Come for coffee tomorrow,' she said quietly before slipping away unnoticed by the others. Matthia finished his dance and faced the table, leaving Voula to struggle to her feet. His face, flushed, eyes sparkling, he turned towards Agapi's empty chair. Angie saw a flicker of disappointment.

When Angie woke, she found herself prostrate on the cushions in the garden. The first glint of sunrise lightened the sky. Someone had thrown a faded pink sheet over her.

She lay still for a moment, remembered the stars and listened to the whirring of birds' wings. The scent of jasmine hung in the air, and the trellis next to her was covered in small white flowers. She admired a blue and yellow butterfly that fluttered down and perched on a discarded watermelon rind.

The remnants of the party were scattered across the table. If only Poppy had been there to complete the family. Angie felt sure she would have enjoyed herself. Stavro's words returned. '*. . . we all hope your mother will come back and see this once more. Remind her of it, Angelika.*' He had sounded so sincere. Poppy was the only one missing. There had to be a way to return her mother to the family circle.

The dawn chorus escalated into a racket and various flying insects, attracted by the empty wineglasses, buzzed over the table. Angie collected a few tumblers and wandered through the motionless strip curtain. Stavro lay, fully clothed, asleep on the sofa. She placed the glasses in the sink, covered her uncle with the sheet, found her keys and set off for town.

The road was busier than Angie expected. Traffic had backed up to the outskirts of Viannos. She sat patiently, wondering if there had been an accident. Her fears dissipated when hundreds of goats shambled and bumped between the vehicles ahead. A huge bell clanged beneath the head of the leading ram. Angie thought of Andreas. When the beast reached her car, it stared into her windscreen for a second, before it turned off the high street and galloped up the mountainside. The herd followed.

Angie showered and changed before she bought fresh bread and a box of baklava from the local bakery. She set off for Amiras again. On the outskirts of the village, she caught sight of Agapi with two bulging carriers.

'Can I give you a lift?' she called through the window, eager to spend some time with her father's sister.

'Good day, Angelika.' Agapi hurled her groceries onto the back seat, squeezed onto the small front seat, and grinned. She directed Angie down a narrow bumpy track that finished just above Maria's cottage, saving a trek up the steps.

They carried the shopping into Agapi's whitewashed house. 'You must stay for coffee, Angelika,' she insisted.

Agapi *must* know what had split the family, and why her mother left, Angie thought. They chatted while Agapi stored her groceries in the old fashioned kitchen.

'What do you like to drink, Angelika?'

'A glass of water would go well with this baklava. I brought them for *Yiayá* but I don't think she'll miss two, do you?'

Angie studied the rough-plastered room while Agapi bustled in the kitchen. Religious bric-a-brac seemed to be the decoration of choice, along with crocheted curtains, and a huge mirror decorated with varnished seashells.

Only one old photograph hung on the wall, an oval portrait in a thin wooden frame. The woman, regal, almost formidable, had a strong chin and high forehead. Her black hair was parted down the middle and dragged tightly back. Agapi returned while Angie was studying the image.

'My mother, Constantina,' Agapi said, placing forks on the table.

'My other grandmother?' Angie said.

Agapi straightened, stared at the window, and then at Angie. 'Has your mother forgiven her, Angelika?'

Angie frowned. 'Forgiven her . . . for what?'

Agapi's eyes flicked away and she retreated to the kitchen, returning with a tray laden with glasses of water, saucers and napkins.

They settled on the sofa with its patchwork cushions at their backs and a striped Cretan rug under their feet. Angie opened the cake box and the scent of honey and toasted sesame seeds reached up and grabbed her appetite. A minute later, they were enjoying the sticky confectionery.

'Is she still alive, *Yiayá* Constantina?' Angie said carefully.

Agapi stared at her. 'You mean you don't know . . .?'

Angie shook her head. 'Know what?'

Agapi blew her cheeks out. Awkward silence filled the room.

Shut out again, Angie thought. She decided to change the subject, and try returning to it later. 'Wasn't it a lovely night?' she said over a mouthful of crushed walnuts and filo pastry. 'Great to see my uncles having a good time too.'

'Don't judge Matthia too badly, Angelika.' Agapi wiped her mouth on a napkin. 'Voula told me he'd been hard on you. He's a very loyal man. He spent his entire life in the shadow of Stavro.'

'You were engaged to him, weren't you?' She bit her lip, tasted honey and felt the heat of a blush rising. 'Sorry, I didn't mean to pry.'

Agapi dabbed at cake crumbs. 'Don't worry, it's not a secret.'

No, but everything else seems to be, Angie thought.

'Everybody knows we were betrothed. He loved me very much and I rather liked him.' Agapi paused for a moment.

Liked? Angie frowned again.

'Things turned bad between our families, in fact, it became impossible.' Agapi put her empty saucer on the table and tangled her fingers. 'My brothers forbade my wedding to Matthia but he refused to end our romance. I'm afraid they treated him very badly.' She paused, staring at the window.

Angie suspected Agapi wanted to say more. She licked her lips and leaned forward, sure she would learn something major. 'Why wouldn't they let you get married? If you don't mind me asking.'

Agapi glanced up, first at Angie and then at the portrait of her mother. She gave a little shake of her head. 'You really don't know, Angelika?'

Chapter 19

ANGIE STARED AT AGAPI. Could the reason for Agapi's breakup with Matthia have something to do with Poppy, or Constantina?

'I don't know anything about my mother's exit from Amiras.' Angie said. 'I understand there was a feud, but no one will explain. *Papoú* told me it's for *Yiayá* to tell the whole sorry story, but it's taking so long.' She hoped Agapi would drop a few clues. 'I'm trying to discover why my mother ran away to England. Mam won't even talk about Crete and gets upset if I do.'

'That's understandable. Poppy wants to forget. We all have demons from those times.'

'But the trouble is she *can't* put it behind her. Mam's still tortured by whatever happened here. We had a huge fight because I wanted to come to Crete.'

Angie took a moment to think of Poppy all alone at home. 'Poor Mam,' she muttered. Her mother would be fretting, cleaning that kitchen over and over, scratching at her hands.

'Agapi, I knew nothing of the war or the massacre. I can't understand why Mam's never talked about *Yiayá*'s troubles. In fact, the whole split-up between the two families is a mystery to me.'

'I see. Look, Angelika, I don't want problems,' Agapi said. 'It's taken generations for things to settle. I advised Poppy to go, get out of our lives and never come back, and she did. I've often wondered if she ever forgave me. We were great friends, I miss her. You can't imagine what she suffered, but for all the heartbreak, she did the right thing. People had died and it wouldn't have stopped. Please tell her: I haven't forgotten her. That I'm truly sorry. And I still regard her as my best friend.'

Angie nodded. 'But why did she go? I can't even guess at circumstances that would cause such a rift in a family.'

Agapi sighed. 'You must wait for Maria. Nobody will go against her wishes. She's a good woman, Angelika, the most respected village elder in Amiras.'

'Can you tell me something about your brother?' Angie said.

'My brother? No, forget him, bah! Don't listen to what anyone says.' Agapi leapt to her feet, her thigh knocking the saucer of cake, causing it to teeter precariously on the edge of the table.

Angie caught it, instantly remembering the apple pie and the terrible argument that took place in her mother's kitchen.

Agapi clenched her fists and stared about the room before she continued. 'What they did to Matthia was unforgivable. Why would you want to know anything about my brother?'

Angie blinked rapidly, startled by Agapi's change of mood. 'Because he's my father and nobody else will talk about him.'

There was an awkward moment while Agapi struggled to recompose. 'Oh . . . yes, of course. Sorry, I misheard you. Thought you said . . . anyway, never mind. Old age catching up and too many questions. What can I tell you?' She dropped into her chair, two red patches flaring her cheeks.

'Well, naturally, I'm curious about everything. I wish I'd known my father and I am desperate to hear somebody say nice things about him. I guess you were close in age.'

Agapi sighed, patted her chest and sat back, a faraway look in her eyes. Seconds ticked by before she answered. 'Yeorgo was two years older than me, Angelika. We were very close . . . so very close.' She swallowed hard, absentmindedly dabbing at crumbs in her lap – and then she brushed away a tear. 'I miss him terribly, even now. It took me a long time to accept that he had died.' She paused and touched her eyes. Angie realised she had been insensitive, not thinking of anyone else's pain.

'I'm so terribly sorry, Agapi. I didn't mean to upset you. You've been really kind and helpful. I'm very grateful. That was a thoughtless thing to say, and very selfish, too. It's a problem I'm trying to deal with. I've been spoiled all my life, but it wasn't until I came here, did I realise how shallow and self-centred I'd become.'

'No, you're not selfish, Angelika. It's only natural that you want to know about your father, and I understand you're here trying to help Poppy. Under the circumstances, all this secrecy must be very difficult for you. I wish I could be more help.' Agapi stared vacantly for a moment, and then she smiled. 'Your father was completely selfless, and a very honest man, Angelika. Yeorgo had integrity and great loyalty to his family. He was a martyr in the truest sense of the word. He forfeited everything he loved, inadvertently even his own life, to save us all from more problems. You've inherited Yeorgo's looks, but I pray you also have his special qualities, his principles and sincerity.'

'I hope so too. It's great to hear positive things about my father.' Angie smiled. 'Thank you, Agapi.' Angie realised she had broadened her shoulders, proud. Of course he had been a good man, she always knew it. She promised herself she would try to become more like him.

Agapi continued, 'He took care of me when my parents were working. We had our own little gang. Me, Matthia, Yeorgo, Voula and . . .' She frowned, clucked, and then chuckled. 'When I think how life was then and how people treat children today – so different. When Poppy came along, she stayed with us from the day she left the breast. I would drag her around and find safe places to dump her while we played our childish games. Anyway, no more questions. Wait for Maria to tell you. I'm afraid of speaking out of turn.'

Disappointed for a moment, Angie tried a different angle. 'I can't imagine what it must have been like for you, betrothed to Matthia and then forced to break the engagement.'

Agapi opened her mouth to speak, closed it again and glanced around the small room.

Angie felt a change of mood in her aunt and, treading carefully, encouraged her to continue. 'It must be difficult to accept that Matthia is married to Voula.'

'Yes, I found it hard at first, Angelika, but they have two beautiful daughters and six grandchildren, and I love them all. So it's rather good the way things turned out.'

'Still . . . to see him almost every day . . .' Angie said softly. 'It must have been heart breaking.'

Agapi took Angie's hands and stared into her eyes. Her face softened and she started to speak, but once again hesitated, breaking eye contact and staring at the floor.

'Go on,' Angie said softly. 'Tell me, Aunty.'

After pulling in a long breath, Agapi let it out slowly and in a voice barely louder than a whisper she said, 'You don't understand, *koritsie*, it's not Matthia I love.'

The information took a moment to register.

'Voula?'

Agapi met Angie's eyes, searching for a reaction, the longing for understanding shining from her face. 'I hope you don't mind me telling you, Angelika. I know it's more acceptable where you come from, but I'd die if anyone here knew. An old woman like me – the locals would say all kinds of things. Are you shocked?'

Angie smiled and gave her hands a squeeze. 'Not at all, just surprised. I'd never have guessed.'

Agapi nodded slowly. 'Good. I've loved her since we were children. I always wanted to tell somebody. I suspect Voula knows, although I haven't told her. Sometimes when our eyes meet . . . what can I say, love is a strange thing, yes? Anyway, it feels . . . well . . . marvellous now that I have said it aloud, actually divulged my secret.' She looked down, shy for a moment. 'I hope you don't mind.'

'Actually, I'm honoured that you've chosen to confide in me,' Angie said, and it was true. Angie kissed Agapi and left another piece of baklava with her. She contemplated their conversation as she took the rest of the cakes to her grandmother's cottage. How tragic, yet selfless, to love somebody all your life and not say anything. And wasn't it easy to misread the situation, and jump to conclusions?

Angie found her grandmother sitting at the cracked marble table in the garden. She had a mound of small green plants before her. 'Good morning, *Yiayá*.' She kissed Maria and caught the scent of Palma violets. 'You smell nice.'

Her grandmother's eyes sparkled. 'Stavro always brings me a tablet of expensive soap from Athens. It's my treat.' The old woman grinned childishly, her frail body growing a little sturdier, strengthened by pleasure.

'What are you doing there? Can I help?' asked Angie, nodding at the leafy rosettes, thinking they looked more like something weeded from a lawn, than food.

Yiayá ignored the question. Her eyes shone with contentment while her scarred hands clutched a knife awkwardly and cut taproots off the plants. 'Sit down, *koritsie*. What time did you leave last night?'

Angie laughed. 'I didn't. I woke up this morning on the cushions. We had a great party and I suspect we all ended up a little drunk.'

'Good. Everyone needed to have some fun. And thank you for the food.'

'Oh . . . I hope you weren't offended. I wanted to save Voula the work. How did you know?'

Yiayá chuckled. 'You're my granddaughter so perhaps I understand you better than you think. I probably would have done the same. Besides, after forty years of Voula's cooking, I recognise her recipes. I suspect what we had last night came from Seli Taverna?'

Angie nodded. 'I hope I have your brains when I'm ninety, *Yiayá*.'

'Be careful what you wish. It's a curse to remember everything with such clarity. Sometimes I've prayed my memory would fade. Now tell me, what's in the box?'

'Baklava, from the bakery in Viannos.'

'Then I suggest you practise your coffee-making skills, before Voula gets her greedy hands on the cakes. What do you say?'

Angie laughed again. 'You love her very much, don't you?'

'Voula's a wonderful wife to Matthia. He's not the easiest person to get on with and, despite being his second choice, she's been loyal to him and a good mother and grandmother.'

'Uncle Matthia's a lucky man.'

'In some ways, but not in others; he was obsessed with Agapi – so besotted, he agreed to wait until she finished her teaching degree – and part of that love has never died. You saw it last night, didn't you?'

Angie nodded, recalling the glance that passed between them.

'But Matthia's been faithful to Voula, and I admire him for that. Of course, he thinks nobody knows that he still holds affection for Agapi.'

'I'm anxious to hear more of what happened, *Yiayá*.'

'You go and make the coffee and, while we deprive Voula of as many baklava as we can, I'll continue with the story.'

Chapter 20

Crete, 1943.

After an hour trudging uphill in the September sun, Matthia collapsed. Completely exhausted, my youngest child was unable to continue. Afraid for him, and realising we were still vulnerable on the mountainside, I knew we had to put more distance between us and Amiras. I don't know where I found the strength to carry him on my back, but I did. Bent double, one step at a time, and desperately thirsty, I struggled on with Stavros, uncomplaining, at my side.

We found water in a gully above the village of Simi. Baby frogs were hopping all over the place. I used Matthia's shoe to scoop the muddy liquid up, and ran it through my skirt into the other one. It tasted disgusting but we had to drink. I looked forward to our goat's milk later and thanked God we had brought her along. The boys quickly recovered and played with the creatures. They needed a break from the slog and their laughter uplifted me.

The track got steeper. Near to midday, we found the old ruined house that Andreas had described. Although far from civilisation and the soldiers, I felt uneasy. It stood close to the path, and had an atmosphere, as if the air around the building warned us to go away. We moved higher up the mountain.

Most of the trees were pines now and, because of the steep lay of the ground, there was a reasonable view both up and down the slope. Apart from a herd of skittish wild goats and a few birds, our surroundings were still. The only noise came from the wind further up the mountain, soughing through the firs. The cool breeze refreshed us.

We found a hiding place, a great, sprawling holly oak. The dead leaves on the ground were hard and uncomfortable with their sharp little spikes but the tree was big, old, and robust. Warm, still, air under the canopy was sweet and musty like stewed tea. The scent reminded me of home. Then I remembered we no longer had one.

The heavy boughs reached to the earth and the inner ones, around the base of the trunk, were dead, dry and brittle. We pushed against them and they snapped away, disintegrating into little more than dust. The boys stamped on them, breaking them into manageable lengths.

Soon we had a space cleared. Inside our woody cave, I laid the blanket that I'd used as a sling to bring the food up to Andreas's cottage. We slept under the boughs until mid-afternoon when Matthia woke us with his wailing. The child had a fierce cramp. Stavro rubbed his bunched calf muscles and I begged him to stop crying.

Our belongings were down the mountain and I was unable to fetch them by myself. We needed things that we took for granted in our daily lives: cups, a cooking pot, and the salt. The boys needed nourishment too, and if the goat wasn't milked soon, she would start making a racket.

'Stavro, do you think you can milk the goat straight into Matthia's mouth if I hold her still?'

He grinned, lifted and dropped his shoulders, and said, 'I'll try, Mama.'

I sat next to the goat and gripped her back legs between my knees, to protect Matthia's face from a kick. The result of Stavro's efforts had us all in hysterics. Matthia had milk in his eyes and up his nose, but a fair amount ended up in his mouth. I'm not so sure all the misdirected milk was entirely accidental. Stavro swapped places with Matthia, and succeeded in squirting most the milk into his own mouth.

When I lay under the goat, with Matthia hanging on to her back legs, Stavro did quite a good job. I don't know if it was the milk, or the laughter, that made us feel greatly uplifted.

While the boys went back to playing with the frogs, I tried to decide what to do about our things. Should I leave Matthia alone and trust the four-year-old to stay put for at least three hours? What if the cramps came back?

'Matthia, I'm going to get our belongings with your brother. You stay here. Collect as many acorns as possible while we're away and have another sleep,' I said.

He wrapped his arms around my knees. 'I want to come with you. Please don't leave me, Mama.'

'Somebody must take care of the goat, and you've become an expert. We won't be long.'

'I wish I was seven, it's not fair!'

'Promise you'll hide, and be very quiet, son?' This was a bad plan and I knew it, but I had to take the risk. I thought about tying him on a length of rope like the goat, but he would have kicked up a fuss.

'I won't move, Mama,' he promised. 'Can I go with you next time?' His big brown eyes turned up to me.

'Of course.' I dreaded leaving him. 'Now give your mother a hug.'

He wrapped his arms around my neck and squeezed. How could I abandon him on the mountainside, little more than a baby?

Stavro and I set out on our journey. We made good progress without Matthia and I reassured myself I'd reached the right decision. False comfort because, deep down, I feared something unimaginable would happen to him in the time we were parted. Andreas's cottage came into view and I sensed Stavro's excitement.

'Will the shepherd be there, Mama? Isn't he the greatest man you ever met?'

In my heart, I knew Andreas's fate, and when I had a moment alone, he would reap my prayers and tears. I smiled at Stavro, realising the shepherd would always live in his memory too. One day, my son would realise what had happened to Andreas on this mountainside, and with all the sadness in the world, he would mourn for his hero too.

'I don't know, Stavro,' I said softly, 'Andreas planned to go up the mountain to his sheep.'

We hid in the bushes, watching the cottage, afraid someone occupied the place. It stayed deathly quiet. I put my hand against the wall and opened the door. Such a feeling of abandonment seemed to come from the stones themselves. Overwhelmed by sadness, I remembered the intimate occasion when he washed me.

We crept inside the hovel. Olive sacks lay on the floor, rucked along the edge where Andreas had lain on his side, watching over me.

I'll pray for you every night, Andreas. I'll always remember the one night of peaceful sleep you gave me. You cared for me at a time when my life was a nightmare, filled with terror and turmoil. Thank you my dear friend.

The cracked cup stood on the table where I had left it that morning. We drank our fill of water, replaced the cup and then continued down the mountain.

Halfway between the shepherd's cottage and the fig tree, we took a moment under the spreading carob, where I had seen the polecat. A great shadow slid over the open ground between the trees, heading in the same direction as us, towards Amiras. My heart almost stopped.

The shadow seemed as big as a man but, knowing no Cretan men remained in the village, it did not make sense. Then I thought about the camouflage clothes that soldiers wore. Perhaps they were very effective in this environment of harsh light. So long as they didn't move, I feared they would be invisible to us. Afraid we were surrounded, I remembered what they had done to the midwife.

We peered between trees, stared into dark shadows made by the strong afternoon sun, but I saw neither man nor animal. My heart hammered and a sharp cutting pain seared my hands. I realised I'd clenched my fists, cracking the flesh open.

For a stupid moment, I thought the shadow belonged to the spirit of Andreas, watching over us. Then, I reprimanded myself for being a superstitious fool. Just when I believed I had imagined it all, Stavro gasped.

'Mama, look!' He stepped into the clearing and gawped, pointing at the sky.

I craned my neck to see between the branches, and then my flesh crawled over my bones.

Oh, dear Jesus Christ . . .

To the west, at least thirty vultures circled slowly on a thermal over the ridge. Their parallel wings, black against the deep blue sky, contrasted with the cream of their ruffs and necks.

Another shadow slithered over us, across the pale ground, and then another, and another as more of the giant birds with their huge wingspan glided in from the direction of the canyon.

One came so close I saw the glint of its eye. Black feathers on the end of its wings spread stiffly like outstretched fingers.

I wanted to sprout wings, fly to the ridge and find Petro. Please God, let somebody have taken his little body and buried him properly. Horrific visions thundered into my head. Those hooked beaks . . . my baby. The world about me spun and my throat closed. I crumpled to the ground, my boy's voice vague, distant, and panic stricken; then everything rushed away.

Consciousness came back with the sound of Stavro's sobs. I opened my eyes, vision creeping into focus. At first, I was poleaxed by fear that we may be encircled by soldiers with their pistols drawn. Then my sanity returned. I realised we were alone.

My boy sat cross-legged next to me, his hands in his lap, fingers twisting and knotting and his shoulders jerking up and down as he cried. Even after all we had been through, I'd never seen him so wretched.

'Don't die, Mama, please don't die,' he blubbered, rocking back and forth. 'I'll try harder, I promise. I'm sorry, Mama . . .' he sobbed. 'Please, God, don't take my Mama, I need her more than you do. And I have a little brother that I can't take care of by myself.'

Bless his brave heart, I thought. 'You have nothing to be sorry about, Stavro. You've been wonderful,' I whispered, wanting to hold his hand but my own looking so repulsive stopped me. Flies, taking advantage of my stillness, were feeding on the congealed blood. He stared at them. 'I just went a little dizzy,' I said. 'Probably shock from the burns, son.'

'You were asleep for a very long time, Mama. I thought you had died and I didn't know what to do.'

'Well, I'm not dead. Anyway, I would be in heaven watching over you both if I was. Stavro, my boy, you do understand what you must do if anything like that happens?' His eyes widened. 'You will leave me where I lay, and go and care for Matthia.' I pushed myself up into a sitting position. 'Now, come on, silly, give me a hug.'

I held him, forced myself not to crush him to me as I thought of Petro. What more could I do to reassure Stavro? I saw myself as a big old roof beam, holding everything up while worms tunnelled inside, eating my strength, and no matter how hard I tried, one day I would crumble and all about me, collapse.

I shuffled onto my knees, blinked away the light-headedness and after a few deep breaths, I got to my feet. We were just about to continue to the fig tree when a great clattering noise rattled over the mountainside. The racket increased. I sensed danger and my heart thumped against my ribs.

'Quick, Stavro! Let's go back a bit and hide.'

We scooted up the slope, panting hard, and stumbling over dry thistles until we found a patch of low shrubs. A gap through the trees ran straight down to the road below, which made it impossible to cross without being seen. We dropped to our knees and crawled inside the bushes, me on my elbows, scrambling for cover. Twigs dragged at my hair and clothes and scratched my face.

Neither of us spoke. Crouched, we peered between the branches, hardly believing what we saw pass along the highway. Soldiers led a procession of their plunder. A string of local donkeys laden with metal items, everything from mattocks to fire-tongs, confiscated from our villages. They trotted in the direction of Viannos. Raki stills, pots, ploughs and all kinds of ironware were stacked high and roped onto the beasts of burden, clashing and clattering through the silence of the mountain road.

Behind this bizarre procession, a six-wheeled sheep truck followed at donkey pace. Not loaded with chattels of iron or copper, this lorry had a human cargo. Beautiful women, aged between fifteen and twenty-five, were packed to standing. Distressed, they wept and hugged each other, or grasped the vehicle's surrounding rail as it lurched along the road. Even from that distance, I recognised them.

My school friends were there, and also my students. The young females of Amiras, Viannos, and the other local villages. Although they wouldn't be able to see me, I felt their despair, their sense of hopelessness. Would they ever return to their homes and the people they loved? What terrible experiences lay in wait for them? One thing I knew for sure, they would never be the same again.

'Where are they going?' Stavro whispered.

I searched for an acceptable answer. 'They're taking them to work, son, probably to cook for the soldiers. We're famous for our fantastic food and you know those Germans are brought up on nothing but pickled cabbage.'

I had done right to leave Amiras, despite our hardship. If we had stayed, I would have ended up in that truck, and my poor boys . . .? Where would they be now?

The Nazis' proximity made it too dangerous to continue to the fig tree. Our possessions were not worth hanging for and I fretted about Matthia. Stavro, glad to turn back towards the shepherd's cottage, scrambled ahead. I looked forward to washing my hands, which were bleeding again, attracting flies whenever they were still.

We darted from tree to tree, staying in the shadows. As soon as we reached Andreas's house, we pushed through the entrance. I had mixed feelings, remembering the big man but glad to return to the familiar place.

We crept inside the room. Something wasn't right, I sensed it at once. Then I realised: the cup was missing. Confused, I gawped at the spot, grasping for a logical explanation. A crash came from outside. I spun to face the door, pushing Stavro behind my back. He cried out and threw his arms around my hips.

A Nazi with the tin bath rocking at his feet and a pistol in his hand. He stood just beyond the doorway. I stared, too terrified to speak. His pale, narrow face hardened as he jerked the gun up and down, beckoning us to go further inside the cottage. He followed, kicked the lower part of the door shut, and spoke in German.

I didn't understand but he kept waving his weapon, indicating for us to sit on the banquette. He sat on the low table with his elbow on his knee and the pistol pointing in our direction.

I tried to think of something to say that he would comprehend. Did they have religion in the hellhole that spewed out these children of Satan? Could he possibly believe in God? I did, so I crossed myself, attempted to prayer-lock my blood-smeared hands and then recited the words of psalm 121, the entreaty that all Greek Orthodox knew. I hoped that even if he did not understand my language, he would recognise the rhythm of the anthem and, in his head, hear it in his own tongue.

'I will lift up my eyes to the hills. From where comes my help? My help comes from the Lord, who made heaven and earth. He will not allow your foot to be moved; he who keeps you will not slumber.'

Stavro crossed himself and joined in the prayer.

What would happen to Matthia if the Nazi killed us both? Was it possible for a four-year-old to survive on the mountain by himself? I imagined him waiting, and us never returning, and I wanted to tell the soldier why he should let us go.

I glanced into his eyes, ice-blue, and saw the dullness of fatigue – a human trait that gave me hope. I should have been consumed by panic but I felt oddly calm. Perhaps the prayer had done it, or exhaustion. We had suffered so much horror in so few hours.

He might kill me and my son, what could I do? I lowered my eyes, leaving our future up to God's will.

The Nazi groaned, muttered something and stared at my burned hands, shaking his head. We sat, motionless, the cottage as quiet as a tomb. I lost track of time. He seemed to come to a decision, stood, and placed the pistol to my temple. The metal barrel pressed at the side of my eye. I could see the knuckles of his fist, fine blond hairs standing to attention and the gun angled towards the back of my head. The rapid panting of my own breath drowned out my heartbeat.

It wasn't the fear of imminent death. My terror, purely distilled and potent, came from the unknown . . . the exact moment when he would pull the trigger, the end of life as I knew it. A second passed, then another, and another. Which tick of a billion clocks would bring that single bullet? Which breath would be my last? I wanted to swallow but couldn't, anyhow what was the point?

I grabbed Stavro and pulled his face hard into my chest. He shouldn't see his mother shot, I didn't want my brains splattered all over him and anyway, he would be next. If I held him tight enough, he might not get a chance to look up before the end came for him too. God take us.

Unable to cope anymore, I cried silently. My last seconds on earth and all I did was snivel – stupid, stupid snivelling. I bit my top lip so hard I tasted blood, and I screwed my eyes tightly and then I opened them as wide as possible. I wanted to die looking down at my dear boy, Stavro.

The German stepped back and, although the barrel didn't leave my temple, I found I could sit up straight, and at least die with dignity. I guessed he did not want my blood spatter over his smart uniform. I waited for the shot, still expecting each breath to be my last, and then Stavro squirmed from my grasp.

He looked the Nazi in the eye and said, boldly, pointing at me, 'Mama, my Mama!' and then he pointed at the soldier. 'You, Mama? You have Mama?' He put his arms around my neck and kissed my cheek. 'My Mama! You have Mama? You don't kill Mama!'

The Nazi shook his head and, very slowly, Stavro raised his hand and moved the gun away from my head.

After God knows how long, perhaps seconds, or even minutes, I dared to glance into the soldier's face, afraid that with twisted malevolence he wanted me to see the bullet coming. He continued to stand over us and, when our eyes met, he lowered the gun and fastened it into its holster.

His mouth worked as if he were chewing tough meat, then he frowned, reached into his tunic and pulled out a fistful of sweets. He threw them onto the table and I realised they were barley sugar twists. In that bizarre moment, I wanted to laugh hysterically, as if laughing would wipe out the irrationality of evil. Then, like a thrown switch in my soul, my emotions flipped.

Given the chance at that instant, I would have bashed him to a bloody pulp with his own gun, killed him myself but not with a simple shot. The need to cause him indescribable pain surged through me. Bastard sperm of Satan! My thoughts screamed in my head, but the violent instincts quelled in seconds, being nothing but my unstable mind at breaking point. The spark that could have ignited an explosive scenario died and left me like a damp fuse. I sat, dumb and trembling, staring at his soft white hands, his nails bitten to the quick, the skin down the sides ragged.

The soldier spoke, pointing at us and then at the ground. Stavro squirmed and I realised I had pulled him to me, suffocating him against my bosom.

I nodded, indicating that I understood we should stay where we were. The soldier stared for a few moments longer, and then he left, reaching through the open top of the door and sliding the wooden bolt home.

'Thank you.' I sobbed quietly, not sure if I spoke to man or God but, anyway, the words hardly formed. I smoothed my son's damp hair from his face and kissed his flushed cheeks.

Again, he turned and pointed to the ground through the top half of the door before he left. I judged the soldier's distance from the fading clatter of the tin bath down the hillside.

Stavro and I were emotionally and physically exhausted. I shook so badly, a few minutes passed before I was able to stand. Stavro had wet himself. We held each other and cried relentlessly. I don't know how long we took to come to our senses, but eventually we did. After drinking as much water as possible, we gathered all the useful things. We hardly spoke, equalised by fear and trust; and understanding each other. We had shared infinite terror. I kept thinking of my little Matthia, all alone. We had to return to him, up the mountain.

We snuck out and I saw a mulberry tree, lopped back a year ago, which produced many long straight branches. The villagers used them for knocking down walnuts in September and, later, for the olives harvest. Seeing it near the shepherd's cottage gave me an idea.

We could make a dragging stretcher and transport all the things we needed. With the help of my knife, we managed to remove the thinner twigs and push them through the sides of a couple of olive sacks. We gathered everything transportable and put it in another sack on the jute hammock.

'But what about Andreas, Mama?' Stavro asked.

What should I say? 'He's gone to his cottage on the plateau,' I lied. 'He told me to take all that we needed, son, before the soldiers raided the place. We've already lost the bath.'

When we were ready, I stood between the mulberry branches and Stavro tied the last piece of rope to the extending lengths and then around my waist. We moved as quietly as possible, up the slope, sucking on the blessed barley sugar. Such had been our slog that nothing but exhaustion ran through my veins. Stavro walked behind, kicking dirt over the tracks we left. The laborious trek uphill, with all that weight to pull, took a couple of hours.

Night had fallen by the time we approached the sprawling holly oak.

Stavro raced ahead. 'Matthia!' he called, pushing through the curtain of leaves and squirming away from sharp spines. We both expected to find him asleep on the ground.

My little boy, the blanket and the goat, were gone.

Chapter 21

Crete, Present Day.

VOULA BOUNDED THROUGH THE plastic fly-curtain, her face scrunched into a pug-like frown and her fists clenched.

'They're arguing again, your sons drive me crazy,' she yelled at Maria.

'Then let them get on with it, Voula. Come, eat baklava and tell us, what's the problem?'

Silent for a moment, Voula gazed at the plate of cakes, her eyes wide and her lips glistening.

'Voula!'

She snapped from her reverie. 'Sorry. I'm cooking for tonight but Stavro insists he can't stay. He must return to Athens. Matthia says our food's not good enough for Mr High-and-Mighty and there's no reason why the city can't wait another day.'

Frustrated, Angie wondered what had happened to young Matthia on the mountain side. Why was he so cantankerous now? Would she ever find out what caused the rift between her mother's and father's families? What made the war story relevant to Poppy's self-exile? What further tragedy finally destroyed her other grandmother, Constantina? It seemed that with each day, more secrets came to light.

Her grandmother's laugh brought her to the present. 'Will the food be ready for lunchtime, Voula?' Maria said.

Voula nodded, her eyes fixed on the baklava.

'Then let's all eat together before Stavro goes back. Now, make the coffee and force one of the cakes inside yourself.'

Angie fingered her engagement ring, remembering that is was a bank holiday in the UK, and wondered if Nick would be home. If Stavro returned to Athens later today, this was Angie's last chance to connect everyone with a call.

'I have to go to Viannos. Do you need anything, *Yiayá*, Voula?' she asked.

'Tell me what you want, Angelika, perhaps I can save you the journey,' Voula said.

'It's a surprise, Aunty. I'll be back in an hour to help with the food.'

While driving back to Viannos, a niggling doubt built up in Angie's mind. Was she doing the right thing? Time was the problem.

Poppy was going to be so upset by Angie's plan, she knew her mother that well, but in the end, Angie was convinced, it was the right thing to do. An unpleasant action for her mother, Angie admitted, but administered with all the love and best intentions in the world.

Once Poppy had recovered from the initial shock, she would see how right Angie was. Like ripping off a plaster to air a wound, so healing could begin. She would be cross with Angie, at first, but apart from that, what harm could come from a simple videocall between Poppy and her parents.

Angie pulled over and stopped to let a wagon come over the narrow stone bridge, just before Viannos.

It must be hard being a mother, she thought, having to hurt your children for the greater good. Vaccinations, discipline, first aid. She'd never thought about it before. If you love somebody enough, then you do everything necessary to make their lives better, regardless of what they might think of you, wasn't that right?

Nobody could love their mother more than Angie loved Poppy. She was determined to do whatever she had to, to bring Poppy and Maria together again, for their own good. Of course, Poppy would be angry at first, Angie felt miserable at the thought, but Poppy would understand her motives and forgive her eventually.

In Viannos, she collected the tablet from her room and then went to Manoli's kafenion. Under the big tree, she ordered a small beer and claimed one of the freshly vacated tables, which was littered with empty coffee cups and overflowing ashtrays.

Angie phoned Nick at the apartment, smiling in anticipation. He would be waiting for her call, and realise it was her even before he picked up the phone.

'Hi, sweetheart, good to find you at home. I've missed you,' Angie said. 'How's it going?'

'Hello, beautiful. I can't remember a week being so long. Work's panning out, difficult to tell how it's going at this stage.'

'Poor darling. You sound tired. I'll bet you've been working all hours.'

'Pretty much, yes. Working today too.'

'I'll make it up to you the moment I get back.' She tried to lift his mood. 'How about a box of the finest local honey cakes and my undivided attention.'

'That's the best thing I've heard all week.' Relieved, Angie caught his chuckle. 'Seriously, darling, I'm counting the days until you get back.'

She giggled. 'I look forward to it, too.' But then her concern returned. 'How're things going with the merger?'

'Like I said, everything's fine.' He lowered his voice. 'I'm not alone, Angie.'

Startled, Angie pulled her phone away and stared at the number. Yes, she had called their apartment. Nick was with somebody in their home. It had better not be that Whitekings woman again.

He raised his voice. 'I'm in a meeting, and I have another one this evening so I can't talk. I can't wait until you come back, love you.'

'Wait! Listen, Nick,' Angie said, trying to speak and analyse the situation at home at the same time. 'Uncle Stavro's returning to Athens later today. I've managed to get wifi connected at *Yiayá*'s cottage.' *Who was in their apartment?* 'Would you visit Mam and Skype us from there in an hour or two, so they can all see each other?' *Where is his meeting this evening?* 'I thought it would be lovely. *Yiayá* hasn't seen Mam for so many years. The reason I came here was to bring them together, remember?' *Was he going out with the Whitekings woman, again?* 'It's really important to me, Nick.'

'You do drop them on me, Angie. I'm up to my eyes. I'll try, honestly, but no promises. Just hold on a minute.'

Muted talking came from the phone and Angie guessed his hand was over the receiver. Why did he do that? They had no secrets . . . did they?

'I'll be finished here at four, so what about four-thirty?' Nick said.

'Fine, or this evening.' She tested him.

'I've a meeting tonight and I have no idea what time we'll finish.'

'At the Meadows?'

She actually heard him swallow, and then a door closed. Their bedroom door? She guessed he had gone in there for privacy.

'Are you there, Nick?'

'I am. Look, Angie, I realise what this looks like –' His voice was hushed, almost a whisper, but angry. 'I'm trying to keep my job.'

'I'm sure you are. You have a business meeting, on a bank holiday evening, at a romantic little restaurant, while your fiancée is away. Just let me ask, Nick; how many people will be at this important meeting?'

'Stop it, Angie! You make it sound as though I'm having an affair.'

'Are you?'

'No, for God's sake! I told you, I'm pulling out all the stops to try and keep my job.'

'I have to go,' she said smoothly and ended the call.

She clenched her fists, screwed her eyes, and muttered, 'Fuck! Fuck! Fuck!' When she opened them, Manoli was standing before her holding the beer. 'Sorry, work problems,' she said.

'Lady, you have too many difficulties. He glanced at the table full of clutter, left Angie with her beer and returned with a tray and cloth. 'A holiday means you leave work at home. Why you bring it with you?' He cleared the table and wiped away the coffee drips and cigarette ash.

'I must be mad, Manoli.'

'This is true.' He straightened, holding the full tray. 'You want mezzé with your drink?'

Angie planned to put Nick right out of her head. Nothing could be gained from fretting, and she had to trust him. That was the first time she had ended a call without saying she loved him. Perhaps she would phone him later, much later, just to check on him. That, she decided, was pathetic behaviour.

She wondered how everyone in Amiras would react to seeing Poppy again. Her mother and grandmother reunited. Although, she was still none the wiser about her mother's exile or unhappiness.

Her thoughts went back to Nick and she felt terrible about her hurtful behaviour. *Grow up, Angie!*

Manoli returned. Perhaps he had information about her family. After all, Angie thought, he was 'very good friends' with Demitri, and Angie needed a distraction from Nick and her worst fears.

'Will you have a raki with me, Manoli?' she asked.

'Raki and beer? The grape and the grain, no, no, no, lady.'

'Then I won't drink the beer; let's share a raki, and my name's Angelika.'

Manoli raised his eyebrows. 'I like you,' he said, throwing one of his lewd winks.

'Oh, behave!' Angie laughed, sensing he put his flirtatious act on for all women. She wondered if the real Manoli ever showed himself. He brought a small bottle of raki, glasses, and a bowl of peanuts.

They chatted, easy banter, Manoli plying her with questions as usual.

Angie decided to interrogate him for a change. 'Manoli, tell me about the Kondulakis family, my family?'

'What you want to know?' He shared the raki between their glasses.

'*Yiayá*'s telling me about the war but it's quite a saga and very sad. She's asked me to write her story, what do you think about that?'

He frowned. 'Is difficult for me to say these things.'

'I speak Greek, Manoli, tell me your thoughts,' Angie said.

Manoli's face changed like a summer storm rolling in, dark clouds consuming the sunshine. He knocked back the raki, refilled his glass, and then spoke in his native tongue.

'If you write about the massacre, you must tell both sides of the story. There are government secrets that have never been disclosed, orders that were given. But it's easier to blame the Germans.' He exchanged a nod with a group of burly men dressed in black army fatigues, sitting on another table. 'What happened here, the account of the burning villages and the holocaust, was a tragedy. But who was responsible and why? That debate is open and still ongoing.'

'I don't understand, Manoli. Wasn't it the Nazis?'

'Let me ask you a few hypothetical questions, Angelika. At that time, Britain was as paranoid about communism as the Americans; the Cretan people were mostly communist. Do you think Britain was going to help liberate a communist island?'

Angie shook her head. 'I doubt it.'

'Britain couldn't have given a toss about this island, except for one thing; the south coast of Crete was the perfect place for British submarines to pick up fleeing British military, and the capitulated Italian leaders.'

Angie imagined a map of Europe. 'Where would they take them?'

'Egypt,' Manoli said. 'The British needed Crete, but not a Crete with socialist tendencies. Essentially, the Cretans had to be turned away from their political ideals, and what better way to do it than for the communist Andartes, freedom fighters of Crete, to be totally discredited?'

Angie frowned.

'Okay. You don't understand,' Manoli said. 'Let's say, hypothetically, there were two groups of freedom fighters in Crete, one lot taking their orders from Britain, the others made up of local communists. It's a fact anyway. But let's say the communist group received orders from the British group to kill the Germans in Simi, which was what they claimed. The actions of that communist group led directly to the reprisals, and the massacre.'

Manoli stood, walked around the table and sat down again.

'Job done! The communists are discredited and hated for causing murder and mayhem. The British led, capitalist Andartes had long since scarpered across the island and deny giving any orders. Of course, they condemn the communists for being hot headed, out of control, fools who caused the deaths of over five hundred innocent Cretans. You must realise that in World War Two, nearly as many civilian Greek lives were lost as the sum total of all the USA and the UK forces combined?'

Angie blinked at him, remembering how small Greece was, hardly larger than England itself, never mind the UK.

'It's true,' Manoli said, reading the doubt on her face. 'More than six hundred thousand Greek men, women and children were killed, while America and Britain together only lost seven hundred thousand, and they were mostly soldiers, not innocent villagers.' He banged his raki glass on the table and then knocked it back. 'But there's more, Angelika.'

Angie lifted her glass, realised it was empty, and watched Manoli fill it.

'The beach, along the way a little,' Manoli stuck his chin toward the distant sea. 'The beach of Keratokampou was perfect for evacuating the British and Italians to Egypt in submarines, but the Germans were up here at Simi, keeping a lookout. The British needed a local distraction big enough to pull all the Germans away from the beaches and lookout posts. The battle at Simi did exactly that.'

'Are you saying the British caused the Germans to send Nazi troops into the vicinity of Viannos, Manoli? Just to clear the beaches and discredit the communists?' Angie said.

'I'm giving you things to think about, Angelika, events you should investigate before you write about the history of Viannos. And ask yourself this: Two thousand enemy soldiers were gathered in this small area, and the British undoubtedly had that information. Their troops were near. So, why did they stand back and allow the atrocity to happen? Our allies should have followed the Nazis to Viannos and wiped them out. It was a great opportunity for them, but they choose to look the other way. Why was that?'

Angie shook her head, trying to take in the facts and unravel the logic.

'Right after our war with the Germans, we had civil war,' Manoli said. 'Then military rule, the junta. Two sides to every thing; the communists and the capitalists; the war and the Colonels. Our villages divided into political groups. You see it, even today, with the doors and the table colours.'

'What? I don't understand – the table colours?' Angie said.

'The kafenions, you can see which political party they support by the table paint. Red, Communist; blue, Democrat; green, Liberal; yellow, Socialist.'

Angie glanced at the yellow tabletop.

'And if you're going to write about your family, well . . . I was very young,' Manoli said. 'Only three years old when my parents were killed and things get changed a little each time they're told. You can't be sure of the truth unless you speak to the people involved.' He thrust his jaw, fists clenched.

'I'm sorry for your loss, Manoli. It's a tragedy to grow up without your parents.' Angie considered his age, perhaps early forties. 'I guess you won't remember my father? Can you tell me what divided the Lambrakis and the Kondulakis families?' She watched his face.

Manoli stared into the branches of the big tree, his mouth hard and his face angry for a moment before he spoke.

'You know the relationship between my father and your father? My mother was your father's sister-in-law, by marriage of course. When they killed her my mother . . .' Manoli's eyes narrowed to slits.

Confused, Angie tried to work out the family connection.

Killed his mother?! Who killed his mother? Was Manoli her cousin?

This was too much information to digest, she needed to think about what he said and work out what he meant. Was it possible that her father and his father were brothers? Manoli snatched a packet of Marlboro from the next table, lit a cigarette and inhaled deeply. 'When they killed my mother,' he said again, blowing out smoke, 'my father never got over it.' His face turned sour, eyes unfocused. 'That debt has not been paid.' He tossed the cigarette packet back to the men on the next table and nodded sharply.

What debt? Angie tried to keep up.

'You shouldn't ask these questions,' he said, breaking her thoughts. 'People spend decades trying to forget, and then you come here opening old wounds. I don't want to talk about it.' He stared into the distance. 'Anyway, going back to the war, you're too British. Nobody would tell you the truth behind the massacre of '43. It's easier to blame the Germans – everyone does – but if you dug deep enough, Angelika, you would find another story. Let it go. You don't know where it could lead.'

Angie recognised bitterness in his eyes and remembered her mother using almost the same words. Could she prompt him to explain further?

The men in black shouted, 'Coffee, Manoli!'

He flinched, his gaze flicked to Angie, irate, yet she suspected relieved to be distracted. 'I'll be back,' he said.

Angie waited but the kafenion tables filled and, knowing he wouldn't have time for her, she returned to Amiras.

It seemed everyone she met had a story about her family. But, at the source of the puzzle, she realised there were dark secrets that nobody wanted to share. She didn't doubt *Yiayá* would tell her, but the old lady tired easily. Recalling the terrible events was so exhausting for her. Angie feared she was putting too much on her dear grandmother, even though they only covered a short episode each time.

And Angie's departure loomed ever closer.

Chapter 22

Disappointed and frustrated by her trip into Viannos, Angie pulled over to the side of the main road, next to the war memorial. Unsettled by Nick and the transitions manager in her home, and then by Manoli's words, she was even more confused.

Was Manoli trying to say the local people blamed the British for the massacre? She wondered if that was true; but if it were, why would her mother run away to England?

Angie stared at the simple marble figures that lined the road. She blinked sadly at the list of names engraved down each slab, wanting to find baby Petro's name, and her great-great-grandfather, Matthia. But if Stavro was leaving for Athens, and Nick managed to get Poppy to call Crete, she had to return to her grandmother's at once.

Again, she hated the idea that she was going to hurt Poppy, but she couldn't go home and see her so unbearably miserable. Her mother deserved more out of life. She had always been completely selfless, bringing up Angie, never complaining. Now, the time had come for Angie to repay that kindness.

At the top of the cement steps, next to Maria's house, Angie paused and stared across the village to the monument. It seemed to beckon her.

'Angelika, come!' Voula shouted.

Angie turned into the cottage garden and found Demitri swinging a long-handled *skapáni.* 'What are you doing, digging in the afternoon sun, Demitri?' she asked.

Demitri nodded at his son, Young Mattie, who leaned on a shovel. 'We're planting your lemon tree, Angelika.' He swung at the hard dry ground between the two olive trees.

The ten-year-old shovelled away loose earth, struggling with the weight. His knees turned in and his back bent. Young Mattie glanced over his shoulder at Angie and she saw the pride in eyes.

Yiayá, *Papoú* and Voula sat in garden chairs and watched. Each gave instructions on how to dig the hole.

'Deeper, Demitri,' *Yiayá* said.

'Wider, for the roots,' *Papoú* said

'Don't forget the fertiliser,' Voula said.

'Not giving me any advice, Angelika?' Demitri asked.

'I suspect you're getting enough already,' Angie said and laughed. 'And I believe you know what you're doing.'

'I'm glad somebody does.' Demitri swung the pick again but a judder went through his body as he struck something solid. 'Feels like another rock.' He levered the *skapáni* blade under the obstacle and pushed. 'Get your shovel right under and push with me, son. Let's see if we can lift it.'

They worked together and then Demitri fell to his knees on the loose earth.

'It's not a rock,' he said, shifting the soil.

The boy knelt opposite his father while they scraped the dirt away. The object was the same colour as the red-brown soil, but it took shape as the dry clods crumbled.

'Virgin Mary, it's a machine gun,' Demitri said.

Papoú crossed himself three times.

Maria placed both hands flat over her face and whimpered.

Young Mattie jumped to his feet, hopping with excitement. 'Let me hold it, Papa. Let me hold it, please!'

Demitri seemed stunned and, while his mind wandered, he let his son take the rusted gun from his hands. The boy pulled it to his shoulder and, grinning wildly, yelled, 'Rat-tat-tat-tat-tat!' as he swung an imaginary death arc over everyone.

Yiayá gasped, horror spread over her face.

Papoú and Voula both launched from their chairs and attempted to protect Maria by blocking her view of the weapon, but she slapped their hands away and then peered up at the ridge.

'Petro, my poor baby,' Maria whispered.

Demitri swung the flat of his hand at Young Mattie, immediately startled when the swipe knocked the child off his feet and sent the gun flying into the dirt.

Maria stared at her great-grandson lying on the ground. 'No, no!' She shook her head, closing her eyes, a warble of hysteria in her voice.

Angie ran into the kitchen and brought a glass of water. When she returned, she found *Yiayá* crying, her sobs broken by stuttered words. Maria grabbed Angie's wrist, ignoring the glass as it fell and smashed.

'You see, Angelika, it's an omen,' the old woman said. 'What happened here can't stay buried. Tell my story; you understand me? Write my story so that the world knows what happened. And tell the truth, promise me that, Angelika.'

Papoú seemed confused. 'Let's move to the table, old woman.'

Yiayá patted the front of his shirt, her tears rising. 'I wish you had seen him, Vassili.' Her face turned up to her husband. 'Your son, he was such a beautiful baby. Why did it happen to us?'

'Who understands God's plan, Maria?' Vassili said. 'It's a mystery,' he spoke in his calm and steady way. 'Anyway, Petro never truly left us, did he? Even today, he's here.' He thumped his heart, the tremor shook brimming tears from his eyes and sent them tracing along the crags of his life-worn face.

Angie found the moment terribly poignant. She filled with leaden sadness, far heavier than painful words or tears. How long could such suffering torture the people she had come to love? An entire lifetime? Her heart went out to her grandparents as she helped them move to the cracked marble table and settle themselves.

Demitri took Young Mattie to the far end of the garden and spoke quietly to him. Angie was moved to see him hug his son and then kiss him on the cheeks. The boy came over to his great-grandmother.

'I'm sorry, *Pro Yiayá*, I was being silly. I didn't mean to upset you,' Young Mattie said, staring at his trainers.

Maria patted his shoulder and nodded.

Voula brought raki; her answer to most problems. Everyone watched *Papoú* pour a half glass and then slide it towards Young Mattie.

Angie recognised the importance of the gesture, a coming of age for the boy. She felt quite proud to witness the occasion. *Papoú* slammed his glass down and said, '*Yammas!*' and Maria, Demitri, and Young Mattie did the same, his eyes flicking to Angie as he sat straight and sipped his drink.

She smiled and threw him a wink, which made him grin. 'I wondered if you could help me with my Greek, Mattie?' she said.

'You speak well, Aunty,' he replied in perfect English.

'Thanks, but I don't understand many of the local words. Perhaps if I wrote the problematic ones down, you could translate them for me? When you have time, of course.'

He nodded, sitting even taller.

Demitri gave her a grateful smile and also sat straighter.

Later, when the rest of the family arrived everyone gathered around the cracked marble table, tension between Stavro and Matthia escalated, flaring and dying over minutiae, each jibe stronger than the last. Angie fretted about Nick, their jobs, the damn woman intruding on her home territory and perhaps encroaching on her future husband.

As if that wasn't enough, every time she looked at Maria, she remembered Matthia had disappeared from his hiding place. She imagined her grandmother's torment and wanted to hear what had happened to the little boy.

On top of everything, she wondered what Manoli had meant at the kafenion: because she was British they wouldn't tell her the truth. What rubbish was that? She struggled to accept that blame for the local massacre lay at Britain's door. But then again . . .

Poor Maria, Angie thought.

Until the appearance of the gun, Angie had accepted the war story as an emotional and tragic tale. Now she realised those past events lived with these people on a daily basis. Just seeing the monument on the ridge every day must bring the atrocities to mind again and again.

Matthia and Demitri sat on the wall at the bottom of the garden having a heated discussion, occasionally glancing her way, their hands animated, angry voices subdued. Stavro looked over at them and frowned. Angie caught his eye. He glanced towards heaven and said, 'Don't worry; it's not your fault.'

What wasn't her fault?

Should she go over and talk to them? She stood.

'Best leave it, Angelika,' Stavro said.

‘I don’t understand,’ Angie said, dismayed, her emotions welling dangerously close to the surface.

‘Matthia needs to vent his anger, he’ll be okay, let him get on with it.’

What’s he angry about now?

Suddenly, Angie recalled the letters from Stavro in the spare bedroom of Poppy’s house. Probably, she thought, Stavro knew Poppy better than anybody if they had kept in touch for so many years.

‘Uncle Stavro, I still don’t know why Mam left here, or what has made her so unhappy. I’ve organised for my fiancé to get Mam to videocall *Yiayá*, on my tablet later, so they can see each other and talk. Is there any reason why he shouldn’t do that? I don’t want to make matters worse.’

Stavro frowned at her, then at the tablet, then at *Yiayá*. ‘You mean, live?’

Angie nodded, trying to read his expression.

‘Now?’

Angie nodded again. For the first time, she saw him looking a little unsure of himself, which stirred her unease. She wondered if she should call off the entire event.

Stavro’s face relaxed. ‘I can’t see any reason why not. I’m sure it would make your grandmother very happy.’

‘But what about my mother? I don’t want to hurt her,’ Angie said.

He thought for a moment, shrugged and shook his head. ‘What harm can it do? It would be quite incredible for us all to see her, but I’m finding it hard to accept that Poppy would call.’

Angie’s worry that she was making a huge mistake, and knowing she was crossing a line, continued to battle with her determination to ease her mother’s pain and unhappiness.

The stress of the afternoon, along with Voula's homemade pasta in fresh tomato sauce, gave Angie a bout of indigestion. Demitri and Matthia returned to the table. The supermarket man offered embarrassed smiles and her uncle glanced daggers at every opportunity.

Angie was grateful for the distraction when her tablet chimed into life.

'It's Nick, everybody, my fiancé. He's at Mam's. *Yiayá*, *Papoú*, come and speak to Mam.' Angie, ashamed of her bout of jealousy, longed to see Nick, and at the same time, she worried about her mother's reaction to the videocall.

Yiayá hadn't said a word since they all sat together. Her face brightened when Angie slid onto the cushion next to her. All the effort to unite her mother and grandmother was about to come into fruition. Angie recognised this moment as one of the most important times in her life.

Her insides felt fluttery with excitement and nerves. At last, Maria and Poppy would see each other!

Matthia pulled a cigarette packet from his pocket and returned to the wall at the end of the garden. Angie smiled in his direction. His grumpiness, bad as it was, couldn't destroy the bond between them all. He would return, she knew it.

Once again, Angie thought about her phone call to Nick. She had been stupid. Nick was as honest and trustworthy as she could ever hope.

Truly sorry she had given him a hard time, she touched her eyes, damming tears as the Skype application chimed. Now, everything would be perfect because her mother and her grandmother were about to be united after forty years.

Smiling, Angie took a huge breath as the picture came into focus.

The anxiety on Nick's face, and the hospital's Accident & Emergency sign in the background, poleaxed her. 'What's the matter, Nick! What's going on?!' she gasped, feeling her skin shrink in fear.

'It's Poppy,' Nick said. 'So sorry, Angie, really sorry. I did all I could.'

Chapter 23

'Nick! What's happened!' Angie cried hysterically.

'They got her back, Angie,' he said breathlessly. 'The paramedics, they got her back; restarted her heart.' He put his hand over his eyes and Angie could see he'd snapped. After a few seconds, he could speak again. 'Don't worry. She's in good hands now. I'm outside the hospital. They made me turn my phone off in the A&E. I've got to go back inside and wait for the doctor to come back to me, but I thought you should know straight away.'

'Mam!' Angie gasped, staring at Nick.

Matthia returned to the table. Agapi had appeared and squeezed onto the end of the seat. Voula pushed up, squashing Angie against *Yiayá*, who also recognised the medical background. They all crossed themselves. The men sat opposite and watched Angie. The women's wide-eyed faces crowded together and peered at the tablet.

'What do you mean, "They got her back", Nick? Exactly what's happened, how is she? I'll get a flight, come back right away –'

'Don't panic, Angie. The worst's over. Trust me, I'm dealing with it.'

'I know you are, I know. But tell me?'

'I tried to persuade Poppy to speak to everyone there, like you wanted, but she wouldn't. I told her the real reason you had gone to Crete was to bring you all together and it was so important to you.' He pushed at the furrows in his brow and blew his cheeks out. 'Poppy got upset, all emotional. She started crying and then the colour drained out of her. I'm not kidding, Angie, her face was grey, and she had awful pains in her chest and down her arm. She couldn't breathe, couldn't stand. I was afraid . . . God! A nightmare. She looked terrible. I guessed she was having a heart attack so I literally picked her up and carried her to the car. Luckily, the traffic wasn't too bad. I raced straight to the General's A&E.'

'Oh Nick, poor you! I'm ashamed, please forgive me. What happened when you arrived? Was it a heart attack?' she stammered. Her mother had nearly died because of her! This was all her fault! Her conniving, self-centred fault! She had caused Poppy too much distress. The videocall was bound to horrify her, Angie had known it. Convincing herself the result would be worthwhile was no excuse.

'I pulled into the ambulance bay, but she was unconscious and I couldn't get her out of the car. The paramedics raced over with a gurney and a defibrillator. She'd gone, Angie. Oh my God! The worst moment of my life.' He choked on the words. 'Give me a minute, will you?'

He lowered the phone and, through her tears, Angie could see people rushing into the hospital. 'But she's all right now?' she asked the moment he came back on screen.

He nodded and sighed and she recognised the awful strain on his face. 'I wish I hadn't put you in this situation, darling,' she sobbed. 'Thank goodness you were there.' Things could have been much worse. She shuddered to think of Poppy on the floor, alone. It was four days before Angie would have returned to London.

Although Nick had done a great job, it should have been Angie taking care of her mother. Would Poppy ever forgive her?

In her selfishness, Angie had marched arrogantly on, never contemplating that she might be making things worse.

One guilty thought after another fell on Angie until she swore to God she would concentrate on being less self-centred and manipulating, so long as her mother recovered soon.

'She's a bit better,' Nick said. 'They've taken her to cardiology. Jesus Christ Almighty, Angie, I never want to go through that again.'

Angie looked up up to see everyone crossing themselves. 'Sorry, sorry,' she said, glancing around the table before returning to her fiancé on the phone. 'Then what happened, Nick?'

'They made me go and park the car. By the time I returned, the cardiologist was with Poppy.'

'How's Mam now?'

'They're doing tests at the moment.' He looked at his watch. 'Call me back in exactly half an hour, Angie, I'll know more then. My battery's low. I've got to turn the phone off and go back inside now. I don't want to miss the specialist. Love you, sweetheart. Try not to worry too much.'

The connection broke. Angie gulped and tried to gather her self-control before she looked into the faces of her Cretan family. 'Poor Mam,' she muttered.

Stavro turned and stared at the horizon. After a long silence, he blew his nose, glanced at his watch and turned to face them again. 'We'll call Nick at two o'clock. Voula, make some coffee.'

Voula scuttled to the kitchen. Stavro demanded everyone's attention, 'Listen, everybody! Poppy will be fine. It's been twenty years since the same thing happened to me and treatment is much better these days. Nick's right, we should try not to worry.'

They all stared at him, wanting to believe, afraid, speechless.

Angie said, 'Mam's never had a problem with her heart before.' She turned to Stavro. 'Do you think it might be hereditary? I think it's important that Nick tells the specialist about *your* heart – I didn't know about it until now.'

'It could be the same trouble, but then maybe not. We mustn't jump to conclusions. There's no reason to think it's a family weakness, or that there's any genetic link. After all, your grand-parents both seem to have strong hearts,' Stavro said.

Voula returned with frappés for everyone. Angie noticed an odd look exchanged between her and Matthia. Voula's shoulders dropped.

'What do you think, Uncle Matthia?' Angie asked.

He shrugged and, without answering, stomped off back down the garden to smoke another cigarette.

Voula handed out coffee and then exclaimed, 'Somebody should tell Angelika! Perhaps it *is* hereditary!' She sounded angry. They all shuffled in their seats, throwing glances at each other before lowering their eyes.

Angie looked from one to the other. Shut out again. She broke the silence.

'I must check flights to the UK, so I'm prepared, in case the doctor thinks I should go back.'

Will you ever forgive me, Mam?

Angie glanced at her watch; time crawled. 'Can I use the house phone, *Yiayá*?'

'You can, *koritsie*. The phonebook's on the living room shelf.'

Ten minutes later, Angie came back into the garden. 'There's a flight at eight o'clock tonight. I'll call Nick, see what's happening.'

Tension mounted, even Voula remained quiet. Nick answered her call and said the heart specialist had returned. He explained that Angie was Poppy's daughter before handing the phone over to him.

'We have everything under control and Mrs Lambrakis is stable,' the specialist confirmed. 'I'm logging her in for a balloon angioplasty tomorrow afternoon. She may need surgery; we're doing tests now, just to be on the safe side we'll be prepared.'

'Thank you,' Angie replied. 'I'm sorry, but what's a balloon angioplasty? How serious is it? Should I get a flight home? Is she in pain?'

'Ah, yes, one thing at a time.' Angie heard impatience in the doctor's voice. 'Briefly, a balloon angioplasty means we'll insert a small balloon on the end of a catheter and inflate it to widen the arterial lumen. It's a common procedure for angina.' He spoke to somebody away from the phone then said, 'We may fit a stent – a small tube to keep the artery open. Should you come home? Not for me to say. There's always a certain amount of risk with any surgery – if she does need surgery. You'll probably feel better if you're here. Mrs Lambrakis is conscious but sedated and comfortable. I'll inform the ward sister that you can see her up until her pre-med. That's if we do decide to go ahead and operate.'

'Does that mean more than the angioplasty?'

'Excuse me.' He spoke to somebody else again, and then said, 'Yes, we may decide on something more, perhaps a bypass. It's impossible to say at this moment. Now, I must go. Try not to worry, it won't make any difference.'

'Her brother has a stent and had a bypass,' Angie said.

'That's useful information.'

Angie thanked the doctor and ended the call, fearing she had forgotten to ask a terribly important question.

She worked out her timescale. 'I'll have to leave Viannos at about five o'clock. I'll phone the airport and book a ticket.' She glanced around the silent faces and remembered Voula's words.

'Uncle Matthia, will you come with me? Mam would love to see you. I'm insured, so it would be a free ticket.'

Matthia's face pinched. 'Why would Poppy want to see me? She hasn't bothered for all these years. Go by yourself.'

'Honestly! You and Mam are so alike. Can't you be nice, just for once?' Angie snarled, at once regretting it. 'Sorry, I didn't mean . . . I'm worried . . .' Hot tears spilled and she swiped them away quickly.

Matthia glared, struggled to his feet and marched out of the garden.

'He'd love to go,' Voula said, 'but he doesn't have a passport.'

'I'd like to come with you, Angelika,' Stavro said, 'but I don't have the money and – forgive me – I can't believe your insurance will cover the ticket.'

'Look, Uncle Stavro, your seat will cost less than my room and the car hire for the rest of the week, so please let me get it for you. I think if Mam saw you again, in person, it would do her more good than any medicine. You'd be doing us all a favour.'

Stavro stood and glanced to where Matthia had stormed from the garden. 'Give me an hour to decide, Angelika?'

'Of course I will – and don't fret about your brother. I'll talk to him.' Angie's organisational skills were underway. She could rise to a challenge and keep calm in a crisis. Now over the initial shock, she could handle the situation as sensibly as anyone.

Stavro nodded and followed Matthia.

'Voula, I need to show you how this works.' She tapped her tablet. 'I'm going to give it to Uncle Matthia so he can call us in England.'

'But you can't leave your laptop, Angelika, they're so expensive,' Voula said.

'No, Aunty, it's a tablet. Don't worry, I want to be able to call you.'

'Will I be able to see Poppy, Angelika?' Maria asked. Angie turned to her grandparents, both visibly upset. They hadn't spoken since Nick's call. Angie told them exactly what had happened.

Maria placed her hand on Angie's cheek. 'I want to go to England and see my daughter, Angelika, but haven't a passport either. Anyway, I don't think I'd make it. Can you fix it so I see her on that contraption of yours? Then I can die in peace.'

Vassili nodded. 'Me too,' he said.

Angie gasped. '*Yiayá, Papoú*, please don't talk like that. It frightens me. I promise that even if I have to catch Mam asleep in bed, you'll see her as soon as possible.'

Maria stared at the tablet, then her eyes met Angie's. 'Will I really see her, Angelika? I can hardly believe it – it's impossible to explain how I feel.'

Vassili also nodded at the tablet. 'You probably take that thing for granted, Angelika, but it's like a miracle to us. My little girl left here so long ago. Often, I sit here and stare at the bus stop.' He lifted his head towards the rickety shack on the ridge next to the monument. 'I imagine how I would feel if I saw her get off the airport bus. And now you say we can speak to her on your television thing.' He shook his head. 'Poppy has no idea how much I miss her. Fathers and daughters, there's always a special bond between them, hey? You'll see, soon enough.' He nodded at her belly.

Angie's eyes widened. *Soon enough?* He seemed to be implying she was already pregnant.

Vassili blew his nose and then told Voula to bring raki.

When the old folk had calmed, Stavro returned.

'I'd like to accept your offer, Angelika. I haven't seen my sister for forty years,' he said. 'And I've never been to London.'

Angie smiled. 'Thank you. I'm so pleased.'

She set up a Hotmail account for Matthia, taped instructions onto the back of the tablet, and then went in search of him.

She found him in the kafenion.

'Uncle Matthia, please, let's call a truce. I can't take this anymore,' Angie said, approaching him.

A group of middle-aged men, playing cards, stared at her.

'Uncle Matthia?'

'I heard you, I'm not deaf.'

'How about it, what do you say? I'm worried about Mam and I don't have time for this aggravation. Can you help me with something?'

Matthia sucked on his moustache and glared. 'How could I help you? You seem quite capable of helping yourself.'

'Why are you always so horrid to me?' Angie pulled out a rickety chair, nodded at the kafenion owner, and ordered a small bottle of raki.

'Uncle Matthia, *Yiayá* is desperate to see my mother, and between us we have the power and the technology to make that happen. Aren't they more important than us? Can we put our differences aside, please, for their sakes?'

Matthia stared at the tabletop.

He's like a sulky child, Angie thought, before she tried again. 'I understand that you love Mam and she loves you. I also realise she's hurt you. Nobody will explain what it's all about and, to be honest, I'm totally pissed off at being shut out. I'm family too and I have a right to know what's going on.' Frustrated when he didn't respond, she took a breath and continued. 'I didn't come here to cause trouble, Uncle, or make you angry. I just wanted to meet you, and my family, and find out if there was a way to lessen my mother's heartache. I love her! Can't you help me?'

'You make us look foolish with your modern ways.'

'Sorry, I didn't intend to embarrass anybody.' Angie put her hand on the tablet. 'This is new technology and somebody had to teach me how to use it. Now I want to show you.'

Matthia glanced up to her face, almost met her eyes, but then diverted to his raki glass.

'You can try, but I'm not saying I'll do it,' he said.

Twenty minutes later, a reluctant Matthia had mastered it. 'Great!' Angie said, 'You've got it, Uncle. I've written the instructions on the back in case you come unstuck. It took a few goes before I understood it, and I got very frustrated, but you'll probably get it right first time.'

He seemed placated, and then he shocked her by gently placing his hands over hers.

'I realise you don't understand, *koritsie*,' he said. 'It's the past, but it doesn't go away, all the pain and regret. If I didn't care, it wouldn't hurt so much.'

Angie heard such sadness in his voice. She looked from his hands to his face and saw the bitterness in his eyes replaced by sorrow. 'Oh, Uncle, I wish I did understand. If only somebody would explain.' She glanced at the kafenion clock. 'But I have to go now. Can we part friends? Please?'

Matthia nodded, slammed his glass down and then raised it. '*Yammas*, Angelika, safe journey.' His eyes locked on to hers. She had a strong impression he wanted to say more.

'What?' she said.

'Come back, before your wedding,' he said.

'I will, as soon as I can.'

'Listen to me, Angelika. It's important ... *Come back before your wedding!*'

Slightly startled, Angie nodded, kissed his cheek and left him alone at the tin table.

Back at the cottage, Angie stared at Stavro's luggage. 'Sorry, Uncle, I had you down for a cabin bag. I didn't realise . . .'

'Ah, I see, but I need a suitcase, Angelika.' His eyes swivelled in the direction of Maria and Vassili. 'Your grandparents want to send things to help with Poppy's recovery.'

'What's in there, anyway?' She caught the mischievous twinkle in his eye, uplifting after all the stress of the afternoon.

'You'll be sorry you asked. All kinds of our local food, olive products, and Demitri's wine, and all Voula's photos of Poppy and Yeorgo. We'll need to copy them and bring the originals back.'

'You're too generous. The gifts will make Mam feel better. Thank you.' She was pleased to have the photographs. She glanced around the cottage, stepped outside and looked up at the ridge. Maria watched her. Their eyes met

'Can I come back, *Yiayá*?'

'I'll be waiting for you, Angelika. Don't leave it too long.'

Angie understood that the words were more than simple politeness. 'Thank you. I'll return as soon as I can.'

'I know, *koritsie*. Don't come alone, I haven't much time.'

Angie listened to Maria's poignant words, wrapped the old lady in a gentle hug and kissed her damp cheeks. 'Thank you,' she whispered. 'I'm sorry I didn't come sooner.'

'It's important, *koritsie* . . .'

'I wish –'

'I know. Go now.'

Chapter 24

London, Present Day.

OUTSIDE HEATHROW'S ARRIVALS, Angie ran into Nick's arms. 'I've missed you so much.' She squeezed him tightly. 'How's Mam?'

'She's okay, doing better. They've decided on a stent.' Nick glanced past Angie. He squared his shoulders and stood taller. 'I think you'd better introduce us. I'm guessing that's Uncle Stavro standing with the suitcases?'

Angie grabbed Nick's hand and tugged him towards her uncle.

'Uncle Stavro, I want you to meet my fiancé, Nick.' The men shook hands, kissed cheeks and slapped one another on the back. Stavro gripped Nick's shoulders and stared him in the face. The head of Angie's family approving the man she would marry. The traditional salute meant such a lot to Angie. Acceptance. Stavro's nod and the twinkle in his eye came as a ray of sunshine on a stormy night.

Nick drove them to the hospital. Angie watched the windshield wipers slap a melancholy heartbeat. Poor Poppy.

She remembered Crete, that star-studded evening, the pleasure of eating with them all, and the dancing. Her grandmother's happiness, and above all, the camaraderie of her family. The occasion brought a strong sense of belonging to Angie's life.

Angie continued to fret about her mother, as she had since the moment she heard the news, in Amiras. The thought that Poppy might have died was like a kick in the chest that she would never recover from. She tried to push the debilitating thought away and, for a moment, concentrate on Nick, as he drove. Her poor fiancé looked terrible, completely worn out. His skin was pale, he needed a shave, and he had dark bags under his eyes like she had never seen before. *He* looked like a heart attack waiting to happen, she thought, horrified.

Nick must be out of his mind with worry about his job. He had enough to deal with, without Angie accusing him of having an affair and his future mother-in-law collapsing at his feet. With the added pressure of house buying and the wedding on top of all that, no wonder he appeared stressed out and exhausted.

In a flash, Angie saw it all. She had asked too much of the people she loved. Hadn't she inherited any of her grandmother's spirit, the selfless need to better the lives of others? Had she ever made a real sacrifice for anybody? Sick and ashamed, she swore to herself she could change, it wasn't too late, and that change would start here and now in the car.

She wanted to tell Nick that their goals, which were really her goals – the house, the job, the wedding, even the babies – weren't crucial. That the people she loved were healthy, happy and above all, united, they were the important things. Together, Nick and Angie could change plans, and work things out. They'd talked about starting their own editing service, but she'd discouraged him, claiming it was better to aim for promotion, at least until they had a mortgage in place. So, her ever-loving Nick had abandoned his plans and taken Angie's advice.

Now, with the shock of Poppy collapsing, and the horrible thought that she could have died, Angie's priorities had taken a sharp turn. She would move back home for a while to take care of her mother. She wondered how Nick would feel. He would come to live at Mam's too, if she asked him, but was that going to add to his pressure?

Angie wanted to be alone with Nick, to talk all these things through, but with Stavro there such a personal discussion would be impossible. Then it occurred to her, what they really needed was a proper date. Some time by themselves – with no distractions – to discuss their future. She would set it up for tomorrow evening. Somewhere special. They would arrive separately, and go home to the flat together. She sighed audibly.

'You all right?' Nick asked, glancing sideways before returning to his driving.

'Yes,' she said. 'Just thinking.' She lowered her voice to a whisper. 'Are you free tomorrow evening?'

'I hope so,' he said forlornly, still focused on the road. 'Why? What can I do for you?'

'A date, after work, 7.30 at Chez Henri? I'll meet you at the bar.' She tried to lighten the mood but the worry about her mother killed the humour and her words fell flat. 'I'll be carrying a red rose.'

'Forget the rose, just tell me what you'll be wearing,' he whispered back, understanding where she was coming from and playing along. 'In detail.' His face lifted with a tired smile, the bags under his eyes bulging in the streetlights.

'We'll get through this, Nick,' she said sadly.

He nodded, keeping his eyes on the road.

They continued to the hospital in silence. Her concern for Poppy gathered strength. Once there, the night sister said, 'You can look in on Mrs Lambrakis for a moment, but don't wake her. You may visit tomorrow until noon.'

Nick's phone rang. He turned it off without looking at it.

‘Thanks,’ Angie said quietly. He put his arm around her and gave a squeeze.

They peeked in on Poppy. Asleep, she appeared drawn with dark circles under her eyes. Her hair, lank, fell away from her face, and an unhealthy sheen glistened on her forehead. Angie felt sick. She wanted to gather her mother in a hug, take away her pain, and ask forgiveness.

Outside the hospital, Angie buried her face in Nick’s chest. Nick, understanding words weren’t necessary, simply held her tightly while she gathered herself together. The north wind gusted around them and, after a minute, Angie gently pushed away from his embrace.

‘Feeling better?’ Nick asked, lifting her chin.

Nodding, she whispered, ‘Thank you,’ and pecked him on the cheek.

On the way home in the car, Angie said, ‘You’re very quiet, Uncle Stavro.’

‘I’m in shock, Angelika. I expected to see a mature version of the sister that left Crete forty years back, but she’s an old woman.’

‘Better not let Mam hear you say that, she’ll kill you.’ Again, Angie tried to lighten the moment.

Stavro didn’t laugh. ‘I can’t believe I made the same mistake again.’

‘Again?’

‘My old brain’s shutting down, *koritsie*. Only last week I searched for . . . someone.’

‘Yes?’

‘Yes, someone special that I hadn’t seen for years. I had a picture of a young man in my head and he must be quite old now. I’m a fool,’ Stavro said.

* * *

The next morning, Angie couldn't concentrate on anything. Despite three aspirins and a strong coffee, a headache pounded across her brow. Nick had gone to work and she needed a diversion from the long day ahead. Nothing could be gained from fretting about Poppy. Yet she found it impossible to put her mother out of her mind.

Stavro wandered into the kitchen.

'Morning, Uncle. Sorry there's no Greek coffee. Would you like tea, or instant?'

'Do you have any NoyNoy, Angelika?'

Angie shook her head. 'I don't think so, what is it?'

'You know, milk in a tin? I mix half a glass with hot water for breakfast. Most villagers do if they haven't any fresh goat's milk.'

'Ah, evap. Yes of course. I'll buy more, later. Sorry, but there's no chance of Mam keeping a goat in her precious garden. She keeps that lawn mowed to within an inch of its life.' They both laughed. 'Let's see now, where's the can opener?' She yanked the junk drawer open. As her hand closed around the kitchen utensil, her eyes fell on the old mobile, an emergency pay as you go that always had credit. She could give it to her uncle, in case he needed to contact her, but then the seed of an idea germinated.

She pulled the phone out, plugged in the charger and checked the credit.

* * *

Two hours later, Angie and Stavro were inside the hospital. The harsh lights, acres of glass and hard acoustics fuelled Angie's tension.

Stavro squeezed her arm. 'Trust me, she'll be fine.'

'I'd rather not shock her by us walking in together, Uncle. Do you mind if I see how she is first?'

'I'll stay in the corridor. Call when you're ready, Angelika. If you don't think she's up to it, I'll wait a few days.'

Poppy was asleep, a monitor pegged to her finger. A colourful bunch of mixed flowers stood on her bedside locker.

Angie worried about her mother's hay fever.

Overhead, a notice said: NIL BY MOUTH and an LCD screen blipped technical information in a language known only to the medical profession.

Poppy looked so vulnerable that Angie wanted to hug her tightly. She held her hand instead. Then she reached into her bag and hooked her fingers over her smartphone. She had called it from the old mobile earlier and saved the number. All she had to do was press redial. She hoped this cunning plan would divulge her mother's secrets without causing more distress. Then she could concentrate on bringing peace to Poppy.

Maria's words returned: *And you think if I tell you what Poppy doesn't want you to know, it will make her feel better?*

Angie hesitated, and then slid the phone behind a water jug on the bedside locker.

* * *

Poppy drifted up from a deep sleep. Remembering she was in hospital, she didn't open her eyes. Poor Nick, she thought, recalling his horror when the crushing pain in her chest spread down her left arm and she could hardly breathe. She didn't have to tell him it was a heart attack. He swooped her up and almost ran to the car. God knew where he got the strength, but he had certainly saved her life. She would always be grateful to him.

Smiling, Poppy thought fondly of him. Angelika had done well. Suddenly, she sensed a presence in the room. She opened her eyes, confused when her daughter came into focus. Hadn't Angelika gone to Crete? Her head filled with questions but she only voiced one.

'Angelika, what are you doing here?' Her throat, dry as sand, meant the words sounded rough.

'You didn't think I'd stay in Crete with my mother in hospital, did you?' Angelika kissed her.

The brush of her daughter's lips did Poppy more good than all the hospital treatments in the world.

'How are you, Mam?' Angelika asked.

'All the better for seeing you, love. Truly, I haven't felt so well in a long time.' The warmth of her daughter's hand in hers gave her strength. 'How was Crete?' she asked, closing her eyes, afraid of what she might hear. Had they told her the truth as they knew it? The monitor on the wall bleeped.

'Mam. I really didn't mean to upset you so much with that call,' Angelika said. 'I'm very sorry.'

Poppy ignored the apology. 'How's everybody?' She *had* to know.

'They made me very welcome. *Yiayá* told me amazing stories about the war. Everyone sends their love and wishes for a speedy recovery. They all said how they missed you, Mam. They've sent a suitcase full of gifts to help you get better.'

Poppy noticed that Angelika's eyes were intense, sparkling, exactly like Yeorgo's. Her heart skipped a beat. The monitor bleeped again.

'They're incredibly generous.' Angelika chewed her lip. 'The presents are at home, but I've brought something from Voula. I thought you might like it on your locker. She told me to say: "Remember the day?"'

Poppy smiled. Voula, always concerned about the welfare of others, always laughing. Memories trickled back, but then she sensed her daughter's tension.

Angelika hesitated, then shoved a crumpled bag at her. 'Sorry it's not wrapped.'

Poppy pulled out a framed portrait. 'Oh, Angelika,' she said, staring at the wedding photograph. Yeorgo, so handsome, stood at her side in the church doorway. 'Thank you,' she whispered. 'This was the most wonderful day of my life. Just look at your father. Wasn't he the most perfect man on earth? And do you know what, Angelika? You are so like him. Not only in looks, but temperament too.'

Poppy's daughter blinked. 'You've never talked about him before, Mam. It means a lot to me, please don't stop. Tell me more.'

Poppy squeezed her hand. She found the effort draining, but worth it. 'What can I say? You know how you feel about Nick, well, multiply that by a million, and that's me and your father.'

With her emotions rising, Poppy realised how precious Angelika was to her, and how her own mother must have loved her, all those years ago. She wondered if she had faded from Maria's memory after so long. For the first time, she really understood the pain that she had caused Maria when she left Crete, swearing never to return.

Poppy tried to recall the last thing she said to her mother. A strange sense of panic came over her when she couldn't remember. Then the moment returned, sharp and vivid. Words shouted over her shoulder as she ran out of the cottage.

Forget me, Mama. Forget I ever existed!

How would she react if Angelika said that to her, or if Angelika hadn't returned from Crete? If Poppy never saw her daughter again . . . she would go crazy. Her eyes brimmed. Who would eat her cherry cake?

'I'm sorry, Mam. I didn't mean . . .' Angelika misread the tears and passed a tissue.

'No, no need. You and your good intentions,' Poppy grumbled. 'You really must learn to mind your own business.' A smile played on her lips as she stared at the picture. 'We were a beautiful couple, don't you think, Angelika?' She wanted to say more to her daughter, but couldn't. 'Put it on the locker for me, so that I can see it.' She fiddled with the edge of the hospital sheet and silence returned to the room.

'Give me your hand,' she said to Angelika.

After spending more than half her life practically alone, Poppy found it difficult to speak while emotional, unless she could draw on anger. She battled to keep her voice steady.

'Angelika, listen to me, the mortgage is paid and the house deeds are in your name, just in case.' Angelika's hand squeezed. 'And if I don't come out of surgery this afternoon,' Poppy continued, 'you go straight back to Crete and tell Mama I *never* stopped loving her.' Breathless, she closed her eyes, panting, relieved the words were said. 'I never stopped loving her. Have you got that? Remember, it's very important.'

'Don't talk like that. There's no "just in case", Mam. You'll be fine.' Poppy could hear her daughter's battle to keep her voice even. 'I promise you, Mam, they do these operations every single day.'

'You never know.'

'That was mad, but very kind, the house thing . . . Thanks,' Angelika said.

'It'll save you doing it later,' Poppy said.

'Stop it, Mam! You'll be home and on the mend in a matter of days.'

Poppy nodded at the photograph. 'He was beautiful, your father. I'd loved him even as a child, always dreamt of becoming his wife.' She squeezed Angelika's fingers. 'That kind of love never fades, but I believe you know that.'

'Please tell me about your wedding, Mam?'

'One day, but not now, Angelika. Perhaps when I get home.' Poppy closed her eyes and recalled the run-up to her marriage, all those years ago.

Chapter 25

Crete, 1962.

Poppy clutched her stomach. The cramping pains of her first period made her want to stay in bed.

'Come on, don't act like a child, you're a woman now, Poppy,' Mama said kindly. 'It's only a few days a month, you'll get used to it.' Her mother wrapped a hot water bottle in an old cardigan, placed it on Poppy's belly, and then gave her the woman's rags to place in her underwear.

Poppy, unsure that she wanted to be a grown-up, couldn't imagine coping with the discomfort every four weeks, for the rest of her life.

Her mother became an expert on boys and lectured her for the entire morning.

'Mama, I won't let them near me, honestly,' Poppy said, dying of embarrassment.

'Just understand, once a boy gets his paws on you, they'll all be after you. They will ruin your name faster than dice roll on a *tavli* board.' Mama seemed angry, the way she said it, but then she smiled and fussed, stroking Poppy's hair and cuddling her.

'Mama, you don't have to worry.'

'I've made you a present to mark the day.' Mama shoved a parcel, wrapped in brown paper, into her hands. Because of the civil war, times were hard and gifts unusual.

Poppy untied the string and opened the gift. She stared at the cloth sewing bag, blue gingham with white embroidery and varnished bamboo handles.

'Mama, it's the most beautiful thing.' Inside, she found a ball of gold-coloured thread and two crochet hooks. 'Will you teach me the craft?'

From that day, everyone greeted Poppy with the respect of a woman. Maria took her everywhere. They became close, more like sisters than mother and daughter. The village women would call out, 'Maria, Poppy, come for coffee,' as if they were equals. Poppy sat at their tables and drank strong, sweet coffee, or ate candied orange peel with ice-cold spring water.

Poppy had always recognised her mother's beauty, and now she wanted to be exactly like her. Maria taught her to cook and crochet. After siesta, Poppy would take a chair into the street with her mother and the other women, while the men played cards or *tavli* and drank raki in the kafenion. She soon learned the hook and made Maria a set of gold antimacassars.

The women's talk, while they worked on their linen, fascinated Poppy. Respectable members of the community gossiped and joked together, mostly about sex. They laughed at Poppy's blushes and said she'd come to understand.

Later that month, Poppy's father and Stavro met the village elders to discuss her future. In isolated villages, marriages were considered carefully for their bloodline. Four local boys were selected but Poppy had already set her heart on one: Yeorgo. Her childhood affection had developed into something more, now that her hormones were sitting up and paying attention. Yeorgo was Matthia's best friend and, although his two younger brothers, Emmanouil and Thanassi, were on the list too, Poppy hadn't hesitated.

'Who will you marry, my girl?' her father said, eyes twinkling, guessing the answer.

Yeorgo, handsome and witty, was a miracle baby. Like Poppy's brothers, Stavro and Matthia, Yeorgo had survived the events of the occupation in 1943. Also, he played the lira, a skill admired by everyone.

Poppy relayed her wishes but feared Yeorgo might not love her.

'I want to marry your brother and have his babies,' she told her best friend, Yeorgo's sister.

'Emmanouil will be disappointed then,' Agapi said.

Poppy didn't care for Yeorgo's brothers, both born after the war. Thanassi, the youngest, was sweet on another girl, but Emmanouil, two years younger than Yeorgo, was a constant bully. Poppy knew Emmanouil wanted her. He had made surreptitious grabs at her breasts or bottom and she had slapped him several times. Once, he caught her wrist, twisted her arm up her back and rubbed his body against her in a lewd fashion, telling her one day he would *do* her and she would love it. Afraid of trouble, Poppy was ashamed, believing the incident was somehow her fault.

Maria and Vassili took Poppy to Yeorgo's house where her future mother-in-law, Constantina, waited. When they arrived, Emmanouil stormed out of the cottage, knocking her shoulder as he passed. On that day, thirteen-year-old Poppy became formally betrothed to Yeorgo who was already a man in her eyes.

'Poppy, let me hug you,' Constantina said, welcoming her into the Lambrakis home.

* * *

Over the next three years, Poppy's love for Yeorgo grew even stronger. Eagerly, she waited for the time they would marry. The marriage was set for her sixteenth birthday and Mama soon started work on her wedding dress.

When Emmanouil was betrothed to Yánna, a friend of Poppy's, Poppy believed he would finally leave her alone. However, the closer it got to Poppy and Yeorgo's big day, the more Emmanouil pestered her, until one terrifying night, a week before her marriage.

The street had been empty when Poppy returned home from Constantina's. A streetlight was out, making the narrow road dark and oddly disorientating. She hurried, startled when Emmanouil leapt out of an abandoned house. He grabbed her arms and herded her through the doorway.

'Why didn't you choose me?' he snarled, shoving her against a rough stone wall.

'Get off me, you pig! You're drunk!' Poppy shouted, pushing him away.

Emmanouil slapped her hard across the face. 'That's for all the times you've whacked me, you slut,' he said.

Poppy tasted blood, realising he'd split her lip. For all his aggravation, he had never before used violence. Suddenly afraid, she tried to sidestep around him.

He crushed her against the wall, grabbed her wrist and forced her hand against the front of his trousers. 'Rub me,' he snarled, before he covered her mouth with his, slobbering, his breath sour and stinking of whisky.

She turned her face away, twisted and writhed. 'Let me go or I'll scream to the entire village.'

In truth, Poppy was afraid someone would hear them and blame her. Her reputation and the good name of her family would be soiled. Emmanouil grabbed her hair and forced her head down while his other hand fumbled with his trouser buttons. She thrashed, gouged blindly with her nails and wouldn't submit to his bullying even though her scalp seemed on fire.

'Give it up,' Emmanouil whispered. 'I'm stronger than you so let's not fight. Be grateful I'll allow you to keep your precious virginity for my brother.'

Poppy panicked, she was no match for his strength and he knew it. The struggle continued until he overpowered her.

Emmanouil clasped one hand over her mouth while his other pushed between their bodies, tugging at the front of his trousers. All of a sudden his fleshy thing sprung out. He stepped back, gripped her hair with two hands and dragged her head down towards it.

'Take it, suck it! Be nice to me and I'll let you go. Nobody will know,' he hissed.

Almost upon it, Poppy felt its heat, the musty smell clouding her face, cloying in her nostrils. A scream rose in her throat but she forced herself to swallow the noise. She clenched her teeth and clamped her mouth shut. Tears raced down her cheeks. Although wanting to reason with him, she daren't part her lips. His penis, hot and hard, prodded her face. Emmanouil yanked on her hair.

'Let me in, Poppy!' he hissed.

Terrified and almost fainting, a sudden change came over her. Anger exploded in her head. Enraged, she made a fist and punched him with all her might between his legs.

He squealed and his legs buckled.

'I hate you!' Poppy said. 'Why can't you leave me alone?'

The instant he let go of her hair, he grabbed her breasts and squeezed so hard she cried in pain. She struggled against him, snatched the dagger from his belt and, using all her strength, she slammed it under his ribs. His mouth hit her head as he doubled over and fell to his knees.

The knife clattered to the floor. Not thinking of the consequences, terrified and desperate to hurt him enough to get away, she swung her foot and kicked him in the face. Then she leapt over his body and ran out of the dark building without looking back.

What have I done?!

Trembling, and afraid someone would see her, Poppy washed his blood from her face and hands at the village spring.

That night she cried herself to sleep, hating Emmanouil, terrified she had killed him. She would go to prison, her family shamed, ostracised. Yeorgo would never forgive her.

* * *

The following day, every hour seemed darker than the last to Poppy, an eternal nightmare, yet nobody spoke of Emmanouil.

'You are very quiet tonight, little one,' Yeorgo said the next evening. He had called her 'little one' since she was a child, and still did although she was fifteen.

'I'm fine, Yeorgo, don't worry.' Her head was spinning from lack of food, lack of sleep, and fear. What should she do? Run away?

Yeorgo remained sweet and romantic, but she made excuses to go home early.

She hardly slept, living in fear of Emmanouil's re-appearance, or the police coming to arrest her for murder. After her midday meal, she took her crocheting and sat on the shady side of the street, watching the dilapidated cottage. Her hands, greased in a nervous sweat, kept slipping off the hook. Her eyes were dry, and her vision so blurred from lack of sleep, she couldn't focus on the loop of silk. Dropped stitches ran through her work faster than the beat of her racing heart. She imagined flesh-flies on Emmanouil's bloodied face. Tiny white maggots expelled from the red-eyed fly burrowing quickly into the corpse. She decided to sneak out that night and bury him right there in the ruin, before he started to stink.

When Poppy saw a group of children playing hide and seek, about to enter the crumbling old house, she leapt up, horrified. What if they discovered his flyblown body?

'Go!' she yelled, running at them. She gathered her courage and decided to look inside the building. She held her breath and stepped through the long grass in the doorway. A cat jumped from one of the worm-eaten beams. Startled, Poppy screamed.

Weeds, growing through the floor, were flattened but, apart from that, she saw no sign of the fight. No blood – no knife – and most importantly, no body.

At Constantina's house that evening, she tried to find out what had happened to Yeorgo's brother.

'I haven't seen Emmanouil for a few days, *Kiriea* Constantina, is he all right?' she enquired casually, her heart thumping against her ribs.

'Hurmph!' Constantina said. 'He's supposed to be in Heraklion searching for work, or so he claims. But in truth, I believe my son's gone to the hospital. You wouldn't have believed the state of him. He could hardly stand when he came home, the night before last. He'd been fighting and for once, somebody got the better of him.' She snorted. 'He breaks my heart, that boy. Perhaps it will teach him a lesson . . . but I doubt it. If I know Emmanouil, he'll be back soon, looking for revenge.'

The rush of relief that she hadn't killed him was powerful, but nothing compared with the idea that he would reappear on a vendetta: it terrified Poppy to her core.

Chapter 26

THE NEXT THREE DAYS dragged out. Poppy's fear of Emmanouil's return gathered momentum. Nobody knew him better than his mother and her words kept Poppy awake at night.

If I know Emmanouil, he'll be back soon, looking for revenge.

She woke on the morning of her sixteenth birthday after having slept in her parents' house for the last time.

The village women came to the cottage at dawn and sang bridal songs, in accordance with tradition. They removed her nightclothes, stood her in the tin bath, and washed her hair and body with perfumed soaps. They anointed her private places with olive oil and a tincture of herbs to numb the tearing pain and make it easier for her husband to enter.

Excited to be the centre of attention and wear such wonderful clothes, she marvelled that even her underwear was new, made by the village women. They also crafted gifts of linen and cooked food for the marriage banquet. The men had worked metal pots and utensils for her kitchen and tools for the garden.

Once dressed, Poppy preened in front of the big old mirror. For her wedding dress, thousands of silk cocoons, unwound and spun, were woven into metres of fabric on the loom. Lace, crafted by Mama and her friends, trimmed the sleeves, neckline and hem. The gown, gloriously slinky and sophisticated, made Poppy's eyes sparkle.

Wedding crowns, garlands of lemon blossom and citrus leaves, were intertwined for Poppy and Yeorgo by the village elders. The two crowns joined by lengths of white ribbon.

'My dress is the most beautiful thing I've ever seen,' Poppy said, twirling. The silk slid against her bare legs, cold, licking her skin and sending a shiver of excitement through her body. She thrilled at the wonder of everything. 'Do I look pretty, Mama?'

Maria cried, emotional because Poppy would be given to her husband's family, officially leaving her and the Kondulakis tribe.

'Aphrodite herself could not compete with you today, child,' Maria said, smiling through tears.

Poppy wore make-up. Powdered rouge blushed her cheeks. Lipstick, which tasted of paraffin wax, framed her mouth. Her eyes were enhanced with mascara, a hard little block, spat on and then applied to her lashes with a tiny brush.

Matthia tugged myrtle branches from shrubs in the gully and spread them in a wide path from the house, all the way down to the church.

Stavro and his friends waited outside the cottage, playing their lira, bouzouki, and mandolin. They drank raki and sang the old Cretan wedding mantinades.

Time to say goodbye
To your parents' bed.
A better place awaits
Next to the man you wed.

And if your groom should die,
His bones to rest in clay,
His heart so full of love
With you will always stay.

As was customary when celebrating a marriage, the village men wore their best beige jodhpurs, highly polished knee-high boots, and a black shirt. They exchanged their usual black *saríki* scarf for the white one traditionally worn at weddings and baptisms. The loosely crocheted *saríki* wrapped about the head and knotted over the right ear. Each man also wound a long red sash around his waist to keep his ornate Cretan dagger in place. Moustaches were waxed and beards trimmed.

Most of the women wore black, as they had since the massacre.

A peal of bells beckoned the congregation and the streets were filled with locals. They rushed from their houses, eager to get a good spot in the church. Young people carried chairs for the elderly, to sit in the churchyard through the ceremony. Trays of cakes were stacked in the portico, to hand out after the marriage.

Agapi came running. 'It's time to go. Come on everybody!'

'Agapi, promise we'll stay friends after I'm married,' Poppy said, suddenly afraid; aware that sixteen was not as grown up as she pretended.

'Of course we will. I have to make sure my brother treats you well.' Poppy hugged her and Agapi whispered outrageous things about the forthcoming wedding bed.

Older women loaded neat bundles of dowry bedding onto the baker's donkey. Constantina had crocheted a white *saríki* for the animal's head. A row of tassels swished above its eyes and its great ears poked out of two holes in the lacy scarf. They tied long ribbons to its mane and tail and patted it admiringly.

The donkey's penis suddenly extended. It almost reached the ground and the girls screamed with laughter. The beast brayed. A matriarch whacked the shaft with her walking stick, which solved the problem, but the animal got skittish and bucked-off the bundles of linen.

'I hope that's not an omen,' Maria said to Poppy, giving the donkey a bucket of water to calm it.

'Start the music before anything else happens,' Voula yelled at Stavro.

Vassili appeared with Poppy's bouquet. He went down on one knee, as was the tradition, and presented the flowers to her. The last gift a Cretan father ever gives *his* daughter because, in a few hours, she will belong to another man.

His black eyes glistened below the heavy tassels of his *saríki*. 'My precious girl, you look like an angel,' he said. 'You brought me sixteen years of joy, Calliope Kondulakis. I have truly been blessed.'

Vassili stood and held her gently in his arms. 'Go to your man with my blessing, daughter, but don't forget your old father.'

Poppy saw Vassili's tears brimming and her young heart broke for the first time in her life. 'I'm never leaving you, Papa, I promise. Please don't be sad.' She kissed his cheeks, his forehead, and his mouth. And with her gentle embrace, his tears broke free.

At six p.m., when the heat of the day had fallen, the marriage took place. A bouzouki player led the groom and all his relations through the village. Poppy heard the locals whistle and applaud vigorously when Yeorgo reached the church.

The time had come for the bride's procession to make its way through the streets. First came the musicians and the donkey, followed by Poppy between Maria and Vassili.

The entire Kondulakis tribe walked behind them; then friends of the family and anyone else that cared to join in the celebration. Crushed myrtle leaves underfoot filled the evening air with exotic perfume. In the churchyard, the beribboned beast, loaded with dowry linen, was formally presented to Constantina. The local women led the donkey to the bride's new home, next-door to her in-laws. At the church, Vassili kissed Yeorgo on the lips and gave Poppy's hand to him.

Earnestly, Vassili said to Yeorgo, 'Make my child miserable for one single second and I'll break your legs before I kill you.' Then he raised his voice and shouted, 'Yeorgo Lambrakis, I give you my daughter, Calliope Kondulakis!'

'My only girl has gone to Lambrakis!' Maria wailed. Her knees folded and she almost collapsed to the ground. The women caught and fussed her, as tradition dictated.

'Where's the pomegranate?' Vassili called out, and when somebody handed the huge fruit to him, he hurled it at the church doorstep.

It split and the seeds that symbolise fertility flew everywhere. Agapi and Voula had lifted Poppy's skirt and red juice splattered her shins. Everyone whistled and clapped but, for a sickening moment, Poppy thought the crimson liquid looked like blood running down her legs. Her belly cramped and a half-realised vision of wailing women thundered inside her head.

Everybody surged into the church.

The building filled to the door, yet people still tried to enter. Constantina spat three times on the step to send the devil away and stop him from interfering in the marriage. The congregation crossed themselves repeatedly and even the icons on the walls seemed a little less miserable.

The service went perfectly until the young priest, Papas Christos, had to ask whoever was smoking to go outside the church. Minutes later, he asked if the women could please find the self-discipline to stop talking. Their *Koumbaros*, the best man, was short in stature and couldn't reach over Yeorgo's head with the wedding crowns. Somebody brought a chair. Even Papas Christos chuckled.

The priest blessed Poppy and Yeorgo and, swinging the thurible, led them three times around the holy table. Still wearing their crowns, joined by the ribbon, they held hands and suffered a deluge of rice from relatives. Poppy kept her head down and placed her free hand over her cleavage to stop the grains sliding inside her dress.

After the first turn, Poppy looked up and beamed at her parents. Yeorgo's brother stood next to them. Her smile fell. Emmanouil glared at her. His mouth was swollen and split. His look, satanic, bored into her with a promise of reprisal that stopped her dead. Aware that she was the centre of attention, Poppy tried to hide her fear. A sneer slid across Emmanouil's face; his dark eyes emotionless as death as his tongue slithered out to caress his bruised lip.

The priest tugged Poppy's hand.

'Keep up, little one,' Yeorgo said, laughing, unaware of the incident. Poppy broke her stare from Emmanouil. On the third circling of the holy table, her heart lurched when she saw he had gone.

After the service, Poppy and Yeorgo stood at the head of the family line. Guests filed past to kiss the bride and groom and wished them 'Happy life!' Their *Koumbaros* held a basket for the wedding money. Each guest left an envelope containing a few drachmas for their marriage gift.

Almost a thousand people attended; Amiras and its surrounding villages, distant relatives, and Stavro's friends from the university in Athens. The line of well-wishers seemed endless. Guests milled around, packing the church yard, despite the *Koumbaros* calling out, 'Move along!'

Voula appeared. 'Long life, you lucky woman.' She kissed Poppy. 'Now I'm going to kiss your beautiful husband,' she said.

Poppy laughed at her friend's exaggerated pout and turned to the next guest.

Emmanouil placed his hands either side of her waist, his eyes bored into Poppy's. He leaned in to embrace her, pressed his cheek hard against hers and whispered in her ear.

'You're driving me insane. I will have you, be ready for us both, first my brother and then me.'

Yeorgo was laughing with Voula, unaware of what was going on next to him. Poppy found it impossible to break away from Emmanouil. Then he said quietly. 'And if you refuse, you'll enjoy the thrust of *my* knife.'

'Never,' Poppy said as a herd of wild horses stampeded over her chest.

Emmanouil squeezed her, reminding her of his great strength, and then he reached for his dagger, drawing it from its ornately moulded scabbard.

'Emmanouil, my brother!' Yeorgo shouted jovially, slapping him on the arm, causing him to let go of the ram's-horn hilt. The knife slipped back into its sheath. Poppy trembled – sick to her stomach.

The guests walked to the village square to eat while Yeorgo and Poppy retired to the marriage bed to consummate their marriage. Determined not to allow the incident with Emmanouil to spoil her wedding day, Poppy decided not to tell Yeorgo about the confrontation. She convinced herself that Emmanouil had simply intended to frighten her with his jealous raki-talk.

They entered their new home, Poppy suddenly shy. Yeorgo lifted her, carried her into the bedroom. The *Koumbaros,* who was a cousin of Yeorgo's, and his wife had decorated the bed with almonds and vermilion bougainvillea bracts arranged in the shapes of birds, flowers and hearts. Poppy gasped, nervous, embarrassed, and full of joy.

'I love you, Poppy, I'm so happy you married me, little one,' Yeorgo said, taking her in his arms. 'I won't hurt you, don't be afraid.'

The warmth of his breath clouded her face. She saw the admiring look in his eyes. He always gave her a sense of beauty.

'I've always loved you, Yeorgo,' Poppy said. 'I'll try to be a good wife.' She wanted him to be proud of her, and she longed to have his children and build a life with him. 'Today's the happiest day of my life,' she whispered before he kissed her.

Yeorgo lifted her onto the bed and, in the flickering candlelight, he carefully undressed her, and himself, garment by garment until they reached nakedness together. He caressed her until she floated, almost fainting with happiness, intoxicated by his touch. Before long, she wanted him with a passion she had never before experienced.

'Please, Yeorgo,' she whispered urgently. 'Make me your wife, I want to give myself to you. I'm yours, forever.'

He made love to her gently, amongst the bougainvillea petals, and only in his final spasms did he lose control, thrusting hard and crying out her name. 'Poppy, you *belong* to me now. You'll always be mine, little one.'

After the consummation, Yeorgo left to drink a raki and smoke a hashish cigarette on the front porch with the *Koumbaros*. The best man's wife came into the bedroom and Poppy blushed because there were red streaks on the new bridal linen.

'Go and wash while I take care of the bed,' she said, trying to steer Poppy into the bathroom.

Poppy didn't understand. 'What do you mean?'

'It's never enough.' She nodded at the soiled sheet. 'We have to make a really good show, Poppy.' She took a small bottle of blood out of her bag and poured it onto the bed. 'I don't know if the rabbit was a virgin, but let's not worry, and never break our secret, Poppy.'

They laughed.

When they were ready, the *Koumbaros* led them back to the reception. They'd been gone for almost two hours, but apparently weren't missed. The entire community ate and drank in the village square.

The *Koumbaros* roared, 'The bride and groom!' Everyone thumped on the wooden tables or clattered the cutlery against the raki bottles and water jugs, and men whistled loudly.

Emmanouil pushed through the crowd, a shotgun in his fists.

Poppy's elation plummeted, she couldn't breathe and clutched Yeorgo's arm. Emmanouil disappeared around their backs. The shots, deafening, exploded behind her.

Poppy clung to Yeorgo. She knew Emmanouil was supposed to fire the wedding volley, but she feared the actions of a man tanked up on alcohol and revenge. Her knees folded. Yeorgo caught her, swept her up, and kissed away her tears. The guests whooped and hollered, enjoying the drama, but Poppy was sure Emmanouil had seen the terror on her face.

Later, calmer, she led the bride's dance, followed by Yeorgo and then family. The party continued until sunrise, Emmanouil always there, somewhere, watching.

At dawn, Yeorgo and Poppy returned to their new home. The bed sheet already hung, unwashed, on the clothesline outside the house. Her virgin blood on display for everyone to see, making her father-in-law extremely proud.

Poppy's wedding day memories faded. Returning to the present, she realised if she had known then, what she knew now, her marriage to Yeorgo would never have taken place. And the love of her life would still be alive today.

Chapter 27

London, Present Day.

Poppy lay back against the hospital pillow. When she opened her eyes, she saw her daughter staring at the water jug, her face flushed and her hand pressed against her chest. Horrified, Poppy wondered if Angelika had developed a weak heart too. She calmed quickly. That would be a cruel twist of fate, hardly likely but, nevertheless, she would talk her into a check-up.

'Are you thirsty, Angelika, would you like a glass of water?'

'No, I'm okay, thanks, Mam.'

'You seem anxious.'

'Ah, yes, well . . . I've a surprise for you, but I am worried you might not be up to it.'

'I'm fine. You're full of surprises today.'

'The shock could be too much for you.'

'Don't keep me guessing. You'll send my blood pressure rocketing.'

'You have a special visitor.'

'You're special.'

'More special.'

'Not possible.' Poppy glanced at the door. 'I hope you haven't brought the neighbours in to visit? And me with my hair a mess and my roots showing.'

Angelika laughed nervously. 'Wait there.'

'Does it look as though I'm going anywhere?' She wanted her daughter by her side. 'Stay,' she pleaded.

Angelika flushed again. 'It's better if I don't, but I'll put my head in again before we go.' She left the room. Muted talking came from the corridor.

The door opened slowly and Poppy blinked at the tall elderly gentleman who stepped into her room. She sensed he had been broad and strong in his younger days, and handsome too. Although the years had been kind, they had whittled away that vitality of youth. Poppy glanced at the photograph next to the bed and then stared at the stranger. He took a step closer, hesitated, his mouth almost a smile, his expression soft and slightly pitying.

Recognition teased her, his identity a fraction from revelation. The ageless eyes, large, brown, with sweeping lashes drew her. Poppy guessed there were few men with such an incredible look about them – and she had loved some of them dearly; one, more than any other man in the world.

With that thought, her mind went crazy, spinning and splintering with impossible ideas. She had never fully accepted Yeorgo's death, and now . . . blood hammered through her fragile heart.

'Yeorgo? Is that you? Is it really you?' Poppy panted, sobbed, unable to say more. She always knew they would be united again, someday. Her dream had come true, that he'd hold her in his arms once more. Even as she started to speak, she saw sympathy flood the stranger's face. Her soul plummeted from the giddy heights of euphoria. He came to her bedside, shaking his head.

'Oh, Calliope, I am so sorry.' He took her hand.

The moment he spoke, using her childhood name, she recognised her brother.

'Oh, Stavro, I'm mortified.' Tears of disappointment spilled down her cheeks. 'Take no notice of me, such a stupid mistake. For a minute, I thought . . .' Poppy tried to calm herself and squeezed his hand. 'It's lovely to see you. Why are you here? Am I going to die?'

Stavro took a tissue from a box on her locker. He sat on the bed, dabbed the tears from her eyes, and smiled down at her. 'No, you are certainly not, Poppy. Angelika kindly invited me and bought the ticket. I hope you don't mind me coming? I couldn't resist after all these years.'

'She's a strong-willed devil, Stavro, but I love her to pieces. You can see Angelika is her father's daughter, she's like him in many other ways too . . . but so stubborn, you wouldn't believe.' They embraced, patting each other, smiling, both slightly shy. 'I'm sorry about before . . . stupid of me,' she said, and then they both let the tears of lost decades fall freely.

Poppy fell into speaking Greek, reeling in the thread of time between them. 'Fancy you coming all this way for me. I don't know what to say. I've missed you all for so long.' She asked about their mother and father and Voula and Agapi.

She glanced at the door. 'Matthia?'

'He hasn't got a passport, Poppy.'

'Will you tell him I miss him?'

'You should do that yourself. He's still angry that you left, even after all these years.'

'I had no choice, Stavro.'

'I know. Such a brave thing to do, to give up so much. And you made a good choice. It did stop the trouble.'

Stavro talked about everyone in Crete but all roads seemed to lead to the family break-up and Yeorgo. At that point, they sat in silence with their individual thoughts, holding hands, squeezing fingers when an emotional moment drifted by, each understanding the other.

* * *

Angie had pressed redial on her phone on the bedside cabinet as she got up from the chair and the old phone vibrated in her pocket even before she had left the room. The moment Stavro closed the door she answered the call, moving a little further down the corridor.

They were bound to talk about what had happened. Angie would hear, understand, work out a way to help heal the wounds – and that would be the end of it.

Her mother and Stavro came through loud and clear.

She heard Poppy tell Stavro about the hard times, working in the kebab house through the night and completing her accountancy module through the day, while bringing up a baby. It had been difficult, Poppy said, but she took pride from the way Angelika had grown up, and her achievements.

'Isn't she beautiful, Stavro? And so clever. She gets that from her father of course. When she sets her mind to doing something, nothing will stop her.' A moment of silence settled on them and then Poppy said, 'If things go wrong this afternoon, tell Angelika I love her more than anyone in the world. She's made me incredibly happy. All those sacrifices, even the ones she'll never know about, were worth it and I'd do it all again, ten times and more.'

Angie's eyes misted. A soldier in army uniform came around the corner at the far end of the hall and, through her emotional haze, she saw the photograph of her father. She lowered the phone and stared at it in her palm, recalling Agapi's words about her father: I pray you also have his special qualities, his principles and sincerity. She shook her head and turned off the phone. How could she stoop so low?

A nurse followed the soldier and glanced at the mobile in her hand. 'Sorry, you can't use that in the corridor; you'll activate everyone's bleeper.'

'The ward sister told us we could make a call from Mam's room. Is that all right? We want to contact her family in Crete,' Angie said.

'Sure, outside communication gives the patients a mental boost. Is your mother Mrs Lambrakis?'

'Yes. Is everything okay?'

'Fine, she'll be up and about in no time. I'm about to administer her pre-med, so you only have another thirty minutes or so.'

Angie followed her into the room. Poppy swallowed the medicine and the nurse left.

Stavro gave Angie his seat and she took her mother's hand. 'Mam, we have to go soon but, well, I made this promise to *Yiayá*.'

'I hope it didn't involve me.'

'I said we'd Skype before your operation.'

'You should have asked me first.'

'She's sitting in Crete with my tablet, waiting. Please say you'll do it, *Yiayá* is demented with worry. She loves you as much as you love me. How would you feel?'

Poppy frowned, chewing her lip. 'I can't, not after so long, and at the drop of a hat.'

'The time will only get longer.'

'I look a mess.'

'The signal's rubbish in Amiras. You'll be in soft focus. Please don't let me down, Mam.'

'Blackmail now, is it? Me at death's door and you with an answer for everything.'

'Mam, stop it.' For an obscure reason, Angie remembered the letter, still in the zip pocket of her handbag. '*Yiayá* wrote this before I even got to Crete. She said I must give it to you.' Angie thrust the folded page at her mother and passed her glasses from the cabinet top.

She had no idea what was written inside, and had forgotten all about it until that moment. They were silent, watching Poppy's tears rise as she read the words aloud. Near the end, her eyes flicked up to meet Angie's, and then returned to the last lines of the letter.

My dearest darling Calliope,

I feel my time is almost done here. God is getting impatient so I wanted to tell you how much I love you, before I leave this world. I move on with a broken heart. I can never express how sorry I am for all that happened, and if I could change the past, I hope you know that I would.

I'm very proud of all the things you have achieved in England, but most of all, I am so happy for your daughter. She could not have a better mother. And isn't she beautiful, just as you were at her age.

Please try and find it in your heart to forgive me, and to return to Crete one day. Your brothers and your father miss you very much, as I do. I hope you think of me with kindness, once in a while. I'll never forget you and, God willing, I will always be watching over you and my granddaughter.

Bless you and keep you safe, Calliope, my only daughter.

All my love,

Mama, XXX

Poppy blinked her tears away, fighting a sob before she said to Stavro, 'I'm quite shocked that Mama seems to know so much about me. Did you break your promise, Stavro?'

He moved over to the window, turned his back on them, and then after a moment he blew his nose. Angie realised he was struggling with his emotions too. He returned to the bedside. 'Absolutely not, Poppy. But I do believe you should find the courage to call Mama. I don't think she has a great deal of time left. I can't see her die of a broken heart.' The tremor in his voice was hardly noticeable. 'You'd regret it for the rest of your life if she passed away tonight. Just say hello.'

The nurse popped into the room. 'Ten minutes, people.'

Angie took her mobile from the bedside locker and called Crete.

* * *

Crete, Present Day.

MARIA SAT AT THE cracked marble table and glared, her jaw thrust out and her eyes narrow.

'The trouble with you youngsters is: you don't listen! Voula!' Voula cowered. 'Go and phone the school,' Maria said. 'Tell them to send Young Mattie home, it's an emergency. Perhaps your grandson knows how to work this contraption.'

Matthia stomped into the garden to join them. 'Is it going yet?'

'Is it hell!' Demitri said.

They all crossed themselves three times.

Matthia scowled and shouted at Demitri. 'You've a laptop and a computerised till giving us chits we don't want and can't read. Why can't you get this thing to work, you fool? It's no bigger than an ant's cock.'

Vassili grinned at Maria.

'Matthia!' Maria scolded and then frowned at Vassili.

Demitri assassinated a smile before it reached the corners of his mouth. 'It's got no keyboard,' he said. 'I have to jab at the right pictures but they don't mean anything to me. It's all guesswork.'

Matthia huffed. 'Can't you just follow the directions?'

They all stared at him.

'They're taped on the back. See what they say.'

Voula appeared from the house. 'The headmaster's bringing Young Mattie home.'

Demitri turned the tablet over and read the instructions aloud, twice. When he turned it the right way up the tablet had switched off. 'I think the battery's flat, where's the charger?'

'It's at our house,' Matthia said. 'On top of the fridge.'

Maria pointed a crooked finger. 'Demitri, you're the youngest, go and find the charger.' She spoke to Voula. 'Get back on the phone. Call electric Orpheus and telephone-man, Pavlo. Tell them to come over here. It's an emergency. We need to have this machine working, out here, with a plug for the charging. It will drain quickly if we're calling all the way to England.'

Voula dashed into the house.

Matthia, about to light a cigarette, hesitated and then said, 'Mama, get used to it, you're not going to see Poppy before she's cut open. It's no good hoping; time's passing.'

'Matthia, I'll boil your head for soup,' Maria snapped.

Demitri returned with the charger and they all relocated in the cottage. The headmaster arrived with Young Mattie and, when Demitri explained the situation, he decided to stay. Voula took a tray of coffees and glasses of raki and mezzés outside and the entire group returned to the cracked marble table in the garden.

Orpheus the electrician turned up with his younger brother. They set about rolling an extension wire from the house. Pavlo the phone technician arrived with his cousin and they moved the router to the bedroom windowsill, the nearest place to the marble table. Pavlo installed a booster so they would still have a signal in the living room, despite the thick walls.

Young Mattie took control of the tablet, his forefinger pecking at the screen like a hungry bird.

'I don't understand,' Maria said. 'Angelika got her boyfriend loud and clear.'

'Somebody had turned the router off,' Pavlo said.

'Voula!'

'I forgot,' Voula said. 'Anyway, it eats your electric, Mama. The lights flashed like crazy, all the time. I feared it would start a fire.'

'You'll be fine now. Don't turn it off,' Pavlo said.

Young Mattie fisted the air gleefully, informing his great-grandmother, 'We have lift-off, *Pro Yiayá*!'

'Talk sense, boy,' Maria said, her mouth dry from the excitement.

'Sorry . . . we're online, *Pro Yiayá*. They can connect with us any time now.'

'I need a wee,' Maria said. 'Somebody help me to my feet.'

* * *

Angie sat on the edge of the bed next to her mother and called Uncle Matthia's new account.

Poppy whimpered.

'You'll be fine, take courage,' Stavro said, taking her hand.

With the third ring, a row of four small dress buttons on faded blue fabric appeared on the screen. One had been sewn on badly with black cotton. *Yiayá*'s thin voice came through.

'Calliope . . . is that you, Calliope? I can see her, everyone, look. Matthia, come and see.' The blue buttons seemed to dance with the sound of Maria's excitement.

'It's *Yiayá*,' Angie whispered.

Poppy panted. Her eyes wide.

Angie worried about her mother's heart. Was this all too much? Surely it was for the best.

Someone else in Crete spoke. '*Pro Yiay*á, you need to move the tablet so they can see us, here, let me hold it.'

'That's one of *Yiayá*'s great-grandchildren, Young Mattie,' Angie said.

The picture shook, and then cleared. *Yiayá*'s face came on screen, wide-eyed, tears trickling, and in the background Demitri's son grinned and Matthia scowled.

'Mama . . .' Poppy whispered. 'Matthia . . .'

The door opened. 'Time to go, people, thank you,' the nurse said.

* * *

Later, Angie glanced at her watch, two o'clock. Her mother would be in theatre. She imagined the green gowns, scalpel, blood; an oxygen mask over her mother's face, a glimpse of white roots below dark curly hair pulled back into a surgery cap. She slugged a mouthful of tomato juice, wishing there'd been vodka in it.

Frustrated and worried, she reminded herself that this operation was performed every day. The procedure hardly ever went wrong. *Hardly ever . . .*

* * *

Angie phoned the hospital again.

Stavro looked up from his newspaper when she ended the call. 'Any news, Angelika?'

'They won't say. It's against their policy to discuss patients over the phone.'

'I'm sure she's fine. Why don't we drive over there?'

Angie noticed the bags under his eyes. He hadn't slept well. 'I'll get the car,' she said.

'Where's Nick? Will he come with us?'

'He'll probably work late, Uncle Stavro. He's trying to secure his job after the takeover. I guess he'll sleep at the flat again so he doesn't disturb us tonight. Nick's considerate like that.'

Her fiancé was spending another evening with Judy Peabody. Perhaps Judy had set her sights on Nick. Who wouldn't? He was gorgeous. Judy had a certain charisma about her too. Angie would cancel her reservation at Chez Henri. They could do it next week, if he wasn't too busy.

For a horrible moment, jealousy and anger swirled up inside her again. Were all these evening meetings necessary or was something going on between them? A last chance fling before his wedding? Cold feet? Angie felt the first throb of a headache, and the increased heart rate of fear. She picked up her car keys, tears pricking the backs of her eyes.

'He loves you,' Stavro said out of nowhere. 'It's written all over him. Don't worry.'

Angie glanced up and caught her uncle's sympathetic smile. She wondered if her entire family was psychic. 'I know,' she said. 'But sometimes I get a little scared. He's my life.'

Chapter 28

After learning Poppy's operation had gone well, Angie and Stavro returned home. When Angie saw Nick's blue Boxster parked in the drive, she squealed with delight. She rushed into the house to find he had dismantled Poppy's bed and was in the process of transferring it down the stairs and into the front room. She threw herself at him, happy beyond words, hardly aware of Stavro's grin.

'What do you think you're doing, Nick?' she said, her hands on her hips and pretend anger on her face.

'I think the technical term is: making an unholy mess,' Nick said.

'Can I assist in any way?' Stavro asked.

'All help appreciated, mate!' Nick replied. 'If you start re-assembling the bed as I bring it down, that would be great.' He turned to Angie.

'A couple of beers for the workers please, serving wench, and then get the shopping from the car boot will you? We should be almost ready for it by then.'

'A bit bossy, aren't we? Did you take a brave pill this morning or something?'

They all laughed.

Angie returned from the car, opened the Debenhams bags, and was moved by Nick's thoughtfulness. He had bought a full set of very feminine, pink floral bedlinen for Poppy's bed, a beautiful box of chocolates, and a range of women's magazines.

* * *

'How's Poppy?' Nick said as he came into the kitchen, hair-tussled from the shower, wearing nothing but a snug white T-shirt and boxers.

'She's a little tired, first day home and all,' Angie said. 'She's settled down for the night with a ham sandwich and the latest Lynda La Plante novel.'

'Who was that on the phone, just now?'

'Judy Peabody. She wants to know when you're available for a meeting.' Angie drizzled Cretan olive oil over a Greek salad and used her fingers to mix it through. Determined not to succumb to another bout of jealousy, she decided to 'woman-up' and have faith in her future husband. 'Ms Peabody asked if you'd call her back.' She concentrated on the food. 'Open a bottle of Chardonnay, will you?

Nick groaned. 'What does she want this time?' he asked. 'I'll tell you, Angie, this afterhours stuff is getting a bit much.' His eyes narrowed.

'Take it easy. She's only doing her job. It's a shaky time for everyone just now, even the publishers. She wanted to know if she could come over here. Something about a contract and some title papers.'

'I hope you said no. I won't have her in our home ever again. I know it upset you when she was in the flat.'

'Nick, if you don't know that I'm on your side, you shouldn't be marrying me. I put her off, naturally.' Angie stopped for a moment. What an idiot she'd been. Of course she trusted him, as much as he could have every faith in her, and that was the end of it.

She placed the Greek salad on the table, nudged him to sit, and slid onto his lap.

Angie remembered how she missed him while she was in Crete. 'I wish you could meet *Yiayá*. She's the most wonderful old lady I've ever known. You should have heard the stories she told me, Nick. How she saved the lives of her children in the war. I'm so proud to belong to her family.' She wanted to talk to Nick about her revised wedding ideas. 'You know, Nick, I think –'

They both caught Stavro clearing his throat in the doorway behind them. 'May I come in?' he said.

Angie slid off Nick's knee and blushed. 'Sorry, Uncle. I hope you're feeling hungry. I'm just waiting for Nick to get dressed for dinner.' She pulled her fiancé up and shoved him towards the stairs. 'Moussaka and Greek salad okay for you?'

'My favourite meal,' Stavro said. 'I don't have it very often, with living by myself.'

Angie opened the oven and lifted a deep dish of minced lamb, aubergines, and creamy egg sauce. Steam billowed up and infused the air with the delicious aroma of meat, cheese and cinnamon.

'Mmm, that smells good, Angelika.'

A moment later, Nick re-appeared dressed in jeans and a crisp white shirt. 'I've decided to take a few days off,' he said. 'I want to decorate Poppy's bedroom while she's out of it. It's late night at the DIY store, so I'm going to nip out after dinner and get some paint and stuff.'

This was a shock, but one that pleased Angie. She was always planning to have her mother's house decorated. Poppy had painted and wallpapered all the rooms herself, thirty years ago, when she bought the property, and it hadn't been changed since.

Angie had planned to have a couple of rooms done for Poppy's birthday, then two more for Christmas. But now with no job and her wedding coming up, she couldn't afford the decorators. She thought they could do it themselves, and that would be fun. They never did anything together these days – always too busy.

After dinner, when Nick had left for the shops and Stavro was settled in front of the TV, Angie crept into the front room.

Poppy lay peacefully still, eyes closed. Angie crept over to the computer desk and slid a couple of sheets of paper from the printer.

'Is everything all right, Angelika?' her mother said without opening her eyes.

'Yes, Mam, fine. Sorry, did we wake you?'

'Don't shut me out, love, I'm not dead yet.'

Angie sat on the edge of Poppy's bed. Even in the dim light, her mother looked terrible, her skin dry and lifeless. Her dull hair, with the ever-growing white roots, fell back from her tired face. Angie took her mother's hand and sat in silence, thinking about her wedding.

She should cancel everything. It seemed the sensible thing to do, and she wished she'd had a chance to talk to Nick about it. Then if Nick did lose his job, it wouldn't be a catastrophe. Slightly shocked, she realised how much her values had changed over the past week. They didn't need a huge and expensive affair to prove that they loved each other. Nothing could change that.

All their problems, her mother's heart attack, and losing her job, seemed to be rooted in her wanting the big fancy wedding with all her relations and friends invited. Now, deciding to cancel, she was oddly relieved to see the back of it. But abandoning her plans wouldn't undo the damage already done.

If only she had taken it more slowly and hadn't tried to reunite Poppy's family in time for her wedding, perhaps Poppy wouldn't have had the heart attack.

If only she hadn't slipped out of work to view a house she'd set her heart on. Bad luck about the emergency meeting, called while she measured windows. Angie guessed it labelled her as unreliable.

Poppy's tired voice broke her thoughts. 'Tell me your problems, Angelika, perhaps I can help.'

'No, nothing, Mam. Everything's fine. I'm thinking about cancelling the big wedding and having a simple registry and restaurant jobbie instead. A better plan, don't you think?' She tried to keep the disappointment out of her voice. She had so looked forward to having a huge family event, just for one special day in her life. 'And the house, well, perhaps it's not quite right for us at this moment.'

'And the rest, spit it out.' Poppy said.

Angie felt a knot in her throat and, despite her determination not to cry, tears gathered. Poppy squeezed her hand encouragingly. 'There's a merger. I've lost my job, Mam, and Nick might lose his. It couldn't have come at a worse time for us.'

'Is that all?'

'Isn't it enough?'

'It's not a catastrophe,' Poppy said. 'Any career that keeps you two apart, working all hours, is no good anyway. Is that why you're going for a smaller wedding? I know you dreamt of the razzmatazz.'

Angie gave a little laugh. 'I'm an idiot. I had my values arse end up, didn't I? Trying to organise everyone to do what I wanted, so stupid.'

'Angelika, part of your problem is you think you can make everything better for people you care about. Better in your eyes, that is. For all your good intentions, you must leave people to sort out their own problems. Just be there if they need you. Even Nick. You have to let him deal with this by himself. He'll ask for your help, or your opinion, or your support if he needs it.'

'Like you and *Yiayá*?'

Poppy smiled softly but didn't answer.

They sat in silence, listening to rain rattle against the bay window. Angie couldn't recall the last time they had been together at home without fighting, and then she remembered Crete.

She closed her eyes, imagined the warm sunshine on her face and the passion for life that seemed to infuse everyone – except Uncle Matthia. In an intense moment, she wanted to be at the cracked marble table with Poppy and Nick beside her, the stars above, and the music in her ears. The night when even Uncle Matthia found happiness. Angie craved these things for the two people she loved most in the world. She wished for them to feel uplifted, as she had.

It seemed so far away, now. As if Angie had exited the cinema and walked home in the rain. She recalled shouting 'Voo-laa!' across the rooftops, hauling air into her lungs and then expelling it in the loudest sound possible. At that moment, she realised how much she underestimated her own capabilities.

'What?' Poppy said.

'Ah, nothing, just thinking . . .'

'About Crete?'

Angie hesitated. 'I loved it, Mam. *Yiayá* was incredible.'

Lightning flashed through the curtains and a moment later, a roll of thunder seemed to hammer its fists on the window.

They were both quiet with their thoughts again.

Poppy broke the silence. 'Why don't you and Nick live here? That posh London flat will rent for a tidy income,' she said. 'I told you the house is in your name and with three floors, it's big enough. When you're not here, the place is too empty. I'll have the top floor. The garden's mine, too; so keep your mitts off. You can get me one of those small greenhouses for my tomatoes.'

Poppy gazed wistfully at Angie. 'I've always wanted a greenhouse, with shelves and a garden chair and a socket so I can make a brew. A heater to keep the winter chill off my plants would be useful too.' She closed her eyes and smiled.

'Good grief, Mam, you've planned it all.'

'Where do you think you get your organisational skills from, Angelika? I'll grow annuals for the front garden and plant up the most amazing hanging baskets. You'll be the envy of the neighbourhood.'

'I'd no idea you wanted to take up gardening on a more serious level.'

'There's a lot you don't know, Angelika.'

She had heard that before.

'I joined the local Potters & Planters Club six months ago,' Poppy said. 'We swap seeds and gossip in a park hut on Wednesday afternoons.'

'I had no idea. To be honest, Mam, I thought you hardly ever went out and I was starting to worry that you had agoraphobia.'

'Ha! No. Bob, the club secretary, came to visit me in hospital and brought flowers from everyone.'

'Ah, the flowers, but your hay fever?'

'Hay fever?' Poppy looked puzzled.

Angie shook her head. 'Lately, I've come to realise how easy it is to misjudge people.' She squeezed Poppy's hand. 'I'm incredibly lucky to have you. Sorry I've been so self-centred lately.'

Poppy patted her hand. 'You're in love, planning your wedding . . . and with what's going on at work, it's understandable. Talk to Nick about the house, see what he says.' She closed her eyes for a moment and squeezed Angie's hand once more. 'And when I'm a little stronger, I want to you to tell me all about Crete. Seeing Stavro has brought me happy memories. Did you take lots of photos?'

'I did. Everywhere I went, I imagined you were with me, Mam. Do you remember the big tree in the centre of Viannos?'

'Oh, I do! It's still standing then? I kissed your father for the first time in the hollow of that very tree. I was fourteen years old.' Poppy's smile grew wider.

'Fourteen . . . Mam, you're shameless.' They both laughed. 'I felt there was something special about that tree. I had my coffee there every morning.'

'I'd like to speak to Mama again. How is she? Really?'

'Considering her age, she's in very good health and her mind is as sharp as a pin. She told me you had your reasons for not wanting me to know things. I respect that, now. I won't torment you again. She told me to tell you she loves you. Never doubt it.'

Poppy nodded. 'She said so in her letter. It's made me think . . .' She was silent for a minute. 'Next time you go . . .' She hesitated, 'I may go with you. No promises, but I will consider it. The doctor said I can fly in a month.'

Angie's jaw dropped, then her hand flew over her mouth. Her mother's words were so unexpected. 'Mam, wow, fantastic! Do you know what I'd really like?' she said through her fingers.

'I guess I do, but don't get carried away now.'

'If the three of us could nip over there, have a quiet little wedding in the village church – where you got married – no fuss.' It all tumbled out and then Angie feared she'd said too much, too soon. In the dim light, she grinned at her mother, excited by possibilities.

Poppy nodded slowly, chewing her lip. After a few moments, she said, 'I'm bored to tears, Angelika. Will you let me take care of the documents, flights, and licences for you?'

'Are you up to it? You're supposed to be taking it easy. We're quite capable, you know.'

'The doctor said no digging or lifting heavy stuff for a few weeks, so a nice bit of paperwork will keep me occupied. I'd like to do it – feel important.'

'I want to tell you about my first day in Crete. I bought a lemon tree for *Yiayá* and when Demitri planted it Voula said I had to give it the first watering and make a wish.' Angie glanced at the curtains, realised the storm had passed. 'I wished that you'd find peace and return to Crete and your family.'

'How sweet, we're a superstitious lot, don't you think?'

Chapter 29

Crete, Four Weeks Later.

MARIA SAT IN THE SHADE of the big olive tree, near the cracked marble table. So, Poppy was coming home to Crete. She stared, blankly, trying to see into the future. Trouble would come, and wounds re-open. Bitter memories resurrected to torment them all, she sensed it. Maria realised Poppy was returning simply because Angelika wanted her to.

In the end, Poppy would do anything for Angelika, just as Maria would for Poppy.

But Angelika had no idea why her mother had left Crete in the first place. Or why, for very different reasons, she had stayed away all this time. Decades of tragedy. But each of those years held an empty space that belonged to Poppy. She thought of Yeorgo. Maria still missed him. What a powerful and handsome man, kind beyond words. Her eyes filled with tears. Such a terrible sacrifice . . .

Maria's daydreaming drifted towards Angelika. She had greatly enjoyed the glamorous young woman's company, and admired her spirit. Maria recognised a certain amount of courage, to go against Poppy's wishes and find her family in Crete. It proved Angelika had that stubborn and determined streak that ran through the Kondulakis bloodline.

Despite painful memories, Maria had, in a strange way, enjoyed telling the story of her survival to Angelika. It took a minute or two before she remembered where she was up to when her granddaughter left for England and Poppy's hospital bed.

Poor Poppy and that precious heart of hers. Forty years had passed since it was so badly broken, so completely crushed. Maria always suspected it would never fully heal. How could it? Whose heart could ever recover from such an abominable revelation? Then, Angelika, close to her own wedding, had opened all the old wounds without realising it. She stared down at her hands and remembered how they would crack open, painfully, and then bleed. No wonder Poppy needed pills to get her to sleep and ended up in hospital.

Ah, yes. Now she recalled their story. She had dragged the items from Andreas the shepherd's cottage up the mountainside after the soldier had come so close to executing her and Stavro. What a terrifying moment. Stavro had saved her life. Her stomach still cramped to think of it.

Maria allowed the horror to drift away from her and fade on the breeze. Over the decades, she found this was the best way to deal with the past. If she tried to forget, push the atrocities out of her mind, it seemed they were always lurking close by, or waiting to be bumped into around the next corner.

Her memory returned to the moment when she had arrived at the big old tree on the mountainside and expected to find Matthia asleep with a pile of acorns beside him.

Closing her eyes, she saw it all . . .

* * *

Crete, 1943.

THE CLIMB BACK UP the mountain had exhausted me. My legs were trembling, and I could barely put one foot in front of the other. The ground seemed to undulate like a rolling sea beneath my feet and I kept losing my balance.

Matthia had to be near; perhaps he had found a softer place to sleep. I dragged the stretcher under the tree branches. Stavro spread the sheepskins we had brought from Andreas's cottage to make a soft bed. Darkness fell, and we were tired beyond anything I had ever experienced.

Whether I collapsed or simply slept, I don't know. My knees buckled and consciousness left me. When I opened my eyes again, dawn light filtered through the branches.

Stavro lay asleep on the sheepskin. Why wasn't Matthia snuggled up to him? It took a few moments for the realisation that he was missing to come back. I speculated about my son's whereabouts and all sorts of terrifying thoughts came to mind.

Could the Nazis have found him? Could he have fallen into one of the many ravines that raked the mountainside? What about wild animals? There were rumours of bears roaming the pine forests, released by Turkish buskers when the creatures grew dangerously large. I hoped he had simply wandered too far from the tree and lost his way. Perhaps the goat escaped and Matthia searched for it. After all, I guessed to a four-year-old, one tree looked pretty much like another.

I scrambled from under the branches. What would make him take the goat and blanket and leave? I spotted a mound of acorns. Knowing how easily Matthia was distracted by bugs and butterflies, they must have taken over an hour to gather. In that case, it was getting dark when my boy left the tree.

Although we called him a little devil, Matthia had always been a good child and usually did as I told him. I ran down to the ruin by the footpath but saw no sign of him. The goat would soon bleat to be milked. I strained to hear it and shouted, 'Matthia!' as loud as I dared. When my search proved fruitless, I returned to our tree and woke Stavro.

'I'm going to look for Matthia. Stay here, under the tree. I don't want to lose you too.' He didn't need telling twice, the poor exhausted boy. 'There are rusks, oil, and water in the bundles, eat and drink, son.' He lifted his head, nodded, and returned to his sleep.

I raced up the mountain, following time-worn animal tracks through the vegetation, stopping to listen for our goat every few minutes. What could have happened? Soon, the trees thinned, their roots like broken fingers clutching crags of rocky ground. Surely he couldn't have come this far, not in the dark.

'Matthia!' I called out; the cold thin air made my voice hard and clear.

'Maria!'

At first I thought I had caught an echo: 'Matthia!'

'Maria!'

I swung around.

Joanna, the baker's wife, filthy and ragged, ran towards me through the trees.

We fell into each other's arms, weeping with blessed relief . . . and also with remorse for the slaughtering we had seen. I knew she had saved my life, keeping hold of me the way she did at the massacre. The Nazis would have murdered me too had I tried to rescue Petro.

'Have you seen Matthia, Joanna?' I said between sobs.

'He's safe, with my daughter, Martha, your goat too. I came looking for you. We're in a cave near the dry waterfall. Where's Stavro?' She paused, staring at me. 'Did they get him, Maria?'

I shook my head, so relieved that I couldn't speak. We walked down to the tree together, united by our ordeal. She told me about the murder of her youngest boy, Harry, her tears tripping on the words. She had seen him amongst the clutch of men;

their eyes met and held, seconds before his seventeen years of life were so cruelly ended.

'Another month and he would have been in the army, safe,' she said.

Her beautiful fifteen-year-old daughter, Martha, had escaped the Nazi cattle truck and was taking care of Matthia. I led Joanna down to the oak tree and woke Stavro. Together we dragged the stretcher up the mountain. Stavro, at the rear, did his best to cover our tracks.

* * *

By midmorning, we were safely hidden in the cave. I hugged Matthia so tightly he cried out and wriggled free. We shared the place with two other families, Stavroula, the blacksmith's wife and her sixteen-year-old daughter, Kiki, who had seen the murder of her fiancé, and Eva, the beekeeper's wife with her fourteen-year-old son, Stefan.

'How did you manage to escape, Stefan?' I asked.

'My *Papoú* helped me, we were captured together. When they shot old man Philipo in the side street, *Papoú* said they were going to kill us all. He kissed me on the mouth and said I shouldn't forget him.' Stefan plucked at the front of his shirt and stared at nothing. 'My *Papoú* was crying, all silent. He told me to take care of *Yiayá* and Mama.' The boy sniffed and thrust his young jaw out, grinding his teeth for a moment. '*Papoú* said I should bend my knees and walk lower and, at the first house we passed with an open door, I should duck in and hide up the chimney.'

He struggled with images still fresh in his head. 'I wanted to hug my *Papoú*, I wish I had, *Kiriea* Maria, because now I can't, ever again. He was the best kite maker in the world.' After a moment, he swallowed hard and said, 'I'm going to learn how to make those kites.'

We both stared at the ground for a beat before Stefan continued.

'When the street narrowed, something happened with the women behind us. They were screaming and it distracted the guards. *Papoú* shoved me through a doorway but a fire blazed in the hearth and a pot of food stood in the grate. I thought I'd feel a bullet in my back. I glanced over my shoulder. *Papoú* did this quick nod thing towards the sky, and then he disappeared down the road with all the other captives.'

Stefan gazed between the trees at the endless blue sky. 'The window to the yard hung open so I leapt through, all the time I thought about *Papoú*. Why didn't he come with me? We could have run away together.'

'Just too old I guess, Stefan. Your grandfather was already at the end of his life, but happy to know that you escaped.'

'I ran to the biggest olive tree, that one with the hollow trunk, and I hid. I heard the commotion, the gunfire and the screaming. It frightened me so much, I didn't dare come out until the middle of the night.'

'You were brave; your mother is proud of you.'

Stefan looked up again, his eyes full of questions. 'Do you think he's up there, my *Papoú*?'

'I'm sure he is, Stefan, and very happy that you are going to make kites like he did.'

He smiled at the sky.

We spent the day in the cave and I slept most of the time. When I woke, I discovered Joanna had taught Matthia to milk the goat properly. That evening we made a plan to try and find the road up to the highest plateau, Lassithi.

* * *

It took four nights, slogging along forest tracks, to reach Lassithi Plateau. We caught and killed a young sheep on the way. I wondered if the creature had belonged to Andreas. Was he watching over us? We also found an apiary – there were many in the pine forests but who would be foolish enough to try and open a hive? Eva was experienced, her hands permanently red and swollen from decades of bee stings.

From a distance, we watched Eva use a smouldering rag to waft around herself, and then clear the bees from a heavy frame of honeycomb. We ate the lot, wax and all, in one go. It gave everyone great energy and the children loved it but several angry bees followed us, pestering with the threat of a sting for the rest of the day.

'Why do you use the smoking rag, *Kiriea* Eva?' Stavro asked.

'When the bees smell the smoke, they think there's a forest fire, so they gorge on honey in preparation for a long flight. You know how you feel when stuffed with food, Stavro?'

The boy stared at nothing and licked his lips. 'Yes, really sleepy, like now with all that honey inside me.'

'There you are then. You're not in the mood to pick a fight with anyone. Neither are the bees.'

We walked on, unsure of where we were. The midday shadow pointed north, so we would choose a landmark in the distance, and head for it the following evening. I think it was luck more than judgement that kept us going in the right direction.

Carrying enough water was a problem. By the second day, we had run out and the youngsters were thirsty. I remembered the shepherd's advice and called everyone together.

'Listen, we must look for small birds. They almost always lead to water.'

This was against our plan of not travelling during the hours of daylight. We were terrified of coming across German troops on manoeuvres, every rustle or snapping twig made my heart leap. But we were parched and desperate to slake our thirsts.

'Mama!' Matthia cried. 'Look, a bird!' He pointed into the branches of a nearby pine.

It took me a moment to find the little brown-speckled creature, and then I saw it swoop across our path and land in another tree.

I waved everyone to come towards me. 'Andreas told me that when the birds fly slowly from branch to branch, it means they are heavy with water. They already drank.' Water had to be near. 'We must keep an eye open for fast birds racing along in a straight line, close to the ground. They will lead to fresh water.'

We spread out and moved cautiously on, until Stefan's shout made everyone jump. 'Hear! Hear! I saw them. There's water!'

'Bravo, my Stefan!' Eva shouted, running up to him, whacking her boy on the back, and then grinning at us.

He hooked his arm in the air and cried, 'Over here!' His voice echoing off the rocky terrain.

'Shhhh!' I said, nervous, afraid we'd be heard.

We dumped our belongings in a pile and followed Stefan through the scrub.

At a time in the distant past, someone, probably a shepherd or keeper of goats, had made a small deposit, about a metre square and half a metre deep, from cement. A spring, hidden on the mountainside above, had its water channelled along lengths of interlocking sandstone blocks. It babbled down into the trough and overflowed, drenching the lush vegetation. The magical sound of that water was music to us. We ran over squelching ground and drank greedily from cupped hands.

The boys, mischievous, flicked water at each other. I suggested that we women should go back for our belongings, and leave the children to play together.

On our return, we heard their screaming.

Terror overcame me, forcing me to my knees. Joanna, Stavroula and Eva did the same, dropping the bundles and hitting the ground. My mouth had dried and I found speaking difficult. I fell so hard, the burns cracked open on my hands. Blood oozed from my wounds like a terrible omen of more suffering and death to come.

'Go back and hide,' I whispered to Kiki and Martha. 'Stay together.' I didn't want the girls to witness any more horrors, and the further they were away from danger, the better.

We women from Amiras Village crept along on all fours, through the undergrowth, unaware of sharp flints that cut into our hands and shins. My heart pounded so hard I feared I wouldn't be able to focus on what might lie ahead.

When we saw the boys, we rolled together, hugging each other, trying to stifle our laughter. The relief was enormous, yet we were reminded of how far our voices carried.

Stefan, Stavro, and Matthia had removed every stitch of clothing and were playing in the water-deposit. Their nut-brown faces and limbs seemed to intensify the luminescence of their white bellies and buttocks. The children, stark naked and full of joy, frolicked and splashed in the dappled sunlight. The sight was truly beautiful for any mother to behold.

As we watched, we realised Matthia, the devil, was the cause of all the squealing. He stood knee-deep in the water, holding his little penis and pissing at Stavro and Stefan.

We four women rolled onto our backs, stared up at the tree canopy and giggled. Such a relief, to laugh. Eva told the boys to keep the noise down, and she put her son, Stefan, in charge.

We gathered our belongings and the girls, and set up camp right there in the bushes. Food consisted of white-mustard plants, wild parsnips and dandelions that grew in the wet ground around the deposit. Drizzled with olive oil and eaten with the last of our rusks, they made a satisfying meal.

When the boys were asleep, we took it in turns to go in pairs and bathe in the water deposit. Oh, that cold fresh water! Wonderful! Stavroula had a small block of green soap, what luxury. I hacked off a chunk of sheepskin, which we used as a wash cloth.

We all washed our hair, and also our underclothes, which we hung on the bushes, hoping they would be dry by morning. I fell asleep that night, thanking Andreas for sharing his knowledge with us. Without his guidance, we would never have found that water.

Two days later, hungry, dirty, and exhausted, we stumbled out of a gorge between the mountain peaks. Spread before us was the plateau of Lassithi. The vast plain – 900 metres above sea level – was dotted with hundreds of white-sailed windmills. We saw clusters of houses, villages scattered among the patchwork of yellow and green fields. Uplifted by the picture-postcard view, we headed for the nearest community, Kaminaki.

The locals welcomed us and were sympathetic, despite their own hardship. News had spread about the mass murders in Amiras and Viannos. We learned similar massacres had happened in all the other villages near to Amiras. More than 500 innocent people, our friends and neighbours, lay slaughtered, and many more were missing.

The women and girls had left the area in a mass exodus, fleeing east, to the town of Ierapetra. They lived in goat huts and begged for food in the streets.

The priest of Kaminaki sent us to three abandoned stone windmills outside the village. 'Stay quietly, my children,' he said. 'We have not been free of trouble ourselves. Seven innocent local shepherds were executed because the Nazis suspected one was a rebel.'

Again, I thought of Andreas and also wondered how many Nazis were in the vicinity. Would we ever feel safe again?

Chapter 30

London, Present Day.

Nick and Angie stood in Poppy's bedroom doorway and admired their DIY work.

Angie slipped her arm around Nick's waist. 'I love the colours; pink, lilac and cream. So pretty and feminine.'

'Like you,' Nick said before he kissed her cheek and ran his hand down her long hair. 'Yuck, what's that? Snot?' he said, staring at his palm.

Angie giggled. 'It's wallpaper paste, you twit. I just washed out the bucket. I'm going to shower and wash my hair.'

'Right, while you're doing that, I'll go and order the carpet, if you are sure about the cream one?' Angie nodded. 'I'll bring something in for tea, okay?' he said.

'Great. I love you,' she said, heading for the bathroom.

The decorating took longer than they'd planned, and Nick had taken another week's leave in order to finish off before their trip to Crete. Although he was supposed to be on holiday, Nick seemed to get more phone calls than usual from work. Hardly a day passed by that he didn't have to nip into the office for a couple of hours. He even took the trouble to shave and change into his best work suit. He was so conscientious, Angie thought. The publishers were taking advantage of his inability to say 'no'.

While she showered, she thought about her grandmother in Crete. Angie would be there in a few days, preparing for her wedding at the weekend. Suddenly, she appreciated how much she missed them all. Wrapped in a bath towel, she looked into the bathroom mirror and grinned.

All her wishes were coming true.

She would marry the man of her dreams, her mother and grandmother would be reunited, and now, she had just realised her period was two weeks late. Amazing. She would tell Nick tonight, and they would do the test together.

Angie plugged Poppy's hairdryer in, threw her long hair forward, and started drying the back.

BANG!

For a moment, she thought she'd been shot in the head. 'Angelika! All the lights have gone out,' Poppy shouted up the stairs.

After sorting the electrics, Angie had bought a pregnancy testing kit on her way to the flat to pick up her own hairdryer. When she turned into the road and saw Nick's blue Boxster parked outside the apartment block, and Judy standing on the step with a set of designer luggage, she drove past and pulled in down the street.

What was going on? She adjusted her wing mirror so she could see the entrance doors. Nick stepped out, pleasure written all over his face. He took the largest suitcase and lifted it into the apartment lobby. Judy followed him with the two smaller ones. The door closed.

Angie sat there for half an hour, deciding what to do. Neither of them came out of the building. This couldn't be what it looked like. After she had put so much effort into convincing herself he wasn't being unfaithful. Was there something going on? Feeling sick ad afraid, Angie returned home. On the way back, she bought the most expensive hairdryer she could find.

Two hours later, Nick phoned. She could hear loud talking and an atmosphere of joviality in the background. 'Hi sweetheart,' he said. 'Sorry I'm not back yet.'

'I was starting to worry,' Angie said. 'Is everything all right?'

'Sure. I got a call from work and popped in, but they'd set me up. The guys had organised a mini stag drink near the office. I couldn't avoid it.'

'Ah, okay. That was kind of them. I guess you won't be home anytime soon then?' She struggled to keep her tone light. 'Shall I pick you up?' He was lying to her! She couldn't believe it.

'You've enough to do. If it goes on too long, I'll sleep at the flat and call you in the morning. No point in spending a fortune on a taxi when we have accommodation just down the road. Sorry about the bad timing, sweetheart.'

Numb with shock, Angie didn't realise she was crying until Poppy said, 'Angie, what's the matter?'

'Nothing. Nick's on his stag do. The guys at work set him up.'

'It had to happen. Never mind, I've a bottle of red and a bag of crisps. We'll have a nice quiet evening in front of the telly.'

* * *

At five in the morning, after a lonely and sleepless night, Angie went down to the kitchen. She found Poppy at the table with her wedding plan folder, and two mugs of steaming tea.

'You've done a brilliant job, Mam. Hasn't the time flown?' Angie said pleasantly, despite her stomach feeling like a bucket of frogs. She had been sick, actually hurled into the loo. Instead of excitement, though, she felt conflicted, confused, and dreadfully hurt.

Poppy smiled. 'Sign this will you?'

Angie lifted the pen and scribbled her signature on the forms wherever her mother pointed. Heaven only knew what she was signing, but if she read them she might hesitate and Poppy would suspect something was wrong.

'Don't forget to organise the flowers for the church, and go over the reception plans with Agapi and Voula. Stavro took most of the wedding stuff back with him. Favours and things. That was handy,' Poppy said.

Stavro had their rings too, as he was going to be their *Koumbaros* – the best man. *He'll be so disappointed when he learns there's to be no wedding.*

'Imagine having a party in the village square, just the same as my own wedding.' Poppy patted her hair and blinked. 'I'll see all my friends again. What do they look like, now?'

Angie hesitated, feeling the weight of her decision bear down. Poor Mam was in for a disappointment, her daughter wasn't getting married. Poppy adored Nick. Angie gulped. She adored Nick too. Tears pricked her eyes. Also, all those kind village people that were cooking for the reception.

Well . . . she thought, why shouldn't that, at least, go ahead? A celebration that a mistake hadn't been made. Festivities to mark the unification of the Kondulakis family. She would speak to the priest – still have a service in church and the party after. She could tell everyone how sorry she was that the marriage was off . . . how terribly sorry. *Oh, Nick . . .*

'Angie?' Poppy said. 'What's the matter?'

'Oh, nothing, just daydreaming. What do your friends look like now? Plump, noisy, mid to late sixties I guess. Lovely people but they'll be jealous as hell when they see your new hairdo, Mam.'

Poppy grinned. 'I want you to be proud of me,' she said.

'Silly, of course I'm proud of you.' She squeezed her mother's hand.

'Pity I can't travel with you today,' Poppy said, 'but I daren't miss my hospital check-up. Anyway, it will be good to go with Nick. Bonding they call it, don't they?'

Hell, Angie hadn't thought about that part. She would have to work something out. Find someone else to fly with her mother. Were Shelly and Debs getting the same flight? Then she realised she hadn't spoken to her friends for days. She should call them from the airport, tell them the bad news.

'I wish I wasn't going so early, Mam, but the nine o'clock flight is the most sensible one. I'd better get my suitcase. The taxi will be here any minute.'

Upstairs, Angie glanced around her bedroom – she had thought the next time she saw it, she'd be a married woman. But no, not now. Her big bed was like an old friend and she remembered hugging her pillow while dreaming about the new boss at work. Three years later, she was on her way to Greece to cancel her marriage to the very same man.

Tears spilled onto her cheeks as she zipped her suitcase. Her mind drifted back to the moment when they discovered they were both avid *Doctor Who* fans. Safely bubblewrapped, inside her luggage, was the perfect wedding cake topper: a groom pulling his bride into the Tardis. She had found it on the web, and although it didn't go with the classic three tiers and columns, Nick would have loved it.

Why did you fall for somebody else, Nick? I love you so much.

Perhaps she should give the Tardis to him anyway. She swore she wouldn't turn into one of those bitter and twisted jilted brides. But what about the children they'd planned together. Who would father them now, if not her darling Nick?

The tears ran faster.

I'll always love you, Nick. Why did this happen to us? Was I just too selfish, for too long? I've been trying to change, honestly. I should hate you, but I can't.

'Angelika, the taxi's here,' her mother shouted up the stairs.

* * *

As the taxi pulled away from the kerb, Angie realised nothing could be gained by sulking. She was bigger than that. She had to face Nick, tell him she wasn't going to marry him before she left for Crete. Return his ring and wish him well. Do the honourable thing. If he was happier with Judy . . . she could live – or at lease exist – with her smashed hopes and dreams.

Her heart was already breaking.

She gave the taxi driver the flat's address, and asked him to hurry. This was one of the hardest things she had ever done. On the doorstep with her keyring in her hand, she found the flat key was missing. At some point, he must have removed it. Technically, the flat was, after all, his. Locked out of his flat, his heart, and his life, she almost broke down on the doorstep. *Oh, Nick!* She rang the bell and looked into the camera over the door. Could she possibly be wrong? Had a terrible twist of circumstances resulted in her believing she had lost him? With all her heart, she hoped this was a ridiculous misunderstanding.

After a long moment, she heard the click of the foyer door as the latch released.

Breathless and trembling at the top of the stairs, she knocked on the flat door. She thought of *Yiayá*, how strong and selfless she was, even today. Didn't she make the right choices, no matter how hard they were? Like leaving her baby on the ridge in order to save her other sons. Angie could be strong and selfless too; well, perhaps not to the extent of her grandmother, but she would do her best. Follow Maria's example.

Her thoughts were knocked out of her when the door opened and Judy Peabody stood before her. Blonde hair – sleep tousled, and her expensive, silver silk pyjamas – rumpled.

'Where's Nick?!' Angie said through her teeth, trying to think what Maria might have done in a similar situation, while she clenched her fists around pure hatred.

Judy lifted her shoulders and turned her palms up. 'Sleeping?'

Angie almost choked with rage. She tugged her engagement ring off and thrust it at Judy, resisting the urge to throw it down the hall with all her strength, or ram it down Judy's pretty, white throat. 'Give him this, will you? The wedding's off!' She glanced over Judy's shoulder, desperate to catch a glimpse of Nick. He didn't appear. Angie swung around and marched down the stairs, unable to see for the pain in her head and the tears in her eyes.

* * *

Heathrow security staff treated Angie like a suspected terrorist. They confiscated her expensive hair mousse and nail polish. When they ordered her to drop it in the bin for 'illegal items', she spitefully sprayed the mousse over the other gleaned toiletries. Then, punished by a three hour delay, she fretted about Nick. Sick of waiting for his call, she turned off her phone.

Throughout the flight, the white noise of rejection hissed painfully in her ears. She couldn't help wondering; what was he doing now . . . and now . . . and now? Until she was so sick of herself she hid in the aeroplane toilet and cried.

Things didn't improve when she arrived at Crete. The airport, dusty and even more chaotic than a month ago, shimmered in the heat. While queuing at passport control, she thought about Maria. How would she take the news that there wasn't going to be a wedding? Angie was loath to disappoint her.

The hour seemed dedicated to flights from the UK and an East Midlands flight landed after hers. The monitor had the wrong luggage carousels listed and, once the tourists realised, they pushed and shoved in the frantic search for suitcases.

Then she had a wonky trolley, hell bent on travelling sideways and catching other harassed travellers' heels. The car hire people claimed to have no knowledge of her advance booking. An argument ensued while the family behind her grumbled and huffed.

Thankfully, her mother had printed the Visa payment and, as all the small cars had gone, she got a free upgrade – but no apology.

Angie raced out of the city, hunched over the steering wheel, jumping amber lights and cursing drivers who seemed incapable of using their mirrors or indicators. On the national highway, she sped to the first garage and found a tanker filling the pumps.

'Twenty minutes,' the attendant said when she lowered her window and caught the pungent whiff of diesel fumes.

'Never mind!' She pulled off the forecourt with a wheel spin. What a rubbish beginning to her trip.

The sun slipped towards the mountaintops, giving the light a peachy warmth. By the time Angie reached the second petrol station, a gangrenous mix of deep red, black and purple slathered the firmament. While she rummaged for euros, a tap on the window made her jump. A man grinned through the glass.

'Manoli, what are you doing here?' she said, relieved to see a friendly face.

'Ah, welcome back, lady! My car is being serviced. You can give me a lift to Viannos?'

'Sure, get in.' She turned the headlights full on and headed for civilisation.

'Why you return so soon? You like it here, yes?'

'I'm supposed to be getting married, Manoli, in Amiras.' Angie took her eyes off the road to see his reaction.

'Congratulations, I will come.'

Taken aback, she looked at him again. 'It might not happen . . . I don't know yet.'

'Be careful!' Manoli stared ahead. 'The edge is dangerous. Many people died here. You see the small churches? Drivers have gone over, into the ravine.'

'Ah, yes, I noticed they're usually on a bend.'

'It is a long drop.'

Manoli didn't speak again until they entered Viannos, which bustled with life. A scattering of locals promenaded proudly down the main street.

'It's good to be back,' Angie said, trying to relax under the big tree with a beer. *Nick and Judy, Nick and Judy, Nick and Judy.* She couldn't even hold a conversation with Manoli, who organised her accommodation once again.

Her scant room – a peaceful haven the first time around – became a torture box of memories. She phoned Poppy, told her about the confiscating security staff at Heathrow, and gave her a list of things to bring to Crete. For the second night in a row, sleep was sparse and interrupted by misery.

* * *

The next morning, just before turning into the village of Amiras, Angie pulled off the highway. She stopped for a moment to compose herself, her nerves were frayed. Nick would have the ring back by now, relieved, no doubt. He must have dreaded telling her because Angie was absolutely positive that he did care for her, in some way. Would she ever be able to speak to him again?

So much had happened since the first time she had driven down this road. She had found her family – but on top of that, she had lost her fiancé, her mother had had a heart attack, and now, Angie suspected she was pregnant. Loath to do a test, Angie was afraid the result would change her direction.

Two mornings in a row she had up-chucked into the toilet at dawn. She recalled her joy, only a couple of days ago, when she realised she might be pregnant. All her dreams had come true. Only hours later, the dream turned into a nightmare. Now, she had lost her ability to think straight. What to do? She had the pregnancy test, but chose to wait until she got to Crete before using it. Delaying tactics, because she hadn't decided on a course of action if the result was positive.

She stared at the war memorial on the corner of the village road. The enormity of the tragedy hit her. Maria's terrible misery, still raw and painful after all this time, multiplied by the suffering of all the other families who had lost their menfolk. Innocent people, their lives turned inside out, for what? She shook her head sadly.

Angie recalled the afternoon when *Yiayá* had relived the horror of the massacre. They had cried together and those tears watered the seed of a bond between them, which Angie was sure would never be broken. She had come to love her grandmother deeply – and she also felt the warmth of her grandmother's deep affection in return.

On this trip, Angie had time to investigate the epitaph, to look for baby Petro and her great-great-grandfather, Matthia, her grumpy uncle's namesake. She stared out at the horizon and felt at home. When Poppy and Maria were finally reunited, would she feel slightly compensated for the loss of the man she loved so much?

She peered up into the deep blue sky and thought about her father. *'I suppose you'll be watching over us, Dad, and I know you'd have approved of the man I was about to marry. I love Nick so much – and for a long time he loved me too. He was wonderful beyond words. I think I'm pregnant by him, so I'm not sure what will happen next. I don't want to use a baby to try and get him back. We both wanted children so badly. What shall I do?*

'I wish you could have come to our wedding, Dad. That's impossible, but I hoped you'd be there in spirit. Now there isn't going to be a marriage, of course. My dreams are shattered, like Mam's. She's been wonderful. She still loves you very much. When she arrives in Amiras, I know she'll be remembering your wedding day, when she walked down the aisle by your side. I don't know if you can give her a 'spiritual hug', is that possible? I'm sure you understand what I mean. I love you, Dad. Always have and always will.'

Suddenly, Angie wanted to be with Maria more than anything in the world. She rushed into the village, parked, and raced up the steps.

'*Yiayá!*' she called into the cottage, ripping through the plastic strip curtain until she was standing before the old lady, grinning like a fool.

'Angelika!' Maria cried, her eyes sparkling.

Angie hugged her grandmother tightly, realising, once more, the noble matriarch was little more than fragile skin and bone. '*Yiayá*, it's so lovely to see you again.' She kissed Maria's soft cheeks and resisted hugging her as tightly as she wanted.

'Welcome back, *koritsie*.' *Yiayá* sat in her usual place on the sofa. *Papoú* grinned from his chair, smiling and clacking his worry beads over the back of his hand. For Angie, it was as if she had never been away. 'Sit next to me, Angelika,' Maria said quietly.

'I'm so glad to be back, *Yiayá*.'

Maria nodded and then rested her hand on Angie's cheek. 'So, you persuaded Poppy to return to Amiras. I've lived in hope for decades, Angelika. My lights went out when she left and, after forty years of darkness, you fetch a beacon of joy. Will I hold my daughter again?' She took Angie's hands in hers. 'I can hardly believe it. The family is going to be almost complete on your wedding day. If only . . . but no, we cannot bring back the dead, only in our hearts. Those who can't be with us for the marriage are sure to be here in spirit, *koritsie*.'

Papoú nodded and crossed himself.

'Do you mean my father?'

'I'm talking about Petro.'

'Of course, I'm sorry.'

* * *

'I'm anxious to hear the rest of your story, *Yiayá*.' Angie said, desperate for somebody to put Nick out of her head before the longing and the hurt diced her heart and threw it to the cats.

'Remind me, where we were?'

'The Nazi had almost shot you, then you'd lost Matthia on the mountainside.'

'Ah, yes, I remember it well, Angelika. I found my son, and the goat with a group of women from Amira who were also running away with their children.'

'Your relief must have been enormous, *Yiayá.*'

Old Maria nodded, her eyes wide as she seemed to stare into the past. 'But our troubles were far from over . . .' she said.

Chapter 31

Crete, 1943.

TOGETHER, WE ALL MADE it to the Plateau of Lassithi, high in the mountains. We were allowed to shelter ourselves in three ruined windmills outside a village.

While our children played, we four women from Amiras Village sat cross-legged on the ground and discussed how we should accommodate ourselves. Eventually, we decided to share a windmill that was almost complete and had three floors. My boys and I took the middle floor, built around the great wooden cogs that were turned by the sails. The sails themselves were long gone, so the mechanism stood motionless.

Eva and her son, Stefan, claimed the narrower level above us. Joanna and Stavroula, with their teenage daughters, slept on the wider ground floor. We could have had a windmill each but felt safer together in one.

We fixed a discarded sail over the doorway. Ten metres away, we used the planks from one of the other mills to build a rickety toilet over a pit. The triangular 'kak-shack' as we called it, much to the delight of the youngsters, was a comical roofless construction that gave us privacy.

Life was difficult, months filled with tension, sickness and hunger. Every day we feared the Nazis would arrive. The windmills were situated atop a ridge on the village perimeter. It became a habit to scan the plateau before we stepped out.

The rains came in mid-October. We shifted our bedding to avoid drips through the leaking roof. Food consisted of snails, wild mushrooms, and young cactus pads which we peeled and boiled. Acorns, carobs, walnuts and figs were collected for our stores. We stewed nettles, found dandelions, millet, wild parsnip and asparagus.

Each day was a dire struggle for sustenance. The flesh fell from our bones. My breasts, which weeks earlier were ebullient with the milk of life, now hung like flat pancakes against my bony ribcage, but we were surviving.

One morning, while gathering carobs, I found myself thinking of Petro. How could I have managed to get our family to this place if I'd had a newborn to deal with as well? I knew that task was beyond anyone's capabilities. They say God works in mysterious ways, and I believe that's true. If Petro had been with us, we may all have perished in the end.

Fleas tortured us. Our fingernails were black, encrusted with dried blood raked from our necks, armpits and groins. The minute tormentors ran riot over the floor and walls and when we slept, they fed, and then sought sanctuary in the nooks and crannies of our bodies. We woke each morning, blood-streaked and disgusted.

I fretted for Matthia. He became listless and uncommunicative, his belly swollen and his limbs stick-thin. I felt sure he would die and the injustice made me bitter. Wretched, I snarled at my friends and snapped at Stavro.

Eva and Stavroula decided to return to the apiary. They came back the next day with four full frames of honey and several bee stings. Matthia wasn't interested, he just wanted to lie on the sheepskins and stare at the ceiling planks.

Joanna trudged into the village and asked if there was a doctor, although we didn't have money to pay. She returned with a solid looking woman, sixtyish and dressed in black. Her name was *Yiayá* Fotiá, Grandmother Fire.

'He has bad blood,' she said after stroking his dry skin, dragging his eyes open and inspecting his tongue. 'We must bleed him.'

I had seen this done to my father. The thought of poor little Matthia going through the process made me sick. Joanna convinced me the old woman knew her job. I did my best to comfort Matthia while my friends made him straddle the centre post of the windmill. They tied his arms and legs on the opposite side of the column so that his body pressed against the wood, which kept him still. I kept talking to him, assuring him he would feel better soon.

Yiayá Fotiá heated her medicinal cups on the fire and then produced a razorblade. My stomach churned.

Matthia cried bitterly.

She sliced into his beautiful white back and then placed the hot glass cups over the wounds. As they started to cool, the vessels sucked onto his skin, drawing his blood from the cuts.

Matthia wailed loudly.

When the old woman had six cups on his back, I could take no more.

'Stop!' I cried, sick to my bones. 'I don't want you to do this.'

Yiayá Fotiá understood my determination.

'He's your child, Teacher,' she said. 'The mother always knows when it's enough.'

Mortified, I realised I should have stopped her after the first cut.

Yiayá Fotiá looked at my hands, now septic in places where the burns were constantly cracking open. 'I'm going to collect the right herbage for a poultice,' she said, and within the hour she returned with a large bunch of *asko zitsára*, hemlock.

Stavro watched her pound the stalks to pulp. 'Don't touch, son, the juice is poisonous,' I said. It stank of rotting mice.

'There's a clump by the cemetery at home, Mama,' he said. 'They have the same purple spots on the stems. Once, we were going to make pea shooters, but the priest came out of the graveyard and said to leave the plant alone.'

The thought of him putting hemlock in his mouth made me shudder. 'Just as well he stopped you,' I told him. 'When they condemned Socrates to death, they forced him to drink hemlock juice so that he died by his own hand.'

Stavro glanced from me to Matthia who lay face down and miserable on a sheepskin. I sensed Stavro's concern and, after a moment, he performed for his poor, sick brother. Writhing on the floor like a dog with fleas, he watched Matthia's face.

'Was Socrates in agony, Mama? Did his belly burst open, squirting his shitty guts all over the ceiling? Arh, arh! And did his eyes catapult out of his head and roll around the floor? While they were there, did he look up all the old women's skirts?' He placed his fingers on his eyes and then flung them out wide.

Matthia managed a smile.

'Stavro, you're too gruesome, son. Poor old Socrates simply fell asleep without any pain, or any of your fine dramatics. And watch your mouth or you'll feel my hand across the backs of your legs.'

'You'll have to catch me first, Mama. Bet ya can't catch me!' Stavro sidestepped around me and the *Yiayá* Fotiá.

Matthia managed a giggle.

'You need to control that one,' *Yiayá* Fotiá said as she plastered the stinking gunk onto my hands. 'He'll give you trouble if you don't rein him in soon.'

Behind her, Stavro put his thumb to his nose and wiggled his fingers.

Matthia laughed.

'Don't go too far, Stavro,' I said, giving him the 'stop it now' look, yet I rejoiced in my heart. Stavro was a very special child.

'I have nothing with which to pay you,' I told *Yiayá* Fotiá as she left.

'You may teach my granddaughter to read,' she said. 'I'll send her tomorrow afternoon.'

* * *

That child must have spread the word. Before two weeks were up, I had six students coming for lessons from 4p.m. to 6p.m.. The payments they made amounted to a drum of olive oil, a bag of lentils, a sack of horse fodder to make porridge, one laying hen, a chair with a broken leg, an army greatcoat and half a parachute.

Our lives improved.

The village priest gave me a box of white chalk and I used soot to darken an area of the wall, to use as a blackboard. The priest also sent a bundle of pencils and a bolt of paper that I carefully folded and tore into squares when the children needed to write.

One morning, while cleaning our floor, I noticed a curl of paper sticking out from under Andreas's sheepskins, where my boys slept. When I pulled it out, I found childish drawings of a baby and recognised Stavro's artistry. I called him to my side.

'What's all this about, son?' I asked, pointing to the sketches.

'Sorry, Mama. Am I in trouble for stealing the paper?'

'You only needed to ask, Stavro.'

'I didn't want to upset you, Mama.'

'Why did you feel it would upset me, is it Petro?'

He nodded, tangling his fingers and looking at the floor. 'I don't want to forget him.' He shook his head and then turned his sad face up to me. 'He's dead, isn't he?'

'I'm afraid he is, son. God decided Heaven was the best place for him. And rightly so, Stavro. He would never have survived the terrible journey we made, would he? We only just managed it ourselves.'

Stavro looked into my eyes and I saw his slight embarrassment.

'Tell me, son,' I said gently.

'I feel like he's slipping away out of my head. He was my baby brother, Mama, and I know it's soppy, but I did, you know, love him.' He swallowed hard.

I lowered my eyes for a moment.

Stavro continued. 'Stefan told me what happened at home, while we were hiding. They shot lots of people. Our friends. Was Petro with them?'

With my heart breaking, and the twisting pain of keeping control of my emotions, I whispered that Petro was indeed one of the martyrs of that terrible day.

'Well, I would want people to remember me, you know, if I'd been killed,' Stavro said, 'because it seems it's all that's left of you, the memory of you in other people's heads. And I got a bit scared when I realised I was forgetting what baby Petro looked like, so I tried drawing him to keep him alive in my mind. I never want to forget him. Ever.'

I chewed my lip, unable to speak. *Oh, Stavro.*

'Are you angry with me, Mama?'

I shook my head and slipped my arm around his shoulders. We sat in silence for a few minutes before Stavro spoke again.

'Anyway, it worked,' he said.

'What worked, son?'

'As soon as I started to draw him, I remembered things.'

'Really? Like what?' I said, smiling, wondering what he recollected.

He gazed at nothing, distant but calm. 'Do you remember how Petro would make fists and do that boxing? He had a wicked look in his eyes, like he was staring at somebody he wanted to punch. It always made me laugh, I watched him for ages. And that birthmark, the dark red bird on the back of his head. It seemed as if it was flying over his brains. And I remembered that sometimes he would screw his mouth up, as if he was whistling a tune that we couldn't hear.' Stavro's eyes sparkled, and there was a moment of silence before he said with all sincerity, 'I wish he'd lived, Mama, he would have made a great brother.'

'We can't change what's happened, Stavro, that's a fact,' I replied, holding back tears. And you do have Matthia, but you're right, we should never forget baby Petro.'

* * *

Although our lifestyles improved slightly, Matthia remained sickly. He became covered in spots that developed into open sores. *Yiayá* Fotiá paid another visit, which terrified Matthia, but I promised him there would be no bloodletting. She said my son had scabies, a highly contagious parasite.

Joanna, Eva and Stavroula said he would have to move out and stay in one of the other windmills or we would all have the dreaded crabs, and wasn't it bad enough with fleas running over our skin and feeding on our blood. They wouldn't have the dirty lice living under our skin, shitting in our flesh.

I told the schoolchildren not to come back and explained why. The next day, a small bald man wearing spectacles appeared and introduced himself as the local doctor. He examined Matthia and said the rash wasn't scabies but simple malnutrition. He gave me food vouchers, nearly useless with precious little in the village shop. Still, it meant the children returned for my lessons and we received occasional payments of eggs and potatoes. Stavro played eating games with Matthia and succeeded in getting him to swallow almost everything put in front of him.

Summer ended suddenly on the last day of October. The air turned cold and, wearing all our clothes, we huddled together under olive sacks. I borrowed a needle, cotton and scissors from one of my pupils' parents and made long trousers for my boys from green tent canvas that the fleeing Italians had forgotten.

Gradually, Matthia grew stronger. We heard the Nazis had left the area and we were able to return to Amiras. We planned to go the week before Christmas but a snowfall blocked the mountain pass.

In mid-January, a break in the weather put carts on the road. We begged a lift from a potato merchant who was setting out to Ierapetra for supplies. He agreed to drop us off at our village. We all climbed into the back of his lorry with our meagre possessions bundled in squares of blanket or sailcloth. Freezing cold, and with our behinds bruised from the long and bumpy ride, we arrived back in Amiras.

Chapter 32

Crete, Present Day.

'Angelika!' Maria said sharply.

Angie stared at her grandparents' puzzled faces and realised she had been daydreaming about Nick. She must tell them the wedding was off. The longer she left it, the harder it would become. She reached for her ring finger to turn her engagement ring, a nervous habit. Then, startled for a moment, she realised it wasn't there. Perhaps Judy wore it? Why was she punishing herself with such stupid thoughts?

'Does your mother know?' Maria said quietly.

Angie's head snapped up, confused, speechless, eyes questioning.

'There's only one reason why you would look so sad, and wouldn't be wearing that beautiful ring.'

'It's only just happened, *Yiayá*. After years of living with me, he's fallen in love with somebody else.' She spoke quietly, holding back the tears. 'I didn't tell Mam, because I was afraid she might cancel her flight.'

Maria patted Angie's hand. 'Very considerate of you. Thank you for that. How long have you and Nick been together?'

'Three years.'

'And you don't think he's worth fighting for?'

'Well, yes, but . . .'

'Then do it, child! I nearly lost Vassili once. I gave up on everything. Don't make that mistake.'

Angie looked across at her grandfather and found it hard to imagine he would do anything untoward.

'Let me tell you what happened, Angelika,' Maria said. 'Then make up your own mind.'

* * *

Amiras, 1943.

BACK IN AMIRAS, we found our village had not suffered as much destruction as surrounding communities. A wagon, laden with wide planks, dropped its load for the repair of the houses that were burned. Many of the women had moved back home, and some men returned from the war in Albania. No one had news of Vassili and I feared I would never see my husband again. Between us, we managed to put a roof on our house, board up the windows, and make a crude door hinged with strips of goat hide.

We found our two big old trees laden with fruit, so much that the branches weighed to the ground. We picked the largest olives for preserving in brine in a terracotta urn. The rest, we took to our local olive factory in the lower village, where the village donkey pulled a millstone around, crushing the fruit to extract the oil. We brought the olive leaves home for goat fodder, the pips to dry in the sun and use for smokeless winter fuel, and the olive pulp to make soap and night lights. Nothing was wasted.

At first, without cooking pots, or a *skapáni* to dig the earth, everything seemed set against us. We needed wood to burn for heat and cooking and although surrounded by trees, we were without saw and axe to cut logs. Before the Nazis left, they burned the crops. No wheat harvest meant no flour, and in turn no bread or rusks.

I remembered Andreas's lessons on how to make coffee and bread from acorns, to take sugar from the carob beans, and to use pine cones instead of charcoal or wood for cooking. I shared all this information with the other village women.

In the spring of 1944, the Germans were retreating from mainland Greece. More of our soldiers trickled home, used up and spat out by the armed forces. In a pitiful state, these men were too sick or weak to be of any further use to the army. Their wives nurtured them back to health and they soon set about making tools and shoes for us all.

In March, six months after the massacre, I was busy at the outside sink carefully removing the eyes from half a dozen potatoes before cooking them. The shoots would provide us with another crop. I concentrated on the job, and didn't notice the stranger until he was well into our garden.

A skinny man, with a beard that reached his chest, wandered onto our land. He walked right through the new tomato patch, flattening the seedlings, but I hadn't the heart to scold him.

This stranger wore the coat of a soldier and, from the way it hung limply from his shoulders, I guessed it didn't belong to him. The garment was far too big. The vagrant's long hair hung in matted tendrils, and his dull dark eyes were sunken deep into his skull. Some mother's son, God love him, I thought. The tragedy and pain he endured must have been enormous to reduce him to that dishevelled condition.

Yet in those eyes that witnessed too much death, there was something familiar. He stood there, smiling; his strong teeth appearing huge in the skull-like face, the breeze ruffling his long hair.

'Yes?' I said, wondering from where he came and what he wanted.

'You've forgotten me so soon?' he asked.

The voice! My darling husband. 'Oh, Dear God, Vassili!' I cried, rushing into his arms.

His thin, bent body shocked me. And the smell of him. He appeared to be far less than half the man that left only a year ago. The small amount of skin, visible on his hirsute face, stretched tight across his bones and ran with sores. His dull eyes were sunken and his broad muscular body was now nothing but skeleton and skin. I sat by the stone oven, pulled him onto my lap, and rocked him like a baby. My beautiful husband, reduced to a starved shadow of his former self.

Over the weeks that followed, I told him of all the things that had happened while he had been away, reliving the events, but Vassili seemed remote and uncaring. He ate ferociously in those first days and then he started complaining. I did nothing right. His behaviour confused me and I should have realised a breakdown had warped his mind. I loved him so much and held him in great admiration, so this new conduct confused me.

In the early days, I didn't understand that war changed more than his physical appearance. He would wake from nightmares, thrashing and screaming. His mind collapsed due to the atrocities and the cruelty he had experienced.

Stavro and Matthia were bewildered. He frightened them with his shouting and they tried to stay out of his way.

In September, Constantina's little boy was baptised. The occasion was hugely uplifting but at the same time, sad for all of us. Her little baby boy Yeorgo had been found seconds from death, under the huge pile of dead men and boys from Amiras. The air almost crushed out of his little body, he lay there, unconscious, for three days. That the baby lived, survived all that was against him, elevated the spirits of the entire village. If he could endure such adversity, so would we.

The baptism was held in the church yard. In accordance with our religious rules, to have a celebration within the first twelve months of a death in the family was unthinkable. They held the baptism exactly a year to the day that Yeorgo was found alive.

So, while we ate and drank and danced in the village square, celebrating Yeorgo's life, we remembered our departed loved ones. Nobody mentioned their slaughtered menfolk, but they were in our hearts and minds. Among the merrymaking, the proud dancing, and forced conversation, many women suddenly broke down in tears. Held tightly by their neighbours, no one asked why, or tried to make them stop. We were simply there for each other, letting our friends vent their grief against our shoulders, and us against theirs, once more.

Each took their turn in bouncing the tot on their knee. Some laughed, some wept, some were still so traumatised they simply stared at him while thoughts of their own departed ran through their minds. I desperately wanted to hold baby Yeorgo, but found it impossible. Too much, too soon. My heart was still breaking. If only Petro had survived, he would have been around the same age.

Constantina came and sat next to me for a while. She was a handsome woman. Her straight black hair, parted down the centre, was pulled severely back into a chignon. Big black eyes under arched eyebrows, and although thin, as we all were, her figure was shapely.

We held hands, hardly speaking. The little tribute was generous of her. Sadly, our eyes met and we nodded occasionally. There was nothing to say that was worthy of words. We were close friends before that September night, but after, I couldn't stand to see her with Yeorgo. I avoided her. Things changed as her boy grew older. He often played with Matthia and I grew to accept him.

Vassili and I became virtual strangers. Our marital situation deteriorated. My husband turned to drink and I became a nagging wife, always on his back complaining. Bizarrely, we protected ourselves by hating each other. Then, one evening, an argument about nothing escalated. He called me a filthy whore and threw a punch at me, knocking me to the ground. With my nose gushing blood, I ran from the house.

When I reached the cemetery, I fell to the ground and cried until exhausted. What was it all for? I couldn't see any good, any joy, any reason to continue with my mortal toil. Vassili had been everything that I lived for, yet my nagging drove him to drink and now he hated me. He blamed me for my sons turning against him, he blamed me for the death of Petro, and he blamed me for the impoverished way we lived. I despaired, my life not worth living. I saw, like an omen right in front of me, the clump of hemlock that Stavro talked about.

Heaven seemed so inviting, so peaceful. I pulled the stems from the ground and snapped them into chunks, stuffing them into my mouth. I thought about all that had gone before. Soon I would be with my baby Petro, and dear Andreas, and also my gentle grandfather, Matthia; a place without hunger, fleas or aggression. I chewed and swallowed, chewed and swallowed, eager for the moment when I would pass from this earthly struggle into the afterlife.

Consciousness drifted away; hemlock, the painless death – until searing pain jabbed at the back of my throat and I heard my husband's voice, pleading, 'Don't die, I love you, Maria! Forgive me!'

Vassili cried, begged, tears of remorse raging down his face. His hand thrust into my mouth, jagged nails stabbing until my stomach rolled and I convulsed in a fit of vomiting. He sat up with me all through that night, holding me, keeping me awake until he felt it was safe for me to sleep.

* * *

The crisis of our lives had passed. Slowly, we learned to trust one another. After a time of growing towards each other like a courting couple, nervous and shy, our love returned. On a warm summer night, we drank a little wine and then Vassili led me outside. He hummed an old song, a favourite of mine, while we danced in the moonlight. We reminisced about life before the war and, just before dawn, I fell into his arms and we became lovers again.

I truly believe that on that night, when we laughed and cried together and lay on a blanket beneath the big olive tree, under the dazzling constellation of Cassiopeia, I conceived my baby girl, Calliope.

Chapter 33

Crete, Present Day.

'PHONE YOUR FIANCÉ NOW,' Maria said. 'Tell him your honest feelings, Angelika, at least do that. Don't shut all the doors. After all that I've told you, haven't you understood anything? The only things in life worth fighting for are those that you love. Fight, girl.' She lifted a clenched fist and shook it at Angie. 'Give it all you have. If you don't value him that highly, you shouldn't have been marrying him anyway.'

Confused, because right up to the moment Judy answered the door of Nick's flat, in her pyjamas, Angie believed she could have been mistaken about their affair.

She walked into the garden and stared at the horizon. What if Nick came back to her? She would always be wondering if something was going on with another woman, or even with Judy who was the sort to make sure she got what she wanted.

But, Angie thought, *she* could be that determined too! Just look at her grandmother. What she had gone through, endured, all fuelled on stubbornness, determination and guts. She returned to the living room, took her phone from her bag, and nodded at Maria.

Back into the garden, she realised she hadn't turned her mobile on since London airport. Five missed calls from Nick. Should she take the pregnancy test before she called him? He had a right to know, didn't he?

But he might marry her for the sake of the baby, and then things were bound to go wrong later. She foresaw separation and custody battles. Why instigate all that unhappiness? Angie never wanted her child to be in the bitter tangle of a divorce.

She loved Nick intensely and would do anything to keep him, except use her child as ammunition. Could that love turn to suspicion, resentment, and eventually hate if they married now? She had seen it happen to friends. It didn't seem possible, but she guessed her colleagues had thought that too.

Angie returned indoors and stared at her grandmother. 'What should I do? I'm so upset I can't think straight.'

'Follow your heart, Angelika.'

'Angelika! Angelika!'

Angie recognised Voula's dulcet tones and much as she loved her Aunty, now was not the moment. Voula crashed into the cottage, her arm outstretched, thrusting a large brown envelope Angie's way.

'For you!' she said.

Angie blinked at the letter addressed to her. Who would send her mail to Amiras? She tore it open and found another, beautiful, white embossed envelope, with Nick's handwriting across the top.

NOT TO BE OPENED UNTIL OUR WEDDING DAY

Angie wondered if this was the big brush-off, letting her down while she was far away and surrounded by her family. When she moved into Nick's mindset, his timing gave her a chance to calm down and come to accept the situation, before they met again. But why save it for her wedding day? She could hardly believe Nick would be that thoughtless or cruel. She hesitated, and then decided as there wasn't going to be a wedding day she might as well open the bloody envelope and be done with it.

Her hands trembled slightly as she peeled back the flap and examined the contents. A rose scented letter, and a cheque for

£400,000. Her jaw dropped and she fell into a seat beside her grandmother. Maria also looked at the cheque in Angie's hands, and then blinked at Angie. In shock, they stared at each other. Voula and Vassili, aware of a drama, watched silently.

Angie opened the letter, exquisite embossed paper that was folded into three. She read in silence.

My Dearest Darling Wife,

I feel as though I have been waiting for our wedding day all my life. I can never explain exactly how much I love you. This cheque is for you to spend, as you see fit, on our future. If you like, open the editing business we talked about, knowing we will start our married life together with no financial worries. I sold the flat at a premium to Judy Peabody. I tried my best to keep it a secret because I wanted to give you a big surprise on your wedding day; but perhaps you suspected?

I have also sold the Porsche Boxter, but this money will be used to do up Poppy's house exactly the way you (and Poppy) want it.

I love you so very much, Angie, you are my life.

Your devoted husband, Nick, XXX

Maria poked a crooked finger at the kisses and said, 'What does it say?'

Angie translated, tears tripping her before she got halfway.

'Voula, raki!' Maria said. Vassili nodded. Voula scuttled. 'You'd better call him right away,' Maria said.

'It's not that simple,' Angie said. 'I gave my ring to the woman I thought he'd fallen in love with.'

Maria threw her head back and laughed. 'That's the funniest thing! Then you'd better call *her* right away then.'

Angie felt sick. He'd sold his flat and his precious Porsche Boxster for her and she couldn't trust him for five minutes. Shame on her. She phoned the flat, hoping Judy was there and that she hadn't had the number changed.

Judy wasn't home. Nick might never forgive her. He was probably cancelling the cheque right now. She called an old friend at Whitekings and got Judy's office number.

Judy picked up. Angie's heart was racing.

'I thought you and Nick were having an affair,' Angie blurted out.

'Is that his fiancée?'

'Yes: Angie. I thought you –'

'No such luck, Angie. It would have been nice, yes, but he wasn't having any of it. He'd rather lose his job, sell his flat, and stay with you.' She snorted. 'I take it you want the ring back?'

'I –'

'Look, Angie, I know we haven't been bosom buddies, but I want you to know: it wasn't me that fired Nick.'

Fired Nick? Then she saw it all. Taking the time off to decorate her mother's house. His recent attention to the *Guardian* appointments page. His sudden interest in their old idea, to start their own writing and editing service. 'Who fired him then?' Angie asked.

'The MD himself. We had a board meeting, first of last month. Nick simply didn't turn up, didn't call in, and his phone was off. When he said he couldn't attend the next meeting either, the MD put him on the redundancy list.'

'Unfortunately, Nick was alone with my mother when she had a heart attack, Judy. His quick action saved her life. He picked her up and took her to hospital. They make you turn your phone off in cardiology.'

'I understand. I'm sorry. How is she now?'

'On the mend, but if Nick hadn't been so quick thinking, there might have been a less satisfactory scenario. He stayed with her until I arrived back from Crete that night.'

'I see. You can collect the ring from my flat at the weekend.'

'I can't, I'm in Crete. Nick and I were planning to get married here on Saturday.'

'Unfortunate coincidence. That would explain his unavailability for the MD's next meeting, on Friday. I'll make sure you get the ring back.'

'Uhm, does he know about it? I um . . .'

'Haven't seen or spoken to him since you gave me the ring. I won't say a word.'

'Oh, um, yes, thank you.'

Angie ended the call, sighed, re-composed herself and said, 'It looks like the wedding's back on. I made a stupid mistake.'

* * *

The next day, Angie encouraged Maria to continue with her story, still eager to learn why Poppy had left Crete. Close to reaching the end of her quest, Angie guessed she was about to understand everything.

'Please tell me about my mother's early life, *Yiayá*.'

Maria chuckled. 'Calliope was a darling, chubby as a cherub and always laughing,' she said. 'Terribly noisy, constantly singing, or shouting, or squealing! How many times did I tell her,

"Young Ladies don't shout"? She remembered for less than a minute. Occasionally she'd shout back at me, "But Mama, I don't want to be a Young Lady. I want to be a Big Boy, like Matthia." He was her hero. Sometimes, if she woke before him, she would put on his clothes and shoes. She'd clomp about the house and tell us she was a boy and her name was Matthia. She had us in stitches with her antics.'

Pleasure flushed Maria's cheeks. 'Poppy hugged everyone she met. Her favourite place was in Vassili's lap. She would scramble up there with no regard as to where she dug her elbows and heels. I often saw him wince and draw his knees up, his eyes watering.' Maria chuckled. 'Poppy would fling her arms around his neck and yell, "I love you, Daddy!" before planting great slobbery kisses all over his face. Vassili adored her.' She glanced over to his chair. 'He still does.'

Angie found herself grinning, but her smile softened when she realised how much Vassili must miss his daughter.

Maria said, 'I returned to teaching after the war. We had forty-five local students aged between six and eleven. School started at 8a.m. and lasted for four hours.

'I had a big playpen for Calliope. It was a huge, open-topped, wooden crate set under the big olive tree. I would dump her in it with a bottle, toys, and her favourite blanket. All Vassili had to do was to keep an eye on her while he worked in the garden.

'One morning, I remember it so clearly, the year was 1953. We had just started teaching English in our Greek schools. I was attempting to give a group of ten-year-olds their first lesson in a language I barely knew myself, when a terrible thumping hammered on the classroom door. I looked through the glass at the top, but saw nobody. When I opened up, to investigate further, three-year-old Calliope rode straight into the classroom on her little tricycle and said, "I need to start school now, Mama! Where shall I sit?" My students thought it hilarious. She was a bossy little madam. Happy days, Angelika, although we had civil war. Our crops were bountiful. We were together, healthy, and life seemed harmonious.'

Maria recounted more tales of Poppy, and Angie realised her mother was a character.

'How pleased I was to have my little girl,' Maria said. 'She came like a blessing, absorbed our happiness, multiplied it tenfold, and then gave it right back. Whatever our difficulties, we found it impossible to be miserable with Poppy around.'

Angie imagined her mother as a newborn, held precious by *Yiayá*. Life seemed to have improved immensely for them all, after the ravages of war and the tragedies they suffered. She stood and drew the lace curtain back. Above the trees and rooftops of the lower village, the church bell tower marked the spot where she would be married in two days' time.

Captivated by Maria's stories, Angie realised that she still didn't know why her mother had left Crete.

She checked online and saw Poppy and Nick's plane had landed. Soon, the family would be reunited. She gave herself a mental pat on the back. The struggle for unification had been tough at times, but worth it. She willed Nick to hurry, longing to be in his arms, and she couldn't wait to see Poppy and Maria embrace.

The old woman smiled.

Angie smiled back. 'I'm so excited, *Yiayá*. It's going to be wonderful.'

* * *

Poppy glanced around the arrivals area of Heraklion airport, her eyes jumping from the WC sign, to the café, to a row of empty seats.

'Do you need the loo?' Nick said.

She shook her head, unsure what she wanted.

'How do you feel?' Nick asked.

Poppy lifted and dropped her shoulders in a shrug. *So many lost years*, she thought. Who would have believed her return to the island? But when she left Crete, she didn't have a daughter whose happiness was paramount. If her heart packed up, she had to leave this world satisfied she had done everything possible for Angelika's future. Stavro had better be right. She hoped enough time had passed since their troubles.

Nick stood in the car hire queue after depositing her and the suitcases under the clock. As if sensing her eyes on him, he turned and beamed. Poppy had taken to him from the first moment they'd met. She smiled back.

The airport had changed beyond recognition. Poppy remembered the old aerodrome, stifling heat and dust that had itched her nose and eyes. A row of temporary buildings had consisted of nothing more than white canvas tents. She recalled the cement skeleton of a new construction, possibly the modern arrivals lounge she sat in now, with its marble floor and modular seating.

Tired, Poppy allowed her lids to slide down. She tilted her face to enjoy the cooling draught from an air-con grille above. Her thoughts slipped back four decades. Recollections of terror filled her head. The last time she passed through Heraklion airport she was fleeing for her life.

The junta officers were sure to administer the worst possible torture before executing her. They would force her to admit she had killed one of their men. Her eyes flew open . . . but she could not stop the ghastly images: the memory of her last shocking hour in Crete. In Amiras, people were bound to remember why she left . . . even though her own mind blocked most of the details.

If they couldn't forget, could they at least forgive?

* * *

Crete, 1968.

'Go! Don't come back, Poppy!' Stavro said, hugging her so tight, crushing her against him. He shoved her ticket and a small roll of pounds and drachmas into the pocket of her short, belted trenchcoat. 'Don't forget us, Calliope Lambrakis,' he used her full name that last time, and then he pushed her through the black rubber doors.

Poppy ran across the tarmac, her Cuban-heeled boots hitting the puddles, soaking the bottom of her orange flares. Fighting tears, she raced up the metal steps, clutching her meagre luggage. The round vanity case, blue patent leather with white daisies, was stuffed with a few snatched essentials.

Her shoulder throbbed, the pain making her squint. She hadn't expected the shotgun's recoil and wondered if it had cracked a bone. Embarrassed to be the last passenger on flight OA41, she kept her head down and hurried along the aisle.

The man next to her, who had stood while she got to her window seat, gave her a cigarette and a booklet of Olympic Airway's matches. Hands trembling, she lit the wrong end, broke off the tip and sucked hard on the raw tobacco.

'Don't worry, it's safer than the bus,' the man said, patting her arm, mistaking her distress for fear of flying.

Poppy pulled the pleated curtain back and stared out of the small round window, watching the propellers gather speed until they were a blur. The plane vibrated with a rebellious promise to defy gravity.

The air hostess wore a stiffly lacquered blonde beehive, false eyelashes, and startling ice-pink lipstick. She asked the passengers to extinguish cigarettes and fasten their seatbelts for take-off. Poppy's hands shook so badly she could hardly manage the lap strap. You're safe now, she promised herself, closing her eyes for a second and crossing herself.

Her respite was short-lived.

The propellers slowed, the steps were returned and a grey army Jeep came to a halt at the base of them.

'God have mercy, God save me,' she jabbered, her hysteria rising.

The door opened and two hefty military police in dark uniforms entered the plane. They came up the narrow aisle like scum in a blocked drain, checking passports and identity cards. Poppy saw no chance of escape.

When the police reached her, she would be escorted off the plane, locked up, interrogated and killed. Her family would be given hell for as long as the junta ruled. Perhaps her brothers would be executed too, for what she had done.

The hostess walked up the aisle collecting IDs from each row of passengers. She handed them to the military police that followed with pistols drawn. By the time they reached Poppy's row, her heart hammered so hard it drowned the drone of the idling engines. She snatched the sick bag, vomited into it and wiped her mouth on her sleeve.

'ID!' the nearest military policeman demanded. Hands trembling, she passed hers to the cigarette man who, in turn, handed it to the hostess along with his own.

Poppy shrank into her seat, staring at her knees.

'Undo your seatbelt, place your hands on your head and stand up!' the officer barked.

Trapped in the plane, Poppy saw no way of escape. Quivering with fear, she followed their instructions.

'Not you, woman, sit down!' the official ordered.

She glanced at her neighbour. The cigarette man, with his hands on his head, turned towards her. From his look, she knew he realised she also risked capture by the military. He nodded, blinked slowly, saying nothing because they both knew saying anything could be interpreted in any way the junta wanted.

Poppy watched the officers and their captive leave the plane. At that moment, all the hell and injustice that she had suffered seemed to mow her down. Life had not been fair. This journey to London wasn't simply an escape from danger, it marked a new beginning – but it had cost her everything. Her lovely home, and those she loved, were gone forever. She thought about her parents, brothers, and her dear, darling Yeorgo. The dreadful situation was more than Poppy could bear.

What would happen to them, her family? As the plane took to the sky, she swore she would never love again, she had suffered enough. She watched her island shrink into the sea and wondered about the life ahead of her. Then, all she could see were the clouds blurred by tears.

'Goodbye Crete, goodbye Mama, goodbye Yeorgo and my poor dead boys,' Poppy whispered, believing she would never return.

* * *

Crete, Present Day.

NICK RETURNED FROM THE Avis counter. 'Let's go outside, Mam, they're bringing the car to the front.'

Nick called her 'Mam', short for the Greek, Mama, and it made Poppy smile. With the wedding only two days away she guessed the time was right. Despite the grin on his face and the mischievous twinkle in his eye, he must be stressed about meeting the family too.

Poppy patted his arm, 'You're the boss, Son.'

As they walked towards the glass doors, Poppy studied her reflection. What would they think of her?

'You look great, don't worry,' Nick said as if reading her thoughts. 'If Angie looks half as good as you when she's your age, I'll be a lucky man.'

Poppy forced a smile, though oddly uncomfortable receiving a compliment about her appearance from her future son-in-law. 'Don't talk rubbish. Now where's the car?'

'Here.' Nick nodded at a small, white, open-top 4x4. 'You get in and I'll load the cases.'

'It's got no roof!' Poppy stared at the Suzuki Jimny.

'That's because we're on an adventure, and anyway, you'll get a better view of the countryside.'

'It's almost dark, and what about the mosquitoes? We'll be bitten to buggery!' Poppy said.

'They'll never catch us.'

'I hope you're not one of those speed freaks. Just mind you stick to the speed limit. Good grief, my new hairdo will be destroyed. I could kill you, you lummox.'

Feeling much better with something to gripe about, Poppy made him unzip her suitcase to find the chiffon scarf she wore over her curlers at night. While Nick had the case open, Poppy gathered the toiletries that she had brought for Angelika and dropped them into her oversized handbag.

Nick discovered the boot was practically non-existent. He released one of the back seats and stowed the cases there. Poppy watched over him like a mother hen. Nick might be forty years old and one and a half feet taller than her, but she believed there wasn't a man on earth that didn't need advice occasionally. Eventually, she sat in the passenger seat, clutching her handbag and complaining about the lack of roof.

'Belt up, Mam,' Nick said.

'You mind your mouth, Son,' Poppy replied, not quite sure if he was joking.

'Your seatbelt . . .'

'I'm not stupid.'

Poppy watched him study the map before they set off.

'Not long now, we'll be there in an hour,' Nick pulled onto the motorway. 'The road takes us almost straight across to the south coast. I can't wait to see Angie.'

Hunched down in the seat, Poppy clutched the front of her scarf with one hand and her collar with the other, not happy with the noisy, draughty vehicle.

'I hope they didn't make you pay full price when you only got half a car,' she shouted above the roar of the wind. 'And slow down! I daren't open my mouth for fear my damn dentures will be blown away.'

Nick didn't reply, or go any slower, but he was still grinning when they pulled into a petrol station. Poppy made him get a cardigan out of her cabin bag while a young lad filled the tank. She tidied herself up and looked at Nick, but his attention was elsewhere.

He stared admiringly at a massive all-terrain vehicle, parked on low ramps in the mechanics' bay. A giant car that seemed to be constructed of mismatched parts that didn't quite belong together, but at least it had a lid, Poppy thought. The wheels were even wider than the enormous Jeep-type body and the row of spotlights across the roof would better suit an articulated lorry. Bullbars protected the front. Despite the mythology, Poppy doubted a single bull ran free in all Crete. Men, why couldn't they be satisfied with anything as practical as a Ford Fiesta?

'Nice wheels!' Nick said to the pump attendant.

'The boss's,' he replied. 'Where you go?'

'Amiras, a wedding, I'm the groom.'

'Congratulations.' The lad glanced at Poppy.

'My future mother-in-law.' Nick smiled.

'You could do with some air in that back tyre,' the lad said. 'Pull over to the hose while I get the pump key.'

Poppy watched him jog back to the glass-fronted shop where a couple of men sat inside, playing *tavli*. He had a few words and they peered up from their backgammon board. She stared at the older of the two and then shrank into her seat.

'Do you know them?' Nick asked as he drove away.

'It's been so long, and the shadows . . .' Poppy replied, clutching on to her scarf and her dignity as Nick raced towards Amiras. The silence seemed awkward, and then they both started so speak at the same time.

'Look, I –'

'Let me say –'

They laughed together and the tension fell.

'Go on,' Poppy said.

Nick took a breath. 'I just wanted to thank you for doing this for Angie. I don't know what your problem is with your family, but I do realise this was a difficult decision for you. We're both very grateful.' He glanced at her.

'Watch the road!'

'And we're sorry we were so full of wedding plans; we didn't notice you were poorly. It was very selfish of us.'

His phone bleeped. He pulled onto the edge of the mountain road, even though the highway was empty.

'It's Angie,' he said. 'I'll put it on speaker.'

'Hi, bridegroom,' Angelika said. 'Where are you? Is Mam okay?'

'She sounds so close,' Poppy said, incredibly happy, but then the engine spluttered and the lights dimmed. The night closed in and she realised the danger of being invisible and alone in such a remote place.

What danger? Don't be stupid, she thought.

'I guess we're about ten kilometres from Viannos,' Nick said to the phone. 'I can't wait to get hold of you.'

Poppy heard Angelika giggle, remembered Yeorgo and their love, and she smiled too.

The engine spluttered again. 'We'd better get going, Nick, or you'll have to find my coat in the suitcase,' Poppy said. 'I'm getting chilly. You'll see Angelika soon.'

'Put my jacket around your shoulders. It's on the passenger seat.' He unclipped his seatbelt and reached into the back.

A light flashed in the rear-view mirror, making Poppy squint. They hadn't seen another vehicle on the road since leaving the city. A row of headlights blazed from above a cab, a HGV perhaps, or that monster truck from the garage. On the speaker phone, Angelika talked about *Yiayá*, but the approaching lights distracted Poppy. A weird feeling came over her then she told herself not to be idiotic.

The truck drove past.

Nick put the little Jimny into gear and raised his voice to the phone on the dashboard. 'Angie, we're on our way, see you soon, sweet –'

'No! No!' Poppy cried.

The monster truck had U-turned and now hounded towards them.

'Jesus!' Nick yelled as it swung at their Jimny. He released the clutch. The Jimny pitched forward. The monster clouted their rear offside. The phone hurtled past Poppy and vanished into the darkness. She slammed against the locked seatbelt with such force she feared her operation scar might burst open and her heart disappear into the night too.

The monster kicked up a cloud of dirt and thundered out of sight at the next bend.

Poppy didn't realise she was whimpering until Nick tried to calm her down and wrapped his arm around her shoulders. 'Are you okay, Poppy?'

Poppy threw her hands over her face and cried out. 'He's going to kill us!'

'No, it's all right, he's gone,' Nick said, lifting his head and staring into the night. 'Take it easy, deep breaths. We're fine.'

She could hear the shock in his voice.

'Are you hurt anywhere?' he said.

Poppy shook her head. 'No, are you?' She rubbed her breastbone, feeling as though the seatbelt had cleaved her ribs apart.

'No, I'm fine. Probably a drunk driver. Bloody lunatic! It looked like that truck from the garage,' he said. 'I'll turn the engine off to let it cool.' He rested his head on the steering wheel. 'Take deep breaths. We'll be okay.'

Poppy rustled up some anger to block her tears. 'Okay? You nearly killed us, you bloody idiot! My insides are mincemeat.' But behind her words was the terrible fear that their attacker would be back. She suspected this was no drunk driver, but there was little point in terrifying Nick. He needed a clear head to get them to Amiras and the safety of the family.

'Me! There's gratitude,' Nick said.

Poppy gripped her handbag, let go of her scarf, and took a swipe at him. 'If this chaos is your idea of an adventure, kindly remember I'm a pensioner with a weak heart. I'll thank you for treating me accordingly. Bugger it, you've completely ruined my make-up.'

'Language, Mam.'

Poppy thrust her jaw out and squinted at him. 'Sorry! Although I don't know why when your terrible driving nearly killed us, and you've managed to destroy my elegant appearance too.' She clutched her scarf and glared ahead, even though they were stationary. The road was deathly quiet.

Nick held his hands out and stared at them. They were shaking. 'Hell, let's go for it, shall we?' he said, re-starting the engine.

Poppy nodded. A vague sense of calm settled on her, until the vehicle burst from an olive grove, its powerful headlights blinding her.

'Hang on, he's back,' Nick shouted.

Poppy hung on to the door handle and braced herself.

Nick hit the brakes. Poppy's seatbelt locked as they swung through a ninety-degree arc. The car, spinning across the tarmac, slid past the truck. Nick braked hard to avoid plunging into a ravine then he accelerated towards Viannos, gaining precious seconds.

From the racket that came from the wheel, Poppy feared it might fall off. The unlit road wound around the mountainside. After another bend, a distant cluster of buildings, illuminated by streetlights, gave her hope .

'Viannos, at last!' Poppy said. Then, to her surprise, she saw the flashing blue lights of half a dozen police cars racing towards them.

'Look, the police!' Nick shouted above the din from the back wheel.

The monster truck raced up alongside, then took another swing at them.

Contact came with a bone-rattling *Bang*!

Poppy's scream morphed into the sound of metal tearing against metal.

Nick, thrown from his seat, made a grab for the roll-bar but catapulted into the night.

Poppy, terrified and blinded by the truck's spotlights, imagined him crushed beneath giant wheels. She screamed, grabbed the handbrake and pulled with all her might.

Without a driver and out of control, the small 4x4 came to a halt in the gravel run-off at the edge of the mountain road.

Through black tree trunks and billowing dirt, she registered the oscillating police lights, now almost upon them.

The monster truck seemed to have disappeared.

But where was Nick?

Chapter 34

In the cottage, Angie ticked things off her wedding list while *Yiayá* and Voula were engrossed in a conversation about candles. She looked at the clock. Nick and her mother should have arrived. She snatched the moment to give him a call from the house phone, knowing he'd use handsfree while driving.

Nick was halfway through saying something when the call suddenly ended. 'Nick, Nick are you there?' she cried. Turning to Maria, she said, 'That's odd, Nick's on his way but I thought I heard Mam yell, and then nothing.'

'Probably a goat in the road,' Maria said.

'He must be near Viannos,' Voula said, glancing at her watch. 'There's a blank spot, no signal on the other side of the mountain.'

'Ah, okay, then I'm guessing they'll be here soon.' Angie tried to keep the glee from her face. The smiles of the other women told her she'd failed. They returned to their wedding plans.

The minutes ticked by. Angie checked the time on her phone. *Where are you, Nick? Where are you, Mam?*

* * *

Voula was using the house phone to call the taxi driver's wife and organise a ride to the church for *Yiayá* and *Papoú*. She made a face, pointed at the phone and pressed the handsfree button.

Maria and Angie listened to a one-sided conversation about the taxi driver's medical condition. They made clownish faces at each other when the taxi driver's wife went into details.

Angie flapped her hand at Voula who got the message and turned off the speaker.

Papoú, in his corner sipping raki, grinned at the women.

'And, instead of confetti,' Angie suggested, 'can we use rice mixed with rose petals from the garden?'

Maria nodded.

Angie glanced at the clock again. A racket outside the cottage drew their attention. Agapi, yelling at the top of her voice, burst through the doorway at the same moment as the phone rang.

'Angelika, there's been an accident! Poppy and Nick!' She turned to Voula. 'Put the phone down, they're trying to call.'

'I've put it down,' Voula said, startled, picking it up again.

'What do you mean, an accident?' Angie said. 'I was just talking to them.'

The colour drained from Voula's face. She thumped herself in the chest and dropped the receiver.

'What, Voula? Tell us . . .' Angie said. It had to be a misunderstanding.

Voula swallowed hard. 'Somebody tried to ram them off the road.'

'No, no . . .' Angie shook her head. 'It's a mistake.'

'That was the police,' Voula said.

'It *must* be a mistake! Why would anyone want to hurt my mother or Nick?' Angie said.

Demitri barged through the strip curtain, red-faced, sweat beading on his forehead. 'You've heard?' He gripped his mobile. 'They think she's not badly hurt . . . Poppy . . . don't panic.' He fell silent for a moment, eyes fixed on Angie, listening to his phone. 'My policeman friend doesn't know any more but he's . . . wait . . .' He stared at the floor, concentrating on the phone. 'They're about to get her out of the car. There's a stretcher . . .' He chewed his lip and nodded. His eyes came up to meet Maria's stare. 'The fire engine's arrived.'

'There's a fire?' Angie whispered.

Demitri spoke into his phone before focusing on Angie. 'No fire. They're going to run a cable to the car to make sure it doesn't slide into the gorge. Standard practice on the mountain roads.'

'That damn ravine again,' *Papoú* said.

Yiayá covered her mouth.

'What ravine?' Angie managed.

'She was rammed off the road. Hold on . . .' Demitri said.

'Mam . . .?' Angie said. 'But where's Nick, is he all right?' She seemed to be watching the entire scene in slow motion.

Demitri spoke into the phone, then listened, nodding at the floor a few times before he spoke to Angie. 'They don't know. There's no man, no driver. They're starting a search.'

Maria, Voula and Agapi crossed themselves.

Angie grabbed Demitri's arm. 'Where could he be? He was with Mam.'

Maria cried, small quivering noises, dabbing her eyes with a napkin. 'I want to see Poppy . . . I've waited so long and now this. She shouldn't have come back. How did they know?' Voula gave her a glass of water.

Angie stared at her grandmother. A sickening feeling rose from the pit of her stomach. Was this *her* fault?

Maria pleaded with Demitri. 'Take us to the hospital. They'll take Poppy there.'

Demitri listened to the phone again and then turned to Maria. 'They're bringing the dogs out from Viannos to search for him.'

'Why, Demitri? I don't understand. How could Nick go anywhere?' Angie asked. She thumbed redial for Nick's number.

'Get *Yiayá* to the car while I call the station,' Demitri said. 'They might have more news.'

'There's no answer from Nick,' Angie said, staring at her mobile. 'It seems to be turned off.'

'There's no signal there,' Voula said.

'There must be a signal if the police can call Demitri,' Angie said.

Voula frowned and then started shoving things into a canvas bag.

'Here, old woman.' *Papoú* gave his stick to Maria. 'Take this to help you to the car.'

'You're not coming to see your daughter, old man?' Maria said

Papoú pulled himself from the chair, moved towards the bedroom, gripping furniture along the way. A minute later, he returned with the 3D Virgin Mary picture.

'I said; you're not coming to see your daughter, old man?' Maria raised her voice.

'Too busy,' he replied, setting the picture on the mantle and lighting a small red oil lamp before it. He sat in his chair, crossed himself and prayer-locked his hands. Vassili met Maria's eyes and spoke quietly. 'I should have killed Lambrakis when I had the chance.'

Angie's head snapped around, hearing her surname. She saw *Yiayá* nod, her face bitter.

'You don't mean somebody from my father's family tried to hurt my fiancé. Why? It doesn't make sense,' she said.

Glances were exchanged, but nobody spoke.

Angie's frustration exploded. 'Damn it! Don't shut me out! I've a right to know what's happening!' she shouted, her arms stiffly at her sides, fists clenched.

Agapi placed a hand on her shoulder. 'Angelika. He wasn't trying to hurt Nick. It was Poppy –'

'Mam! But why? My God. I practically forced her to come here. Nagging and nagging. Now look at the danger she's in. If anything happens . . . You should all be ashamed, knowing she was at risk but keeping quiet.'

Demitri looked up from the house phone. 'They've found Nick,' he said.

'And . . .?' Angie whispered, her outburst imploding.

Demitri stared at the floor and listened. Finally, he nodded and said, 'He's okay, perhaps a broken leg, but that's all. Difficult to be sure. The ambulance will take them to hospital.'

'Oh, poor Nick! Come on, *Yiayá*, we've got to go,' Angie said. 'Let's get your shoes.'

Demitri stayed on the phone. 'More news,' he called out. The room stilled again. 'The medics have treated Poppy in the car. She seems to be all right, badly shaken and perhaps whiplash.'

Vassili closed his eyes and rocked in his chair. His lips moved in prayer.

Chapter 35

DEMITRI HELPED *YIAYÁ* INTO a wheelchair and Angie lugged the canvas bag Voula had packed. The gang of three passed through the hospital's automatic doors together, ready to deal with whatever awaited them. A long queue snaked from a desk in the lobby. The cool air smelled of bleach and body odour and every sound echoed.

'This way.' Demitri pointed to a counter.

A strip light flickered and buzzed over an enquiry sign and, below it, an exhausted-looking woman with greasy hair asked what they wanted. She directed them to a waiting room with worn-out seats, a barred window and an ancient vending machine.

The building was as tired as its residents. Angie's nerves were frazzled and, before she realised it, she had bitten the nail extension off her ring finger. A damn omen, there probably wouldn't be a wedding now. It didn't matter so long as Nick and her mother were okay. She was prepared to sacrifice anything and everything for that outcome.

Demitri reached through the bars and opened the window. He lit a cigarette, held it through the grille and blew the smoke out.

Angie tried to make *Yiayá* comfortable with the cushion at her back and the shawl around her. She eased the shoes off her grandmother's feet, and replaced them with slippers, appreciating Voula's forethought with the packed bag.

An hour passed. They drank Fanta Orange straight from the cans. Maria fell asleep in the wheelchair. Demitri opened a fresh packet of Marlboro Lights and stood at the window.

'I don't suppose you can tell me what this is all about?' Angie asked him.

Dimitri's eyes widened. He glanced at Maria, lit a cigarette, and shook his head. 'Don't ask me,' he said.

A nurse rushed into the waiting room. She sniffed the air and frowned. Demitri dropped his cigarette into an empty orangeade can. The nurse glanced at sleeping Maria and frowned again.

'Sorry we've been so long,' she said. 'You may see your family for five minutes. They've had x-rays, tests, and they've made a statement to the police. We'll keep them in overnight. Mrs Lambrakis will probably be discharged in the morning. Mr Kondos needs another x-ray. If all's well, he'll go home later tomorrow. I believe you're getting married the next day?'

Angie, unable to speak, placed her hand on her chest and nodded, hoping her face said all the gratitude she felt.

The nurse smiled and patted her shoulder. 'Relax, they'll be fine. No damage that won't mend. Your wedding's quite safe.'

At that moment, she couldn't care less about her wedding.

They were led to a small room with two beds. Both had faded rose-print curtains around them.

'The doctor's with Mr Kondos, you can see him in a minute,' the nurse said while drawing back one set of drapes to reveal Poppy in the hospital bed. The rattle woke Maria, confusing her.

Poppy made a mewling sound. 'Mama . . . Angelika . . .' She held her hands out towards her mother and daughter.

Yiayá also reached out. 'My child, oh, Poppy! Dear God. It's been so long.' They were both crying and the sight of those tears pushed Angie over the edge. She broke down too.

Demitri lifted a chair away from the bedside so that Angie could push the wheelchair up close. Maria and Poppy, arms outstretched, reached for each other. Angie imagined their love arcing between outstretched fingertips.

In the silence of the room, all that could be heard were the powerful sobs of the three women. It took several minutes for their emotions, bottled for too long, to dissipate.

'I've hoped and prayed for the day I'd see you again,' Maria said and then, shaking her head, 'So many lost years. Ever since Angelika arrived to tell us of her approaching wedding, I've thought about yours, Poppy. So long ago.'

'I never stopped thinking about you, Mama,' Poppy said. 'But, after Emmanouil and everything, I hoped you had forgotten me.'

Angie sat up.

'Never!' Maria said. 'When we get out of here, you must tell us what happened on the day you left.'

Angie's jaw dropped. 'You mean you don't know why my mother ran away from her homeland?'

Maria cast her eyes to the floor. 'There were lots of rumours and accusations, none of which I believed, but Poppy had fled Crete. How could I discover the truth?'

'That's the trouble, Mama,' Poppy said. 'Even I can't remember. I've tried many times, but what really happened on that day to make me do that terrible thing, well, it's simply locked out of my memory. A complete blank.'

Carefully, Angie said. 'Mam, will you tell us what you're supposed to have done?'

Poppy shook her head. 'Not here, not now. Give me time to re-trace my footsteps. After the wedding, perhaps?' Her eyes were begging. 'Let's forget all this strife for the moment and just be happy together.'

'I don't understand,' Angie said. 'How can something you've forgotten ruin the rest of your life, Mam?'

'Yeorgo said it was to do with shock and stress, and he'd seen it happen to fellow soldiers.' She absentmindedly scratched the back of her hand.

Angie reached out and took Poppy's hand in her own and exchanged a glance with *Yiayá*.

Poppy continued, 'When your father came to England, looking for me, he arrived at Aunty Heleny's with an armful of flowers, and chocolates.' She gave Angie a fleeting look and then stared at the wall. 'Before you were born, Angelika.'

Maria nodded and said, 'Go on.'

'He took me to a specialist who told me I had, urm, *psychogenic amnesia*, or something like that,' Poppy said. 'Apparently, it could clear up and my memory come back today, if the right trigger set it off, or it could just as easily stay blank for the rest of my life.' She glanced from Angie to Maria. 'The doctor claimed I didn't want to remember what happened. The shock to my mind was so intense my memory's simply blocked it.'

Angie thought it sounded like post-traumatic stress disorder and couldn't imagine what might have caused it. In future, Angie would be more sensitive about Poppy's health, both physical and mental. But her priority right now was to make sure everyone was out of danger.

She sat on the bed and took her mother's and grandmother's hands. The three women made a circle. 'It's awful that it happened like this, but to sit with my mother and grandmother for the first time in my life, well, it's a dream come true.' Their hands squeezed hers. 'I'm sorry I caused all this trouble, Mam. I'll cancel the wedding in the morning. Having a big family wedding isn't worth risking lives for. You're all far more valuable to me than that.'

Nick's voice came from behind the other drapes. 'Cancel the wedding? After all this? No you bloody won't!'

Angie looked at the opposite bed drapes and grinned.

Poppy pulled her chin in, indignant. 'He's right, you can't cancel,' she said. 'I'm not wasting this damn haircut, it cost a fortune.'

Yiayá perked up and crossed herself several times. 'Virgin Mary, you'd all better watch your language in the church.'

The nurse, wearing a broad smile, drew Nick's curtain back and left with the doctor.

Nick's leg, plastered to the thigh, was supported in an over-bed sling.

Angie winced, imagining her fiancé's pain. 'Poor you,' she said, longing to be by his side but feeling the grip of her mother and grandmother.

He jerked his head. 'Coming over here?'

She looked at Maria and Poppy, who simultaneously nodded and let go of her hands.

She rushed to his bedside and kissed him. 'You had me worried,' she said, 'being late for your wedding destination.'

'Sorry,' he said. 'Traffic. Close the curtains.' He threw a wink over Angie's shoulder at the two older women. They laughed and dabbed at their tears.

* * *

In the car on the way home from the hospital, Maria thought about her daughter. Half a lifetime had passed, taking with it the youth and great beauty that Calliope had all those years ago. But despite being in her sixties now, she was still a very handsome woman. Maria felt herself grow, strengthened by pride.

She recalled the awful day she last saw Poppy. The shocking events of that month hardly compared to those of the 1943 massacre but, just before Poppy ran away to London, things took a terrible downturn. One catastrophe after another, until Maria believed someone had put a curse on her family.

Constantina had died. She hadn't been well for years, her mind still tortured by the atrocities that happened twenty-five years before. However, recent revelations had sapped what little sanity she had left. Tragically, she had escaped all the pain and heartbreak by killing herself. Poppy, not without her own personal sorrow, was devastated. She had loved her mother-in-law dearly and took her death hard.

Everything deteriorated into a downward spiral, one horror after another, and Maria could see no end to their suffering. Then Poppy left, ending their strife in an instant. Peace settled over Amiras once again.

Nobody mentioned Poppy's name. There was no: *How's your daughter?* called across the supermarket. Maria and Vassili removed photographs of Poppy and Yeorgo from their walls and placed them in the bedroom drawers, face down, and everyone else did the same.

In the comfort of the car, Maria closed her eyes. She drifted back to that terrible month of conflict, confrontation, and loss, the outcome of which led her to now.

* * *

Crete, 1968.

THE SIROCCO BLEW IN from the south bearing thick yellow dust from the Sahara. This malevolent warm wind hit the coast of Crete each year. Locals called it *The Sick Wind*. Cursing and spitting, men washed the cloying dirt from their car windows twice a day. The women, if they had to go outside, wrapped their heads in muslin scarves that covered the lower half of their faces. Washing lines hung empty, and the landscape paled. Everyone hated the Sirocco wind.

To make matters worse, a terrible outbreak of measles had already claimed the lives of two Viannos children and one child from Amiras. The schools were closed for three weeks, to try and stop the spread to other villages.

Staying inside the cottage, to escape the stifling atmosphere in the garden, Maria sat opposite her future daughter in law, Agapi Lambrakis, and a small mountain of garden peas. She popped a pod and thumbed the contents into a bowl. 'That was good,' she said. 'Six big ones.'

Agapi, also shelling peas, smiled. A quiet girl; slim, nervous, and frail-looking, but with the most amazing thick, dark hair that fell almost to her knees. Maria had noticed her narrow hips, and worried about her childbearing qualities. She foresaw problems, but Matthia was smitten. Maria understood if she tried to turn Matthia away from the young woman, he would become even more determined.

'Yánna, and Voula have agreed to be my bridesmaids,' Agapi said, talking about her wedding plans. 'Poppy was going to be a bridesmaid too, but with the baby and everything, well . . .'

'I understand, Agapi.' Maria nodded, pushing down her own emotions and not wanting to discuss Poppy.

'Emmanouil didn't want Yánna to be a bridesmaid, but for once she stood up to her husband and said we were all best friends, so why shouldn't she?' Agapi paused. 'Did you know Yánna's pregnant again?'

Maria looked up from the peas and nodded.

'She would have had the baby by the time we got married.' After a moment's glum contemplation, Agapi continued. 'But now, with Mama's death . . .' at this point they both crossed themselves, 'we have to postpone for the year of mourning.' Her eyes reflected misery. 'I feel as though I'll never get married, *Kiriea* Maria.'

Maria reached across the table and patted the back of her hand. 'The year will fly by, trust me,' she said. 'Anyway, it gives you time to finish your university studies. I never approved of you abandoning your schooling to marry my Matthia. Education is a precious thing, Agapi, and I can see the day when women will work after they're wed. Real jobs with wages.'

The cottage door flew open and Emmanouil, dressed in his junta military uniform, grabbed Agapi by her long hair and dragged her, screaming, out of the house.

'You ever go near a damned commi Kondulakis again, Agapi and I'll kill them myself! Every last one of them. I swear!'

Maria jumped to her feet, grabbed the broom, and set about Emmanouil with all her strength. *Madman,* she thought.

He let go of Agapi and turned to Maria. 'Tell Matthia to stay away from my sister, or I'll kill him *and* Stavro. The engagement's off!' Emmanouil blasted at Maria who took another swipe at him.

Emmanouil snatched the broom from her hands, snapped it over his knee and threw it to the ground. 'I mean it!'

The following day, Maria remembered, events took place that changed everyone's lives. Naturally, Matthia and Agapi had met in secret, or so they thought. Maria had known, but it was only when Agapi came crying hysterically that she realised Emmanouil had known too, and intended to keep his word.

'*Kiriea* Maria!' Agapi wailed. 'Where's Matthia? My brothers have made a plan to kill him! They've done something terrible!'

'Don't worry, Agapi, Matthia has just run Yánna into Viannos on his motorbike. He's not even here in the village. There's nothing to worry about.'

How wrong had she been?

* * *

By the time Demitri, Maria, and Angie arrived back from the city hospital, midnight had come and gone in Amiras. The hospital trip, and seeing Poppy after so long, had clearly exhausted Maria. Demitri said goodnight to everyone before leaving, and once Voula had put Maria to bed, she left too.

Papoú sat quietly by the fireplace drinking raki until he was alone with Angie. 'How was Poppy?' he asked.

'She's good, *Papoú*. They're letting her come home as soon as she's seen the doctor, tomorrow morning.'

He nodded. 'Good. The police phoned,' he said. 'We can sleep easy tonight. They've got the *malákas* who drove into them, he's locked up in Viannos.'

Angie noticed his tired, red-rimmed eyes. 'Who was it?' she said. 'I need to know, and to understand why.'

'I asked too, but they wouldn't say. You know how it is?'

Frustrated, Angie shook her head. 'No, actually I don't!' Her words came out more harshly than intended. 'Sorry, I didn't mean to –'

Papoú interrupted, 'They're afraid of reprisals, Angelika. They'll tell us tomorrow at the station. First, they'll probably make us sign an order to keep the peace. Anyway, he won't be sleeping much tonight. Demitri's friend said he was one of the

Neo-Nazi mob and they've put him in a holding cell with three big Albanian immigrants who are awaiting deportation.'

Papoú patted the cushion beside him. Angie dropped into the seat, held his hand, and they sat in comfortable silence for a while.

'You look tired, *Papoú*. Let me help you to bed. Can I sleep on your sofa?' Angie said. 'I can't face the drive back to Viannos tonight.'

He nodded. 'There's bedding on the kitchen table. You can leave the front door open, it's a hot night.'

Angie helped him out of the chair and when he stood, he cupped her chin between his thumb and forefinger and stared into her face.

'It's uncanny, but you're the double of Poppy forty years ago,' he said, shaking his head. 'A phenomenon. God and his mischief.' He huffed and continued. 'I loved my girl more than anyone could ever know. It was impossible for me to go and see her in a hospital bed tonight. You can't imagine the happiness she brought me, Angelika. I can't think of her, or even hear her name, without smiling.'

His eyes glazed over and Angie suspected he was considering the past. 'What Poppy did, when she discovered the truth, was noble beyond words. She broke all our hearts, and her own. Nevertheless, we were all extremely proud of her. You should be too, Angelika. She's a very special person.'

Overcome with emotion, Angie couldn't speak. Still none the wiser as to what had gone on, nevertheless, her mother had shone through and claimed an even stronger grip on everyone's love.

She supported *Papoú* to the bedroom where *Yiayá* snored softly.

'Leave me, *koritsie*. Close the door,' he said.

* * *

The next morning, Angie heard Voula and Agapi sounding-off in the garden. The moment she stuck her sleepy head through the lengths of multi-coloured plastic, a camera flash blinded her.

'Damn!'

'Are you the bride?' a reporter called.

'Leave, before I call the police,' Angie said. She jerked her head sideways at the screeching bookends and the two women, both wearing scarlet lipstick, waddled into the cottage.

Angie closed the door, turned the big old key and thrust it into her pocket.

'Sit down!' She pointed to the sofa which proved not quite wide enough for both bovine rumps. Her first thought was to bully them into telling her what she needed to know. But everything seemed to have caught up with her and she felt decidedly shaky. She dropped into her grandfather's chair and lowered her voice. 'Aunties, I'm the only person here who doesn't know what's going on. I'm sick and tired of all the secrets and it's simply not fair to keep me in the dark like this. Now who's going to start?'

They stared at her, then at each other. Agapi placed a protective arm around Voula.

'Angelika,' Maria's voice came from the bedroom. 'Let them go. I have all your answers.'

The ninety-year-old came into the living room in her long cotton nightgown. 'Sorry, *Yiayá*, but I need to know why my mother and fiancé are at risk. They could've been killed last night. I'm the one responsible for them facing this danger, whatever it is.' She thrust the door key at Agapi. 'Go, before I change my mind.'

The women bounced to their feet, both panicking to get out of the room at the same time, wide hips bumping and shoving against the doorframe.

Maria sat at the table. 'Make me a drink, *koritsie*, and I'll tell you everything.'

Angie suffered the tedious affair of making Greek coffee, then she grabbed a glass of cold milk for herself and sat opposite Maria.

'There isn't time to tell you everything now, before you get married, *koritsie*,' Maria said. 'But let me try to help you make sense of the most important parts. Those concerning your mother. I'm sure she'll fill in the details and answer your questions after the wedding.'

Angie nodded intently.

'So, a long ago, there was some strife between us: the Kondulakis tribe, and your father's family: the Lambrakis family, which reached a head when one of them tried, and nearly succeeded, to kill Matthia.'

At last Angie was getting to the bottom of it all.

'The events of that year had been awful, especially for poor Poppy, she had suffered so much that she took it upon herself to try and stop any further reprisals.'

'Mam suffered. How? Why? What happened?'

The phone rang. Angie picked up and heard Poppy's voice. 'They're letting me out. Will you send the Amiras taxi to fetch me?'

'Thank God, that's great, Mam. Do you know how Nick is? I was thinking I'd come and get you both. Or at least you could come home together in a Heraklion taxi. They're lined up outside the hospital.'

'It's not the way, Angelika. We keep the money in the village, and besides, you've too much to do today. Nick's perfectly fine, apart from a broken leg, and we're quite capable of making our way home.'

'Mam. There's a row of taxis waiting right there. You'll have to wait over an hour for this one.'

'Angelika, don't argue. I want *our* taxi. I know his father very well. Nothing bad will happen. If I use a Heraklion taxi, next time Mama needs a ride, ours will arrive late and be more expensive.'

'All right, Mam, if you're sure. I'll call you back in a moment. Is there anything you need?' Angie caught sight of Maria going back into her bedroom and sensed a difficult day.

'Of course there is,' Poppy said. 'A wedding outfit for tomorrow! According to Demitri, my suitcase has gone missing. He thinks it's in the boot of the hire car, in a garage that's closed for the weekend. Have you booked a hairdresser to come to the house? I need some proper food, and do you have any nail polish?'

'Yes, Mam. Don't worry. We'll get you fixed up and looking great.'

'I don't want to let you down, Angelika.'

Exasperated, Angie called the taxi driver to make sure he was free, and then phoned Nick to see what time the hospital was letting him go.

Ten minutes later, she had both her mother and her fiancé organised. They were travelling back to Amiras together in the Amiras taxi that, luckily, was almost in Heraklion with a fare. Next, she found the number for Viannos police station and gave them a call.

'Hello, my name is Angelika Lambrakis. Last night my fiancé and my mother, Calliope Lambrakis, were attacked just outside Viannos.'

'Yes, Madam. I attended the incident myself. What can I do for you?'

'Ah, thank you, sir. Well, it's like this, they are coming home from the hospital in a taxi in a couple of hours' time. I want to confirm that the perpetrator's still behind bars and my family is safe?' Angie heard muted talking and guessed the officer's hand was over the receiver. A moment later, he answered her question.

'Yes, madam. Mrs Lambrakis can rest assured, Mr Lambrakis will be held, here, until he attends court on Monday.'

What?!

'Who? What did you say?' Angie couldn't believe her ears. Did he just say: *Mr and Mrs Lambrakis, in the same sentence?*

She heard more muted talking before he came back to her. 'Sorry, madam. I can't discuss the case over the phone. But we need your fiancé . . .' there was a pause, followed by paper rustling, before he said, '. . . Mr Kondos, to come in and verify his statement, this morning if possible. There was an amendment he didn't initial, a minor detail.'

'It might be this afternoon, because . . .' Angie, so shocked at hearing her own surname relating to the criminal, and then the Mr and Mrs. All sorts of things came flying into her head, which she instantly rejected.

'Madam?' the policeman said.

'Oh, sorry, yes . . . my fiancé and my mother are still at the hospital, in Heraklion, but we'll come as soon as possible.' She replaced the receiver and stood with her hand over her mouth.

Mr and Mrs Lambrakis? Breathless, she wondered what it all meant. None of it made sense. Then she remembered *Papoú*, the night before. Amidst the shock and mayhem, what was it he had said? *I should have killed Lambrakis when I had the chance.* Why?

Papoú shuffled into the lounge. 'Make me a coffee please, Angelika.'

She stared at him. *Mr and Mrs Lambrakis?* Why couldn't she get the words out of her thoughts?

Although Angie wanted the explanation from Maria, the moment she had her grandfather settled, she had to race to Viannos for a shower and change.

She returned to Amiras just in time to see Poppy and Nick's taxi arrive at the cottage. She jumped out of her hire car and, with her arms wide, rushed to embrace them both.

Demitri and the taxi driver helped Nick over the uneven ground. Angie linked arms with her mother and they walked together. As they neared the cottage, Poppy faltered and stopped.

'Are you okay, Mam?' Angie slipped her arm around her mother, realising this was a monumental moment for Poppy.

Poppy swallowed hard and said, 'I'm a little nervous about going back into the house, Angelika. I don't know why I'm so anxious.'

'It's all right. Take your time. Whenever you're ready, Mam.' Angie gave her a squeeze. 'I'm so proud of you and, before we go in, I want to say that I appreciate the enormous effort this has been for you. I couldn't ever dream for a better mother.' Angie kissed Poppy's cheek. 'Thank you. *Papoú*'s in there, desperate to see you. He was too upset to come along last night, so he sat in the corner praying for you until we returned.'

Poppy placed a hand on her chest and took a breath, reminding Angie of her first visit when she came up the steps with Demitri. 'One step at a time, Mam. We'll go in together.'

She kissed her mother on the cheek again. 'I'm here for you. Anything you want, any time, just say.'

Poppy nodded, standing in the street, chewing her lip and looking slightly startled. She started scratching the back of her hand.

The moment was broken by a huge shriek, followed by Voula running at them waving her arms over her head. To Angie's astonishment, Poppy also screeched, grinned, and mirrored Voula. They ran towards each other, laughing and crying and hugging. Maria appeared outside the cottage doorway. Voula backed away and Poppy rushed to her mother. They fell into one another's arms, wide smiles and copious tears replacing Voula's racket.

'I need a chair,' Maria said when the emotional greeting had exhausted itself. 'Your father's waiting inside. Go to him, Poppy. His heart's aching to see you. Angelika, help me into the house.'

Angie slipped her arm around *Yiayá*'s waist and slowly guided her back inside. The frail old woman stopped and said, 'One of the happiest days of my life, Angelika. Thank you, *koritsie.* You made this happen.'

Angie filled up. 'Nothing, nothing,' she said, in keeping with the Cretan response to a compliment, but more proud than ever before.

Angie longed to be alone with Nick. Inside the cottage, he winked across the room as she entered with *Yiayá*. With his plastercast on the low round table, he sat next to Demitri who was already pouring out glasses of raki. Angie hoped he would remember they had to go to the police station later. Poppy sat next to her father, holding his hand.

'All right, *Papoú*?' Angie said.

He nodded, tears still wet on his craggy cheeks. 'I've prayed to the Blessed Virgin every night since '68 that one day my Poppy would sit next to me at this hearth. A long wait, *koritsie*. You won't understand this but, when Poppy was born, I couldn't stand on two feet. A little girl. The day, and the time, and the baby, were so precious; especially after the loss of Petro. When she left for London, I felt my feet were lead, every step was a toil. Always wondering. But now I'm on air again.' His eyebrows shot up, a look of amazement on his face. 'My daughter's back. I can die a happy man. Thank you.'

Angie couldn't speak.

Voula brought more raki, and then plates of mezzé. Tiny meatballs, stuffed vine leaves, dips and rusks, plates of giant beans in sweet herby sauce, and olives, matchsticks of raw carrot, and tiny florets of raw cauliflower sprinkled with salt and fresh lemon juice, and many more. The small plates of food were arranged around Nick's foot, on the low table, which caused some giggles. Delicious smells filled the room and in the warm celebratory atmosphere everyone chatted and laughed and ate.

The day seemed to go into fast-forward and often verged on chaos with more people calling to welcome Poppy.

Despite only being across the room from Nick, Angie longed to be in his arms again. *Yiayá* escaped the party and sat under the olive tree, quietly crocheting. There hadn't been a moment to sit with her since the morning, and now Angie had to take Nick to the police station. She still had no real idea why her mother had left the island or what caused the feud. Perhaps the police could answer her questions.

Chapter 36

ANGIE HAD PARKED NEAR Agapi's house, so Nick didn't have steps to deal with. After the hubbub of the cottage, they both relaxed in the car. Halfway to Viannos, Angie pulled over.

'Are you all right?' Nick said.

She nodded. 'I just wanted a moment alone together.' She looked into his eyes. 'Nick, I think it's important that we don't have any secrets, don't you?'

He frowned, nodded, pulled some slack on his seatbelt.

'When I arrived here, Voula gave me the letter from you and, well . . . I was broken hearted. I thought you were dumping me, so I opened it. I thought . . . well, I feared . . .' She shrugged. 'You and Judy . . . I feel completely ashamed. I'm so sorry I doubted you.'

Nick burst out laughing. 'Angie, I can't believe you! My big surprise is ruined then? All those surreptitious trips to the solicitors, wasted. Packing all our stuff and moving it into storage. I thought you'd guessed when she phoned about the title, and the contract.'

Angie blinked at him, suddenly making the connection. 'I thought she was talking about a novel . . . I had no idea.'

'I guess keeping the flat sale a secret was a stupid idea,' he said. 'By the sounds of it, one that could have gone horribly wrong. No more surprises from me, okay?' He reached over and, looking concerned, stroked her cheek. 'I'm lucky you didn't simply walk away. What an unbearable thought.'

'When I feared you were leaving me, I was devastated. *Yiayá* told me I shouldn't give up on you. She said I should fight for the things I love.' She leaned over and kissed him before she put the car into gear and drove on. 'It must have been terrifying for you and Mam in that open-top car. I'm still not sure exactly what happened,' Angie said, changing the subject as she headed for Viannos police station.

'How did you know?' Nick said. 'If you hadn't called the police, we'd be dead.'

'What? I didn't call the police. They phoned us.'

Nick was quiet for a moment. 'That's bizarre, I can't figure it out. Who told the police if it wasn't you? We hadn't seen another car. I thought you'd heard the smash while I was talking to you. It's the only explanation.'

They travelled in silence until Angie pulled up at Viannos Police Headquarters. The new building had fresh paint splashes on the windows and pink marble floors. Although the desks were in use, the legs were still swathed in bubble wrap and stacks of files and folders lined the corridor walls. Several had toppled and Angie imagined the chaos of a document search. The stink of cigarette smoke competed with the smell of fresh paint.

A police officer led Angie and Nick to a room divided across the middle by a row of bars; a table and four chairs were on their side of the division. Angie stared at the back of the man who had almost killed both her mother and fiancé. He faced the wall behind bars, his legs spread and hands behind his head. A police officer yanked the guy's hands down, slammed cuffs on, and spun him around.

'You!' Angie gasped. 'I don't believe it.' She stepped back. Her legs hit a chair which tipped and clattered to the floor. She turned to the policeman. 'It's a mistake, I know this man. He's my friend.'

'There's no mistake, madam,' the officer said.

'Manoli,' Angie called out. 'Tell them they've got it wrong.'

Manoli gave Angie a cold stare, his eyes narrow and empty, and a fat lip appearing painfully fresh.

'They haven't got anything wrong,' he said flatly.

'What?' Angie stared at him. 'Why would you terrify my mother and my fiancé like that? You could have killed them. My mother's just come out of heart surgery.'

'Your mother doesn't have a heart. She murdered my father,' Manoli sneered.

'Don't say such stupid things,' Angie said.

'It's my right, an eye for an eye,' Manoli said.

'You're talking rubbish. Mam wouldn't hurt anybody. She's a good woman.'

'How would you know? Poppy destroyed our family.'

'And you pretended to be my friend?' She squinted at him, her anger rising. 'Do you think we haven't suffered enough, Manoli? I grew up without a father, and my mother lived all her life without the man she loved. It's a good job these bars are between us!'

'Why? Get your own back, would you? That's the trouble with the Kondulakis family, they always have to go one better. I grew up without a father, too. Your mother killed him . . . and Matthia killed my mother! I told you, that debt has never been paid.'

Angie reeled, *a debt that has never been paid*. The truth was, she really did want to hurt him and for a moment, her feelings scared her. 'Manoli, you're being ridiculous. I'm sorry your mother and father died – but it's got nothing to do with my family.'

'Ask them!' Manoli shouted.

Angie blinked, this was absurd. 'You're insane,' she said.

Two officers manhandled Manoli out of the room.

'Ask your mother,' he yelled over his shoulder. 'Murdering whore!'

A policeman righted Angie's chair. 'Sit down, please.'

He pushed several papers towards Nick. 'The charge will be attempted murder. We want you to go over your statement, Mr Kondos.'

'Of course. Tell me, how did you know about the attack? They said somebody phoned you? We'd like to thank them.'

'He's here now. You can thank him yourselves.'

Nick turned to Angie. 'What do you think?'

She nodded, still shaken by Manoli's accusations. 'Perhaps he can throw light on all this.'

When the officer returned with their Good Samaritan, an old man hobbled slowly into the room.

Nick extended his arm.

Angie stared. 'You?' she said, shocked for the second time.

Never having seen him before, Nick shook his hand saying, 'Thank you, sir. I owe you my life.'

Chapter 37

THE PENSIONER STRUGGLED INTO a chair. Angie recalled her first day in Crete. The old man had stood in the middle of the road, holding up traffic. He had come to her table under the tree and welcomed her. Manoli had served him coffee.

'Who are you?' Angie asked.

The old gentleman reached over and took her hand in both of his. 'I told you, Thanassi Lambrakis. I am your father's brother.'

Angie gasped. Now she remembered his name, but her father's brother, her uncle? 'Then you must be Agapi's brother?' Angie remembered Agapi's agitation when she asked her to talk about her brother.

He nodded. 'Manoli's my nephew. I own the petrol station you called at when you first arrived in Crete.' Thanassi bowed his head. 'I'm sorry for Manoli's behaviour. He's crazy . . . his father, Emmanouil, was too. Manoli wanted to make vendetta for Emmanouil's death. It's the custom.' Thanassi stared at the table top. 'I followed you into Viannos that day. I craved vengeance too. I loved Emmanouil.' He looked into her eyes. 'When I saw you close up, so beautiful, the double of your mother, I realised revenge was stupid, so I came and shook your hand. Do you remember?'

Angie nodded.

'Manoli has talked about his parents' death, and vendetta, since that first day you came here.'

Angie gulped. 'Really? My God, he wanted me to rent one of his rooms.' She thought back. 'He was very friendly, but occasionally I did get a feeling it was all an act.'

'It's good that you didn't stay over the kafenion. Manoli is obsessed.'

Thanassi spoke to Nick. 'Manoli comes to the garage to play a game of *tavli* with me each evening. When you and Poppy left the petrol station, he took his shotgun and followed you. I had no choice but to call the police.'

'I don't understand,' Angie said. 'All this talk of revenge – my mother didn't really kill his father, your brother Emmanouil, did she?'

'Poppy's never denied it.' Thanassi glanced at the window.

The policeman brought a tray of frappés and then sat at the table with Nick's statement.

Thanassi took a glass and sucked noisily through the straw before adding, 'Nobody knows what happened that afternoon, but if this feud is to stop, we should all forget the past, let it go.'

Angie stared at Thanassi. The old man met her eyes, blinked rapidly and turned away. His face seemed to warp as he shifted in his chair.

'Is that why my mother left Crete?' Angie said. 'I don't know anything about this. Please tell me.'

Thanassi nodded, sighed and pulled a set of small jet worry beads from his pocket. 'It all started with the massacre in '43.'

Impatient, and thinking she had learned everything about the war from Maria, Angie encouraged him. '*Yiayá* told me about the tragedy. But what made my mother leave Crete, and why did Manoli want to kill her?'

Thanassi's face hardened suddenly. He snapped the beads over the back of his hand with a hard clack.

'I know my timing isn't great,' Angie said, worried he wasn't going to open up. 'But we're getting married tomorrow, we have too much to do and so little time. Will you come to our wedding, please? There's nobody from my father's family, except Agapi. I'd be proud to have you there, Uncle Thanassi.'

His face softened and he smiled at them both. 'Yes, I'd like to attend your wedding, Angelika. Perhaps it would put an end to this feud, but see how Matthia feels. A long time ago . . . I nearly killed him, I fear he may still hold a grudge.'

'Please tell me about it. I need to know,' Angie pleaded.

Thanassi scratched his grey moustache and frowned. They sat in silence while he gathered his thoughts and, after a minute, he cleared his throat.

'My mother, Constantina, had a nervous breakdown because of the massacre. She lost more than anyone, on that day: her grandfather, father, two brothers, an uncle, and her pregnant daughter. The Nazis gutted her in the street. I'll never forgive them. Poor girl. Everyone was affected but my mother never got over such a loss. Me and Emmanouil – Manoli's father – were born after the war. Although my mother recovered to some extent, thanks to the miracle of finding Yeorgo alive, the horror of that day never left her.'

Thanassi smiled at Angie but his eyes were dull with sadness then he stared at the small barred window of the interview room.

'Yeorgo was always her favourite.' His smile turned into a frown but again, she noticed the deadpan eyes. 'Agapi was betrothed to Matthia but we stopped the wedding. I'm sorry for what we did to him.'

'Why?' Angie asked. 'I believe Uncle Matthia loved Agapi very much.'

'Politics, your mother's family were Democrats but Matthia still backed the communists and broadcast the fact. The man's a born rebel, a bloody anarchist.' He scowled for a moment. 'Secretly, many villagers were commies but, with the support of the British, the junta outlawed the party. Emmanouil and I became junta military police. Do you know about the politics, Angelika?'

'Not a lot, I'm ashamed to say, but Manoli did explain some things.'

'Just because he's a hot-headed crackpot doesn't mean he lied about the government's secrets. I'm talking about the British government. I understand you're a writer?'

Angie smiled. 'No, Uncle Thanassi, I work – worked for a publishing company.'

Nick squeezed her hand.

'That's a pity. I was hoping you'd write about what happened here. Our history's very colourful.'

'I'm thinking about it,' Angie said.

Thanassi nodded and continued. 'Emmanouil forbade our sister's marriage to a communist and, in truth, we could have had Matthia thrown into prison and tortured. Emmanouil had bragged that he would marry Poppy, but she chose Yeorgo. She was hardly more than a child, but still the most beautiful woman around.' Thanassi paused, rolling the beads between his fingers. 'It made Emmanouil crazy because he loved both Yeorgo and Poppy, but at the same time he hated them both, so he vented his frustration on Matthia.'

'I didn't know any of this,' Angie said.

Thanassi continued, 'My mother's mind collapsed. And then, just after her second grandson died . . . Stavro came to see her. A great argument took place and, for my mother, something snapped. The final straw, they say. She swallowed all her anti-depressants at once. In the end, whatever the cause of her torment, she only found peace in death, you see.'

Angie didn't see. She had lost the thread and it all seemed jumbled.

Thanassi continued. 'My brother needed someone to blame. Stavro was in Athens most of the time, so Emmanouil did his best to make Matthia's life hell. Matthia was no angel. He started stupid pranks against us too. It escalated; each piece of revenge stronger than the last.'

Thanassi dropped his head into his hands. 'I need a moment,' he said quietly.

Angie sensed the dawn of a big revelation. The air in the room stilled although the window hung open. Nick's hand covered hers but she found it impossible to look away from Thanassi. When he looked up, his eyes were full of tears.

'Emmanouil's son, Manoli, that fool who served you coffee every day and then tried to kill Poppy . . . he was three years old when he contracted the measles. We had an epidemic here, many children died. His mother, Yánna, was pregnant with her second child.' He stopped speaking for a moment.

'Yes?' Angie said.

'Yánna needed medicine from Viannos, for Manoli. Matthia offered her a lift into town on his motorbike.' Thanassi swallowed hard. 'They swerved off the road at the first bend. A tree saved Matthia, but Yánna and the bike crashed over the edge and fell to the bottom of the ravine. They found her dead with a broken neck. They tried to save the baby, but . . .' Thanassi shook his head. 'It died, a little girl.'

'God, *God*! You mean Uncle Matthia killed Manoli's mother? Oh . . . oh, I can't believe it, that's terrible, awful. So, that's why Manoli wants to kill my mother?'

Thanassi took a breath. 'Everyone thought so, Angelika. When they brought Matthia to the police station, we used our truncheons and boots on him. We beat him almost to death. Even when he was unconscious, Emmanouil kept kicking him, screaming abuse, completely out of control because his wife and baby were dead. In the end, we had to pull my brother out of the cell and lock the door until the doctor came. Matthia nearly died before we sent him to prison. Then, Poppy went to see Emmanouil . . .'

The old man placed both his hands flat over his face and Angie saw his Adam's apple bobbing in his scrawny neck.

'Sorry,' Thanassi said after a few moments. 'I was very close to Emmanouil and Yeorgo. I miss them both.'

'Please. Take your time,' Nick said. 'Can I get you another drink?'

Thanassi declined. 'The truth is, Emmanouil had caused Yánna's death and, I'm ashamed to say, I'd helped. We'd doctored the front steering on Matthia's bike, not expecting Yánna to go on it.'

Angie's jaw dropped. She stared at the old man for a moment while this latest revelation sank in. 'Sorry, I'm really confused. Let's see if I've got this straight,' she said. 'Emmanouil was your brother, Thanassi? He was also my father's brother, and the brother of Agapi, as well as being my uncle, and Manoli's father? Is that right?'

Thanassi nodded.

'And Manoli – who must be my cousin – knows that his father, Emmanouil, caused his mother's death, and Matthia wasn't responsible?' Angie asked.

Thanassi shook his head. 'Manoli was too young to understand, and then the time never seemed right. Emmanouil couldn't bear the consequences of his own actions. He wrote to Yánna's family to explain but, I'm ashamed to say, I found the letter and I still have it.'

'So for all these years, Manoli has believed that Matthia killed his mother, Yánna?'

Thanassi nodded. 'I'll give you the letter. I can't have it on my conscience any longer. After we had almost beaten Matthia to death, Poppy came looking for Emmanouil.'

Angie chewed her lip, afraid of what Thanassi was about to tell her next.

After a long pause, Thanassi continued. 'Who can know what happened? Poppy was seen going into his house. A shotgun fired . . .' Thanassi dropped his worry beads on the table and crossed himself. 'It blew Emmanouil's head clean off his shoulders. I was the first person there. I . . . well, there's more but it doesn't matter now. After Yianna's death, there was an inquest. I confessed that I had helped Emmanouil to "fix" Matthia's motorbike. I was sent to prison, and Matthia was released. By that time, Emmanouil was already dead. If this vendetta is to end, it must stop today. No more blame or reprisals.'

Thanassi lowered his hands, silent for a moment. 'Although several people, including me, saw her running from the house after the shotgun blast, there was nothing to prove Poppy had killed Emmanouil.'

Angie shuddered. Nick squeezed her hand.

Thanassi continued. 'Poppy disappeared from Crete that day, never to be seen again.' He turned his attention to Nick. 'It seemed to confirm her guilt in the village. And now she's returned for your wedding. She shouldn't have. She must have realised the risk she was taking.'

* * *

'I don't want to go back to Amiras right now, not after hearing all that,' Angie said when the police had finished with Nick and his statement. 'I wish I'd been told all this before. It's terrible. I mean, the way Thanassi described Emmanouil's death, it made me sick to my stomach.' She contemplated her mother for a moment. 'I can't imagine how Mam feels. No wonder she blocked it from her memory.' Angie thought about Poppy and the last couple of months. 'I feel dreadful pushing Mam to reunite with her family. She must have been terrified of coming back. There must have been another way. I was so determined, but I had no idea of what I might instigate. It could have ended so differently.'

'I think it was pretty brave of Poppy to come back. She must have known the danger she put herself in. Where's your apartment?' Nick asked.

'Fifty metres up a narrow backstreet. It's a bit steep, will you manage?'

'Good practice.'

* * *

Inside her room, breathless from the climb, Angie locked the door. 'Alone at last,' she said. 'Make it all go away, Nick. I want to forget, at least for a while.'

'Are you sure you wouldn't rather talk about it?' he said, dropping the crutches and taking her into his arms.

'I'm so tired of words, of trying to work it all out. This week was supposed to be about us, and our love, and bringing people together.' Everything seemed to well up inside her. The happiness of finding her family, seeing her mother and grandmother embrace, and relief that the accident hadn't been worse. She realised she was trembling, and then sobbing.

'Don't ever leave me, Nick,' she whispered. 'Not like my father left my mother, all alone without the man she loves. Promise me? I don't want to grow old looking at an empty chair.' She wrapped her arms around his waist and squeezed him as hard as possible.

'Angie, of course I'll never leave you. You've had a difficult time, sweetheart. I imagine you were frantic when they told you about the crash. Come on,' he smiled, 'let's make some use of that bed, shall we?' He shrugged out of his cream linen jacket and hung it on the doorknob. 'I've missed you for every hour we've been apart.'

'Nick, remember I said I can't keep secrets from you?'

He nodded.

'I don't think we'll have another moment alone before the wedding, so I have to ask . . .' She still struggled to say it. The words stuck in her throat: *Did you sleep with Judy Peabody?* More than anything, she was terrified of the answer. What if he said yes and then asked her to forgive him? She'd rather not know, because if he had, she would have to leave him, and how could she possibly live on the outside of his life? Just the thought caused her to panic. More than that. To imagine life without Nick made her irrationally sad. Who else could be the father of her children? No one compared. She considered the letter she was not supposed to have opened yet.

'I really was afraid you were having an affair with Judy Peabody,' she blurted out.

'Sweetheart, don't doubt me now. Haven't I proved that I'll do anything for you, that you're the only woman for me? You should know I'm not a man to compromise. You're the best, Angie, simply the best.' He took both her hands in his. 'I confess I did spend some time with that woman outside of work, but not in that way. I showed her the flat twice, and met her a third time, at the flat, just before my stag do; on the day we exchanged contracts. That was to hand the keys over.' He sat beside her on the edge of the bed.

'Sorry I doubted you.'

'I should tell you, I did keep some secrets from you though. Only because I thought you were stressed enough with Poppy and the wedding.'

'If you're going to tell me you've lost your job too, I already know. I don't care, Nick. My priorities have changed drastically. That we're happy together, for the rest of our lives, that's what's important.'

'You're right, I did lose my job. But yesterday, before we went to the airport, the MD called me in. He said he had heard why I had missed the board meeting, and why I couldn't attend the next one. He said he liked a man with integrity, who knew what was important; and not only did he reinstate me, but he gave me a promotion!' Nick grinned.

'Wow! Congratulations. It's only what you deserve after all the extra work you put in.' Angie realised Judy must have gone straight to the MD after Angie had told her what had happened. Perhaps she wasn't so bad after all.

'After the meeting, Judy gave me something for you. Pass it over, will you? It's in my jacket pocket.'

Angie fetched the small bubble-lined envelope and sat beside him while he ripped it open.

'Will you marry me, Angelika Lambrakis?' He slipped her engagement ring onto her finger and kissed her.

They stretched out on the bed. 'I think I'm pregnant,' Angie said quietly, staring at the ceiling, allowing tears of relief to fall freely.

His silence seemed to fill her chest to aching point. In his arms with her ear pressed against him, she heard his heartbeat. She wanted to look into his face, but was afraid to see the truth. Eventually, he spoke.

'How long have you known?'

'I'm not exactly sure. I haven't done a test yet. I have the kit in my bag.'

Nick's silence filled the room again. He let go of her and, wincing, shifted his plaster cast so he could lie on his side and look at her. 'Let's not do the test until after we're married, what do you think? We can do it together.'

She nodded, searching his face for a reaction, and then it came all at once.

With his grin wide and eyes sparkling he said, 'You make my ordinary life completely wonderful, Angie.' He was silent for a beat. 'Our own baby, wow. A real family. I can hardly take it in. It's impossible to say how happy I am. Thank you for loving me, darling.'

'I *do* love you, Nick. You're my world.'

* * *

Angie's phone rang; the noise loud in the sparse apartment. 'It's Mam, what time is it?' she said, wriggling out of Nick's arms.

He looked at his watch, the only thing he was wearing. 'Six-thirty.'

'She'll kill me.' Angie answered the phone.

'Hi, Mam . . . Where have I been? I promised I'd get you an outfit for the wedding didn't I? Wait until you see it. Back in twenty, love you, bye.' She ended the call, kissed Nick lightly on the lips and then dragged her going-away ensemble out of the wardrobe. Good job the clothes were a little stretchy and Poppy was only half a size larger. She found the matching shoes and handbag and threw them all into a carrier.

'You'll have to dress me,' Nick said, grinning cheekily.

Angie glanced at his naked body. 'You're taking advantage now.

'I will if we have time.'

Angie shook her head. 'Next time you make love, it will be to a married woman, Nick.'

* * *

Half an hour later, back in the cottage, Angie gave Poppy her outrageously expensive trousseau.

'It's red, red, I can't wear that! I can only wear black. I'd look like a tart.' Poppy glared.

'No, Mam, you're not wearing black for your only daughter's wedding. It's a celebration of life. Anyway, you couldn't look like a tart if you tried.'

Poppy squinted at Angie and then grumbled her way into *Yiayá*'s bedroom. Five minutes later, she reappeared in the crimson dress and jacket. Everyone applauded.

Maria, damp eyed and smiling, held out a hand. 'Poppy, my daughter. I'm so proud of you.' She lifted Poppy's hand, kissed the palm and then curled her daughter's fingers to keep hold of the kiss. 'It's not much, but it's all I have.'

'Oh, Mama!' Poppy turned to Angie. 'Thanks for all this, Angelika. I'd never have done it without you.'

'Wait,' Maria said. 'I forgot, I *do* have something for you, Poppy. I've kept it for so long and dreamed of the day when I'd give it back.' She turned to Angelika. 'In the top drawer of the pink cupboard in my bedroom. A brown paper bag.'

Minutes later, Poppy opened the brown packet and pulled out a blue gingham sewing bag with varnished bamboo handles. 'Oh, Mama! I remember when you gave it to me.' She giggled childishly. 'I recall how much I didn't want to be a woman.'

'The pillowcase you were working on when you left is still inside. I hope you get around to finishing it this time,' Maria said.

Angie watched her mother and thought about Thanassi. What had really happened to Emmanouil? She decided to get Emmanouil's letter from Thanassi and show it to Manoli, so he understood the truth. Yánna's death was an accident – a dangerous prank gone horribly wrong – a prank that might just as easily have killed Matthia.

She wanted to talk to Poppy about Emmanouil, but with the wedding tomorrow, now was not the time. They had all been through enough.

Papoú was shunted down to Voula's cottage and Poppy slept with Maria. The silk wedding dress that *Yiayá* had made for her daughter hung from a nail on the bedroom wall.

Outside Demitri's house – where Nick would sleep – Angie kissed him goodnight.

'Is this your idea of a quiet marriage in Crete?' he said, pulling her to his chest. 'It's pure madness.'

'I've come to love them all to bits, but I'm really happy that we're going to the other side of the island for our honeymoon.'

'Nothing but sun, sea and sand, Angie. Are you sure you won't go crazy with nothing to organise?'

'I'll have you, darling. That's all I want. I'm relieved the mayhem's over, Nick. Tomorrow will be perfect, you'll see. Don't forget we're doing the pregnancy test, after the wedding, but before the reception, so we can drown our sorrows if it's negative.'

Nick pulled a face and groaned.

'What? It was your idea.'

'Yes, but I just had this horrible flash of the whole family waiting outside the bathroom door for the result. You didn't tell anyone, did you?'

Angie laughed. 'No, of course not.'

Nick grinned. 'You realise if it's negative, I'll have to spend the entire honeymoon trying to change the result?'

'Oooh!'

Chapter 38

A COCKEREL CROWED NEAR ANGIE's bedroom window at five in the morning. *My wedding day*, she thought. She stretched, happy that they had chosen to marry in the village. Today was going to be wonderful. She just knew it.

Angie pulled her sweats on and set out for a jog down the steps and past the Amiras cemetery. The air was still cool from the night. Dawns muted colours; a pastel blue sky displaying wisps of pink feathery clouds, and the distant sea, a shimmering turquoise watercolour.

Scrub land surrounding the village glinted silver-green dew on clumps of wild sage. Exposed rocky areas leading up to the hilltop chapel, *Agios Charalampos*, were daubed with swathes of delicate mauve and cerise anemones. The perfume of dawn; jasmine, honeysuckle, and night-flowering cactus, rich and enchanting, hung drowsily in the air. Long-haired goats, their tin bells a distant clatter, shifted into the strengthening sunlight, from the shadows of the church. The morning's silence was further shattered by a rooster's boisterous crowing, and the priest's donkey braying for its oats.

Doors squeaked open, and Angie heard village people greet each other with obvious enthusiasm for the day ahead. She strode easy, her head full of imaginings; telling her children about the day Mummy and Daddy got married. They would hear how she wore their grandmother's silk dress, had a bouquet of wild flowers, and a reception that consisted of a street party for the entire village.

She ran onto the national road and then turned back down into Amiras at the war memorial, gathering speed on the downhill slope. She sprinted past the kafenion, and caught sight of Matthia who sat alone at an outside table, smoking. Full of joy, she had an urge to hug him.

'Uncle Matthia, isn't it a fantastic day? What are you doing here at this time in the morning?'

Matthia scowled, rested his forearms on his knees and grunted. 'I can't sleep.'

'Have you any news from Uncle Stavro?'

Matthia drew on the cigarette and stared at her. 'No.'

Angie pulled a chair from one of the other tables and sat beside him, the sweat on her back chilling. 'If he hasn't returned by this evening, will you give me away?'

He drew on the cigarette again. 'No, I won't.'

Angie's euphoria fell, she felt his anger and hers rose to meet it. She guessed he resented being last on her list. 'Look, you can be a grumpy old git, but I'm not going to let you spoil my wedding day. Please, stand in for my father. It's supposed to be an honour,' she said good-humouredly.

Matthia dropped the cigarette and screwed it into the ground with his foot. 'I won't. You shouldn't be getting married, not here in this church. It's not right. Whose mad idea was this, anyway?' He stood and shoved the cigarette packet into his pocket.

'What do you mean, *it's not right*? Why? Tell me.' Angie clenched her teeth. Matthia was nothing but a nasty old man. Then she wondered if he was still bitter about the things Thanassi had told her. 'Look, sorry, I shouldn't have snapped. Let's sit down and you can explain what's upsetting you, Uncle.'

He glared at her. 'I can't tell you, Poppy made me promise.' He stomped away. 'You shouldn't get married,' he said over his shoulder. 'People remember. You're an unholy child – it's a disgrace against God . . .'

Angie's jaw dropped. She went after him. 'What are you talking about? What a horrible thing to say on my wedding day!' She grabbed his arm and spun him around. 'Why shouldn't I marry the man I love, have his children, live happily ever after?'

Matthia reeled and staggered. Angie caught him, saw tears brim in his tired old eyes. Her apprehension rose.

'You think I don't care about you, Angelika. You're wrong, I seem to be the *only* one that's concerned. You don't understand. I won't see you suffer like Poppy has,' Matthia whispered. He knuckled his eyes and turned away.

Confused by his emotion and ashamed of her heavy-handedness, Angie told herself, grumpy or not, Matthia was a frail old man.

'Never mind what my mother made you promise, I have a right to know. Exactly what you are concerned about? It's my life. Why shouldn't I marry Nick? Tell me, Uncle.'

Why couldn't he let the past go? Despite what Poppy may or may not have done, why would it make Angie unholy? What rubbish was that?

Matthia hesitated, closed his eyes and said slowly, 'I'm too old for all this, but I can't let you have your wedding without knowing the truth, Angelika. You should know the facts before you make your decision.'

'What do you mean? Why shouldn't I get married in the church?' Angie repeated.

Matthia's hard features collapsed like a melting candle and, with incredible sadness in his voice he said, 'It's wrong for you to marry because . . .' He sighed, blinked slowly and then peered into her face. 'Your mother and father were brother and sister, and all your brothers were born dead . . .'

Angie gasped, stared at him and forgot to breathe. She ran through the sentence again, and again, trying to make sense of it. She let go of his arm, and failed to grasp the rest of his words. Matthia's speech became a distant mumble and her body swam though the rising heat of the morning, every movement a nauseating crawl. Darkness invaded the corners of her eyes. Close to passing out, Angie staggered to the edge of the street, slammed both palms against the wall of a house and vomited into the gutter. While she gagged, the statement thundered around her head. Her mother and father, brother and sister . . . her mother's weak heart, Stavro's weak heart, all her brothers – born dead? What brothers?

Thanassi's words came back: *And then, just after Constantina's second grandson died . . .*

'No, no, it's not true . . .'

Angie started to run, holding her belly that continued to cramp, her head reeling with the enormity of Matthia's statement. The unthinkable – the disgusting, outrageous, impossible statement. It had to be a lie. Yet deep down, Angie feared he had told her the truth. Her own mother, Poppy, *no*!

Confused and angry, she raced up the steps and into Maria's cottage. The empty room said it all. They knew. Driven by secrets that no one dare tell her, the family hid away while she came to terms with the fact. *Her mother and father were brother and sister.*

Had Matthia always known he had to tell her? It explained his animosity towards her from the start. His words tumbled around in her head.

Today was her wedding day.

Poppy emerged from the bedroom. 'Angelika, what on earth is the matter? Calm down. Have you had a fight with Nick?'

All Angie's confusion and fears blasted out of her.

'No!' she paused, gathering her thoughts. 'Uncle Matthia told me, Mam. I know everything. You and my father . . . brother and sister! How could you do this to me? God knows what would have happened. You know we're desperate for children, I might even be pregnant already – I think I am – what am I going to do? Why didn't you tell me? You've ruined everything,' Angie yelled the words, tears streaming. 'What in God's name will I do, Mam? I love Nick. We hope to start a family. I'm supposed to be getting married today . . . Our wedding, our future, all damned to hell. Why did you keep such a *terrible* secret from me?'

Poppy's face turned grey and her mouth worked but no sound came out. She clutched her chest, took a step forward and, shaking her head, managed to gasp, 'Don't tell Nick. Forget what Matthia said. It's not true. I'll kill him. He can't hold his mouth shut for five minutes. Just forget it.' Her words spluttered out angrily.

'Forget it – how can I? Don't be so stupid, it's disgusting! How could you have been so selfish, to keep something like that from me?'

'I'm not selfish. How do you think this has been for me, all these years? Why did you go and dig up the past? I warned you. We were happy. You brought it on yourself. Just don't tell Nick,' Poppy warned.

'I can't not tell him. You can't keep secrets from the people you love.'

Poppy staggered back against the wall, cupped her hands over her mouth and juddered air through her fingers. 'Don't do this to me, Angelika. Trust me. Haven't I been a good mother to you? Didn't I love you with everything I had?'

Angie hardly heard her. 'I'll have to cancel the wedding. I have to tell Nick. Get advice, blood tests, DNA stuff . . . God! What if we're unable to have children, Mam? What if I'm already having Nick's baby? Uncle Matthia told me about the others, my brothers, born dead. Brothers I didn't know I had. How many more secrets are there? And how many times would you have watched me go through childbirth . . . knowing? I can't believe you!'

'Take no notice. I've told you, Matthia's a stupid old fool who doesn't know anything!'

'Is that so? Then tell me the truth, did you marry your brother, Mam?' In blind panic, Angie couldn't grasp the logistics. Her mind was going crazy with the thought that she might be pregnant, and what were the consequences of her being born from an incestuous relationship.

'I . . . I . . . oh, God forgive me!' Poppy broke down, stumbled into a seat and rocked back and forth with her hands flat over her face.

Angie leapt from the sofa. Poppy reached out and brushed her arm.

'Don't touch me! There's no excuse for this!' Angie yelled through her tears. She stormed through the door and down the steps, sprinting along the village street until she came to the olive grove. Behind her, Poppy cried her name.

'Angelika, Angelika, please!'

'Leave me alone,' Angie shouted. She ran up the slope and into the grove, throwing herself under the biggest tree.

Overwhelmed by anger and confusion, she had to decide what to do.

Naturally, she had to tell Nick. Or did she? What if she didn't tell him? Was it possible to deceive the man she loved, as Poppy had deceived her? Perhaps the risk was minimal. Angie had no idea. But a threat would hang over her pregnancy and the joy of having a baby would be marred by worry.

Now it all made sense. Why her mother never wanted to talk about Yeorgo. Why he left her for a life in the army. Why she ran away from Crete. But who was Angie's father? Was it Stavro or Matthia? Her stomach churned.

Angie stared into the tree branches and recalled Maria's story. Would her grandmother have told her? She thought so; they just hadn't got that far. She sobbed, her face puffy and her vision blurred with tears. Why hadn't Poppy warned her? All this time she had kept that terrible secret? Angie remembered the wretched arguments when she wanted to connect with her family. Poppy must have gone through hell when Angie said she was going anyway.

Her mother called out, 'Angelika! Angelika!' And then Poppy came into view. Still in her slippers, she ran along the road where Maria had seen the soldiers on that terrible day in 1943.

Chapter 39

Thessaloniki, Greece, Present Day.

On the morning of Angelika's wedding, Stavro glanced at his watch: seven-thirty. His last chance to find Yeorgo before the marriage ceremony. Although a little early to go knocking on a stranger's door, these were unusual circumstances. This was the fifth Lambrakis doorbell he had pressed in two days.

The clock was ticking. He hoped there was a flight from Thessaloniki to Crete that afternoon. If not, he was in big trouble. He had received a list of retired soldiers with the name Lambrakis from the pension office, and his investigation had started in Athens. No luck. He continued his search around Thessaloniki, where three of the names on his list had already passed away.

In two of those cases, the widow had failed to inform the correct department. One soldier's wife suspected Stavro came from the fraud squad. The old woman attacked him with a broom. *Hadn't her man given everything to his country? He'd died in poverty and wasn't he entitled to more than that?*

Now, in the city of Thessaloniki, Stavro stood before the last address on his list. If he drew a blank here, he would take a break from the search for a while. He found it too time consuming and expensive. He glanced up at the apartment's name, etched over the glass door, and pushed through. Doors seemed heavier these days.

The central light didn't work, and the cream marble floor was grimy in the corners. The wall to his left contained the lift, and straight ahead, two apartment doors. To his right stood a block of overflowing mailboxes, and the occupants' doorbells. Stavro slid his forefinger down the list of names. His hand trembled a little. Condensation bubbles obscured some of the writing behind the Perspex and, to make matters worse, he had forgotten his reading glasses. Forgetting things seemed to be a common occurrence lately.

Somebody came into the lobby and walked towards the lift.

'Excuse me. I'm wearing the wrong glasses. Can you see a Lambrakis here?' Stavro pointed to the call buttons.

The stranger peered at the list. 'No, I don't see . . . wait, it's number nine, shall I call?'

Stavro nodded, his tongue stuck to the roof of his mouth.

The stranger, a fat effeminate man with pursed lips and a flabby face, eyed him. 'Is there anything else I can do for you?'

Stavro realised he'd been propositioned. 'No thanks,' he said.

He stared at the small speaker next to the button. Would he hear Yeorgo's voice? Would he even recognise it after so long? Nobody answered. He pressed again, holding his breath. The lift arrived for the stranger and a pensioner exited and walked towards the doors.

'Yeorgo?' Stavro said.

'Sorry?'

'I'm looking for Yeorgo Lambrakis,' Stavro said.

'You'll find him at the kafenion around the corner,' the old man replied flatly.

* * *

Amiras, Crete.

FROM DEEP INSIDE THE olive grove, Angie watched Poppy run along the village street.

'Please, Angelika!' her mother cried. She stopped and sat on a plastic crate at the side of the road, hugging herself, rocking, distraught. A woman emerged from one of the houses and spoke to Poppy. Moments later she fetched her a glass of water. Sunlight flashed off the tumbler like a silent explosion. Another woman joined them.

Although her insides were cold and fluttery, Angie's sweats had dried and fresh perspiration prickled her forehead. She sat on her haunches, her hands on her knees, watching Poppy on the road below. How could she possibly make sense of such shocking information? In those few seconds, with the delivery of Matthia's words, her life had come adrift. She wasn't the person she thought she was. In fact, she didn't know who she was at all.

What had really changed? Poppy still loved her, she didn't doubt that. And despite this catastrophic news, she still loved her mother. But biologically, she didn't know where she stood, didn't know about inherited problems. Perhaps there were none. She could find information on the web, quickly, before the wedding.

Angie knew she had to tell Nick as soon as possible. They could research this morning, together. They had time. How would he take the news? Incest, God, how awful. How could Poppy have hoped to cover this up?

She felt sick again. Anguish rising. She imagined a baby with a genetic heart deformity, growing in her womb right at that moment. Lost in the horror of her own speculation, she considered her choices. Broken hearted, she knew she wasn't prepared to take chances with her child's health.

This was all Poppy's fault! Her distress built until all she wanted to do was yell at her mother. Angie gasped, suddenly startled by a bright yellow and blue butterfly, fluttering about in front of her face. The insect landed on the back of her hand, opened and closed its scalloped wings. She stared at it, her troubled mind emptied by the magical incident. When the butterfly flew between the trees and disappeared, Angie got to her feet, calmer, but not wanting the locals to gawp at her.

'Mam!' she shouted down to the road.

Poppy wailed and the two women helped pull her up. She hurried into the olive grove and threw her arms around Angie. 'I'm so sorry that I didn't explain. I didn't want to tell you, ever . . . I'm so ashamed.' She broke into fresh tears. 'Don't hate me, Angelika. Please, not after everything . . . not after I've lost everyone I love, except for you.'

'I don't hate you, Mam – I couldn't, Angie whispered, her throat hard and painful. 'I was upset . . . I'm still upset. It's an enormous shock, to be told such a thing. I can't get my head around it. God . . . Mam . . . Let's sit on the ground.'

'No.' Poppy stepped away, dried her face on her sleeve and then placed trembling hands on Angie's shoulders. 'I must explain, now. Please don't hate me . . . don't hate me.'

'Mam, I told you, I was distressed. I'm still in shock, but hate you, *never*, you're my mother.' Angie started to sit.

'No, wait, it's difficult to say . . . but I have to tell you . . .' Her eyes left Angie's face and she glanced frantically around the grove and then peered at the cobalt sky, chewing her lip. She seemed to search for the right words. 'God help me to speak the truth,

Angelika, I never wanted you to know because, because . . .' She let go of Angie's shoulders and collapsed to the ground, choking back sobs.

Angie dropped beside her, afraid for her mother and her weak heart. 'Mam, come on . . . Please, Mam . . .'

'I'm not your Mam! You're not my daughter! Do you understand? You're not from my womb – I wish you were, and I've loved you as if you are. God knows, Angelika, I've loved you with everything I have, all your life, but you're not my child. My babies died, both of them. I wouldn't have let you go through that for anything.'

Angie couldn't speak. It was as if her world had been ripped from under her.

'I'm sorry, Angelika. Truly.'

'What? No . . . wait. That can't be right, Mam. Don't say such things. Of course you're my mother!'

'You're not my baby.'

Angie stared at Poppy, confused. 'But . . . what do you mean? Who am I then?'

'You are your father's daughter. The man I've loved all my life. The man who's like a knife in my breast. The man I miss with every single breath, who held me in his arms a lifetime ago and said goodbye. Yeorgo is your father: Yeorgo. There's no genetic risk when you have children.'

Angie swallowed hard. This was all too much. If Yeorgo was her father, who was her mother?

'I may not be your baby, Mam, but you *are* my mother and you'll always be my mother. Don't take that away from me. But I need to know everything. No more secrets. Please. Will you tell me the truth?'

Poppy nodded. 'Help me up, love.'

'Come on then.' Together, they stepped out of the shady olive grove and into the sunlight. A string of media vehicles drove past them, into the village. 'It's your daughter's wedding day, Mam,' Angie whispered and a smile squeezed through her tears. She hugged Poppy. 'I'm sorry for what I said. I couldn't hate you, never in a thousand years. You're my mother.'

* * *

Back at the house, after making some tea, they sat in silence on the sofa.

'First, let me hold you, Angelika,' Poppy said. 'I've always been terrified of you finding out.' Poppy held Angie tightly, ending with a fierce squeeze before she let go and took a long breath. 'Today's taught me what I must have put my own mother through. I have to make my peace with her.' She sat quietly for a moment, wringing her hands. 'I don't know where to start. To remember so much pain . . .' Fresh tears trickled down her cheeks. Angie, heart-breakingly sorry for her, brushed them away.

'Try the beginning, at a happy time. How about before you married?'

They sipped their tea, listening to the tick of the old clock.

After a few minutes, Poppy spoke. 'We grew up together, Stavro, Matthia and myself, the youngest. I was baptised Calliope, after my grandmother, but everyone shortened my name to Poppy. After the war, when our soldiers came home, many children were born in the village and the younger ones all played in the field, regardless of age differences. Stavro said I'd had another brother, Petro, but he'd died when he was only a few weeks old, long before I was born.'

'*Yiayá* told me about the terrible massacre and what happened after.'

'Stavro was always a grown-up to me, but Matthia and I were close, he looked after me while my parents were teaching or working the fields with Stavro. We grew all our own food. We were often hungry and had no shoes, but I remember having a happy childhood.'

'*Yiayá* said those times were hard, even after *Papoú* returned from the war,' Angie said.

'Difficult, yes, but the village was like one family because of what we'd survived.'

The reminiscent smile fell from Poppy's lips and she dropped her head into her hands, sobbing quietly. Matthia stumbled through the doorway, clutching his chest, his face pallid.

'I'm sorry, Poppy, I had to tell her.'

Poppy raised her eyes. 'You did right. I'm the one that's sorry. But it's okay, you see I . . .' She turned away, biting on her lip. Reluctant to speak, her voice dropped to a whisper. 'I'm not Angelika's real mother.'

Matthia's eyes widened. 'What? Why didn't you tell me, Poppy?'

'I was ashamed. Angelika is Yeorgo's daughter. You put Yeorgo on a pedestal so I didn't want you to know the facts. I've missed you so much. We were close, Matthia.' She turned to Angie. 'Nobody knew, Angelika, I realise you don't understand, but Yeorgo and me, we had no idea we were siblings and when we found out the truth, you can't imagine what it did to us. We weren't bad people.'

'Mam, I'm not trying to blame anybody, I just want to know – who am I? Tell me about your wedding day, take it from there.'

'My wedding isn't important, what's significant is what happened after.'

Chapter 40

Crete, 1965.

FOUR MONTHS AFTER OUR WEDDING, I missed my period. I couldn't wait to tell Yeorgo. Everyone had anticipated the news and whenever I met Mama, she would squint at me sideways, looking for signs.

The evening I told Yeorgo, I had cooked a special rabbit stifatho and put a single red rose in a glass on the table. When Yeorgo saw it he grinned, suspecting. I thought he had better eat before he heard my announcement, having an idea how things would proceed after. We chomped away at the stew, his eyes meeting mine, waiting for me to speak.

'Get on with your food, Yeorgo,' I said, trying to keep a straight face.

'Are you teasing me, little one?'

For all my careful cooking, I ate without tasting a mouthful. Before long, Yeorgo banged his fork down next to his empty plate.

'I've something important to tell you,' I stammered, my cheeks burning.

Yeorgo cocked his head to the side. His brown eyes questioned mine and a grin spread across his face. He reached over and took my hands.

'Yeorgo, I think I'm pregnant.'

'Poppy!' he whooped with joy and leapt up, catching the corner of the table with his thigh. It tipped; plates and glasses skidded and crashed onto the floor. In an instant, his arms were around me, twirling me in the small room that seemed to explode with our happiness.

'Put me down!' I squealed.

Yeorgo placed his hands on my belly. 'I hope it's a boy, but if we have a girl, she'll be as beautiful as her mother and I'll be even happier,' he said. He lifted the lid off the bench seat, letting the cushions fall on the broken crockery scattered across the floor. My husband snatched his hunting rifle, raced through the doorway, and fired into the evening sky. What a racket!

Children, playing in the street, clapped their hands over their ears. Dogs barked, and neighbours came rushing out of their houses. Everyone knew the reason for the volley. Men slapped him on the back and shook his hand.

'Bravo, Yeorgo!' they shouted as if I had nothing to do with it. I stood in the doorway, blushing and laughing.

Constantina helped me to clean up the mess before she accompanied me up the village steps to tell Mama. I hardly felt the ground beneath my feet. Mama had guessed from the noise. We found her smiling, under the olive tree with her arms outstretched.

Yeorgo left for the kafenion to celebrate, and two men brought him home at midnight, so inebriated he couldn't walk. They took his boots off and got him onto the bed. He muttered, laughed, and then snored so loudly that sleep was impossible.

'I've such a headache, Poppy,' he said the next morning, bleary-eyed and clumsy.

'Serves you right, getting that drunk. I hope that's not the example you'll be setting our child,' I scolded.

Yeorgo peered at my belly, grinned, winced and hugged the top of his head.

'You got up in the night and pissed into the wardrobe,' I said. 'Disgusting. You've ruined my beautiful wedding shoes.'

'Virgin Mary, I didn't . . . I'm sorry, Poppy.'

'That was bad enough, but to take all your clothes off and then dash outside to vomit over the geraniums . . . It's a good job nobody saw you, what a ghastly sight.'

'Don't tell my mother . . .' Yeorgo said.

'I will – unless you clean up the sick yourself.'

He raised his bloodshot eyes and stared at me in horror. 'I can't do that. I'll be a laughing stock.'

'Your bad luck, your choice.' I had to turn my back so he wouldn't see me smile. I made as much noise as possible that morning, clattering dishes and pans, chopping herbs, pounding a pork chop with the tenderiser, taking mischievous pleasure when I saw him wince.

Yeorgo cleaned the patio, diving indoors whenever someone walked down the street, desperate to avoid the shame of being caught with a mop in his hand. Papa arrived at noon and dragged him back to the kafenion. He laughed, shaking his head when he understood the size of my husband's hangover.

I prayed for a baby boy and for nine months I was ecstatic. My labour pains started in the middle of the night. The first cramping woke me and I lay in the dark, smiling to myself. By the time the sun came up, the contractions were intense and I wondered how much stronger they would become.

Yeorgo realised his child was on the way.

Although a little afraid, myself, I laughed at Yeorgo's panic. He raced through the village to get the midwife, swearing I would drop the baby at any moment.

Twenty-four hours after that first contraction, Elias appeared. He was so beautiful with his thick black hair, tiny feet, and fists that gripped my fingers. I gazed at him in wonder. His wide brown eyes blinked at nothing in a big new world and his cherub mouth puckered on an imaginary teat. Someone ran to the kafenion to tell Yeorgo while Constantina washed my face and cleaned my body.

'Thank you, *Yiayá*,' I said, exhausted but delighted to give my mother-in-law her first grandchild. Everyone agreed Elias was an unusually handsome baby boy. I held him to me, happy beyond words. My life had become perfect, married to a man I had always loved, and now giving him a son. Nobody could know my joy; it was so intense. As I rocked him, I imagined all the things that would stem from this day.

Elias would go to school, and then university, even if I had to scrub floors to get him there. He would grow into the most handsome and intelligent of men, like his father. Later, he would marry and produce the most gorgeous grandchildren, and in our old age, he would support me and Yeorgo, and surround us with security and harmony. I saw all this as I lay there with my beautiful infant.

The midwife wanted Doctor Petrinakis to look at Elias right away. When Papas Christos arrived and baptised him, I sensed something was wrong. My friends, who had stayed with me through the labour, seemed to disappear into the shadows. Everybody spoke in whispers. Yeorgo returned from the kafenion and sat on the edge of my bed. The room emptied.

He took my hand and hardly looked at his child. 'Poppy, they want me to tell you . . . something is wrong with the baby. His heart is not beating properly. He won't survive the day.'

'No, they're mistaken, Yeorgo! Elias will be fine, look, our baby's perfect.' I refused to believe it. It couldn't be true. I had the idea that my love alone would strengthen our little boy.

Yeorgo reached out to caress his child, but stopped before his fingers touched Elias. 'You have to accept he's going to die, Poppy,' he said gently. 'There's nothing we can do except hold him for the short time he has with us.' His hand fell back to his lap and he hung his head. Fat tears rolled down his handsome face. I'd never seen Yeorgo cry before, and it broke my heart into pieces.

All my joy turned sour. Lost to the unfairness of it all, I held the little mite to my breast. I didn't know exactly when Elias breathed his last breath. His life faded away and, at some point, he was no longer with me.

I refused to part with his tiny body. Yeorgo stayed with me, silent, just staring at his boots.

Maria came into the room and peered into Elias's face. She laid a hand on his cheek and after a moment said, 'He's gone, Poppy. You have to give him to the doctor now.'

'No, not yet, Mama. I don't want to let him go. He needs me to hold him. Permit me to keep him a few moments longer . . . please?' I cradled his small body. 'Don't let them take him, Yeorgo.'

I refused to believe his short time on earth had ended. Elias had such a peaceful expression.

'Perhaps he's just sleeping, too tired from the terrific journey.' I kissed his cherub lips and blew a little air into his mouth, calling on God and his angels to give Elias the breath of life.

I hummed cradle songs that I'd learned especially for him, and I rocked him gently as the weight of grief slid slowly into my heart.

The doctor and the midwife left. The women sat with me until dawn, and then they carried my baby away.

I felt such shame and apologised to everyone. They said the baby's death wasn't my fault, but who else was to blame? Elias's funeral took place the next day.

Doctor Petrinakis tried to console me. 'Poppy, Elias had a heart deformity. Nothing would have saved him. You did everything right, don't hold yourself responsible.' But the only person that I could blame was myself.

* * *

Before a year had passed, I found myself pregnant again but, this time, I saw suspicion in everyone's eyes. Nobody looked at my expanding belly, afraid they would put the evil eye on my baby. I had mixed feelings when Yeorgo received his national service papers.

The kafenion had the only village phone and, after two months away, Yeorgo called to say he had leave. I waited at the war memorial on the ridge, peering up the road for the city bus. I longed to see him dressed as a soldier. Stavro had taken a chair to the bus stop for me, and Constantina lent an umbrella for a little shade.

'I'm *so* proud of you,' I said when Yeorgo stepped off the bus in his smart uniform. He took off his cap and kissed me, right there by the roadside. He looked incredible, although I missed his thick dark hair. They had shaved Yeorgo's head, army style, to stop the spread of lice in the barracks.

I noticed a strange mark on the back of his head. 'What's that?' I asked curiously.

'It's a birthmark,' Yeorgo said. 'I've always had it, but nobody saw it before the short haircut. Does it bother you?'

I shook my head. 'No, it makes you special. Let me see properly.'

He bent, and I examined the liverish shape. 'It looks like a magnificent bird flying over your brains,' I said and laughed. 'I love it as much as the man beneath it. I've missed you terribly, Yeorgo.'

He kissed me again and replaced his cap.

'Can we visit Mama before going home? She's eager to see you in uniform. Look, she's watching us.' We saw her sitting under the big olive tree in the garden. When we stopped walking and looked up, she stood and waved.

Mama was always fond of Yeorgo. Even when we were children he often shared our meal.

Together, we walked through the streets of Amiras. Men came out of the kafenion, shook Yeorgo's hand and admired his uniform. I was wearing my best clothes, already tight around my expanding belly. When we arrived at the cottage, Maria was all grin and sparkle, waiting in the doorway. We linked arms and, respectfully, Yeorgo removed his cap and bowed slightly to Mama. I was dizzy with happiness. But when we passed into the house, Mama had a terrible fit.

She collapsed onto the floor, kicking and screaming, calling on God and all the saints. I feared for her life, she seemed unable to breathe and her face lost its colour. My heart raced with fear.

'Yeorgo, get the doctor!' I yelled.

I thought my mother had epilepsy, would swallow her tongue, and die right there and then. Yeorgo ran for Petrinakis. Mama eventually recovered but Petrinakis spent more than an hour with her in the bedroom.

We heard them talking, sometimes shouting, but couldn't quite make out what was said. Occasionally, Mama would yell, 'No! Don't, you can't!'

That day changed everything for Yeorgo and me.

Chapter 41

Crete, Present Day.

Poppy leaned against Angie and scratched the back of her hand furiously. Angie caught hold of her mother's fingers, brought them up to her face and planted a kiss in each palm. She knew this was the terrible stigmata that Poppy had endured for as long as Angie remembered.

'The truth is, Angelika, Maria had recognised the birthmark of my brother, Petro. Yeorgo was Petro. For twenty-five years Mama had believed him dead, and there he was, standing in front of her and married to her daughter.'

Angie stared at her mother. 'The birthmark . . . of course, I'd forgotten. *Yiayá* told me, right at the beginning of her story.' Angie's mind raced, trying to guess where this was leading. 'So Petro hadn't died.' She swallowed hard and asked the all-important question. 'Are you telling me Petro is my father, Mam?'

Poppy nodded and dropped her head into her hands. Small whining noises came from between her fingers and her shoulders shook as the struggle to control her feelings failed.

'Mam, it's all right. You can cry.'

Baby Petro is my father? Angie could hardly grasp the information.

'It's been a lifetime, Angelika,' Poppy said. 'I've had it all knotted up inside me. It's such an enormous relief.'

Angie slid her arms around Poppy. Matthia pulled a packet of Marlboro Lights from his pocket and then sat outside the door. Poppy allowed her emotions to vent.

Angie filled time by making coffee. Who was her mother? Now she understood that Petro was her father – baby Petro – the information was so huge and unexpected. *Yiayá* had told her about the beginning of his life, knowing he was Angie's father. She took a drink out to Matthia, rested a hand on his shoulder and stared across the valley with him.

'Do you know who my birth-mother is, Uncle Matthia?'

He shook his head, drew on his cigarette and blew the smoke out. 'I believed Poppy was, that's why I was against you getting married.'

'I thought you hated me,' Angie said.

'Just the opposite, I couldn't see you suffer like my sister.'

Poppy recomposed, dried her face and plumped the cushion beside her. 'Sorry, I'll try not to cry anymore, love.' She attempted a smile. 'Until that moment, when Mama saw the birthmark, she truly believed her baby had died in the massacre. She'd grieved for him and eventually accepted his death.'

'*Yiayá* told me about that cruel day and her struggle to save Stavro and Matthia. Those evil Nazis – to murder Petro and her grandfather, Matthia – then to beat her and rape her. No wonder she tried to kill herself.'

The shock on Poppy's face registered. Angie glanced at the doorway and saw her uncle open-mouthed.

'You didn't know?' she whispered. 'I'm so sorry . . . so thoughtless of me.' Too late, she remembered *Yiayá*'s request. To keep the story to herself until after *Yiayá*'s death.

Poppy sighed. 'Beaten and raped, poor Mama, and I'd no idea she'd tried to end her own life. How awful. I'm ashamed that

I added to her troubles. She never burdened us with all that. I made things worse, blaming her for not telling me Yeorgo was Petro.'

Angie imagined how she would cope if somebody told her Nick was her brother. She flashed back to their glorious love-making and felt sick.

'Stavro had seen the birthmark,' Poppy said. 'He remembered baby Petro had an identical one so he asked Constantina how Yeorgo had survived the massacre. My mother-in-law changed from that day. Perhaps she had always doubted herself.'

'Stavro must have dreaded hearing it all,' Angie said. 'What happened?'

'The details are gruesome, Angelika, you don't want to hear.'

'I'd rather you didn't leave anything out, Mam. *Yiayá* would have told me if there'd been time.'

'Constantina said the Nazis stood guard for two days. Before they left, they bayoneted the corpses to make sure nobody was alive. The bodies – a hundred and fourteen men and boys from Amiras – were stinking in the September heat. Starved dogs came at night, and the vultures circled overhead by day. Constantina told Stavro that the spilled blood had turned black and sheets of bluebottles covered everything. The poor women; their loved ones already decomposing. Mostly they used clothes and shoes to identify the men.' Poppy crossed herself.

Angie didn't want to imagine the awful sight and waited for Poppy to work her way through the story.

'When they were allowed to take the bodies, everyone was weak from days without food and, of course, there were no men to help.' Poppy's shoulders drooped. 'The women were alone, not just here but in all the villages around. To make matters more difficult, the Nazis had taken everything made of metal.

There wasn't an implement left to dig a grave. They had to scratch a hollow out of the baked September ground with their bare hands or pieces of flint.'

'How on earth did they manage?' Angie asked.

'Constantina took the blanket off her bed and a length of rope and found her father's body first. Most of her neighbours had lost their voices from the wailing. Flies lifted from the mens' corpses and worried wounds on the womens' faces where they'd raked the skin away in anguish. Constantina stumbled among bloated bodies, searching, pushed over by other hysterical women. The crows had taken her father's eyes.'

Matthia sighed. 'Agapi told me Constantina would wake in the night, screaming about the maggots between her fingers. The back of her father's head was missing and, despite the loss of his eyes, she wanted to bury him whole. When she scrabbled around, feeling for pieces of skull, she found her hands were crawling with maggots.'

Poppy's face contorted in disgust. 'Constantina managed to pull her father away and roll him onto the blanket. She tied him up and then looped the rope around her waist. One by one, she dragged her men to their plot and buried them under rocks she hardly had strength to lift. Animals were digging at night. Then, the women found a live baby. They say Constantina went crazy.'

'What about the real Yeorgo, did somebody bury him?' Angie asked.

'Nobody knows; the dogs, crows and vultures were relentless. It's too terrible to consider.'

Cigarette smoke drifted into the room.

'Constantina's first daughter, Marianna, was also killed that day,' Poppy said. 'Eighteen years old and full term, she was about to give birth. Two Nazis held her up while a third one ripped her clothes apart and bayoneted her belly open, in the street. She bled to death. Poor Constantina, it's impossible to imagine what she suffered.'

Matthia came inside. 'Go on,' he said. 'It needs to be told.'

Poppy continued. 'Years later, we heard the order from the German commander had been to kill all the males over sixteen, and anyone found outside the village. The Nazis went on a killing frenzy. Everyone blames others for the bad things that happen.'

Angie remembered Manoli saying the British started it all because of the communists in Crete.

'Ha!' Matthia interrupted. 'Power, brings out the worst in all nations. This sort of evil is still going on, but we choose to look the other way. War changes people. The English have done worse, and the Americans, and most of the others . . . sorry, Poppy, go on.'

'All this happened before I was born. Most of it I learned from Constantina, who seemed to get some relief by talking about war time, and especially the miracles. The women discovered three children, unconscious but alive. One was the baby boy.'

Poppy sniffed and wiped her eyes. 'They had found your father, Angelika, the man I came to love. He was nothing but a tiny infant, dehydrated, badly bruised and hardly breathing. No one doubted Constantina. She genuinely believed he was Yeorgo. The women rejoiced. The miracle of finding a newborn alive lifted everyone's spirits. Constantina still had milk. The baby latched on, and the bond was made.'

'And *Yiayá* struggled up the mountain trying to save Matthia and Stavro, sure that Petro was dead,' Angie said.

'Eventually, Constantina nursed Yeorgo back to health and all the bruises cleared except for the one on his head, which his thick dark hair covered. They simply forgot about it. Babies were kept well dressed in those days. They wore a long flannelette nightgown and a bonnet for the first three months. Nobody knew about Petro's birthmark apart from Mama, Stavro and the midwife. People were superstitious about such things, the mark of the devil, and so on. They weren't talked about.'

Angie nodded. 'And the Nazis hanged the midwife on the road to Pefkos, the next day.'

'You know so much more than me,' Poppy said. 'Mama told us little. I heard tales from Stavro, about a shepherd, and the fleas, and when they cut Matthia, but that's all.'

Angie slipped her arm around her mother. 'So Petro grew up as Yeorgo and died in the army after I was born. Ironic, after surviving the massacre. When did *Yiayá* break the awful news that Yeorgo was your brother Petro?'

'She didn't. She told the doctor on that day she saw Yeorgo's birthmark. However, because I was already four months pregnant, she forbade him to tell me. She claimed it wouldn't change anything, and we must hope the baby was normal. I can't imagine her torture while I carried that child.'

'It's a wonder she kept her sanity,' Angie said.

'When my second child arrived, stillborn, I nearly lost my mind. The doctor said he also had a heart problem and hadn't a chance. Yeorgo had returned to the army when we had the thirty-day memorial service. Stavro and Mama had a terrible argument in the cottage after church. Neighbours came to me, and told me to go there quickly.'

'Didn't she tell you?' Angie said.

'No. She yelled all sorts of things at Stavro. He took me back to Constantina's and I learned the truth. My mother-in-law attacked Stavro; she called him a liar and threw him out.'

'Constantina went crazy and wasn't the same from that day,' Matthia said. 'Doctor Petrinakis prescribed a drug, an anti-depressant, but she deteriorated rapidly. She seemed to turn into a half-wit and wandered for miles. She didn't wash, talked to herself and stared at nothing. Then the feud started. Emmanouil said we'd broken his mother's heart by claiming she'd taken Maria's baby, and hadn't she borne enough grief in her life?'

Chapter 42

MATTHIA DELVED INTO HIS POCKET and pulled out his cigarettes again. Angie noticed the frayed edges of his trousers. She glanced down and saw the hems were also on their last legs. She thought of all the food she'd been given: cakes, raki, wine and olive oil to take back to London. Yet her old uncle was in rags.

He opened the cigarette packet, counted the contents and put them away again. 'Thanassi and Emmanouil blamed us for their mother's madness. They both hated me anyway, because I was a communist and refused to lick their junta boots.'

Poppy glanced at her brother and then took Angie's hand. 'The fight between our families escalated. Someone set fire to our woodpile and poisoned the dog. They accused my brothers of putting sugar in their petrol tank, and poisoning their chickens, and so the nonsense continued. Perhaps Matthia did kill their hens, I wouldn't be surprised. He'd always been a bit of a devil.' A smile flickered as she exchanged a knowing look with him.

Matthia shrugged and lifted his hands in a gesture of non-committal.

'One morning, I found Constantina dead in her bed. She had taken all her pills at once,' Poppy said. 'Yeorgo came home for the funeral and Stavro told us the truth. On that day, our hearts were shattered. The man I'd loved all my life . . . my brother. We'd broken all God's laws.'

Angie realised she was crying. Poppy squeezed her hand.

'The feud escalated until the motorbike accident,' Poppy said. 'Emmanouil blamed Matthia for the death of his wife and unborn child. The situation worsened.'

'Thanassi told us about Yánna and the beating they gave Matthia,' Angie said, glancing at her uncle.

Poppy nodded. 'Yeorgo returned to the army, and I tried to talk to Emmanouil. You know what happened next.' She brought her bunched fists together and closed her eyes. 'I shot him. God forgive me.' She panted for a moment. 'I can't remember it, I swear. I've tried so hard, but it's been wiped from my mind. Why would I do such a terrible thing?' Poppy asked.

'They threatened to kill somebody in retribution for Yánna's death, Poppy. You were afraid for Yeorgo,' Matthia said.

'I don't know . . . A few nights before Yánna died, Emmanouil caught me alone and apologised for the way he'd bullied me over the years. I'd put up with a lot from him. He blamed his anger on my choice of husband. He claimed I should have married him. He frightened me, him and his temper. He said he loved me and always would and that I drove him crazy. For a moment, I felt sorry for him, but then he swore if I didn't go to him willingly, he would take me anyway and kill my family.'

'He was dangerous, Poppy. You should have told us.'

'Less than a week later, his wife died,' Poppy said. 'Emmanouil had almost kicked Matthia to death, and I'd killed Emmanouil.' She reached out and took Matthia's hand. 'Although I don't know exactly what happened at his house . . . I remember going there, opening the door . . . but then . . . running away and begging Stavro to lend me some cash. I've tried to fill in the blanks, but can't.'

'You asked me first, Poppy,' Matthia said.

'Asked you what?'

'For the money to leave Crete.'

'No . . . I don't recall,' Poppy said.

Matthia frowned and glanced about the floor. 'You telephoned me at the hospital and said you were desperate. You had to get away, urgently, but you never told me why. I refused. I've regretted it every day since. You knew I had savings for a new motorbike.'

Matthia sighed deeply. 'You killed him because of what he did to me, and I wouldn't lend you the money to escape the junta. I'm ashamed of that. How can you not remember, Poppy? You haven't spoken to me for nearly forty years because of it. Broke my heart it did. I wish I hadn't been so mean.'

'Matthia, you're wrong. I never held a grudge, not for a moment. I've missed you. Why didn't you write? I thought you were angry with me.' Poppy laughed. 'You were crazy about bikes. Mama said you shouldn't go to her for sympathy when you cracked your skull. Still, after what happened to Yánna it's not surprising she was against you getting another bike.'

Matthia shook his head as if trying to clear his thoughts. 'But I thought . . . I don't understand.'

Poppy looked at him curiously. 'You mean you believed, after all these years, that I didn't contact you because I was angry that you didn't lend me the money?'

'Why else? We were so close.'

Poppy frowned.

Angie glanced at the clock. 'What happened to Constantina's family, Mam? I know Thanassi is still alive. He's coming to the wedding if Matthia will allow it. They told us at the police station that Thanassi had phoned them – not an easy decision for him to shop his nephew. Thanassi saved your life, Mam.'

Matthia spoke. 'He wasn't a crackpot like Emmanouil, but they did tell me to stay away from their sister. Agapi was shipped off to the university in Athens. I never heard from her again until she retired and came back.'

Was Agapi her mother? Angie didn't think so.

'Stavro gave me the money to go to England on condition I kept in touch,' Poppy said. She stared at Matthia for a moment, her brow furrowed as if questioning herself before she continued. 'I made Stavro promise not to tell anyone where I'd gone and I disowned Mama before I left. I blamed her for everything. I was consumed by grief; two dead sons, the man I loved turning out to be my brother, and then killing Emmanouil . . .'

But who's my mother? Angie thought.

The old clock struck eleven, seven hours to her wedding. Tick, tick, tick. She heard a commotion in the village square. Tables and chairs were dragged out. Men knocked a wooden stage together for the bouzouki and lira band, and her heart also hammered.

'Let's sit outside so that we don't disturb *Yiayá* and *Papoú*.' A little fizz of excitement almost nudged Angie's curiosity and sadness to one side. Soon she would be Nick's wife.

They sat at the cracked marble table, the sun warming their damp faces, lifting the mood another notch. 'How come you left for England, Mam?'

'Stavro knew many people in Athens. The Mandrakis family had recently moved to London so he telegrammed them, asking for help. They owned a kebab house, one of the first all-night places in the city. They gave me a job, the night shift.' Poppy gazed into the distance. 'England was so different from Crete. The Beatles, Queen Elizabeth; Harold Wilson was the Prime

Minister and there was much trouble about Ireland that I didn't understand.

'In Crete, because of the junta, we only had military music on the wireless but in England they had Radio Luxembourg. Also, all the women around my age wore the mini skirt, which was banned in Greece. I listened to pop music all night while I worked, Writing down the words to songs when we weren't busy. I sang them while I served customers and practised the twist behind the counter. The customers loved it.'

'I missed you. Especially when I married Voula,' Matthia said, bringing her back to the misery. 'On my wedding day, I raised my glass to absent friends, thinking of you and Yeorgo.'

Poppy placed her hand on his cheek. 'There's been so much misunderstanding between us.'

She turned to Angie. 'I was lonely, but I learned English and spent a lot of time in front of the TV. They put a man on the moon, I couldn't get enough of that. The Mandrakises took me into their family. Aunty Heleny had a daughter two years younger than me, Valentina, wild but very beautiful. Men found her irresistible.' Poppy laughed. 'When she worked in the kebab house with me, we would sing and dance all night long. Heleny's business got so busy we had to employ extra staff.' Poppy sighed, the smile falling away. She cupped Angie's face in her hands and nodded. 'Valentina was my best friend in England.'

Matthia stared at his sister.

Poppy continued. 'Your father found me in London but, although I loved him with all my heart, living together became unbearable. He stayed for a week. We fought all the time. Being intimate was impossible, knowing we were siblings so I said I never wanted to see him again – which wasn't true. I told the man I adored to divorce me and find another woman.'

'That must have been so painful, Mam.' Angie took her hand.

'It broke my heart, Angelika. I loved him, I still do. The hardest part was packing his case. To fold his personal things into his bag seemed so final, it cut me up badly. Oddly enough, I wasn't too concerned about him finding another woman. To tell the truth, I hoped he would. Whether he did, or he didn't, made no difference to me, so if it added to his happiness, then it was some small consolation to me.'

Poppy sat in silence for a moment, tears trickling. 'When he was going, he put his brown suitcase by the door and said, "Come here, little one." He took me in his big strong arms. "I'll never love anyone like I love you, Poppy Lambrakis. I've given you my heart and I refuse to take it back. It's broken, but that's not your fault. Promise you won't forget me?" He kissed me, properly, for the very last time. My insides were twisted with pain. I longed to tell him how much I loved him, but doing so would just make matters worse.

'He said, "You're my moon and stars, Calliope Lambrakis, my moon and stars." And then he turned and walked away.'

Poppy closed her eyes and slowly shook her head. 'Why did it have to happen to us, Angelika? I didn't deserve such a cruel blow, nor did your father.'

Angie couldn't find the words to comfort Poppy – it was so much to take in.

'He never re-married, and I never saw him again.' Poppy sniffed and stared into the distance. 'I see him in my imagination, talk to him in my dreams, but no, I haven't set eyes on him since that day. Occasionally, I have a feeling he's close, watching me, but that's just my way of dealing with it.'

'How awful. I'm sorry I said those terrible things,' Angie said, full of remorse.

Poppy picked at a loose thread on the bottom of her cardigan. 'Yeorgo said if he couldn't live for me, then he'd die for his country, and he signed up for a life in the army. He returned to Greece with Valentina who was going to visit her grandparents in Athens. Valentina had a crush on Yeorgo. She said I was mad to send him away. Nobody knew why we were divorcing. When Valentina came back from Greece a month later, she was pregnant.' Poppy turned to face Angie.

'*She* was your real mother, Angelika; Valentina, Aunty Heleny's daughter.'

'No, Mam. You're my real mother. Valentina gave birth to me. Can you tell me; what happened to her?'

'Valentina had kept her pregnancy a secret until she went into early labour at home. We had no time to get her to hospital. The doctor did an emergency caesarean to save your life. She had eclampsia. They did everything possible. I'm sorry, Angelika. Although she was pregnant with Yeorgo's child, she told me he still loved me, and I should always keep him in my heart.'

Angie nodded and slipped her arm around her mother's shoulders.

'I'll never forget your father, Angelika. And the miracle of you . . . oh, Angelika, you can't possibly understand how much that meant to me. I helped to deliver you. I cleaned your little body and watched you to get a grip on life. Before your mother left this world, she thanked me, and made me promise to keep you safe. She told me to make sure you were happy, until the end of my days.'

'She'd be pleased to know what a good job you've done, Mam.'

'Near to death, Valentina confessed to her mother that Yeorgo was your father, and that I was to raise you as my own child. I wondered if Yeorgo had told Valentina why we'd parted.

I did bring you up as my own, Angelika. I love you unconditionally, because you're my husband's child.'

Angie found herself lost for words.

'I prayed for years that Yeorgo would return,' Poppy said. 'But nobody heard from him. Most of our soldiers that were sent to Cyprus didn't return.' She smiled. 'He'd be proud of you, Angelika.'

'I'm glad baby Petro didn't die, Mam. It's hard to imagine I'm his daughter and one day – maybe soon – I hope to have his grandchild, *your* grandchild.'

Poppy continued. 'Only Stavro knew the truth about Valentina, and he swore he wouldn't tell. Back then, I didn't think of the consequences. It wasn't until you started asking about your father and later, wanting to come to Crete, that things got difficult.'

'Didn't *Yiayá* know?' Angie asked.

'No, and as the years went by, I even convinced myself you were mine. Seeing you grow, the double of your father, was a bittersweet experience, but I wouldn't have had it any other way. I was blessed to be able to hold on to the most precious part of him – his only child.'

'And nobody has heard from my father since?'

Poppy shook her head. 'I think we have to accept things.'

'There must be a tomb for the Unknown Soldier in Cyprus, Mam. Let's go there together one day and lay some flowers for Dad?'

'Yes, I'd like to do that. It would give me a sense of closure after all these years.'

'Angelika! Poppy!' Voula and her granddaughters, laden with bulging carrier bags, came waddling up the steps.

Angie laughed and dried her eyes. 'Are you okay, Mam?'

Poppy nodded. 'I'm glad you know. I nearly died when you were searching for your birth certificate. I feared you'd hate me if you discovered the pretence.'

'Never,' Angie said. 'There's no pretence. You're my mother and that's that.'

Poppy blew her nose. 'Like I said, I can't give you away, ask Matthia or Stavro, they're next in line after your father.'

They turned to Matthia. 'If Stavro isn't here, I'd be proud, Angelika.' He patted her hand.

Maria came out of the house. 'Well, I'm glad that's settled. It took long enough.'

The three of them stared at the old lady.

'Sorry, did we wake you, *Yiayá*?' Angie said.

'You woke me with your racket hours ago, inconsiderate lot,' Maria said.

'Mama, can you forgive me?' Poppy hugged Maria and helped her into her chair.

'Enough . . .' Maria gave Poppy a cynical glance. 'It's been a long time. Perhaps we can put all this behind us now. I couldn't tell Angelika or Matthia. You had to do it, Poppy. I'm glad you found the courage.'

Angie stared at her grandmother. 'You knew, *Yiayá*?'

'Of course I knew. I told you on the first day you came here, *koritsie*, I'm not the stupid old woman you may think.' In her eyes, a spark of anger glinted and died.

Chapter 43

Thessaloniki Greece, Present Day.

STAVRO FOUND THE KAFENION and, inside, glanced around for Yeorgo. Two guys played *tavli*, neither of them old enough to be his brother. A young woman in a revealing vest top and short shorts cleared a table. She lifted an empty coffee cup and a full ashtray onto her tray and then threw Stavro a questioning look.

'Hello, I'm looking for Yeorgo Lambrakis. Is he here?'

She glanced at the tray. 'You've just missed him. Can I get you anything?'

Stavro stared at the empty seat. 'Will he be back, do you think?'

'Probably, he's gone to buy a paper.' She straightened, placed her hands on her hips, pert breasts pushed against stretchy fabric. Stavro realised he was staring and flicked his glance back to her face.

'Okay, I'll wait. Greek coffee, medium sweet.'

He pulled out the chair that he suspected his brother had just left and watched the sweetest bottom he had noticed in a long time swing provocatively until it disappeared behind the counter.

Yes, Yeorgo, I'd come here for my morning coffee too.

By nine o'clock, Stavro battled with impatience. The kafenion had filled. He stared at each face that came through the door but didn't recognise Yeorgo.

'Do you have a phone book?' he asked the waitress. When she brought it, Stavro looked up the airport number, holding it at arm's length to get the small print into focus. He called flight information and wrote details into his notebook. He had to get the rings and wedding crowns to Crete, so the two o'clock flight from Thessaloniki to Heraklion was his only option. He glanced at his notes. The later Heraklion flight was at five o'clock – far too late.

Stavro tore a page from his book and wrote:

Yeorgo Lambrakis,

My good friend. Your daughter, Angelika, is getting married in Amiras today at six o'clock. The reception is in the village square. I have been trying to find you for many years to ask you to return to the family. We all miss you, especially Mama, Poppy and Angelika. Please come home!

Your loving brother, Stavro.

To arrive at this point – so close – and still leave for Crete alone, sickened him. He folded the note and passed it to the young woman. 'Please give this to Lambrakis. It's very important. I have to go. I've a plane to catch.'

She unfolded the piece of paper and read it. Her eyes widened. 'I'll make sure he gets it as soon as possible.'

Stavro dropped five euros onto the table and scooted back to his apartment.

* * *

Aboard the Aegean Airways plane, Stavro fastened his seatbelt and watched the flight attendant. He should have written his phone number on the note, and he also forgot to take down the kafenion's details. His memory had let him down again. Being realistic, what were the odds of this person, who had one of the commonest names in Greece, being his brother? Slim, he thought.

Stavro recalled the last time he saw Yeorgo. He remembered his face so clearly. A clean-shaven and handsome man with wide brown eyes, a square jaw, and a slight cleft in the chin. They had hugged and slapped each other's backs. They were alike in many ways. Once the truth was out – that they were brothers – he questioned how everyone had missed their similarities in both looks and personality. He wondered if Constantina had recognised the resemblance between them and always feared her mistake.

A few months after Angelika's birth, Yeorgo had turned up at Stavro's apartment in Athens and stayed overnight. They had drunk too much raki and talked until dawn. When Yeorgo left, he took Poppy's letters and the picture of his baby daughter. Stavro had tried to get him to visit London, knowing how much Poppy still wanted to see him despite her hard words.

'I've already been,' Yeorgo had said, staring at the photograph of Angelika. 'I went to London, laid flowers on Valentina's grave and watched Poppy pushing a pram around the park. I kept out of sight; better that way, no point in causing more upset.' His shoulders dropped and he stared into the distance. 'She'll come to terms with everything and deal with it.'

Stavro topped up their glasses – a feeble gesture when he wanted to do so much more.

'*Yammas!* Health and happiness to my baby girl,' Yeorgo had said with an overly bright smile, slamming his glass on the table before knocking back the clear liquid. 'I couldn't see her, tucked away in the pram, so I'm grateful for the picture. Angelika's a pretty little thing, isn't she? Poppy seemed happy. She was smiling and chatting to other mothers who peeked at my baby. I don't want to spoil things for them. You know how much Poppy wanted a child and I couldn't wish for a better mother for Angelika, could I?'

Yeorgo had paused and swallowed hard, the photograph trembling in his hand.

Stavro saw his brother's heart breaking.

Yeorgo continued. 'I'll set up a trust fund for Angelika but I'll have it paid into your account, Stavro. I know you'll see they get it. Say it's from you. It's kinder if they don't think of me.'

When drink had the better of them, Yeorgo confessed he believed himself responsible for the death of the woman he had always regarded as his mother. Constantina had loved him with everything she had, no one could doubt it. The truth, that she had taken another woman's baby and left her own to the dogs, had destroyed her.

Once Yeorgo returned to the army, Stavro had an odd feeling his brother had come to say goodbye. He never heard from Yeorgo again.

* * *

The seatbelt sign stayed on inside the Aegean aircraft. Stavro gripped the armrests. A couple of passengers crossed themselves as the plane continued through turbulence. In the back of Stavro's mind, a spark of fear flared and died. He was safe. Planes seldom fell out of the sky. His skin seemed to tighten over his body with each anxious moment. The aircraft galloped across the firmament like a disorientated carthorse. The flight attendant answered the internal phone and had a conversation with the cockpit. She replaced the receiver, strapped herself into a pull-down seat at the front of the cabin and then stretched for the mike above her head. The plane banked and dipped, slightly out of sync with Stavro's stomach.

'Due to high winds at Heraklion airport, we're turning back and heading for Athens. All passengers will be transferred to the first available slot for Heraklion. The captain apologises for the inconvenience but would like to remind everyone that it's for their own safety.'

Stavro glanced at his watch; three o'clock. Was there any chance he would make the wedding? A dull pain in his chest grew stronger as time ticked by. In forty-five minutes, they'd be inside the Athens terminal. Even if the winds at Heraklion dropped immediately, it would be an hour before he was outside that airport and then he had to get to Amiras.

The plane continued to toss around like a brick in a tumble drier and the pain in Stavro's chest grew a little stronger.

Chapter 44

Amiras, Crete.

Angie and Poppy stared across the cracked marble table at Maria.

'But how did you know, Mama?' Poppy said.

'Matthia, fetch me the big pink chocolate box from the top of my wardrobe,' Maria said.

Minutes later, Matthia placed the tattered box, tied by a length of yellow ribbon, in front of them.

'This pile of mementoes is your wedding present from me, Angelika. It's your life story in a chocolate box,' she paused. 'Now will somebody make me a coffee or do I have to do everything myself?' Maria said.

Voula, who had joined them after organising her granddaughters, was uncharacteristically quiet. She jumped up and waddled into the kitchen.

Angie and Poppy delved into the collection of mementoes and found bundles of letters, a pair of scratch mittens, a baby's shoe, photographs of Poppy holding a sleeping baby, Angie's first steps, Christmas dinners, Girl Guide badges, school plays, university graduation and so much more.

'Where did they come from?' Angie asked.

'From London, of course,' Maria said.

Poppy unfolded one of the letters, her eyes scanning to the bottom, and then she gasped.

'Good grief . . . they're from Aunty Heleny – Valentina's mother!'

'Yes, Valentina's mother and Angelika's grandmother. A very *good* woman. She knew Poppy had come from Amiras, and learned my name from Stavro. She sent me a letter to say my daughter was safe and well. We corresponded.' Maria nodded. 'When she'd lost her own daughter she understood the pain I'd suffered after Poppy left. Until last year, she sent me a letter and photographs every month, bless her.' Maria picked up the baby shoe, stroked it affectionately and smiled. 'After Heleny died, it made me crazy not hearing about you both. So, I was about to send a letter to England, but then Angelika turned up like a miracle.'

'Heleny was always snapping us with her little camera. We used to call her paparazzi,' Poppy said.

Angie wagged a playful finger at her grandmother. 'So that's why you were working on my dowry linen, you already knew I was getting married!' She nodded to herself. 'I thought you looked a bit shifty when you let slip what you were crocheting.' She turned to Poppy. 'Think about it, Mom. Nick and I got engaged before Aunty Heleny died.'

Maria's eyes twinkled.

Poppy studied the photographs and read letters until Voula appeared with the coffees. 'Matthia, why are you still with the bride on her wedding day?' She whacked the side of his head, playfully.

'Drink your coffee, Matthia, then go to the men's house or you'll bring us bad luck,' Maria said.

Angie moved to the chair next to him and recalled the first time she had done that. 'Thank you, Uncle Matthia. It took courage to tell me the truth.' She reached for the cup in his hand. 'Now go away and join the men. And be careful with that smile – it could become a habit.'

Matthia sat there grinning at them all.

'Virgin Mary . . .' Maria crossed herself three times. 'Will somebody get my son out of here? We've a dress to put onto the bride, and food to bring out.'

A microphone bellowed up from the village square, 'One-two. One-two. *Alpha-Beta,*' followed by a screeching whistle and then the strum of a string instrument.

They all grinned at Angie. She laughed, delighted when Voula's granddaughters appeared from the cottage in their traditional Cretan costumes.

'Bravo! Right, we'd better get ready,' Poppy said.

'It's about time you took control.' Maria glanced at the empty table. 'Fetch the food out here, and bring some glasses. Let's open the sparkling wine.' She pulled herself up from her chair. 'I'm going to take it easy now, leave it to you girls. Voula, help me get ready. Angelika and Poppy should have ten minutes together.'

Angie's phone rang.

'How's my bride doing?' She heard a smile in Nick's voice.

'Hello! Listen, you're not supposed to speak to me until we're wed. You'll bring us bad luck, the evil eye.' She giggled, they both thought the Cretan superstitions were quaint.

'I'm not speaking to you. I'm speaking to my phone. I love you.'

'You love your phone? I knew it. Have you been drinking, bridegroom?

'No, have you, bride?'

'Just about to start. Is Stavro there?'

'No, a bit of a panic about that, nobody's heard from him for three days,' Nick said. 'Matthia has just arrived. He said to remember Stavro has a weak heart.'

'Trust Matthia to drop that on us, like we need the extra stress. You don't seriously think something might have happened to him?' Angie asked, concerned.

'No, don't worry. Matthia just likes a bit of drama. There's no reply from his apartment phone and his mobile's turned off, which probably means he's on a plane.'

'Don't forget, he's our best man.'

'I've just remembered – he's got the rings,' Nick said. 'Hopefully, there's a simple explanation – one of those stories that will be tagged onto our wedding forever. Don't fret.'

'All right bossyboots!' Angie said, playfully. 'Did you hear from Thanassi?'

'He's speaking to Matthia. I think they're settling their differences. Got to go, I love you, bye.'

* * *

'Still no sign of Stavro?' Angie asked Voula half an hour later.

'Perhaps he's with the men now,' Voula said. 'I'll send one of the girls down.'

Twenty minutes passed before Voula's granddaughter returned and said, 'Uncle Stavro has disappeared and Grandpa Matthia said he'll give Angelika away. But he asks will you all stop making him feel like a stand-in.'

The house phone rang and Voula bobbed inside to answer it, returning a minute later. 'Stavro called to say his flight was diverted. He's on his way. Can we put the nuptials back an hour because he has the *stefana* and the rings?'

'I keep meaning to ask, what's the *stefana*?' Angie said.

Poppy explained. 'They're supposed to be a surprise from me. That's blown it! Silver wedding crowns joined by lengths of ribbon, never separated after the marriage ceremony.' Her eyes clouded. 'When me and Yeorgo wed, we stuck with tradition and had wreathes of citrus leaves and blossom. Anyway, we didn't have the money for anything else. I kept ours. Now they're all dried up and wrinkled like me, but still tied together.' She closed her eyes and pinched the bridge of her nose.

'Will you stop the snivelling, Poppy? Have a drink.' Maria huffed.

'It's too early for me to start drinking, Mama,' Poppy said.

'Virgin Mary! Do as you're told for once, child.' Maria slid her glass towards Voula, who popped the champagne cork. It landed on the roof, rolled down the tiles, bounced off Maria's head and fell onto the table. Everyone started laughing. Maria held on to her dignity and ignored them.

'What do you mean: Stavro is going to take another hour? Where's he coming from, Timbuktu?' Maria said. 'He's usually very reliable. I can't believe my son is messing up everyone's plans.'

'I've no idea where he is,' Voula said. 'He just told me we must wait for him because he has the rings.'

'It's the bride who's supposed to be late.' Maria slapped the table. 'Somebody inform the priest and the band, and the women organising the food. Tell them it's the *Koumbaros*'s fault, so they don't put a curse on Angelika.'

Voula's grandchildren went back down the steps. Angie longed to see Nick. So much had happened since they were alone together.

'If nobody needs me, I'm going to get ready,' Poppy said.

'Angelika,' Maria squeezed Angie's hand and looked up toward the small chapel on the hill, *Agios Charalampos*. A herd of goats had gathered before it. The bells around their necks clanged mismatched chimes across the valley. As grandmother and granddaughter gazed up to the skyline, an enormous shaggy ram came to the forefront. It stared down at them, still for a moment as if searching, and then it slowly bobbed its massively-horned head.

Maria nodded back at it. 'Bless you, Andreas . . .' she whispered.

Angie and her grandmother were still gazing up when four burly policemen came around the corner of the cottage.

'Calliope Lambrakis,' the leader called out.

In her stunning red outfit, Poppy stepped into the garden and whimpered. She nodded at the policemen.

Angie rushed to her side.

'Step away, please,' one officer said to Angelika.

The officers surrounded her mother. One of them took her handbag, holding it awkwardly. 'Place your hands behind your back,' another said.

Poppy bowed her head and stared at the ground while he snapped on the handcuffs.

'Calliope Lambrakis, I have a warrant, issued by the public prosecutor, against you, for the murder of Lambrakis Emmanouil. You may read the warrant if you wish.'

Poppy gulped and shook her head.

'You have no obligation to say anything and your silence cannot be used against you,' he said.

'No!' Angie cried out. 'You can't arrest my mother; I'm getting married today! *No!*'

'Sorry, miss, I have no choice,' the policeman in charge said. 'Bring me her passport.'

'It's in my handbag,' Poppy said quietly.

'Quickly, Voula, phone Demitri and Matthia, right away,' Maria said.

'Let me say goodbye to my mother and daughter, please,' Poppy said.

The officer nodded.

'I'm coming with you,' Angie said. 'I can't let you go through this alone.'

Poppy shook her head. 'No, you and Nick must marry. Raise your glass to me at the reception, but until then, forget about me. I'll be thinking of you, Angelika. We've come so far, haven't we, love?' Her eyes filled and her lips trembled as she said, 'I'm truly sorry your real mother can't be here, but don't let this stop your wedding, promise me. I want you to have a wonderful day, do it for me, please.'

'Mam, stop talking rubbish, you're my real mother, I couldn't love anyone more.' She gave Poppy a fierce hug and kissed her cheeks. 'We'll find a way out of this, I swear.'

'Mama,' Poppy said, turning to Maria. 'I'm sorry for all the trouble I've brought upon you. I've never stopped loving you. Can you forgive me for running away? I should have faced up to this long before now.'

'There's nothing to forgive,' Maria whispered, dabbing her cheeks and then embracing her daughter. 'You knew you'd have to deal with this sooner or later, Poppy. It's brave of you to return, and I'm so very proud of you. We'll do everything we can to get you out of there.'

'Oh, Mama, I don't deserve you,' Poppy said.

Angie held Maria who sobbed quietly. Together, they watched the police lead Poppy down the cement steps to a waiting police car.

* * *

Poppy sat on the back seat with her hands cuffed behind her. She stared at the scenery, remembering olive harvests when families gathered and everyone worked in harmony. Now that the truth was out, despite her predicament, a sense of peace settled on her.

Angelika would marry Nick and she would have her 'happy-ever-after'. Nothing else mattered. Poppy hoped for grandchildren. Perhaps she shouldn't have left Amiras all those years ago, but then she would have been executed for murdering Emmanouil, and would never have had the joy that was Angelika. Despite the heartache she had caused her family, she had no regrets.

She thought about her mother. If Maria hadn't left the village in 1943, she would have been there when Petro was found, and everything would be different. Poppy wouldn't have fallen in love with Yeorgo, if he had grown up as Petro, her brother. She still loved Yeorgo. That she found out he was her sibling, after they were married, made no difference to the way she felt. Society's rules had no claim on her heart.

The pain of living without him had been almost more than she could bear but she had Angelika – his daughter – and that was the most glorious twist of the whole sorry story.

The patrol car entered Viannos and drove past the big tree, then down a side street next to the town's church. She saw the modern police station building loom up ahead. They double-parked and she struggled to get out of the car.

'Young man,' she said to an officer. 'Please may I have the cuffs in front of me? I've just had a heart operation. It hurts to have my hands behind my back.'

The policeman, tall, overweight, sweating in his dark surge uniform, studied her for a second. He rested his hand on his gun holster. 'Will you behave?'

She nodded. 'I swear. I won't be any trouble.'

He took the cuffs off and clipped them onto his belt.

Sounds echoed inside the new building. A tired looking policewoman with unruly blonde hair tied back, shifted boxes of files from the corridor into several offices. She offered Poppy a sympathetic smile. The air was fuggy with cigarette smoke and paint smells.

The policeman took her into a small interview room and offered her a seat. Her chair legs screeched against the pink marble floor. Five minutes later a middle-aged man in civilian clothes joined them.

'Is there anything you want to tell me?' he said.

Poppy shook her head.

'You realise we have to do this?'

She nodded.

The policewoman came in and put two glasses of frappé on the table.

'I'm going to take your statement. Do you want a lawyer?' the man said to Poppy.

'No,' she said and glanced at a clock on the wall. Angelika would be changing into the wedding dress that she had worn to marry Yeorgo. 'Is there any chance I will see my daughter get married, sir?' she said. 'I swear I won't run away. Anyway, you have my passport . . . it's an island, where could I go? It's really important to me, and to her. Her father's dead.' Poppy's throat ached with hope and a sob escaped.

He rubbed his fingers over his mouth and then shook his head.

Chapter 45

HERAKLION, AT LAST! STAVRO unfastened his seatbelt, grabbed his hand baggage from the overhead locker and raced to the front of the plane. With a bit of luck his suitcase would be first off and he could grab a taxi. He pulled out his mobile.

'Please wait until you're inside the terminal, sir,' the flight attendant said.

Stavro pocketed the phone.

They had to sit on the tarmac for ten minutes while a plane from Thessaloniki landed. Eventually, Stavro and his fellow passengers were bussed to the building. He watched the luggage carousel, wishing he had only brought hand baggage but Heleny's family in Athens had sent too many wedding gifts.

Calm down, he told his racing heart. He had to accept he wasn't likely to make the actual marriage, but at least he would be at the reception to greet the bride and groom. He patted the lump in his jacket pocket and wondered what they would do for rings.

Stavro's suitcase see-sawed under the black rubber strips and then slid onto the carousel. He dodged travellers and knocked somebody's shoulder calling, 'Sorry' without looking back. The handle felt great in his hand. He yanked it up, dragged the bag outside the terminal and then raced to the taxi rank.

'Amiras, Viannos, quickly as possible! I'm the *Koumbaros* of my niece's wedding. I'm late and I have the rings in my pocket.'

He threw his case into the boot of the silver Mercedes and dived into the front seat.

The taxi driver grinned. 'Okay, let's burn rubber!' he said.

Again, Stavro calmed himself, no point in arriving *dead* on time, as the Greeks were fond of saying when they were late. The pain in his chest returned.

The driver blasted his horn, yelling '*Malákas!*' at anyone in his way.

Work on the dual carriageway across Crete had stopped with the financial crisis, and three small villages interrupted the motorway. The cabdriver knew shortcuts. They bounced over rough ground and then hurtled through a gap that somebody had cut into the crash barrier, hair-raising but it shaved precious minutes off the journey.

Glancing at the speedometer, Stavro saw they were travelling at 110 kph. He phoned Matthia.

'I'm in a cab on my way. Hold things up until I get there.'

'It's already been put back till seven,' Matthia said. 'Where've you been? Poppy was arrested for Emmanouil's murder. She's in Viannos police station, but she insists the wedding goes ahead. Thanassi said he'll deal with it, but I don't see what he can do.'

'Poor Poppy, after all she's been though. Tragic if she misses Angelika's nuptials. I'll try and think of something,' Stavro said.

'Poppy's told everyone about Valentina, and the Yeorgo–Petro thing.'

'Good, how did Mama take it?' Stavro's phone signal died. His watch said: six thirty-five.

The sun headed for the horizon. Racing up close behind them, another taxi blasted its horn and flashed its headlights.

The taxi driver cursed. They were flying down the outside lane of the empty road, steep mountains to their left and a ravine to their right. The vehicle pitched and dipped over subsidence and then bounced back on to a level surface, only to swerve violently to the left to miss a void where the tarmac had fallen away.

Stavro glanced into the wing mirror. The car behind came closer, honking and flashing. 'Let him pass,' he said, afraid of instigating an accident.

The driver huffed, lurched over, and the other taxi flew by, disappearing into the distance. They came off the straight road and snaked around the mountainsides. Stavro checked his phone repeatedly. Almost at Viannos, he got two bars. He called Matthia.

'What's happening? I'm just coming through Viannos, where are you, Matthia?'

'We're starting down the aisle and I'll burn in hell from the looks I'm getting from Papas Christos,' Matthia said.

'Ignore Papas Christos. Go back outside the church. We'll be there in minutes.'

The taxi slid to a breath-taking halt. A head-to-head with a sixteen-wheeler in Viannos's narrow thoroughfare. Stavro wished he had time to call at the police station. Poor Poppy, what a cruel twist of fate.

The taxi driver lowered his window, thrust his entire upper body out and yelled, 'I've got the *Koumbaros* and we're late for the Amiras wedding, *Malákas*!'

Motorists dashed to their cars, pickups crunched gears, shifting back so he could bump up the pavement and let the truck pass. Stavro found himself rocking back and forth in his seat, willing everyone to move faster. Arms waved, people shouted, hands rolled in guidance. The taxi driver pulled his mirror in and the truck squeezed through with centimetres to spare.

Under the big tree, people clapped boisterously as the taxi lurched onward. The driver hooted the horn, warning deaf old jaywalkers to get out of the way. Once through Viannos, they had to slow once more. The vehicle that had blasted past them earlier was parked on a bend, the driver pissing into the ravine. They managed to drive by and, with one kilometre to Amiras, Stavro phoned Matthia.

'I'm just coming into Amiras. Is there any news about Poppy, Matthia?'

* * *

The square interview room contained four chairs and a simple one-drawer desk. The plain-clothes policeman and the uniformed policewoman sat opposite Poppy. The man, restless and uninterested, recorded the interview. The woman completed a form using small neat letters, her eyes flicking up with each question. When she had finished, she introduced herself.

'I'm PC Katarina. Do you prefer to be called Calliope, or Poppy?'

'Poppy,' she said.

Katarina glanced at the man who sat back with his arms folded. 'This is Detective Inspector Spanaki from Athens CID. He's standing in for the chief, who's away.' She turned towards him. 'Are we ready, sir?'

Spanaki flicked a switch on a recording device. He stated the time and date and the names of those present and then nodded.

'Tell us every tiny detail about that day, Poppy,' Katarina said. 'Even the things you think aren't relevant. You'd be surprised what can trigger a recall. Take your time, start when you're ready.'

Poppy glanced around the room. 'I don't know where to begin,' she said.

'What's the first thing you remember?' Katarina said.

Poppy gathered her thoughts, evoking that distant day. 'It was the second of April, 1968,' she said, tilting her face towards the recorder. 'I recall fretting about what to wear for my confrontation with Emmanouil. Silly really, considering Yánna and her baby were dead and Matthia in hospital, yet it seemed important.' Poppy closed her eyes and concentrated. 'Eventually, I chose my newest outfit; a candy-striped sweater over homemade orange flares.'

'Is this necessary?' Spanaki said. 'I've got a plane to catch.' He stared at his watch.

Poppy felt the heat of a blush.

Katarina squinted a silent curse at Spanaki and then nodded at Poppy. 'Go on, as I said, *every* detail is important at this stage.'

Poppy thought for a moment. 'I painted my nails tangerine, and backcombed my hair into a bouffant,' she said. 'I used sugar and water to set kiss-curls against my cheeks.' She met PC Katarina's eyes and half smiled. 'I was a cool-cat, hip, very with it. The clothes and make-up were important, they made me feel strong enough to stand up to Emmanouil.'

'I understand,' Katarina said.

'I walked to Emmanouil's house rehearsing my speech: I was sorry he'd lost his wife. Yánna had been a good woman, everyone liked her – she had been one of my bridesmaids. Fate had been unkind and I completely understood Emmanouil's need for revenge. I was going to tell him our family would make the first move in the truce. There would be no reprisals for the terrible beating they gave Matthia. That would be the end of it.'

'And you rehearsed all this, on your way to his house?' Katarina said.

'I did. I was very afraid, but I had to try to stop the vendettas.'

'Don't think about that now. Concentrate on what you saw, and the sounds you heard as you went along the street. See if you can return there in your mind.'

Poppy placed her hand on her stomach. 'I had this fear trying to rise up inside me, but I pushed it down, determined to complete my plan.' She took a breath. 'I threw my shoulders back and lifted my chin. I clearly remember doing that.' Poppy sat taller. 'The street was empty. Nobody called, "Come for coffee!" yet I sensed my friends were behind me. I reached Emmanouil's house.' Poppy shrank into the chair and felt herself shaking. 'I can't . . . I . . .'

'Okay, take two steps back. Tell me what you smell.'

Poppy closed her eyes again. 'Honeysuckle. I recall thinking Yánna wouldn't be pleased.'

'Why not?' PC Katarina said.

'She was very house-proud. Their home and the street outside were always spotless.'

'And how was it that day? What did you see?'

'Emmanouil's door was turquoise planks in a frame painted Greek-flag blue. A folded olive-sack improvised as a doormat. Fallen honeysuckle blossom lay scattered over it. It hadn't been swept for a week. The door handle was a twisted iron ring.'

Poppy's fingers curled. She felt the contrasting rough and smooth of corrosion and gloss paint. 'The sun was on my back and I could feel its warmth in the handle.'

'You're doing great,' Katarina said. 'Go on.'

'"Emmanouil!" I called, twisting the handle to go in. "Emmanouil!" He didn't answer so I pushed the door . . . Oh, no . . . No!' Poppy's eyes flew open.

'Go on in, Poppy. Tell me what you see,' Katarina said quietly. 'You can smell honeysuckle. The street's quiet. The door handle's warm.'

Poppy lifted her hand and pushed the imaginary turquoise door. Her voice trembled. 'There's fine dust on the door, it's silky against my fingers. We'd had the Sirocco, the Sick Wind, for a week. "I've come to offer my condolences," I called out, but then I couldn't get into the house.'

'Why not? What stopped you?' Katarina said.

Poppy shook her head. 'It's no good. I can't remember.' She dropped her face into her hands.

The door burst open, hitting the empty chair and sending it skidding on the polished floor.

'Thanassi, what are you doing here?' Poppy said.

'*Malákas!*' Spanaki pulled the desk drawer open, snatched an ashtray and a packet of Silk Cut and said, 'We're in the middle of an interview, get out of here.'

'I've come to help,' Thanassi said and then turning to Poppy. 'Forgive me, Poppy. I've always known what happened to Emmanouil, but as you weren't here there was no need to tell.'

Another policeman came barging into the room. 'Sorry, sir. He asked where Mrs Lambrakis was. Before I could get around the counter, he was racing down the corridor.'

Spanaki stared at the young officer, then at Thanassi. 'And you couldn't catch him, Olympian as he is?'

'I was up the ladder trying to stop the strip-light flickering, sir.'

'I've come to tell you what really took place,' Thanassi said, shoving the empty chair towards the table.

'Get out!' Spanaki yelled at the policeman. 'And take this old fool with you. Get him to make a statement at the front desk.'

'Don't say anything,' Katarina said to Thanassi. 'We're conducting a formal interview.'

The policeman tried to steer Thanassi through the door but he wouldn't budge.

'I did it, Poppy, it was me!' he said.

'Sir, you're corrupting our investigation. Please leave!' Katarina turned to the young officer. 'Take him to the other interview room. We'll be there when we've finished –'

Spanaki interrupted. 'Katarina, let him tell us what happened. Get it over with. I've got things to do.'

PC Katarina rolled her eyes.

Thanassi fell into the empty chair and reached for Poppy's hands.

'I hid the string, Poppy, and the wood that was nailed to the table. And I took Emmanouil's letter, his confession,' Thanassi said. 'I've been out of my mind since you came back to Crete. I didn't believe you'd ever return so I let everyone believe you'd killed my brother.' He turned to Spanaki. 'She didn't kill anybody.'

The door closed behind the young officer and silence returned to the interview room.

'String? What string?' Poppy muttered, and then her eyes widened. The interview room disappeared as her memory of those lost minutes returned. 'Of course . . . there was a length of twine tied to the inside door handle. It slid through a bent nail on the doorframe.' She turned to Katarina. 'That's what stopped me from entering. I thought the catch must have broken.' She stared at the interview room door. 'I tried to pull a little slack and unhook it from the nail.'

Poppy placed a hand over her mouth and cowered in her seat. In her head, she heard Emmanouil's voice coming from the gloom inside the room.

'Wait!'

She shoved the door, opening it a little more. A shaft of sunlight illuminated Emmanouil. He wore days of beard growth and black clothes, his hands were prayer-locked, eyes closed, lips moving.

She hadn't understood, stared at his face and tried to enter the room. Then she saw the shotgun fixed to the tabletop.

In that small space, the flash and the sound of two deafening blasts seemed to rip the brains right out of her head. The gun recoiled with such force, it slammed the door against her shoulder before it ricocheted back into the room. Bright sunlight streamed into the house and revealed the carnage. Poppy, choking on the stink of burned metal and flesh, knew she was screaming but couldn't hear anything above the ringing in her ears.

She turned away from the blood, and the stench, and the smoke. Gripping the top of her arm, she ran, and ran . . . and it seemed that she had been running from that moment for forty long years.

Poppy forgot the police, and the wedding, and lost herself in the exploding memory. She sobbed, trying to reject the picture of her brother-in-law's dying seconds. The image so grotesque, her mind had blocked it. His face had disappeared into a splatter over the whitewashed wall, even before the rest of his body, in the chair, tipped back.

With no recollection of the shotgun fixed to the table – and feeling the terrible recoil pain in her shoulder – she concluded that she had pulled the trigger.

Spanaki lit a cigarette, got up and opened the window. Honking horns, people shouting, and revving engine noises told of a commotion on the main street. He glanced at his watch again. 'Sounds like the street's blocked, now.'

Poppy stared at Thanassi and then faced Katarina. 'I remember everything.' She slid the backs of her fingers under her eyes, wiping away her tears. 'I didn't kill Emmanouil. He'd rigged his shotgun so that when the door opened, it fired.' She glared at Thanassi. Her forty wasted years of dishonour and distress morphed into pure anger.

'Poppy, can you forgive me?' Thanassi asked. 'It wasn't that I wanted to get you into trouble. I simply didn't want Manoli bearing the shame of his father's suicide. I knew Emmanouil very well. He couldn't watch his son growing up without his mother and sister because we'd caused their deaths.'

'You bastard!' Poppy cried, pulling her hand back and delivering a vicious slap across his face. 'You let me, and my family, think I'd murdered him! What sort of person are you? I've been parted from my parents for all that time, because I thought I had killed somebody. How dare you ask for my forgiveness?! I know you didn't intend to harm Yánna, Thanassi, but let's not forget, you did try to kill my brother, Matthia.'

Thanassi, stunned for a second, nodded while rubbing his stubbly old cheek. His wrinkled hand shook violently.

'Take it easy,' Katarina said to Poppy.

'It's true, I admit it,' Thanassi said, his eyes wet and his lips trembling. 'But Matthia had cut the brake line on our truck. It was only luck we found it. My entire family were going into Viannos the next day. We could have *all* gone into the ravine. That's why Emmanouil wanted his revenge.'

Poppy's mouth fell open.

'After Emmanouil's death, I confessed to what we'd done to Matthia's motorbike. I was sent to prison for three years for involuntary manslaughter and malicious intent to cause harm.

But I didn't say why, Poppy. Matthia would have been locked up for a long time too, if I'd spoken out.'

'So all this happened in 1968?' Spanaki said to Thanassi. 'You were convicted and sentenced for your part in the crime?'

Thanassi nodded.

Spanaki addressed Poppy. 'And you didn't commit a felony apart from leaving the scene of a crime?'

'A crime?' Poppy said.

'To attempt suicide was against the law in those days and carried a prison sentence.' Spanaki shut down the recorder and faced Katarina. 'Shall we bring this to an end? There seems little to answer for. I'm sure you can deal with the minutiae.'

'Yes, sir,' Katarina said.

Spanaki nodded at them all, picked up his cigarettes, and left the room.

'Poppy, we'll need a fresh statement. What time's the wedding?' Katarina asked.

Poppy glanced at her watch. 'Any minute now. Please . . . it's so important to me, and my daughter. You can keep my passport; I can't go anywhere.'

Katarina squinted at Thanassi. 'Mr Lambrakis, you will be held for further questioning. We'll probably charge you for withholding evidence.'

'You destroyed my family,' Poppy said quietly, anger curling her lip. 'How could you put an end to so much love and unity, to preserve the false reputation of a bastard like Emmanouil. He had made my life hell ever since I was a little girl! You may have idolised your older brother, but let me tell you, Thanassi, he was a bully and a filthy paedophile.'

Katarina and Thanassi stared at her.

'I don't know what to say,' Thanassi said, staring at Poppy, then casting his eyes down shamefully. 'Sorry seems inadequate, but what else is there? Let's just clear it up. I've paid my price –'

'Paid your price?! When you've spent forty years in isolation, away from your family and all those who love you, then you will have paid your price, Thanassi,' Poppy said through fresh tears. 'How could you? All those years I was ostracised by my village and my loved ones. You knew I was innocent and said nothing!'

'Poppy, if you think I haven't been punished enough, so be it. Who cares? I've no family left except for Agapi, and she hates me; and Manoli who's locked up because I never told him the truth about his father.' He nodded at Katarina. 'She really should be at her daughter's wedding. The bride has no other immediate family.'

Katarina stood.

Poppy's anger died, her heart bursting with hope. Could she get to the church before the end of the ceremony?

'I'm truly sorry, Poppy,' Thanassi said. 'If you can't forgive me, I understand. I thought you were happy in England. Please don't be hard on Manoli. He's never known the truth. Did Angelika tell you, Emmanouil left a letter explaining everything?' He reached into his jacket pocket and passed over a heavily stained envelope.

'Don't touch it!' Katerina cried. 'We have a procedure. I need to contain it in case it's needed for evidence. Just place it on the table.'

Poppy trembled, exhausted.

'I didn't show anyone the letter,' Thanassi said. 'I was going to give it to Angelika, but now I believe I should take it to Manoli myself, if they'll let me,' He nodded at the officer. 'I'll tell my nephew what actually happened. He'll come to terms;

the young find it easier, don't they? Manoli's a hot head, but he's not really bad.'

Thanassi had known that Poppy faced execution for killing a military policeman. 'Would you have remained silent if I'd been caught by the junta police, Thanassi?'

He shook his head.

She remembered the young man who worshipped his older brother. Only a couple of days back, he had sent Manoli to prison in order to save Poppy from further acts of revenge.

Calmer now, she looked into Thanassi's face and recognised a reflection of her own wasted years. She had lived with four decades of torment and regret. A life of misery that should have been joyous, should have been spent with the man she loved so dearly. If Yeorgo had lived, oh how she wished . . . now that they were old, they could have lived their days in happiness together. Her tears rose. How she wanted to be held in his arms once more; to feel the strength of him, hear his voice, listen to him as she played the lira. In her head, she heard him play *their* song, 'Stars Don't Cry For Me', and fresh tears rolled down her face.

You're my moon and stars, Calliope Lambrakis, my moon and stars.

For forty years, alone in her bed at night, Poppy had thought of the man she loved, and remembered his last words to her before he turned and walked away forever. Every night since, hugging her pillow, she told Yeorgo's spirit about her day. She recounted her thoughts and wishes, and shared her fears. This was the only way she could get through another night without him.

She swallowed hard, reached across, and took the hands of the man who regarded himself as Yeorgo's brother. 'I forgive you,' she said. 'I forgive you, Thanassi.'

The old man nodded, his eyes brimming. When he blinked, the tears ran down his tired old face and splashed onto the table.

The feud had finally ended.

Katarina touched Poppy's shoulder and jerked her head towards the door. 'Come on, let's see if we can make the wedding. You'll have to return for your handbag later . . . there's too many forms to deal with.'

'Good luck,' Thanassi said.

'Thank you,' Poppy replied.

They left Thanassi with the police officer. Poppy followed Katarina out of the back exit, and into a patrol car. Katarina pulled the wing mirror in and turned on the siren. 'Belt up,' she said. They lurched down an alley behind a taverna. Scavenging cats scattered.

'You're going the wrong way!' Poppy cried.

'Trust me.' Katarina licked her lips, raked an elastic band from her bottle-blonde curly hair and shook it free. 'I've always wanted to do this. Yee-ha!' She grinned and ploughed through a strip of red and white tape that closed the entrance to road works.

The back of the car fishtailed as it spun into a turn on the loose, brown dirt. The half-constructed bypass joined the main road just before Amiras. They raced through the village, siren blaring.

* * *

Angelika and Matthia were in the church porch. Poppy got out of the police car and couldn't speak at first. Neither could Angelika. They rushed towards each other, hugged and kissed, and then Poppy shook her head and whispered, 'It's over; I didn't kill Emmanouil. I can't tell you what a relief . . . oh! It's indescribable.'

'Thank God, Mam,' Angie said. 'I never believed you would kill someone, anyway. But what a turn of events. I couldn't stop thinking about you, all alone in that police station. I'd already booked a taxi to take us straight there after the church.'

Poppy faced Matthia. 'Emmanouil committed suicide. Thanassi helped to bring my memory back, and he has proof. A letter Emmanouil wrote just before he died.'

'Poor, poor Mam. Thank God it's over. You must be completely exhausted.' Angie squeezed her mother and planted a kiss on her cheek. 'Let's get you into church, so you can tell everybody. *Yiayá* is out of her mind with worry.'

'Just a minute! You mean Thanassi knew?' Matthia shouted in rage. 'All this time he knew and he kept quiet!' His eyes narrowed. 'I'll kill him, the bastard!'

'Stop it, Matthia. Let it go. It's over. I'm tired out by the emotion,' Poppy said quietly. 'Put your hand on your heart and swear the vendetta has ended, Matthia, forever. No more reprisals. Thanassi has made a confession and is in prison. From what I heard, it's lucky you aren't locked up for attempted murder too.'

Begrudgingly, Matthia placed his hand on his chest and swore an oath.

Poppy nodded. 'Thank you. Now, I'd better get inside.'

She hurried through the church doors. The organist struck one long note of Mendelssohn, before she realised her mistake.

Poppy lifted her head and walked to the front. In the outfit as red as her namesake, she had prime position at the beginning of the first pew with her father and mother to her right. Voula stood next to Maria, and then Agapi.

Maria and Vassili took Poppy's hands.

'I didn't do it,' Poppy whispered. 'I'm free to go. I'll tell you everything later.'

The relief was clear on her parents' faces. Both Maria and Vassili dropped back into their seats and smiled at each other.

'Stay sitting,' Poppy said. 'Nobody expects you to stand.'

Voula leaned across. 'What happened?'

'It's all over,' Poppy replied. 'I didn't kill Emmanouil.'

Agapi stretched even further forward. 'Did I hear right? You're innocent?'

Poppy nodded. Her eye caught the microphone, between the metre-high wedding candles. She slipped out of the pew and had a quiet word with one of the churchwardens who turned on the mike.

'My dear friends,' Poppy stammered, embarrassed by the sound of her own voice. The priest poked his head out from behind the rood screen, his eyes wide and mouth open. The warden spoke to him quietly.

Poppy cleared her throat and started again. 'My dear friends and neighbours, most of you know why I left Amiras. I have just returned from the police station. Before my daughter gets married I want to tell you all that I was not responsible for the death of Lambrakis Emmanouil. The matter has been cleared up at the police station. The truth is Emmanouil sadly took his own life, after the death of his wife and child.' She crossed herself. 'May they rest in peace.'

In a stage whisper, someone near the front said, 'Poppy didn't kill Emmanouil!' and the sentence passed through the church, rustling like leaves in a breeze, and interspersed by the occasional, '*Bravo!*' And then somebody started clapping and before

Poppy could stop it, the entire church was applauding and Maria and Vassili were beaming at her.

When the congregation calmed down, Poppy took her place and noticed that Maria now looked tired and bewildered. 'Not long now, Mama,' Poppy said.

'What's happening? I can't keep looking over my shoulder, I'll get a crick. Why haven't they started?' Maria said.

The parishioners stirred. Matthia came dashing down the aisle and had a few words with the groom.

Voula smiled at Matthia and Nick and then whispered across to Poppy. 'Don't they look fantastic?'

Poppy glanced at the two men standing in the aisle in their pale grey suits; Nick's missing a trouser leg, his plaster cast bright in the dull church light. Fortunately, Angelika had bought chain store outfits for the groom and the Kondulakis men, explaining the four Marks & Spencer's suits, with shirts, ties, and shoes, had cost less than the Armani job Nick had originally planned for himself.

Matthia had eventually agreed to wear the outfit, but only to please Poppy. Nevertheless, they all noticed his swagger in the new clothes as he returned to Angelika, outside the church.

Chaos seemed to accessorise every wedding day, Poppy thought. She caught a glimpse of Voula and Agapi squeezing hands. The action caused her an odd glow of warmth. Aware of something more than affection between her oldest friends, she smiled and nodded to each of them.

The priest of Amiras stood in the arch of the rood screen, brown eyes staring from his wildly hirsute face. Poppy remembered Papas Christos's nervousness when he conducted her wedding, one of his first. Memories of her own marriage returned. Dear Yeorgo . . . despite the short and difficult time they'd had together, every moment had been worth the heartache of the following years.

With a smile on her lips and her vision misted with tears, Poppy studied her Timex, staring at the second hand as it ticked towards seven o'clock.

Papas Christos cleared his throat, stepped into the central aisle and gazed over his parishioners. When the congregation fell silent, he rolled his eyes heavenward, appearing to seek divine inspiration. Then Poppy realised he was simply checking his position under the Kriti TV boom mike. He turned on the loudspeaker and gave the microphone a couple of swift taps.

Poppy got to her feet, faced the church doorway, and saw Angelika resplendent in the wedding dress that Maria had made all those years ago.

Matthia stood tall with the bride on his arm. He tugged on his tie and polished a shoe against the back of his leg.

Poppy squeezed Maria's hand and, as is customary with any bride's mother, she let her tears fall. Angelika and Matthia started their slow walk accompanied by a buzz of admiration and a few bars of Mendelssohn.

Then, a catastrophe. Matthia's phone rang. He stopped, fumbled in his pocket and answered the call. An angry exchange took place that everybody strained to hear. Eventually he closed his phone and spoke to Angelika. They turned and walked out of the church. The congregation murmured, silenced, and then everyone listened to another undecipherable conversation coming from the porch.

Papas Christos paled. His mouth clamped so tight it disappeared between his beard and moustache.

Matthia returned alone. Was the wedding cancelled? Poppy sniffed, didn't know what to think. Her brother hurried to the groom's side. A discussion took place between the two men, with no regard to the fact that they were in church and standing only a metre in front of Papas Christos.

Poppy sensed the priest's dismay. He slid the microphone down its stand and whispered something to the verger. Unfortunately, the microphone picked up the rumble of the priest's belly and transmitted it, loud and clear, not only through the church but also over the rooftops of Amiras.

Young Mattie giggled loudly. The infectious laughter spread until half the congregation were laughing uncontrollably and the other half shushing the guilty.

Papas Christos glowered.

* * *

Stavro pressed his phone to his ear and shouted over the taxi driver's blasting horn. 'We're here, in the village! Where are you, Matthia?'

'I'm outside the church of *Agios Yeorgios* with Angelika, but Papas Christos is furious and everyone's getting fidgety,' Matthia said. 'The police brought Poppy back. They've dropped the charges but she must return to the station on Monday to make another statement. They kept her passport, but at least she's here.'

'Matthia, you must wait for me, I've got the rings!'

The driver turned onto the village road, still blasting his horn.

'Is that your taxi making the racket?' Matthia said.

'Yes, were almost there.'

Stavro chuckled to hear Matthia shout, he guessed into the church, 'It's my brother, the *Koumbaros*. He'll be here any minute.'

'Which way?' the taxi driver asked.

Stavro pointed to a narrow street leading to the church of *Agios Yeorgios*. The cab tore off the road and through the ornate iron gateway at a ridiculous speed. The congregation overspill scattered. The vehicle crossed the churchyard and screeched to a sliding halt between alarmed reporters and cameramen at the porch.

Stavro leapt out.

'Go to Nick's side, Matthia, I'm following you with Angelika.' He turned to the bride. 'Are you all right, *koritsie*?' Then he realised he'd forgotten to give Matthia the rings. He would slip them to him when he left the bride with the groom.

'Let's go, Angelika,' Stavro said.

The taxi reversed, and the congregation overspill squeezed in behind the last pew.

The organ seemed to hesitate before giving Mendelssohn another rendition.

Poppy turned to see Stavro, with Angelika on his arm, step through the doorway. Parishioners nodded their approval and Mendelssohn, played with gusto, drowned murmurs of admiration. Angelika and Stavro had almost reached the groom when a voice bellowed from the open doors at the back of the church.

'Stop!'

Chapter 46

ANGIE COULDN'T BELIEVE THE pandemonium of her wedding. Villagers, wearing their wide smiles and Sunday clothes, had lined the street to the church calling, '*Bravo!*' and '*Happy life!*' They clapped heartily as the marriage procession passed. Reporters made the most of the occasion, constantly taking pictures and shouting, 'This way, please.' A TV camera had filmed her arrival at the church and then ... things got crazy.

Angie stood three quarters down the aisle for the second time, staring at the back of a man with a plastercast on his left leg and a crutch under his arm. Nick should have become her husband an hour ago, yet still she waited.

Now another irreverent voice halted the proceedings.

Angie decided to pay no attention to this latest interruption. She slid her arm out of Stavro's and was about to continue alone, when she saw Poppy turn to face the door. Matthia, her grandparents and even her groom were peering at the back of the church. The priest and entire congregation gazed past Angie.

This wasn't how it was supposed to be.

Angie turned and squinted through the sunbeams at the figure in the doorway. Stavro grinned, squeezed her hand and nodded like a restless horse.

'I knew it!' he whispered urgently. 'Let's return to the porch.'

Not again . . . This is simply unbelievable, she thought.

Rooted to the spot, Angie wondered what could delay her walk down the aisle for a second time. She remembered her grandfather's words, 'Be patient, Angelika'. She looked at the unfamiliar man silhouetted at the back of the church.

The sun, setting behind him, showed the tall upright figure only as a stark shape. Shafts of blinding sunlight radiated through the open doorway, gilding his outline.

'Stop,' the stranger repeated, calmer now that he had everyone's attention. 'Stavro, would you allow me to give my daughter away, brother?'

Poppy's voice, hardly more than a whisper, broke the complete silence.

'Yeorgo? Oh . . . Oh, I can't believe it, my dear husband!'

Maria cried out with both hands on her heart. 'Petro . . . Petro! It's my baby boy, my son, Petro!' Vassili held her to him, and together they stared disbelievingly at Yeorgo.

Stavro stepped away from Angie and stood with Matthia in the front pew. The sun-drenched spectre came into the church and took his place at Angie's side. His mature, handsome face, radiant; his eyes fixed on the bride.

'Petro . . . Yeorgo . . . Dad . . .?' Angie muttered, unable to believe her own words. 'Surely you can't be? Is it true? This is . . . well, just remarkable.'

He nodded. 'You can thank your Uncle Stavro. He found me and persuaded me to return for your wedding.' He embraced her. 'You've grown since the last time I saw you.'

Angelika drew back and recognised a reflection of herself, and Uncle Stavro, in his features. 'When was that, the last time you saw me?' she asked.

'I was in the back of the school hall, when you won your award for writing.'

The priest cleared his throat. 'Are we ready?'

Overwhelmed by the moment, Angie linked arms with her father and walked proudly towards Nick.

Matthia, at the far end of the front pew, leaned forward and said to Stavro at the other end, 'Is that really Yeorgo?' When Stavro nodded, Matthia exclaimed, 'Jesus, God!' and three rows of congregation crossed themselves repeatedly.

Angie and her father arrived at Nick's side. 'You look amazing. I love you.' Nick said, his eyes shining.

She turned to her future husband and said with all sincerity, 'I love you more,' and after a shaky breath she whispered, 'I know this is really inappropriate, but would you give me a moment with my parents?'

Nick's jaw dropped. 'Angie . . . this is our wedding day.'

She nodded, 'I know.'

Nick threw his head back and started laughing. 'This is the maddest day of my entire life,' he said. Then turning to the scowling Papas Christos, he apologised, and squeezed onto the end of a pew, his plaster cast sticking out into the aisle.

Angie reached for Poppy's hand and pulled her into the aisle. For the first time in her life, Angelika Lambrakis stood between her parents, holding their hands. She closed her eyes and remembered all the Easters, throughout her childhood, that she had cracked her red egg against her mother's and wished for this very moment.

She turned her face up to the priest. 'Papas, would you bless the three of us, before I leave my parents' family, to live with my husband?' She heard her mother's gasp and felt the squeeze of her hand.

Papas Christos commenced with the blessing. Angie looked over to Maria and saw her smiling and weeping. She gave Angie an understanding nod, which Angie returned. When the blessing was over, Angie placed Poppy's hand in Yeorgo's and they took a step back. Nick, smiling broadly, hauled himself back onto his crutch and hopped to Angie's side.

'I knew we should have run away together,' he whispered.

'What, and miss all this chaos on the happiest day of my life? No way,' she whispered back, still unable to grasp that her father was in the church. The day that had seemed to be turning into a nightmare, now surpassed her wildest dreams.

'Who gives this woman, Angelika Lambrakis, to marry this man, Nickolas Kondos?' the priest said.

'I do. Her father,' Yeorgo said with immense pride in his voice. He stepped between them, took Angie's hand, and placed it in Nick's.

He turned to Nick and said with all seriousness, 'Make my daughter miserable for one single second, and I'll break both your legs before I kill you with my bare hands.' Then Yeorgo kissed Angie chastely but firmly on the lips before stepping back to Poppy's side.

'He means it,' Angie whispered, smiling.

'I do believe he does,' Nick replied.

Somebody shouted, 'Bravo, Yeorgo!' Someone else whistled, and another called out, 'Opa!'

The priest flapped his hands at the congregation.

Angie's tears reached their tipping point.

Yeorgo embraced Poppy and then Maria who, stroking his hair and patting his face, almost fainted with pleasure.

The priest pulled the mike closer to his mouth and said, 'Is everybody *finally* ready for this wedding?' He paused, watching his flock nod and mutter, 'Yes, yes,' before he continued. 'Then let's join these two people in holy matrimony!'

* * *

After the marriage service, Nick and Angie rushed to Maria's cottage. They squeezed into the small lean-to bathroom.

'Where's the kit, wife?' Nick said.

'In my toilet bag, on top of the cabinet, husband.'

They both giggled. Nick lifted it down and tipped the contents into the wash hand basin. 'Angie, this looks complicated.'

'No, I just have to pee over the stick. Can you hold my dress up for me?'

'Sure, what about your knickers, do you want help?'

'No, I'm not wearing any.'

'What?! My God, you're going to burn in hell! Knicker-less in the church! Got to be a huge whopping sin.' He laughed uproariously.

'If God knows everything, then she'll understand about VPL.' Angie chuckled at Nick's vacant look. 'Visible Panty Line.' Angie sat on the toilet and peed over the wand. She passed it to Nick and they both stared at it.

'Nothing's happened,' Nick said. 'We drew a blank then. Not about to become parents.'

'No, we have to wait three minutes. If we see a blue stripe, we're pregnant.'

'Where's your watch?'

'Didn't bring one. Where's your phone?'

'Demitri's house.'

'Clock!' they both said together before shuffling into Maria's living room.

Nick held the pregnancy indicator behind him as they watched the second hand on the old clock turn three times around the face. It seemed to take forever. 'Right, on three,' he said. 'One, two, three!' He whipped the wand from behind his back.

Angie squealed. Nick grinned.

* * *

At the reception in the village square, everyone stood and applauded when Nick and Angie arrived. Every time bride and groom kissed, the guests hammered their forks against their wineglasses, making a glorious racket and coming precariously close to a mass shattering.

The moon rose and arced over the celebration. A tiny pipistrelle bat flitted around the streetlamp catching moths. Dogs and the roosters were respectfully quiet.

Through the balmy night, three musicians playing bouzouki, lira, and guitar, performed on a makeshift stage under the starlight. After the traditional wedding dances, Angie had a quiet moment with her mother. They sat facing each other, knee to knee, holding hands.

A long note from the lira came louder than earlier music, and they both looked up, towards the source of music. Yeorgo sat centre stage, drawing his bow across the ivory inlaid instrument.

'For the two most beautiful women in my life,' he said into the microphone. 'My daughter, Angelika Lambrakis, sorry, Angelika Kondos; we have some catching up to do.' He played a couple of notes, smiling down from the stage. Angie stood and blew him a kiss, and the guests whooped and clapped.

'And my wife, Calliope Lambrakis.' His face softened, eyes crinkling. 'You are my moon and stars, Calliope Lambrakis, my moon and stars.' And with that statement, he played the slow intro to their favourite song, 'Stars Don't Cry For Me'.

Everyone got up, danced the *Sitarki*, and sang along. Poppy, her face wet with tears, waved a napkin over her head and led the dance. Angie followed, then Nick and most of the guests. They danced in a spiralling circle in Amiras village square. Both mother and daughter smiled at Yeorgo, fighting emotion, happier than they'd ever been before.

The festivities were still going strong at 3a.m. It was then, while Angie was talking to Nick, she noticed Poppy moving away from the party. She slipped down a side street off the village square.

'I'll be back in a moment,' Angie said. She gathered up her skirt and followed her mother. Once past Voula's cottage and around the next bend, she saw Poppy disappear into another narrow road.

When Angie caught sight of Poppy again, she was struggling with a huge rusted key in the lock of a faded dusty-rose-pink house. The place looked as though it hadn't been lived in for many decades. Poppy slipped inside and moments later, Angie recognised the flicker of candle light. She hesitated, wanting to respect her mother's privacy, but then she heard a heart-wrenching howl. Such pain. Angie couldn't stand it. She rushed through the door.

Angie found herself in one large room with a stone floor. Kitchen, dining table, bed and sofa, all thick with dust, were arranged around the walls. Poppy sat on the edge of the bed, hugging her belly and crying.

Angie guessed this was where she had given birth, and held her dying babies. Her heart went to her mother, because one thing Angie was sure of, Poppy was absolutely her mother in *every* sense of the word.

'Mam! Mam, don't cry. What's the matter?' she said, slipping her arm around Poppy and holding her close.

'I don't want to go back,' she cried. 'I can't, not after all this. The man I love is here in Amiras. It's been so long. My parents. My loving brothers. Angelika, it will break my heart to be parted from any of them, or you either. And now I'm torn between all that I've missed, and you, my precious girl.'

'What do you mean, Mam?'

'I don't want to leave Yeorgo, and my friends and family, Angelica. But I love you more than anything. How can I remain here when you're returning to London? Will you stay? Please. Come and live here in Crete, please!'

Angie blew her cheeks out. 'I can't, Mam. England is my home. But you must remain in Amiras. It's your birthplace, *your* home. One thing *Yiayá* taught me; we women are strong enough to do whatever we want.' She gave her mother a hug. 'It took a little effort to get you here, Mam; and you were extremely brave to come. So, stay. Be happy. See the stars again.'

Poppy gazed at Angie and nodded.

'Anyway,' Angie continued. 'Think about it, you're less than a four hour flight away, and we can call one another every Sunday.' She smiled and kissed Poppy's cheek. 'I'd feel better if you were with my father and my grandparents. And we'll visit often. But I must warn you: you'll have to come back to London next March.'

'March . . . why?'

'Because I want you with me when your grandchild is born, Mam.'

EPILOGUE

London, Nine Months Later.

ANGIE RAN HER HAND over the soft down on her baby's head and watched the alabaster eyelids flicker. She wondered what her baby girl could be dreaming about. She lifted baby Maria from her crib and smiled at the infant. Although only six weeks old, it was plain to see Maria had the regal beauty of the Kondulakis women.

Angie slipped her nursing bra open and held the baby to her breast. The infant latched on and suckled. Breastfeeding hadn't been easy. Angie had struggled through the first week, almost giving up. But now, she found feeding times were the most intimate and rewarding moments of her day. With her daughter snuggled to her bosom, Angie padded into the kitchen in her dressing gown and slippers. She filled the kettle, and then sat and enjoyed watching her baby girl. Life, she decided, could not be more perfect.

Once Maria was changed and settled, Angie switched on her laptop to see which new manuscripts looked promising. She loved working from home, and so did Nick. After fifteen years in publishing, they had opened their own literary agency and editing service. They couldn't be happier.

She usually woke Nick with a coffee at eight, and then he took over as househusband, leaving Angie to work in her office, Poppy's old bedroom.

While filling the coffee machine, she heard the jangle of a Skype call. Who could this be at seven in the morning? When her mother's avatar popped onto the screen, Angie remembered Crete was two hours ahead.

Poppy had returned to Crete after baby Maria's birth just in time to see her father one last time.

Papoú had died of simple heart failure, sitting next to Poppy at the cracked marble table, with a glass of raki in front of him. Poppy had taken a small framed photo of Angie and baby Maria for her parents, and *Papoú* had stood it on the outside table. He clattered his *bastouni* against the marble and said, 'Long life, Angelika and baby Maria!' Everyone banged their raki glasses down and then gulped the clear liquid.

With his family having a good time around him, and his worry beads hanging slack from his fingers – nobody knew the exact time he had left the party. He died smiling mischievously, on a star filled night; Demitri and Yeorgo's music in his ears, and his grandchildren dancing under the big olive tree.

Angie was glad Poppy had returned in time. She ran her fingers through sleep tousled hair, and then clicked on answer, smiling in anticipation of seeing her dear mother.

'Hi Mam, how are you and Dad . . .?' Angie's smile fell when the distraught look on her mother's face registered.

'I'm sorry, Angelika . . .' Poppy sobbed, her red-rimmed eyes blinking back tears.

'*Yiayá*?' Angie whispered.

Poppy nodded. 'We guessed she wouldn't last long after your grandfather's heart failure, but it's still a shock.'

Angie gulped, struggling to speak. 'I'm so sorry. What happened, Mam?'

'We had my father's thirty-day memorial yesterday. Stavro came from Athens and we spent the time together. Mama said to say thank you. Your wedding re-united the family. She also said,

"Tell Angelika not to forget her promise. She is the guardian of my story; she mustn't let it fade away." You were in her thoughts right to the end, *koritsie*. You made her very happy naming the baby after her.'

Poppy sniffed hard, fighting her emotions before she could continue. 'Mama went to bed at eight o'clock last night and passed away in her sleep. She's smiling, like *Papoú*, Angelika, I've never seen her as relaxed and peaceful. I'm waiting for Papas Christos.' Poppy dropped her head into her hands. Angie found herself crying too, wanting to say comforting words to her mother, but finding herself overwhelmed by grief.

Poppy moved out of the way and Yeorgo took her place.

'Hi, Dad.' Her father's face blurred through her tears.

'Hello, *koritsie*. Sorry for this news, but your mother wanted to tell you herself. Everyone sends love and blessings for the baby. The priest's just arrived. Are you okay?'

Unable to speak, Angie nodded, then managed to say, 'Thank you, Dad. Will you call me later?'

'Of course I will, Angelika. Try not to be too upset. It had to happen and Mama wouldn't have wanted it any other way. She had spent the afternoon with Young Mattie, helping him with a school project. Survival skills, believe it or not.'

Angie closed her laptop and sat in the silence of the kitchen, remembering her first trip to Crete. How nervous she was at the prospect of meeting her grandmother, the beautiful, warm-hearted, and brave Maria. *Yiayá* was a teacher in the truest sense of the word. Angie had learned so much from her, not just about making coffee from acorns, but about the value of life, and love, and above all; trust, respect, and sacrifice.

* * *

Angie placed her mug of tea next to the keyboard, opened a Word document, set the font to Times New Roman – double spaced, and typed:

Maria Kondulakis and the Holocaust of Amiras.

At six o'clock in the morning, on the fourteenth of September nineteen forty-three, hunger woke me. In the dark, I listened to the breathing of my boys, Stavro and Matthia, beside me. Would my husband, Vassili, at war in Albania, remember his oldest son's name-day today? Should I cook the last of the beans to celebrate the feast of The Holy Cross, Saint Stavro, or should I plant them? This war couldn't last forever. I ought to plant them but the thought of boiled beans flavoured with wild greens, herbs, olive oil and a splash of lemon juice made my belly rumble.

Baby Petro stirred in his little hammock above me.

THE END

Turn over for the author's personal story of what inspired her to write the novel . . .

THE STORY BEHIND THE NOVEL

FOR ME, THIS BOOK STARTED when my husband, an electrician, applied for early retirement in the UK. After some research, we decided to move to the Greek island of Rhodes. Fate played a hand, and we ended up buying a lovely villa near Agios Nikolaos in Crete.

After being a workaholic and an entrepreneur all my life, I thought I would die of boredom in Crete. My solution was to set myself a challenge: to accomplish something new, and difficult, each year. As time passed, I learned diving, sailing, self-sufficiency, painting, building, photography, writing and so on. One of my challenges was to drive all over Crete taking pictures and, on one of these travels, dusty and thirsty, I ventured into the kafenion of Amiras. An elderly gentleman told me he had an old house for sale for very little money. The property was a ruin – it barely had a roof and had a goat inside – but it had garden all around and an amazing view down the mountain and out to sea. I bought it as an investment.

Several years later, my husband and I decided if we didn't make the move to Rhodes, we would never get there, so we put our villa on the market. It was a shock when we sold the villa straight away. We had eight weeks to move out.

Remembering the ruin in Amiras, we decided to 'do it up', and live there while we found the perfect place to build our house in Rhodes. A few months later, with the cottage comfortable, I started on the jungle of a garden.

When clearing a bed for strawberries, between an ancient olive tree and a gnarled, mature, lemon tree, I dug up a rusted old machine gun. Wow! I called my son, Peter, and his partner, Nicky (they had moved into the lower village of Amiras) and, with the gun, I met at the kafenion, which rapidly filled with local men. We were told many moving stories about how war affected the village people, especially in 1943. I took the gun into the nearby town of Viannos and handed it over to the mayor, for the museum. Photographs of the house, the gun, and the handing over ceremony can be seen on my website: www.pmwilson.net

Over the following months, one by one, the village matriarchs told me *their* personal stories about the terrible day of the massacre of all their men and boys, and how they survived. Shocking stories of abuse, tragedy, bravery and survival. I was both honoured, and humbled that they shared these stories that I felt needed to be told.

I started to research, and was astounded by the results of my investigation. This is what I discovered:

On 14 to 16 September, 1943 a campaign of mass extermination was launched by the Nazis against civilians in around 20 villages in the remote mountain area of Viannos, Crete. This resulted in the murder of over 500 peaceful villagers - mostly, but not exclusively, men and boys – by the Wehrmacht units.

All the houses were looted, and everything of value or made of metal was confiscated. A white powder was thrown into many of the houses and then ignited, causing the complete destruction of property in many of the villages. The Nazis then burned all the September field crops, so that there was no food for the surviving women and children through the encroaching winter.

The mass extermination cleared the area, and was one of the deadliest in the Axis occupation of Greece. The attack had been ordered by General Friedrich-Wilhelm Müller and claimed to be in retaliation to a battle in the nearby village of Simi, between German soldiers and a small band of Cretan resistance.

Friedrich-Wilhelm Müller (29 August 1897 - 20 May 1947) was a general in the German Army. He was a recipient of the Knight's Cross, and of the Iron Cross with Oak Leaves and Swords, awarded by Nazi Germany to recognise extreme battle-field bravery or successful military leadership. Müller was notorious for having been a most brutal commander of occupied Crete. The infamy earned him a nickname: The Butcher of Crete.

The mountainous area of Viannos, in the district of Heraklion, is situated to the south of Crete and looks out over the Libyan Sea. After the Battle of Crete in 1941, Crete fell to the Axis (Germany, Italy, Japan) and Viannos and its surrounding villages, including nearby Amiras, became part of the Italian zone.

The Italians had hardly bothered the Cretan villagers, apart from stealing the occasional chicken and flirting with the women. This led to the presence of several resistance groups (*andartes)* in the area. The largest group was led by a communist, Emmanouil (Manoli) Bandouvas.

Increasing activity of the resistance, and rumours that the Brits planned to invade Crete, led the Italians to construct fortifications on the coast. The Axis also built a garrison in the local mountains, with good lookout views over the Libyan Sea and surrounding area. Three German soldiers were posted at Kato Simi, supposedly in charge of collecting potatoes for the provision of occupying troops.

(In my opinion, this was a weak excuse as the potato growing area was the Lassithi Plateau, central to the mass of Axis troops in the area of Heraklion. It was generally believed that the true reason for the troops at Simi was to keep the surrounding area, particularly the coastline, under surveillance.)

The Germans had a station of forces in the villages of Tsoutsouros and Arvi on the coastline below the Viannos area.

An armistice, signed on 3 September 1943 by Walter Bedell Smith and Giuseppe Castellano, was made public on 8 September. The armistice stipulated the surrender of Italy and her forces to the Allies. After the armistice, the Italian commander, Angelico Carta, and members of his staff, were smuggled from the south coast of Crete, accompanied by British Special Operations Executive (SOE) Patrick Leigh Fermor, to Egypt. Rumours that the Allied forces were about to take, and liberate, the island of Crete intensified.

Bandouvas organised an attack on the German lookout post at Simi. According to the locals, he had been ordered to do so by the British led resistance (SOE). British sources later claimed he had acted without consulting them, anticipating that the Allies would soon land, and that he hoped to emerge as a national hero. The claims of Bandouvas were also denied by SOE agents, Patrick Leigh Fermor and Thomas James Dunbabin.

(The local Cretans claim that Bandouvas naively fell into a trap set by the British who, preparing for the post-war era, aimed to wipe out the increasingly popular local units of pro-communist EAM/EL; and they also hoped for a distraction big enough to take German attention away from the coast. Several local women asked me why their Allies allowed the holocaust of Viannos to happen. 2,000 enemy troops, gathered in that small area for four days, and their supposed allies chose to look the other way while grandfathers, husbands, sons and brothers were tragically murdered.)

With most of Greece having fallen under the Axis, the Greek Communist Party (KKE) had called for national resistance. The KKE together with minor parties of the Left formed a political structure called National Liberation Front (EAM). They were joined by other Greek resistance militants. The Greek People's Liberation Army or ELAS, was the military arm of the left-wing National Liberation Front (EAM) during the period of the Greek Resistance.

(My personal view, after talking to one of the last living members of Bandouvas's local resistance, is that I am inclined to believe the first reason, that Bandouvas was given instructions. Who could have foreseen that his actions would turn into such a catastrophe? This is because; Crete was strongly communist. Britain and the USA were passionately anti-communist and probably didn't feel they could be seen liberating the communist population of Crete. Yet, they needed Crete in order to gather, and submarine to North Africa and Egypt, fleeing Italian leaders, Cretan runners, and escaping dignitaries. Discrediting the communist resistance, and promoting the British led resistance, may well have been a tactic to swing the Cretan's away from their socialist ideals. The ambush in Simi also caused a distraction from the submarines arriving from Cairo and North Africa on the coast below, providing a double solution to the Allies problems.)

Whatever the truth, the fact is on 10 September, when the Italians were fleeing Crete, Bandouvas' *andartes* killed two German soldiers stationed at their post in Simi and threw their bodies into a ravine. The bodies were soon discovered. (Another fact I find hard to believe as the landscape around Simi is extremely rugged with deep, impassable gorges and ravines.)

News of the incident seemed to reach Müller almost immediately. An infantry company was dispatched to Simi to investigate.

Bandouvas, realising the village of Simi was in danger, felt he had no choice but to defend it. With forty of his men, he set an ambush in the valley approaching Simi and waited for Müller's troops. They arrived early on 12 September and the battle of Simi commenced.

Despite their initial surprise, the Germans managed to retreat and a fierce battle lasted until the late afternoon. In the end, Müller's troops were defeated, having suffered several losses and many wounded. Twelve German soldiers were captured. Bandouvas's men suffered at least one loss, and never admitted to any casualties. They withdrew into the mountains.

The following day, a large force numbering more than 2,000 German soldiers gathered in Viannos. Exasperated by the loss of his men, and wanting to set an example to fleeing Italians who may have considered joining the partisans, Friedrich-Wilhelm Müller ordered his troops to destroy the area of Viannos, execute all males beyond the age of sixteen, and kill anyone, man, woman, or child, found outside the village boundaries.

(I ask myself if the true reason for Müller's orders was because he knew the Italian commander, Angelico Carta, had been smuggled away via that area, and Müller's harsh action would prevent the rest of the Italian army in Crete – who were based in Neapolis – from trying to leave by the same route? The Italians would disguise themselves as Greek villagers.)

German forces surrounded the region, invading it simultaneously from various directions. They cunningly reassured the Cretans that their intentions were peaceful, which persuaded many of the men to return to their homes. On the following day (14 September), the Nazis conducted mass executions, impromptu shootings, torture, arrests, lootings, arsons, vandalism and demolition.

The exact number of victims remains unverified. Sources agree that the final number exceeded 500 and consist of the inhabitants of villages: Kefaloryssi, Kato Simi, Amiras, Pefkos, Vachos, Agios Vassilios, Ano Viannos, Sykologos, Krevatas, Kalami, Loutraki, Myrtos, Gdochia, Riza, Mournies, Mythoi, Malles, Christos and Metaxochori.

Around 1,000 buildings, mostly houses, were destroyed. Some hostages were taken and later executed by shooting or hanging. The surviving villagers were forbidden to bury their dead or return to their villages, most of which had been burned to the ground. It took the villages many years to recover. Some never did.

In 1946, Müller was tried by a Greek court in Athens for the massacres. He was sentenced to death on 9 December 1946, and executed by firing squad on 20 May 1947 along with former General Bruno Bräuer, on the anniversary of the German invasion of Crete.

No one else was ever brought to justice, nor any substantial reparation paid to the families of the victims. Today, each village has a war memorial dedicated to their dead, and a poignant monument, commemorating those who lost their lives during that week in September 1943, has been erected at the village of Amiras.

Each year, on 14 September, a memorial service is held at the monument in Amiras and the names of the dead are read out. More than a thousand people attend, some after travelling half way around the world.